WHAT ANNOYED PRINCE AEID

more than his softhearted efforts to rescue a woman from a very common fate was the fact that he had held in his arms the most beautiful woman he had ever seen, and he—fool—had actually *handed her over to another man.*

He had to find out who she was, what she was doing in Katha, whether she was safe. . . .

The guards would be looking for the Blue Avenger now; Prince Aeid would be known, recognized. In any case neither the Blue Avenger nor Prince Aeid could wander openly through the Naian Quarter knocking on doors and inquiring after the health of a pretty Naian maiden whose name he did not know.

Prince Aeid examined the rattling, shouting street below. "I need another disguise."

GAEL BAUDINO

THE DOVE LOOKED IN

BOOK II OF *WATER!*

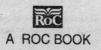

A ROC BOOK

ROC
Published by the Penguin Group
Penguin Books USA Inc., 375 Hudson Street,
New York, New York 10014, U.S.A.
Penguin Books Ltd, 27 Wrights Lane,
London W8 5TZ, England
Penguin Books Australia Ltd, Ringwood,
Victoria, Australia
Penguin Books Canada Ltd, 10 Alcorn Avenue,
Toronto, Ontario, Canada M4V 3B2
Penguin Books (N.Z.) Ltd, 182–190 Wairau Road,
Auckland 10, New Zealand

Penguin Books Ltd, Registered Offices:
Harmondsworth, Middlesex, England

First published by Roc, an imprint of Dutton Signet,
a division of Penguin Books USA Inc.

First Printing, January, 1996
10 9 8 7 6 5 4 3 2 1

Copyright © Gael Baudino, 1996
All rights reserved

Cover art by Tom Canty

In memory of
Rikki, Darzi, and Snuffles,
the three ferret-friends;
together and at rest,
18 December 1993.

Q: What are you rebelling against, anyway?
A: Whaddaya got?

Chapter One

"—gnao!"

Whazzat? Huh? Hmmph. Ga. Urgh. Hey ... dammit ... the cat. Sheet's caught, what the hell? Honey ... dammit, your hair's in my face and—

"Mrkgnao!"

—that damned cat's at it again. How come someone just doesn't, like, *shoot* the fucking thing ... ugh ... dammit, honey, roll over and gimme some sheet and don't gimme no sheet (Hey, half asleep and I can still churn them out, huh?) about it.

And, God fucking dammit, all those feeps up and down the street have those goddam *pit bulls,* and I know they got them 'cause the goddam things try to goddam *eat* me all the time, so why don't they try and eat that goddam *cat* for a goddam change? Huh? I ask you? Hey, are you listening to me? Look, I *know* it's four a.m., but I need to talk to you. Bull*shit*! You've got enough sleep so that you can fucking (not a bad idea, really ...) listen to me for a while. Just sack in. You can go in late. They won't mind. They haven't said anything yet, have they?

"Mrkgnao!"

Every goddam night it's the same goddam thing, and here I was just dreaming up (Get it? Dreaming up?) another scene. It's dynamite! They'll love it! Honey? Are you listening to me?

"Mrkgnao!"

Love to get my hands on that pussy (Hey, get it?), but I really think I've got it this time. Dy-no-mite! You been keeping track of all of this? Honey? I mean, I wouldn't have had you do up that drawing of Robin Hood's costume if I wasn't serious about it. Oh, hey, yeahyeahyeah, sure, and about you. Didn't you know that an artist only shares his work with someone he's real serious about?"

"MRKGNAO!"

JUST GET FUCKED AND GET IT OVER WITH, CAT! Goddam cat. Anyway, where was I? Oh, yeah, that girl who used to be an old woman is, like, heading back to wherever she came from. But she doesn't have much food or water. You know: tension time.

She examined the mixture and, satisfied that the dye was evenly distributed, reached over to a nearby shelf, picked up a bottle, and shook several drops of an oily substance into the sawdust. Immediately, the scent of rosemary rose from the bowl.

Just hold still, will you? Look, I like my hand on your tit, OK? Hey, I thought you said you loved me. I mean, I let you move in with me, and . . .

"MRKGNAO!"

Oh, shit! It's . . . it's a goddam earthquake! Get out of my way! I've got to get to a doorway or something! Christ! Feel that! It's the big one for sure!

"MRKGNAO!"

"Waaaaaaaterrrrrrr! Come buy my waaaaaaaaaaateee-eeeeeeer! Oh, such good water, my friend. Fresh from the well."

"Leave me alone. I am not buying water from you today."

"Ah, but you will. Perhaps not today, but tomorrow

you will buy! Everyone buys! Everyone always buys! And—

Hey, are you listening to me?

"—OOF!"

And the scattering of jugs and brass cups frightened a cat out of its hiding place beneath the shelves of a nearby market stall, and to the jangle and clank and glug of cups and spilled water, it added its own cry:

"MRKGNAO!"

Something comes to hand. Panas' hand. Chisel. No: here only a tin pot.

Clang!

—Stop that demonic yowling, Beshur said, or I will not feed you!

The cat had followed him even here, forsaking its pampered existence at the Novices' House for this run-down corner of the Naian Quarter. Beshur had racked his brains over the reason for it. Why? Perversity? Had the cat realized that its presence would be most annoying were it living with a renegade and apostate Panasian who had come within a hand's-breadth of the priesthood?

—Mrkgnao! it said, sticking its tail up in the air and looking at him as though to indicate that he should know very well what it wanted.

—Sandstone! he shouted.

The cat sat down and began to groom itself.

And do they miss me? They must miss me. Three days now and they have surely noticed that I am gone. After all, I was the best scholar among the novices of my age. Surely they have missed me. They would not *dare* do otherwise. And yet it surely is strange that I have heard nothing. No searches. No patrols. No questions being asked. Of course, the Naians here would tell them nothing. Ignorant idiots! Pumice! *Pumice!* (It feels very good to be able to swear. Like a man. Yes. A man. No more novice. A man.)

—Pumice!

Here, walk like this.

But would they? Would they? It would be . . . but no questions. Why? Closing in? *Ignoring* me? *Me?*

Fretting suddenly at the thought that what he had not wanted was turning out to be exactly what he *had* wanted, he rose from the rickety stool and, reaching up to adjust the head cloth that he wore more to keep his scalp hidden until his hair grew in than from any sense of decorum (since it was well known—and very obvious—that the Naians had no decorum whatsoever), paced about the small room.

"Leave me alone. I am not buying water from you today."

But that is a relief . . . I suppose. Perhaps it is because they do not wish to search the Naian Quarter. That must be it. Yes, I have not heard of a search because they are not looking here. Of course. But one would think that they would at least . . . I mean . . . look a *little*. Maybe? And I their best scholar. (Lifting and carrying for hire . . . a scholar!) Who else but their best would have noticed? The text changed. I know it did. But who changes it? And what . . . what is it changed *from*?

The Library of Nuhr. Must look. Find out. See. Panas' chisel riving open the stone, digging the quarries. Beshur will rive, too. Get into Library. How? In Nuhr. And not a priest.

Beshur had sat down again (for, in truth, the room was so cramped that there was not much room in which to pace), and the cat had, without his noticing, jumped up into his lap, purring.

Only priests.

And he was absently petting the cat now while it arched its back and purred, its tail thrashing back and forth.

Death to all others who enter, and they guard it

closely, but there must be some way in. I am a scholar after all, and I am clever, else I should not have noticed the changes in the text. (Lifting and carrying, indeed!) But—

The cat, deciding in a very feline way that it had gotten enough petting, turned, and, very gracefully, sank its teeth into Beshur's hand.

—GAAAAAAAAAAAH! he said, and, rising, he flung the cat across the room.

It landed with a clatter amid the pile of dusty wicker cages that had, at one time, seen use as containers for the insignificant brassware made and sold by the Naian merchant downstairs. Dust rose, Beshur cursed, and the cat leaped.

"MRKGNAO!"

Obadiah Jenkins flinched at the cry of the cat that prowled somewhere outside the tent. As a good Puritan, he loathed cats, finding in their sensual and promiscuous existence only a single, solitary virtue: the ability to catch mice. Eventually, though, someone was going to invent some godly mechanism that would do the same thing—and possibly do it better—after which the cats could go the way of the Indians and the Quakers.

"And the children of Israel sighed by reason of the bondage," said Mr. Wool, whose store of Biblical quotes could apparently be made to apply even to the vocalizations of cats, "and they cried, and their cry came up unto God."

Jenkins went to the entrance of the ambassadorial pavilion and pushed out through the flap . . .

"Mrkgnao!"

. . . looking as much for the cat as for some sign that camp would be broken soon. But no, the cat was hiding somewhere, and the camp, having partaken of a late (and lengthy) breakfast, was making its preparations for departure in a leisurely manner that would have brought the efficient and utilitarian-minded Jenkins close to swearing out loud ... were it not for the fact that he was already close to swearing out loud. Mindful as he was of his position as a minister, though, Jenkins did nothing more than clamp his teeth firmly together, stare fixedly at the recalcitrant camp, and wish fervently that some great and appropriate catastrophe—a tidal wave, for instance, or a flood—would come along and obliterate the entire country.

Beshur had sat down again (for, in truth, the room was so cramped that there was not much room in which to pace), and the cat had, without his noticing, jumped up into his lap, purring.

"Mrkgnao!"

And where was that cat? No matter. He would find it eventually, just as he would find other things. At present, though, with the cold desert night already dissipating before the heat of the fast-rising (and, by now, much-risen) sun, he wanted to be off, and he felt that if he had to spend even a single additional day traveling through the interior wastes of Kaprisha, unable to mark the miles save by the passage of identical dunes (and, this being the case, Abnel's people might well have been leading him around in *circles*), then he was going to ... going to ...

"Mrkgnao!"

But as the cat (still hiding) cried again, Jenkins saw not only Mather approaching the tent—his steps so uncertain that the ambassador could only surmise that he had either been drinking or had suffered so great a generalization of his constant spasms that even his gait was now affected—but also, among the folded and convoluted peaks of the distant mountains, a flashing as of gems ... or, perhaps, of windows.

"Good morning, Mr. Ambassador," said a suety voice.

Jenkins flinched involuntarily. Abnel. "Good morning, honored Gharat."

Abnel was standing almost at Jenkins' elbow, and the ambassador noticed that the high priest was looking at Mather with an expression of satisfaction. To be sure, there was nothing particularly remarkable about looking at Mather: Mather was, after all, approaching the tent. But ... that look of satisfaction ...

Jenkins flinched again, for a suspicion was beginning to form in his head ... along with a sense of nausea in the pit of his stomach. And that Bakbuk, too ...

Abnel, white-robed and gold-filleted, raised a fleshy arm (And were those *bruises* on his wrist? Almighty God! It was all becoming clear in all its monstrousness!) and pointed at the flashing from the mountains. "Katha," he said.

"MRKGNAO!"

It was just like any other morning, except that she had been allowed to sleep in, which was odd, because a ten-year-old girl had better things to do than to lie in bed all day. But no one had awakened her, and so she had dozed throughout the morning hours with the cat curled up beside her (and, like cats, children never seemed to get enough sleep, (so her grandmother had said), and both were likely to sleep the whole day away unless they were kept busy, which was why ten-year-old girls had things to do in the house so that they might prove themselves worthy of a good husband with a good chisel to call his own, which made the fact that she had been allowed to sleep doubly odd because her grandmother had lived in the house since her grandmother's husband had died some years before, and her grandmother could be counted on not to let a ten-year-old girl sleep through the morning with the cat beside her and the sun creeping in through the window lattices).

Jenkins flinched involuntarily. Abnel. "Good morning, honored Gharat."

And so it was odd indeed, but she mused and dozed as the morning wore on, and she did not hear footsteps approaching the room in which she lay, did not hear someone enter. Her first clue, in fact, about why this morning was different from all the rest of the mornings of her ten years of life came only when several pairs of hands seized her, held her, and spread her legs as she caught a glimpse of a blade hanging in the sunlight and the cat fled.

"MRKGNAO!"

And the cat stepped daintily out from beneath the long table upon which Fakik (Yes, you have met Fakik before, though not by name.) was rolling out dough, preparing yet another . . .

The cat jumped up on a box and poked its head above the edge of the table.

. . . experiment.

"Now you just go away," said Fakik. "I need you to go away. That is all I need you to do, cat. Just go away. I do not need your help. I have had enough help to last a lifetime. I am unmanned because of help. Indeed: look at me! I can hardly stand. I did not need that. I did not need that at all. Now I am unmanned, and all because of help. Curse that Kuz Aswani! It is he who should have been unmanned! Go away, I say!"

"Mrrrrrk?" A gray paw reached out, dabbled in the scattering of flour.

"Go away, cat. I do not need that. I need to find a recipe. I need to find a sweetmeat recipe, and it does not include cats. Not at all."

But here Fakik stopped his rolling and leaned toward the cat, which, in turn, looked up at him with green eyes.

"I tell you this, cat, because I am unmanned and unwived both, and I do not need to be all by myself. I need a confidant. That is what I need. And therefore, I need *you* to be my confidant. I do not need your help, but I need you to be my confidant. Do you understand, cat? I need you to understand that."

"Mrrrrrk . . ."

"Yes, I see that you understand."

". . . gnao?"

Fakik shifted slightly to the side in order to ease the ache in his very empty groin. "I need to find a recipe for sweetmeats that will win for me once again the favor of the king. Do you understand that?"

"Mrkgnao!"

"Yes, I see that you do. That is good. I need that. Good. So you see, I must experiment. And then, one day, I will present the sweetmeats I have made to the king, and he will taste them, and he will immediately say, 'Bring to me the chef who made these wondrous sweetmeats.' And so I shall be brought forth, and the king will forgive me for the spilled compote (Curses upon your head, Kuz Aswani!) and will magnify me greatly in the eyes of my fellow . . ."

He looked down at his groin, winced.

It was just like any other morning, except that she had been allowed to sleep in, which was odd, because a ten-year-old girl had better things to do than to lie in bed all day.

". . . ah . . . men. And I shall be given lands and gold, and perhaps . . ."

"Mrrrrrrrr . . . rrrrrk?" Again, the paw dabbed at the flour.

"Now, none of that. I do not need that. And . . . and perhaps one or two of those boys with the powdered faces, because, as you can see (But you cannot see, can you, even though I need you to see?), I am unmanned, and therefore cannot find fulfillment among women, and—"

And, just then, with a great leap, the cat sprang onto

the table, its paws sinking into the dough that Fakik had carefully rolled out. And then, just as the head chef lunged forward to seize the malefactor, the cat pulled itself free and went hurtling over his shoulder, straight into a tottering pile of pans, pots, plates, spoons, and even a few miscellaneous articles of insignificant brassware that had somehow found their way from the shop of a Naian merchant of Katha to the kitchens of King Inwa Kabir himself; and then, as the pile fell with a great clatter and crash, the head chef to the king, Fakik by name, lost his balance and fell facefirst into the same dough from which, a heartbeat before, the cat had pulled its paws.

"MRKGNAO!"

"Here now, puss: off with you. Go find some of those rats below. Unclean, heathen wharves: infested with the vermin. They're all over us now. Go do your job, missy!"

"Mrrrrk!"

Tail up, the cat flicked around a corner and was gone.

Elijah Scruffy turned to his first lieutenant. "A game of chess, Turtletrout?"

"With pleasure, sir."

Turtletrout pulled at the fastenings of his shirt as the cat poked its head in at the half-open door.

He looked down at his groin, winced.

"My God! The door! SCAT!"

"MRKGNAO!"

Blue. Blue cloth. Blue thread. Blue patches and tatters. The desert air and sun had been hard on the blue, as had sleeping on the ground and getting poked and prodded at by both Abnel's guards and the Freedom Fighters of Khyr.

An upper room was all I could find, but it is good enough. Upper rooms are best (Ouch! Needles are sharp here in Katha! Sharp? Coffee? Ah . . . stupid . . .)

for they let you see what happens below. Everything below and to the front of me is lost . . . hmmm . . . read that somewhere, but cannot now remember where. No matter. Good enough. (Ouch!) Takes a woman's hands to do this, but that would mean that I would have to take someone into my confidence, and that I cannot risk.

Slowly, squatting on the floor of the tiny room, Aeid repaired the tears and the rips and affixed new tatters in place of those he had stuffed into the waistbands and shoes of the hapless guards of Nuhr. Outside, the streets of Katha were rattling and banging with all the noise of a holy—and very commercial—city.

Good for me to do this, though. Good for a man to have a trade. I could be a tailor. (Or an embroiderer? Valdemar . . . hmmm . . . and Haddar with that . . . that thing. Must inquire.) King of France. Locksmith. Cobbler? No: that one is dead, poor thing. Name? Forget. (Sabihah? Rubies? Oh, pumice!) Overthrow kingdom, have a trade. Aeid? Oh, the tailor on the next street over. Name of Darzo. And where are *they*? Still off in desert. Moving slowly, but coming. Yes, they will come, and we will have Americans in Katha. Who would have thought it? Sacrilege. Terrible. And yet I sympathize. (Ouch!)

And, from the window, yellow eyes peered at Aeid.

Elijah Scruffy turned to his first lieutenant. "A game of chess, Turtletrout?"

"Mrkgnao!"

Cat too much like Abnel. Fat and knowing. But knowing . . . nothing. Temple tax on everyone . . . yes, that is something that I would expect from Abnel and his (Oh . . . what about my . . . ?) excesses. That reactionary, bigoted idiot! I shall be glad when I can smack him right in the face . . .

And here Aeid was sewing faster and faster, his

needle winking in and out of the blue fabric like light-ning in a clear sky.

... and him bringing the Americans to the holy city of Katha! Here! Why, the wool they wear—

Oh ... wait a moment ...

Aeid considered, his needle hanging above the blue cloth. The cat watched him from the window, yellow eyes unblinking.

... wait ... the Americans ...

... no ... wait ...

"MRKGNAO!"

"Ow!"

The smith shook his head at Umi Botzu. "It is still hot," he said. "You must be careful."

Umi Botzu, stinging finger in mouth, could not but agree. "Yes, very," he said.

"I just finished it this very moment."

"Yes ... yes ..."

In truth the device looked wonderful (though it was indeed a trifle hot). A closed vessel with three wheels affixed. A tiny valve to close off the single aperture. And, yes, it was hot. Well, it would be hotter still when it was in use!

"Very good ... very good ..." said Umi Botzu, and for a moment, he was lost in wonder at the bare fact of its reality. But then he suddenly clutched the device tightly (burning himself in the process) and pulled away from the smith, who, along with his cat, was looking expectantly at this sorcerer-turned-scientist.

"Tell no one about this!" said Umi Botzu.

"Mrrrrk?" said the cat. Or perhaps it was the smith. Compared with the bright morning streets of Nuhr, the smithy was dark, and it was a little hard for Umi Botzu to tell which of the two had spoken. After all, if a man could become a ferret, then perhaps a smith might speak like a cat.

No ... wait a minute ... Kuz Aswani only *thought*

he was turning into a ferret. But perhaps the smith only *thought*—

No matter: Umi Botzu reminded himself that, regardless of ferrets or cats or the reality or unreality of various metamorphoses, he had magic of the most potent kind in his hands, and to the sandy wastes with impotent and doltish counselors like Kuz Aswani!

And here Aeid was sewing faster and faster, the needle winking in and out of the blue fabric like lightning in a clear sky.

"I said . . ." Umi Botzu realized that he was addressing the cat. With an effort, he fixed his eyes on the smith. ". . . tell no one. I will give you gold . . ."

The smith nodded. "Of course."

"Much gold."

The smith nodded more enthusiastically. "Of . . . of course!"

"Much, much gold!"

"Yes!"

Umi Botzu examined the device again. "In a few days."

The smith nodded resignedly. "Oh . . . of course . . ."

But, ever the scientist, and therefore in sympathy with the common man (and how Elijah Scruffy had ever brought himself to utter that potentially lethal and utterly republican sentiment out loud, Elijah Scruffy himself still did not know, though Umi Botzu, ignorant of republican sentiments and, therefore, of their implications, had swallowed it without judgment or comment . . . just as he had swallowed everything else that Elijah Scruffy had said), Umi Botzu opened his purse and poured its contents out onto the counter of the smithy. A few coppers, a silver coin . . . some lint.

The budding scientist leaned forward, whispered, "More to come!" and then turned and made his way into the bright morning streets of Nuhr, his belly (and, perhaps, groin) all atremble with the thoughts of what he was going to do with the (still warm) device he clutched tightly under his arm. Behind him, smith and cat exchanged glances and, perhaps, words.

"*MRKGNAO!*"

But the cat was not at all interested in Kuz Aswani. Cats were, in general, not at all interested in the doings of ferrets (Yet another sign that the spell was growing on him!), and this one obviously did not intend to be an exception to the rule. Sleepily, it examined him from its sun-warmed windowsill (safely out of reach of even a determined ferret . . . or so it thought) and yawned.

On the patch of sunny garden grass that he had come to favor for his morning naps, Kuz Aswani uncurled himself and stretched. Were it not for the fact that he was still too big to be quite the proper ferret (despite the fact that he *knew* that the fur on his belly was spreading, that his sharp nose was turning even sharper, that his eyes were assuming—hour by hour, minute by minute—the beady, determined, even *mischievous* oh-what-a-lovely-room-allow-me-the-pleasure-of-rearranging-it look of a genuine ferret (for he assumed that a potent sorcerer like Umi Botzu would be satisfied with nothing less than the genuine article), he would have been pleased to join the cat on the windowsill, and he would even have been willing to keep his wiggling to within a degree acceptable to feline tastes. Or at least to try.

The cat eyed him. Kuz Aswani could read its thoughts, could see that it was satisfied with and even proud of its inaccessibility. Well, that was just like a cat. Prideful creatures, all of them.

"Mrrrrr . . . k."

"Fftfftfftfftfftfft." Kuz Aswani whiffled softly as a thought came into his ferrety head. Yes, he was indeed too large to share the windowsill with the cat, but the windowsill—without the cat—could contain him adequately. And so if the cat were not there . . .

The cat looked down at him disdainfully.

But Kuz Aswani—shrewdly, ferretishly—then considered that, though he was still too big to *join* the cat, he was just the right size to be able to *reach* the cat . . . and thereby to have the windowsill all to himself.

A few coppers, a silver coin . . . some lint.

And so, standing, he reached up and plucked the startled and indignant cat from its perch; and as it ran away, tail held high, he clambered up to the window, forgetting (in a most empty-headed and ferrety way) that windows, be they low or high, cat-occupied or not, must, by nature, lead somewhere. In this case, the window led into the kitchen of the king's palace, where Fakik, unmanned and desperate to regain the favor of Inwa Kabir after having been disgraced by the excesses of a certain ferret, now found that same ferret at his window, found that same ferret losing his balance, found that same ferret falling into the already-cat-trampled, experimental dough that was still lying on the floured table, ready to be shaped, cut, and formed into sweetmeats . . . if cats and ferrets would ever leave it alone long enough.

"MRKGNAO!"

The old pilgrim, Charna had decided, was grotesque. Simply grotesque. Badly-aspected. A Scorpio? Nonsense: the woman must have gotten her birthday wrong, which was something to be expected of someone so old. Old and feeble. Dim-witted. It was a tragedy that someone like that had not died yet, and Charna was sure that if it was ever her own fate to be so badly-aspected as to be unable to remember her own birthday—or, for that matter, to be so grotesque as to be as old as that pilgrim—she would certainly prefer to be dead.

But the pilgrim was, doubtless, just that. Dead.

Badly-aspected, grotesque, and dead. It was most unfortunate that she had not stayed in Katha, for even one
so badly-aspected could be of some use to others, but
as it had turned out, she had made herself of no use to
anyone, and had, in fact, wasted more of Charna's time
than Charna cared to think about.

"Mrrrrr . . . k?"

"Fftfftfftfftfftfft." Kuz Aswani whiffled softly as a
thought came into his ferrety head.

She patted the cat that came nosing about her feet,
then went back to stirring the bowl of colored sawdust
on her lap. To be sure, sawdust was annoying to work
with, but the community seemed incapable of appreci-
ating anything else, and regardless of whether Charna
found her surroundings grotesque and badly-aspected
or not, she still had to buy food and pay vendors; and
therefore, if colored sawdust was what people bought,
then colored sawdust was what she would sell.

Satisfied that the dye was evenly distributed, she
reached over to a nearby shelf, picked up a bottle, and
shook several drops of an oily substance into the mixture. Immediately, the scent of rosemary rose from the
bowl.

Stirring, stirring, stirring . . . done!

"Grotesque," she muttered as she thought again of
the Naian pilgrim. "In the middle of the night," she
muttered as she spooned the fragrant sawdust into pots.
"I will need . . . *someone* when the Gharat arrives," she
muttered as she stoppered the pots and, with a stick of
pigment, wrote upon them, in large letters: *LOVE*.

Chapter Two

Consider the following scene:

Katha, just outside the gates. A fine, clear day. The year is 1798, the season draws toward autumn. Within the city, up on the rooftops where we can see him (And how *does* he manage to remain unnoticed in that outrageous costume of his?), is someone we know well: the Blue Avenger. He is skulking about among the semi-precious pinnacles and eaves—just scouting out the territory and keeping in practice, thank you—planning what might be considered an interesting reception for a certain Gharat.

Outside the gates, on the north road ... well ... ah ... the north *path,* southbound now and returning from what might be considered an eventful journey, is a young woman who does not look quite twenty. She is obviously a Naian, for she wears the distinctive medallion of Naian women and her head and face are bare. She is also obviously very beautiful. And, judging from her walk (which is interrupted by slips and shuffles and touched with a general feeling of disorientation), she is obviously suffering from both hunger and thirst.

You all remember Sari?

In addition to these two, and earning his living as a common porter, there is also a young man who keeps

his head cloth very carefully arranged in order to hide
his shaved skull (which is beginning to become both
stubbly (because of his growing hair) and itchy (because of the stubble)). This is Beshur. No, you cannot
see him right now. Quite correct: he is behind the wall,
in the city, within, in fact, the Naian Quarter. His turn
comes later.

All right. That is the scene. Begin!

Even through the fuzziness of hunger and thirst, Sari
could not help but feel that she was, once again, re-
peating herself. She had started out her journey as an
old woman, hungry and thirsty, she had continued her
journey with periodic, incapacitating bouts of hunger
and thirst that had, invariably, made her dependent
upon the goodwill and succor of others (who, invariably, seemed to have had more than goodwill and succor on their minds), and now here she was again,
hungry and thirsty, approaching a city and hoping that
someone would show enough goodwill to succor her
... perhaps even enough to leave it at that.

Nevertheless, behind her chagrin at the repetition
was a kind of dim satisfaction, for, had she been an old
woman, she would have doubtless perished the day before: her planning, her tacit, unconsummated suicide,
would, it seemed, have been wonderfully successful.

Yes, indeed. But, really, it had nonetheless been successful in ways of which she had never dreamed, and
therefore it was neither totally tacit nor completely
unconsummated. Sari, the old woman, was dead, gone,
vanished. That was what she had wanted. But what she
had not wanted—nor looked for—was her transformation into this young slip of a thing who, despite all
odds, and in accordance with the will of the Goddess
(whose intent she found painfully obvious), was going
to gather together community after community of

Naians, bring them to the foothills of the Mountains of Ern, and set them to clearing the Caves of Naia.

She staggered and caught herself on a boulder. Very funny. From what she had seen of community after community of Naians, she might as well have been ordered to herd a flock of cats.

Squinting into the bright sunlight that her spinning head made all the brighter and more dazzling, she made out the city of Katha and judged that she was a trifle closer to it than she had been the last time she had looked. Or at least, she thought she was closer. It was somewhat hard to tell. She had estimated a suicide for an old woman, but she had, it seemed, come perilously close to a suicide for a young one, and unless she kept moving, she was going to find that she had succeeded in both cases.

And what would Naia say then?

Sari almost giggled. In fact, she did indeed giggle, though the sound came out in a whisper. Naia had, without saying a word, already said all sorts of things. And She had done a few things, too. Sari could not help but wonder what she might turn into next.

She was quite unwilling to find out.

But she decided that she did not have to worry overmuch about finding out so long as she fulfilled her promise. And she decided also that, considering the circumstances, she was indeed fulfilling her promise when, sight blurry and steps uncertain, she lurched off the path at the very last minute, spun, fell forward, and careened directly into the wall of the city three feet from the gate, her medallion clanking loudly against the polished blocks of jasper and quartz that (Oh, wonderful!) Panas Himself had set into place.

Her mouth parched, her knees weak, her too-perfect nose smarting, Sari could not help but giggle again. Panas! Ha! Had she met Panas that moment, she might have snapped her fingers in His face.

She felt someone take her arm. "You are not well," said a male voice.

She peered at the guard who had obviously been drawn away from his post by her gyrations and subsequent collision. "I am . . . ah . . . that is . . ." Her mouth was dry enough that her words sounded like crumbling ash. ". . . well, yes: that is true."

"Come with me." And the guard began to lead her toward (so she estimated by the contrasting shades of light and dark that were all that the combination of glaring sunlight and thirst-distorted vision allowed her) the gate.

"Thank you," she ashed out the words as best she could. "May Naia bless you."

"Oh," said the guard. "I believe that She . . . has."

Sari blinked at his statement. "Really?"

"Oh, yes."

"How strange . . ."

But when the glare of the sun was replaced by the comparative dimness of the passage through the gate, and then by the comparative darkness of a room within the thick wall of the city, and when the guard abruptly took hold of her shoulder wrap and ripped it loose, sending her medallion clattering to the floor and leaving her naked from the waist up, she began to comprehend, even through her fuzziness, just how the guard had come to the conclusion that Naia had blessed him.

Very odd. But . . . how revolting! Why, she was old enough to be his . . .

Oh. Oh, yes. That.

She felt more shock than fear. It was probably the hunger and thirst. She was going to be . . . and she a Naian . . . happened all the time . . .

"And no medallion," the guard chortled. "Very convenient. Apostate Panasian women get exactly what they deserve!"

"I . . . I am not a Panasian!" she managed, reaching

for her medallion, not finding it, remembering that she had heard it fall to the floor.

His hands were already cupping her breasts. "Oh ... really ... mmmmmm ... ?"

She shoved him away and bent, feeling sightlessly for her medallion, consumed by the disoriented belief that, should she recover it, she would be safe from the guard's intentions. As luck would have it, her fingers found the palm-sized disk of bronze almost immediately, and she straightened just as the guard stepped forward. Halfway up, though, her head met an obstruction, and the guard's annoyed oath turned into a sputter and a muffled sound that resembled an *Urk!* forced out between clenched teeth.

Sari staggered back, but she caught herself and held up the medallion triumphantly. "See," she said. "I am a Naian."

The guard was strangely silent and motionless. Then: "Urk!"

She peered at him, could make out nothing but a blur. "Are you not well?"

"Urk!"

She began to suspect that he was indeed not well, and, with a concern that was oddly disconnected with the fact that she was bare to the waist because of his actions and intent, she found herself casting about in her mind for herbal remedies.

"Urk!"

She could think of nothing, though. No matter: the door was slamming open and heavy steps were approaching. "What? What did you—?"

"PANDERMAL PUSTULES FOR THE PRURIENT PANASIAN PERVERTS!" came another voice as the door slammed open yet again.

"Urk!"

"What?"

Sari suddenly realized that she was in the room with

two men—Ah ... no, she decided, that would be three now, would it not?—and that she was uncovered. Still fuzzy, she had temporarily forgotten just how she had come to be in that condition, but mortification overcame her, and she quickly bent to pick up her clothing.

The second guard was running toward her.

She straightened. Again, her head met an obstruction. Again there was sound that resembled an *Urk!* forced out between clenched teeth.

"Amazing!" said the third voice.

"Urk!"

"Urk!"

"Ah ..." Sari stood up with her medallion in one hand, her clothing in the other, and her bundle ... somewhere. "Ah ... help?"

"With the greatest pleasure!"

"Urk!"

"Urk!"

A blue presence—*very* blue—loomed up out of the dimness that passed for her sight for the moment. Hands that were male—*very* male—nonetheless wrapped her clothing about her expertly ...

"Urk!"

"Urk!"

... dropped the reknotted cord of her medallion about her neck, and pressed her bundle (There it was!) into her hand.

A pause. Then, two swift thumps followed by two crashes, and she was led out into the passageway into the city again.

She had hardly been in the sunlight for a moment before an arm caught her about her waist and she was lifted. She was vaguely aware of shouts and the clash of weapons, and then she seemed to be flying through the air.

"Where ... ah ... oh ..."

"We are going to the Naian Quarter, pretty woman,"

said the voice that came out of the blueness. "I saw
that you were in distress, and I could not help but
come to your assistance."

Pretty lady? But she . . .

Oh. Oh, yes. That.

"Ah . . . thank-you . . ."

"It is my pleasure!"

Remember Beshur? All right, then.

Fruits. Nuts. Dates. Perfumes. Bolts of cloth, even
of wool (and I wonder what they use *that* for)! I carry
them all, and they do not know. Shoulder worn raw by
evening, and did Panas . . . no, a foolish thought. What
of Panas? Do I care? A figment, no more. Fig . . . mint.
Yes, both in this box I am carrying, and does the slave
with that woman know that I could . . . a man, a
woman . . . yes, but a priest . . .

Almost. Gone now. Left. Apostate? Do I believe
otherelsewise? Or not believe at all? Oh, is He real
then?

Giggling.

And yet I believe. Shaved head week after week.
Panas like a husband to his eunuch wives (Here, walk
like this, and . . . uh . . . agh . . . sandstone! I am still
thinking about it!), and they believe! Yes! They believe! And so do I.

Wish that I did not. Futile. Priest. Almost.

Look up. Be cheerful. Paid more.

Sun on mud. Dried mud. Poorer sections. They come
here to buy cheap, and that is what they get. Panas
picking mud from under his toenails (And I am doing
it again, but pumice up its asshole.) and flinging it
away. Oh, look here, here is a place to live. Good
enough for them. Just look. And these now returning to
their stone houses and their resident priest . . . yes?
Yes? Could have been me. Intelligent. Best scholar of

my class. Best scholar of all. Oh, yes? Oh, we have someone who would be ideal for your household. A hundred thousand settels a year, and he is yours. And after hours, creeping into the wife, they say that Naians are better because they are not cut up—softer—but I do not know (Walk like this ... pumice!) for I have never ...

This turning ... and now this turning. Ahead is the gate. I will go among my Panasian brothers again, and they will not know me. At least, I hope they do not, and ...

... what?

—Ack! he cried as a bright blue figure suddenly appeared atop the wall that bounded the Naian Quarter. In one arm, the figure carried the limp form of a woman. In the other, it held a rope. Somehow, it was contriving—one-handed—to fasten the rope to the top of the wall, but though Beshur was not sure how the feat was being accomplished, it was being accomplished indeed, for a moment later, the figure used that very rope to swing down to the ground inside the Quarter. (Remember: $T=2\pi\sqrt{l/g}$. There *will* be a quiz.) The figure hit the ground running and managed to put about ten yards between itself and the gate just as what looked to Beshur (who, technically an apostate, naturally worried about such things) like over fifty priestly guards exploded through the gate, their courses naturally a little on the random side but decidedly convergent upon the bright blue figure.

—Ack! Beshur cried again.

But while Beshur could not help but notice that the guards were running toward the blue figure, he also could not help but notice that the blue figure was running away from the guards. Scholar as he was, though, his observations did not stop there, for he noticed further (and, to be sure, with frightening clarity) that the blue figure, in its single-minded quest to elude the guards, was running directly toward *him*.

(Here ... walk like this.)

Beshur looked about quickly and noticed that his client—to whose husband belonged the contents of the box that he was carrying—had, along with her slave, taken one look at the bright blue figure and, having immediately come to much the same conclusion as the tax gatherers of Nuhr, had turned and vanished ... somewhere ... leaving Beshur to face a blue figure (with woman) pelting toward him and bringing with it a gaggle of priestly guards (with swords).

—Ack! Beshur cried yet again, only this time he dropped the box, turned, and ran back the way he had come, back into the depths of the Naian Quarter, zigzagging through the mazy streets and byways, ducking through the shade of the awnings that belonged to the industrious Panasian merchants who had been doing a splendid business that day by setting up shop in the Naian market square and offering, at only *double* the price, exactly the same wares as the few Naian merchants offered in the Panasian market square.

But each time he cast a frightened glance (Here, walk like this.) back over his shoulder (desperately fighting, at the same time, to keep his head cloth in place), he saw that the blue figure was following him. Now, had Beshur possessed sufficient leisure to ponder this strange coincidence, he might have come to the conclusion that anyone who had obviously taken such pains with such a brilliant and distinctive costume as the pursuing (and pursued) blue figure must have had some not-inconsiderable experience in the art and practice of eluding priestly guards, and therefore, the fact that the blue figure was invariably choosing the same streets, byways, and awning shadows that Beshur chose must, *de facto,* have spoken highly of Beshur's own innate craftiness ... which would, doubtless, have been speaking highly of something very obvious (at least in Beshur's opinion), considering that he had been a scholar at the head of his class and the most talented novice ever to pass through the priestly school.

As it was, though, Beshur did not have any leisure at all for such pondering. He was merely (Here, walk like this.) frightened—panic-stricken, in fact—and running; and behind him was *still* the blue figure (with woman), and behind the blue figure were *still* the priestly guards (with swords).

And both the figure (with woman) and the guards (with swords) were gaining on him.

Another turn, another byway. Here was an inviting alley, though it was a trifle choked with a mound of rubbish and crystals that had obviously been deemed not quite interesting enough to possess any kind of magical power. Up one side of the glistening pile, then, went Beshur, who subsequently skidded with a bump, bump, bump (which Mr. Milne would make famous in another 128 years) down the other side, lost his balance at last, and fell assoverteakettle up against the wall of a house.

The alley was a cul-de-sac.

Several things went through Beshur's mind, not the least of which involved speculations as to what his fate might be (Here, walk like this.) should he be discovered by the priestly guards. These speculations drove him to his feet and sent him back up the pile of rubbish and castoff crystals, but though he attempted to descend the other side without mishap, experience proved to be no guide for his feet, for—bump, bump, bump (Are you listening, Mr. Milne?)—down he went again, tumbling and spinning, losing his head cloth completely in the process and fetching up against the feet of the blue figure (with woman), which, well ahead of the guards (with swords) was just then turning *into* the alleyway, Beshur's uncanny and, save for this last instance, extremely clever ability to decide upon actions suitable for evading the minions of the law making itself apparent once again.

Beshur, unwrapped and dazed, looked up. The blue figure sized up the situation.

"Good. Well then. Here, my man, you take this woman and I will be off."

The woman groaned.

Beshur found himself suddenly in possession of both the woman and the woman's bundle as the blue figure, now freed of its burdens, dashed farther along the street off of which the alleyway had offered such an illusory escape. For a moment, the figure turned back in the direction of the priestly guards (with swords) who were just now coming into view around a corner, and waved its hands. Beshur heard its cry—

"FELDSPAR FINGERS UP THE FILTH FA-VORED . . ."

—but he had already turned and begun climbing once more the mound of rubbish and uninteresting crystals that blocked the alleyway. Once on the other side (so he told himself as he slipped and stumbled up the treacherous slope), he and the woman he carried would be concealed and safe. They could come out later, when the guards had given up the search, and he could . . . ah . . . that is . . .

He crested the mound wondering what he was supposed to do after that.

"I am thirsty," the woman murmured. Her voice was soft, dry, and she sounded as though, yes, she was indeed thirsty. "Please . . . some water."

Water. Mud. Naians and mud. Always mud. Runzen men have fish scales when they are born. Maybe Naians come into the world covered with mud. Illustrative symbology of the ephemeral existence of—

But just then his foot misstepped yet again, and he and the woman both went tumbling down the far side of the pile, coming to rest against the same wall of the house that Beshur had encountered before.

The woman groaned.

—Fear not, Beshur said. We are safe here. No one will . . .

And just then, an upper window opened, and two arms appeared. As was the custom in the Three Kingdoms, two hands were attached to those two arms, and, as was sometimes the case in the Three Kingdoms, the two hands held a basket. Before Beshur could finish his reassurances, a shower of rubbish and uninteresting crystals fell on him, bouncing off his stubbly head.

—. . . find us here, he finished.

The woman groaned, but Beshur was suddenly struck by how utterly beautiful she was, and it was then that he discovered that his priestly training, thorough as it was, had not succeeded in suppressing quite a number of instinctive reactions.

"Oh, I am thirsty," said the woman.

—Yes, said Beshur, of course. As soon as . . . ah . . .

A rattle, a clash, and the priestly guards (with swords) swept by the mouth of the alley in pursuit of the blue figure.

Aeid pondered the ripped and torn remains of his Blue Avenger costume. It appeared that he would be plying the trade of tailor again. But what annoyed him more than the necessity for needle and thread (and there simply was no way around it: he *had* to do it himself), more than his inept and almost-catastrophic encounter with the priestly guards, more than his soft-hearted (and, as above, almost catastrophic) efforts to rescue a woman from what he knew to be a very common fate for women in general and Naian women in particular, was the fact that he had, for several minutes, held in his arms the most beautiful woman he had ever seen, and he—fool!—had actually *handed her over to another man*.

"Pumice!"

He did not know where she had come from, or what she was doing in Katha. He did not even know her name. All he knew was that he had ... well, he had been over that before.

Another man!

And what a little scrubby thing he had been, with a stubbly head (Stubbly? That warranted some consideration.), a pinched, scholar's face (Pinched? Scholar's? Hmmm ...), and hands so blistered that he could not have been a week at his porter's work. Odd. Very odd. But humiliating! And he had the girl now!

Fuming, Aeid paced up and down the room, dragging his tattered tatters behind him. Who was she? He had to find out. Already, in contrast to his forgetfulness regarding women like Sabihah or Najmat, or ... or ... or whatever their names were, he was remembering with uncanny clarity every detail of her face, her clothes, her words. Yes, he had to find out who she was, what she was doing in Katha, whether she was safe ...

He went to the window. The guards would be looking for the Blue Avenger now; Prince Aeid would be known, recognized, and subjected to the restrictions of public adulation; and, in any case, neither the Blue Avenger nor Prince Aeid could wander openly through the Naian Quarter, knocking on doors and inquiring after the health and identity of a pretty Naian maiden.

Leaning on the windowsill, he examined the rattling, shouting street below him. "I need another disguise," he muttered. "Pumice."

Give the equation describing the period (**T**) or a pendulum in terms of a given length (**l**) and gravitational factor (**g**).

Chapter Three

*If the gun has not been fired immediately before-
hand, that is, if it has been left loaded and ready, the
sponging out may be omitted; indeed, should be omitted. However, should the gun have been discharged, it
is most important for the sponging out to take place,
else the corrosive effects of the discharged powder will
most certainly affect the fabric of the gun adversely.*

Hmmm ... hah ... PIGS! What do they know of
holy work? A book of instructions! That is all they
give me. Take, this, they say, and go practice on the
guns. Guns! On Kanez! Well, then they will have their
guns, and I will have my work, and all for the glory of
Panas (blessed be He!).

*Take up the sheepskin swab and plunge it briskly
into a bucket of water.*

Hah! The PIG! The swab is too big for the bucket!
Only the end will fit! Very well, I will put only the end
in, and sandstone and pumice to the devils who made
this thing and made it badly!

*Upon withdrawing the swab from the bucket, insert
the end into the muzzle of the gun and thrust it down
the bore. Twirl it, and then bring it out. There may be
evidence of burned matter on the swab when it is
brought out of the bore. This is normal.*

Twirl it! PIGS! They tell me to thrust sheepskin into

the God's gun! Sheepskin! Why, that is as good as putting wool into the face of a priest! And ... twirl it, it says! Pah! What do they know? Twirl a great heavy gun! Well, I will spin the swab instead, and may Panas (blessed be He!) forgive them for their sacrilege!

Once the swabbing is finished, the cartridge may be introduced into the gun by means of the aperture afforded by the muzzle. Either end may be introduced first.

Ah! And by pushing this penis of a cartridge into the cunt of the gun, we reach the explosion of orgasm! But the God's ... ah ... urmmmm ... hah ... PIGS!

Once the cartridge is within the confines of the muzzle, the rammer is used to thrust the cartridge down the length of the bore until it lies beneath the touchhole. Thrust the priming iron down through the touchhole so that you may ascertain the presence of the cartridge.

Thrust! Yes! Thrust! Ummm ... ma, ma, ma! Yes, there it is! I can feel it! Oh! Priming iron! Ha!

PIGS!

Once the cartridge is seated properly, the time has come to shot the gun. Select a ball from the garland ...

Garland? Garland! Hah! They give me these orders, and they say to me, read and obey, and then they do not give me a garland. Whatever it is. No matter, here is a round thing that must be what they call a ball.

... and introduce it into the gun by means of the muzzle, following the same procedure as was previously followed with the cartridge. Ram the ball home smartly.

Smartly! Smartly! Hah! I am intelligent. I can "ram the ball home smartly"! Now, that explains why I was put in charge of the gunnery of Kanez. I am unclean, and therefore handle sheepskin (PIGS!), but I am intelligent, and I can ram the ball home smartly! Hah! *That* kind of priest!

Now that the ball is rammed home, take the wad from its cheese ...

Cheese? Cheese? I eat cheese. I scrape cheese from under my foreskin. I do not take wads from cheeses! What do these PIGS mean by that. Wad ... hmmm ...

Oh, here.

... and ram it down over the ball.

huh ... huh ... huh ... PIGS!

And now, the gun should be run out.

Run out? Why not run in? And I alone? Bah. This is good enough. I do not know what this running is. A gun cannot run. And even if it could, I would not want to chase it, for I would certainly not want to catch it. But this is holy work. Yes, I must remind myself. This is God's work. This is for the preservation of the most holy Library. This is the word of the Gharat, and therefore the will of Panas (blessed be He!) Himself!

Run the gun out. Ah, well ...

At this point, priming powder should be poured into the touchhole and about on the surrounding pan, and see that thereafter the powder is bruised with the nozzle of the power horn. This will allow for an adequate contact with the slow match when it is introduced to the powder.

Introduced! Powder (Dub-dub-dub, there it is.), may I present slow-match! Slow-match, may I present pow—!

Haddar turned back and forth, examining himself in the mirror. Very nice. Very nice indeed. Perfect in fact. Well, not exactly perfect. The beard was always a problem. A wom-	Aeid turned back and forth, examining himself in the mirror. Very nice. Very nice indeed. Perfect in fact. Well, not exactly perfect. the beard was always a problem. A wom-

an's face cloth would hide the offending article, but it was not a question of face cloths or of hiding at present. For Haddar to be satisfied, indeed, for the effect to be satisfactory at all, the beard would have to go.

That in itself, though, was also a problem, for the beard was an emblem of his status, and, in fact, no one would recognize him without it. Which was, he supposed, the idea. But to do away with the beard meant a burning of bridges, a total immersion in a new role, and Haddar was not sure that he was ready to so completely abandon his former life in order to gain a satisfaction of which he still was not entirely certain.

The beard ... the beard. A decided problem, but the urgings he was feeling were slowly eating away at that problem as though it were a fragile sandbar, or, rather, were submerging it beneath the chaotic waters of a satisfaction that,

an's face cloth would hide the offending article, but it was not a question of face cloths or of hiding at present. For Aeid to be satisfied, indeed, for the effect to be satisfactory at all, the beard would have to go.

That in itself, though was also a problem, for the beard was an emblem of his status, and, in fact, no one would recognize him without it. Which was, he supposed, the idea. But to do away with the beard meant a burning of bridges, a total immersion in a new role, and Aeid was not sure that he was ready to so completely abandon his former life in order to gain a satisfaction of which he still was not entirely certain.

The beard ... the beard. A decided problem, but the urgings he was feeling were slowly eating away at that problem as though it were a fragile sandbar, or, rather, were submerging it beneath the chaotic waters of a satisfaction that, even though uncertain, held in its reckless abandonment of the past a strange, Dionysian attraction.

To be seen completely as ... *other*. To exist in a mixture of terror and fulfillment. Oh, to be sure, he could find excuses for the absence of the beard, should the necessity arise. And, in any case, his status would provide some protection. But still ...

Thoughtful, intent, even a little excited, Haddar reached for the razor ...

even though uncertain, held in its reckless abandonment of the past a strange, Dionysian attraction.

To be seen completely as ... *other*. To exist in a mixture of terror and fulfillment. Oh, to be sure, he could find excuses for the absence of the beard, should the necessity arise. And, in any case, his status would provide some protection. But still ...

Thoughtful, intent, even a little excited, Aeid reached for the razor ...

In the course of only a few weeks, Umi Botzu's house had undergone a remarkable transformation. The rope webs were gone, the windows were open, the rooms were clean. The flowers at the front gate, coaxed along by the hands of one who was determined to acquire the dignified title of scientist (without understanding in the least what it meant), were blooming fiercely.

Upstairs, in the sunny room in which Umi Botzu conducted what he called his *research*, tables were arranged in precise and regular order, and though, as was the custom of the Three Kingdoms, they stood not more than a foot above the floor, they were polished and clean, and arrayed upon some of them were a number of reasonable—and occasionally workable—facsimiles of Elijah Scruffy's curiosities. Here was a Leyden jar, here was a strange little thing that Umi Botzu called his gyroscope (even though a pot of beans could be counted upon to demonstrate more precession than Umi Botzu's gyroscope), here were small glass disks that, though they still remained perfectly transparent when turned at right angles to one another, would soon, Umi Botzu was sure, turn as dark as those he had seen in the captain's stubby fingers.

Power. It was all a matter of power. Power, indeed, was his already, and more was coming to him every day. The curiosities arrayed on the tables were evidence of that, as were the tables themselves (the mark of a potent sorcerer ... or so Umi Botzu understood from what Captain Scruffy had said), as was, perhaps most of all, the device that he had brought back from the smithy that morning.

Oh, but it was a lovely, potent thing, gleaming with the polish that only fine steel could take! Umi Botzu had demanded that especially fine steel be used for its construction, since Captain Scruffy had assured him that only a vessel capable of withstanding the pressure of the mightiest of magics was sufficient for this ultimate manifestation of arcane power. (True, Captain Scruffy had referred not to magic but to *steam,* but Umi Botzu recognized magic when he heard about it.)

He set the device on one of the tables and spent some time sitting and admiring it. The smith had done a splendid job, more than likely because Umi Botzu had promised to pay him well. And Umi Botzu *did* intend to pay him well. He really did. Soon. Very soon. Just as soon as he mastered his new powers sufficiently.

But there are few men who can bear to feel for very long the tingling spur of anticipation, and Umi Botzu, not being one of them, stood up after only a minute or two and began to relieve the solitary magnificence of the steam engine with a number of other articles. First came a small flask of pure water which he carefully poured into the body of the engine through the single, tiny aperture that the smith had left. Then came several low lamps that he had selected for their ability to fit beneath the shining body of the steam engine. Then came an ordinary lamp, but one already lit, for the eventual firing of the low lamps. Then came a number of thick, wooden baffles that were actually sections sawed out of his roof beams: these he placed about the edge of the table, for when the steam engine began to move, it would move quickly, and Umi Botzu did not want it to run off the tabletop and crash onto the floor. For much the same reason, he spent a few minutes closing the doors of the house and fixing screens over the open windows, for as he had seen the rapid movements of Captain Scruffy's engine, he knew that his own (which was, of course, much newer and better) might well be able to crawl up a wall and effect some kind of egress from the house were it not prevented in some way.

But, preparations finished, Umi Botzu lit the low lamps and arranged them carefully together, after which he positioned the engine so that their flames licked the underside of its body.

Power! Yes!

Minutes went by. Tense, anxious minutes. Minutes filled with anticipation (which, as aforesaid, Umi Botzu did not appreciate at all). He leaned closer to the device. "Yes," he whispered. "Come, beloved. Come. Come!"

And, indeed, the engine seemed to respond to his entreaties, for wisps of steam began to issue from its single aperture, and, very softly, a sound like rustling began to emanate from it as the water within approached a boil.

"Yes . . . yes! Power! Mine. Come, beloved! Come!"

The magic was growing, was, indeed almost upon him. With a shaking hand, Umi Botzu reached out and closed the valve on the aperture, thus meeting the last condition necessary for the magic . . .

. . . and the movement.

The steam, confined to the interior of the engine's body, no longer issued forth, but the sound of rustling grew louder. Umi Botzu watched the wheels that were brazed to the side of the engine, waiting for movement, waiting for that first, stirring quiver that presaged climax and fulfillment.

Leaning closer. Watching.

The rustling turned into something that sounded like a creaking. His eyes fixed on the wheels so steadfastly that the machine as a whole seemed to shimmer and waver before him, Umi Botzu leaned forward even more, bringing his head so close to the engine that his face stung with the heat.

"Yes! Power!"

The creaking grew. Umi Botzu found that he was clenching his teeth, clenching his fists, straining, willing the engine to move. Yes, this was magic.

"Move! Move! Move!"

The rustling rose to a new urgency, the creaking turned into a long, sustained groan . . .

"Yes! Move! The power is mine! Mine! Mine! Pow—!"

Sleeping there. Heaped temptation. Curve of her rump sticking up. Hair all over. Talked about that once. Boys. Smucking. (Here, walk like—*No!*) Hair. Never have a woman. Never. Just . . . what? What do they do in the priests' house? Careful not to let the boys in the schools do it, but what among themselves? So careful about the Texts. The Texts! So careful, and yet . . .

. . . changed. Library. Must go and look. But . . . same thing. Careful with the Texts . . . and they changed. Discouraged the boys, and they themselves . . .

The girl on Beshur's makeshift bed stirred, and, with

difficulty, rolled herself onto her back. The curve of her buttocks was replaced by the curve of her breasts. Large, liquid brown eyes opened, stared up at the ceiling, flicked to the side to examine the room.

Well, she is awake. What do they say about Naian girls? They all want it? Sniggering at night. *They* wanted it, too. Didn't they? And I myself . . .

No. No.

"Where am I?" she asked.

Oh, by Panas! That voice. Come in my robes! And now I am a man! What? Shall I? She wants it? Yes?

—You are in Katha, he said, keeping his distance.

"Katha?"

—Yes.

She stirred some more, started to lever herself up but stopped midway and bleared into the air for a moment as though worried that something might be hanging above the bed. But there was nothing. Sitting up, then, she rubbed her face.

—I gave you water, he said. You were thirsty.

"I was," she said. "I traveled the last day without water."

That voice! A man would go to her, hold her. Hold her *down*! Yes. And then he . . .

—Are you hungry? he said.

"I . . . I think so . . ."

Brown eyes. Her brown eyes. Her scrotumtightening* brown eyes. From under a fall of hair, she watched as he went to the wooden box that he used as his larder and pulled out a loaf of bread.

"And some water, too, please," she said.

—Yes. Surely.

Always wanting something. The others spoke the truth. A man. And with that woman here in the room. And she a Naian. And who would blame me. But . . .

does she want *me*? Well, of course. I mean . . . why would she not?

In fact, he pulled out not only a loaf of bread but also a piece of cheese that he had been saving. There was water in the jug. He set them all before her.

—Here, he said.

"Thank you," she said.

Of course she wants me. Yes. Feed her, and she is mine. Like that cat over there.

"Mrkgnao!"

She smiled at the cat.

Thank you. Yes, just like the cat and, oh, what . . . ? Oh, sandstone! Arrange my robes. Will she notice?

She drank, paused, drank again. "My name is Sari," she said.

—I am Beshur, he said. A scholar.

She smiled, looked at the jug in her hands. "I feel as though this has happened before."

—I am only a porter temporarily, he said, and . . . what?

Again, the large brown eyes. "As though you have given me water before."

Reincarnation? Preestablishment by the God? (Sandstone! Still there! Long as a camel's leg! Will she notice?) No, Goddess for her. But . . . predestination? The act thought of is at one and coexistent with the act perpetrated. In the mind of the God . . . ah, I mean, the Deity, I give her water before the act, and that is a giving nonetheless. Now I give her water, and it is again. What is she thinking? (Down! Damn you! Oh, pumice!) Does she . . . ?

A MAN!

"Mrrrk!"

He glared at the cat, annoyed.

—Before?

She shook her head. "I cannot remember clearly. It is not important."

And then she laughed.

Madmen . . . and madwomen. Prophets. Soothsayers. Warned us about this. Naians? All of them. Those crystals. *All?* No, could not be. But she is here, and she is . . .

"Where am I?"

—In Katha, he said.

"I mean, where in Katha?"

—In the Naian Quarter, he said. In my room.

"The Naian Quarter," she said. Again, her brown eyes lifted to him. Her hair was a river of night. "Good."

—Good?

He shifted his robe again.

"I have . . . something to do."

Yes, she has something to do. Something to do with me. I found her. I rescued her. I saved her. (Down! Ah . . . no. No! *Up!*) Surely she must be grateful for (Here, walk—*No!*) that. And she can show—

A knock came to the door as he was reaching for her shoulder, his lips already half parted as though he were about to nibble a peach. He stared at his hand, hovering inches above her bare skin.

The knock came again. Her brown eyes flicked to the door, and Beshur was sure that she had flinched.

Frightened of a knock on the door . . .

He realized that his palms were damp with a sudden nervous sweat.

. . . and that means she must be hiding, too. From what? (Here, walk like this.) No, could not be. She is already . . . no, not Naians. Softer, they say. I must find out. But . . .

The knock came a third time. Thwarted in his pursuit of something of which he was himself not entirely sure, Beshur turned away from the eyes, the skin, and the hair, and went to the door.

—What do you want? he shouted.

"Now," came the voice of the shopkeeper from whom Beshur had rented the room, "I would not intrude, for Naians do not intrude upon one another. We are all Children of the Goddess, are we not? And therefore, we should not take it upon ourselves to intrude upon one another. But I am a professional, and therefore I have to earn a living, do I not? And therefore, I must ask you, Beshur: Who do you have in your room?"

—I have who I have!" Beshur said. It is none of your business!

"But it *is* my business, is it not?"

Fool. Wants more money from me. I have no money. I am a priest. Gone now. Out here, with woman, and no priesthood. Hands against me. No one understands me. Money they want.

"For I am renting you a room for yourself, not for anyone else, am I not?"

—She is not staying long!

"Mrrrk?"

"Ah, but if she is staying at all, then I must adjust your rent, must I not? And two are more expensive to keep than one. Know that I am not asking this because I am greedy, but because I am a professional, and I must earn a living, must I not?"

—Pumice to you!

"Ah, what a thing for one Naian to say to another! Naia might become angry at times, for She is a mother, and She must become angry, must She not? But it is not for us to—"

Must send him away. Want her here. Have little money . . . wait . . .

—She is my wife! he said.

Behind him, the girl stirred, sat up, stood up.

"Well, now, that is different, is it not?" said the vendor of insignificant brassware. "For if she is your wife—"

"I am not his wife!"

It was the girl. Standing there, holding her disheveled clothing to her front, she was suddenly crying out: "I am not his wife! I am not anyone's wife! I am Sari, and I am a daughter of my mother, and I am here because the Goddess sent me!"

Silence.

"Mrrrk?"

"Ah! It is so wonderful to see you again, I cannot tell you how delighted I am to set my old eyes upon you, though I am sure you understand that I cannot see you as clearly as I would like . . . the embroidery you know. And I am old! Yes! Old! The years have taken much from me, and I am flattered, flattered so much that you have come to see what an old man can do for you.

"The last shipment? Poor quality? Oh, I am so sorry to hear that. I cannot tell you how sorry I am, but, as you can see, the quality is not at all less than that expected—no!—*demanded* by one of the great powers of the world. Yes! Powers!

"What? You do not care about the great powers of the world? Well, I can certainly understand that. I only meant, as an old man—Yes! Old!—who once served on one of the great ships of one of those great powers, that in my estimation (and my estimation is, as I am sure you will admit, not an inconsequential one, seeing as how I was once an officer on one of those great ships), the quality of the shipment was excellent.

"You can see for yourself. See these barrels! All of them. The next shipment. Too many? Well, I must . . . ah . . . keep some in . . . ah . . . stock. Yes! Stock! In case you want more. Why, when I was a young and dashing lieutenant on board the *Frères Marseillaise,* I was known for making sure that there was always a stock of such things on hand. For . . . for emergencies!

And now that I am old (and I am very old, as you can see, an old man, living out my life, losing my sight—the embroidery, you know—but not losing it so much that I cannot tell a good shipment from a bad one), I still hold to the practice of my youth, and I keep a . . . a . . . a . . . stock! Yes! A stock on hand!

"Oh, I am so terribly sorry, but I must disagree. I have already made up to you for the first shipment that you declared unsatisfactory (even though I disagreed with your estimation), and I simply cannot go on supplying you with merchandise to replace that which has shown itself to be satisfactory in practice, even though you declare that it is unsatisfactory in word. Why, I must, after all, provide for myself in my old age, for I am growing old—Yes! Old!—and I am losing my sight . . . the embroidery, you know.

"No, not a word more. I simply cannot. Please! Kindly release me from your grasp! I simply cannot! No! And I am old! An old man! And please be careful with that torch, for it is waving about so distressingly—Yes!—and there is no telling what might happen should it come into contact with the pow—!"

Chapter Four

2) *Color and Gold may be used both for the beauty of them and, in places where there is little light, to increase legibility.*

Hearken all ye to the words of Panas, the Builder of the World, the Raiser of Cities, the Ordainer of Municipalities, the Shaper of Society. May His blessings be bestowed upon His people for all time, and in all nations may there be great and endless praise raised to Him.

Those who are magnified, let them be magnified with *Color and Gold,* all in their degree, for as *each subject suggests its own treatment,* the beauty and material gain of those upon whom all depends should shine forth in accordance with their degree. And thus has Panas (blessed be He!) ordained silk for the king and his family, linen for his closest nobles, cotton for his officers and those of honorable degree, and coarser stuff for all the rest. And let their magnificence shine out in *places where there is little light* for thusly are the unworthy convinced of their unworthiness and thereby prompted to better themselves, and thusly are the great honored in their greatness and thereby urged to be greater still.

And as those who order the temporal affairs of men are endowed by Panas (blessed be He!) with the privilege and the right of outward luster, so those whose au-

thority lies within the subtle but potent realm of the spirit are also graced in an appropriate manner, for their right and privilege, while being exceedingly great among things spiritual, extend to the equally subtle realm of the mind, and therefore, let to their hands come the possession of all right and proper tools of the intellect, wondrous discoveries, devices of all sorts, whether to the lay masses their use appears magical or not, worldly or not, for such is the wisdom of the priesthood that all these things, by nature, will accrue to the glory of Panas (blessed be He!). And lest ignorance prompt questions which can do not otherwise than blemish the spotless dignity of the priesthood and of Panas (blessed be He!) Himself (blessed be He!), let such acquisitions be kept in secrecy.

SO BE IT
ARDANE!

With something that was at once akin to both a crack and a roar, the explosion of Citizen Valdemar's stock of gunpowder fanned out across the length and breadth of Nuhr, its intensity increased by the thick stone walls of the shop that, having initially contained it, could not be inevitably yield ... with catastrophic results.

Walls crumbled, roofs flew high into the air, once broad and reasonably clean streets filled immediately with rubble that included porcelain tiles, bricks, granite, marble, and enough semiprecious crystals (now broken along their appropriate fracture lines) to keep the residents of the Naian Quarter happy, fascinated, and occupied for what would doubtless be several centuries.

Fortunately, the King's Palace was far enough away from the detonation that it suffered no damage to its actual fabric. Not so fortunately, however, there was incidental breakage. In the kitchen, for instance, the

tower of stacked pots, pans, plates, serving dishes,
platters and even a few miscellaneous articles of insignificant brassware that had somehow found their way
from the shop of a Naian merchant of Katha to the
kitchens of King Inwa Kabir himself collapsed and
half buried the hapless Fakik in a heap of metal, jew-
els, and grease, his brilliant but still-experimental recipe for ingratiating sweetmeats brought yet again to
sudden and unlooked-for ruin.

Higher up, both in status and in altitude, the guards
who habitually stood before the ornate doors to the
chamber of King Inwa Kabir discovered not only that
those doors—upon which they had become very used
to learning surreptitiously—had been abruptly jarred
open by the shudder that suddenly ran through the palace to the accompaniment of a very loud and very prolonged *boom!*, but also that, having been so jarred
open, said doors no longer afforded any vertical surface upon which to lean, surreptitiously or not. Deprived of their support, therefore, the guards tumbled
backward into the royal chamber, flailing their way
across the room and tripping at last over the cluster of
servants and slaves who, kneeling on the rug, were trying once more to remove from its fibers the last of the
spilled and much trampled raisin compote.

The guards were punished, of course: Panasian law
was very clear about things like that.

Elsewhere, windows shattered, shelves collapsed,
frightened camels and horses made appropriate noises
and gestures, people who were indoors ran out, people
who were outdoors ran in, and Haddar, who was just
then in the process of removing the last of his
beard . . .

. . . dropped the razor.

HADDAR'S FANTASY

Things like this always go wrong. Either the razor
falls and gets caught by the blade, or it falls and it

lands where it is not wanted. Well, in this case, it falls where it is not wanted, or, at least, where one might suppose that it is not wanted, though with Haddar done up in women's clothes as he is at present, it is rather difficult to tell exactly *what* he wants.

If he wanted *this,* though, he has it: the razor falls neatly, spinning a little, and as the counselor instinctively tries to jump back and away from it, the injury he sustained in the course of his encounter with Citizen Valdemar's infernal device betrays him and actually pitches him *forward,* just in time for the razor (spinning, of course, *backward*) to open a long slit in his skirts, plunge in even deeper, and (yes, well . . .) sever his penis at the root.

"GAAAAAH!" goes Haddar, grabbing for it as the razor (Is it chuckling now: a sniggering little metallic *tee-hee?*) drops to the polished floor, but—too late!— the penis is already crawling down his leg like a stoat seeking escape from a farm boy's trousers. In a moment, it has dropped to the floor, and now it is squirming across the marble as fast as it can, a four-inch (well, all right, *six*-inch), streak of quickly-escaping erectile tissue.

Haddar is after it in a heartbeat, to be sure, but as he lunges for it, he trips on the unfamiliar skirt he is wearing (now made doubly unfamiliar by the slit) and falls at full-length on the floor, his freshly-shaven and still-stinging chin now stinging doubly from its bounce on the hard marble. The penis, though, after having visibly started at the sound of the crash, actually *pauses* and looks back with a coy expression that Haddar would swear has something of the comether to it . . . before it darts snakily around the leg of a table and into the next room.

Back on his feet in an instant, Haddar, skidding on rugs, crashing into tables, and nearly braining himself

on the doorpost, follows the penis into his study. As
luck would have it, though, his study is filled with
scrolls and papers and shelves behind or under or in
which his prepositional organ will, doubtless, find refuge; and as though that is not bad enough, there are
what must be over a hundred pigeonholes in the wall in
back of the low table that serves as his desk, most of
which are filled with documents of various ages, each
one affording yet another shelter for an errant penis.

Slowly, holding up his skirts in readiness for a pro-
prietary dash, Haddar scans the room, glares at the pigeonholes. It is here. It *must* be here. It is lurking . . .
somewhere.

But though he cannot help but feel that he should be
making a better show of this search, caught as he is
half in and half out of his woman's role, Haddar is (as
might be expected) dithering. To be sure, he is the
chief minister of the Three Kingdoms, and as such, he
possesses a reputation for considerable acumen and
perspicacity; but, shaven and skirted as he is, he is just,
after all, a weak, silly woman, and he cannot be expected to make much of a show of doing *anything*,
save calling weakly for a man to come save him. In
fact, as far as he is concerned, it would be a relief *to
be free of acumen and perspicacity both*, for, yes,
Haddar longs for the dullness of femininity, for the
predictable blandness and acceptance of an open cunt's
quotidian receptivity. No problems. No questions. No
doubts. Just open wide and swallow.

And so is Haddar's ability to find his penis seriously
compromised, for, in truth, if he is a woman, he cannot
possibly do a particularly good job of finding it (for
more than the immediately obvious and structural reasons), and, in any case, he is not at all sure that he
wants it back in the first place.

But a rustling behind an embroidered hanging causes

Haddar (reverting, for the moment, to masculine efficiency) to pounce. Too late! His penis, having betrayed
itself, is already fleeing at top speed across the room,
and it is obvious that it is making directly for the pigeonholes, intending to lose itself in the maze of wood
and paper.

Terrible and frustrating as this is, a worse thought
forces itself into Haddar's double-tracked mind: might
there be a hidden egress from the pigeonholes? A
chink through which a determined bit of *corpus
spongiosum* can wriggle? He does not know. It could
be. And how then, if the penis makes good its escape,
will he explain its appearance to the rest of the palace?
What will he say about yet another lurking mischief-
maker that, like Kuz Aswani, will surely pop out of
some hiding place at the most inopportune moments
and frighten everyone with a *chuckle-chuckle-chuckle*?
Or something even worse?

The penis is moving quickly indeed, but just before
it reaches the pigeonholes, Haddar, desperate, dives for
it and manages to clamp his hands about it. For a moment, the penis strains warmly against his grip, but
then it twists around, eyes him balefully, and sinks a
set of (at least they feel like ... by Panas (Blessed be
He!) they *must* be!) one-inch fangs into the counselor's
wrist. Haddar screams and lets go, and as the organ
scampers off into the pigeonholes with a swish and
rustle of paper, he holds his dribbling wrist and curses.

It is war now. All-out, total war. The penis must be
made to submit.

Slowly, he tears a strip from his skirts and binds up
the gash in his wrist, and then, methodically, he begins
to hunt through the pigeonholes, his logical, masculine
mind reducing the lattice to a rigorous pattern of
search paths. Somewhere, deep within the pattern, the
penis (from the sound of it) continues to scurry from
compartment to compartment, but no matter: unless

chance or fate has provided some unknown escape for it (And, indeed, what random chink or cranny could exist in a palace laid out and built by none other than the God Himself?), it will be caught.

Select, examine, move, repeat. Slowly, Haddar eats away at the refuge of his escaped genitals. One by one the pigeonholes are searched. Compartments are splintered by the imperious thrust of his fist. Papers fall to the floor, scattered thoughtlessly by his single-minded pursuit. Someone else can pick them up: Haddar has more important things to do.

And, yes, there it is: an uneasy stirring. He is close! Close!

Down the rows, across the columns, grabbing papers out, plunging his wounded hand in (Stupid ass! Has he forgotten about the fangs?), feeling for that movement, that quiver of life . . .

. . . and there it is!

Haddar gasps, strains, but the penis squirms out of his reach and plunges deeper into the compartment, which now seems to go back *much* farther than any of the others. In fact, Haddar is into the pigeonhole all the way up to his shoulder, and its end is *still* beyond the reach of his fingers. Maddeningly, he can hear the penis pattering farther along into the depths of the . . . what? Wall? Of the palace? Where does this pigeonhole *go*, anyway? (The possibilities are infinite, and infinitely discomfiting. The women's chambers, perhaps? The audience room? Perhaps the grand hall?)

But then, as Haddar strains, reaching, he suddenly finds himself falling *into* the pigeonhole, falling (impossible, true, but this is his fantasy) sideways, the compartment opening up and engulfing him as a man might open his mouth and swallow a sardine.

On his hands and knees now, his skirts catching under his knees, hampering him with voluminous cloth, Haddar scrambles along the passageway, hearing always, just ahead of him, the *pudda-pudda-pudda* of penile flight. But the farther in he goes, the less he can recall about what he is chasing and why. The walls open out, widening into a veritable cavern, but the darkness of this place is absolute, and there is now a thickness to the obscurity that seems to lave the ambisexual counselor in ignorance, a fast-rising tide that is, slowly, stripping him of his thoughts, leaving him to pad along without any concept of what might lie ahead, with only an empty groin to see him through his journey.

If he could think, he would be sure that somewhere ahead is an ending to his yearnings, a quiescent place of waking sleep in which he can drift through his days without care. But, in fact, he is already almost there, for as the passage leads him on into a darkness unrelieved by any sort of conscious light, he feels himself lifted and borne along by a blind current, carried deeper into darkness, deeper into instinctive night.

—The Library, Beshur said, is everything. Some say that the entire world is mirrored in the Library, for within it are all things of worth from the entire world, and what is of no worth is, of course, of no concern. You see, I am a scholar, and I know these things.

Sari yawned before she could stop herself.

—But you are tired, Beshur said. Doubtless it is because of your ordeal in the desert. You should rest.

Sari nodded. It was easier to nod and agree (fifty years of Panasian womanhood had not been wasted on her) than it was to admit boredom with the very mention of the Great Library of Nuhr. Unfortunately, the Library, like ethical dilemmas (both parts of which inevitably appeared to Sari to be identical) or the length of his stubbly hair (which stubbornly refused to grow appreciably in the course of an hour), was Beshur's obsession, and he spoke of it constantly (when he was not

dithering over an ethical dilemma or prodding surreptitiously at his stubble). For some reason, he was determined to enter the Library, even though he would be
faced with an automatic death penalty were he caught.

"I am a little tired," she said, "but I have some
things I must do today. I cannot lie about in your
rooms like an invalid forever. Today, I must go out."

—And do what the . . . Goddess asked you to do,
Beshur said.

He began to pace back and forth, the wafer-thin
floorboards creaking under his steps.

—You are obsessing, he said. You must be reasonable. I am a—

"Scholar," she finished for him, "and you know
about these things. Yes. Perhaps." There was annoyance in her voice that she could not suppress. "But I
must go."

Beshur did not notice.

—At any rate, he continued, the Library is many
things. And I will go there. I *must* go there.

He left off pacing: now he was standing over her as
she sat on the bed that he had given over to her use.

—I *must*.

Sari looked up, nodded patiently. "Yes," she said.
"And you will."

It was easy to agree with his manias. Perhaps it was
no more than just another instance of the idiotic cour-
tesy that had entrapped her before, that had nearly
caused her to succumb to Charna's plots. Beshur had,
after all, given her food and a place to sleep, and had
taken care of her while she recovered her strength. He
had his ways, certainly, but he was a decent fellow,
quite unlike either Maumud or the Naian men that she
had met since she had left her village . . .

Her village. She nearly giggled. What village did
she have? A new body, an old heart, a command from
the Goddess Herself . . . what indeed? At times, she

was almost giddy with the knowledge of what had happened to her, and in the course of the few walks she had taken through the Naian Quarter, she had frequently been forced to make an effort to control her laughter. Crystals, and wind chimes, and superstition—all badly aspected, of course!—and here was Sari, an old woman made young again, feeling once more the flutterings of ovulation and flow, occasionally detecting a faint stirring in her belly at the sight of a particularly good-looking man in the street . . .

She put her hand to her face, and this time she did indeed giggle.

Beshur was still standing over her.

—It is a holy place, he said. It is not a laughing matter.

"Holy," she replied, still giggling in spite of herself. "Yes. I am sure of it."

But when she looked up, she saw an expression on his face that she did not understand. No: that was a lie. She understood it very well. She understood it *too* well.

Oh. Oh, yes. That.

She stopped giggling. "Excuse me," she said faintly. "I . . . ah . . . must go."

Beshur continued to stare down at her, his lips half parted. Sari had the curious sensation that she had just been transformed again. Into a piece of fruit.

But at last Beshur stepped away.

—All right, he said.

A flutter of skirts, a swish of hair, and Sari bolted from the room.

Heart pounding, belly (Was it? Really?) stirring, she rattled down the steep, wooden stairs to the ground floor, raising a cloud of dust from the unswept treads as she went. Down in the shop was the dealer in insignificant brassware—she remembered both shop and dealer well—and he did not fail to look up when he heard her coming.

"Ah!" he said. "It is a fine day, good wife, is it not?" (Despite her vehement denials, he could not be disabused of the idea that she was Beshur's wife.) "But I am afraid that I must tell your husband that I will have to raise your rent anyway, for I am a professional, am I not? And I must make a living, must I not? And I find that even when two are married, two are more expensive to keep than one, are they not?"

Sari stood at the base of the stairs, feeling unsettled, feeling young, feeling just a little too perfect in her appearance. She knew what the dealer was seeing. A fine end for the Children of the Goddess!

"I am going to buy supplies," she said, thinking with a shudder of the look that she had seen on Beshur's face. Did she really want to go back there? But no: she was safe enough. Beshur would undoubtedly debate endlessly and inwardly about the ethics of what he wanted, would sideslip into another examination of his stubbly hair, and from there would return to his obsession about the Library. He would leave her alone.

"Supplies?" The dealer stared at her.

"I am an herbalist," she said. "it is time that I paid my own way."

"Herbalist?"

"Yes."

"Your . . . own way . . ." The dealer stared some more. "You mean . . . you mean your husband *lets* you?"

A flutter of skirts, a swish of hair, and Sari bolted from the shop.

Once she was out in the street, she leaned against the side of the building, her hands to her too-smooth face. Between her fingers, she could see the cracked and mazed residences and shops of the Naian Quarter, with every wall and floor and roof misaligned just a fraction of a degree from the perpendicular. All in all, the sight gave her a mild sense of vertigo, though none of the Naians ever seemed to take any notice of it.

The smell of incense. The tinkle of wind chimes. And, faintly, from the distance: *Hunna-hunna-hunna-hon!*

Here she was. In Katha. And young. And with a mission. Naia had said it as clearly as if She had spoken the words aloud. *Clear the Caves.* Unfortunately, the Goddess had not thought it necessary to inform her daughter as to how she was to gather together a group of people who seemed to make a virtue of disorganization, transport them to the Caves, and convince them to move large amounts of rock from one place to another. And, peering through her fingers at the cracked walls, smelling the incense, listening to the random tinkling of the wind chimes (whose ephemeral and relatively trivial nature seemed to her to symbolize perfectly what she had seen of contemporary Naianism), Sari felt the hopelessness of the situation.

Hunna-hunna-hunna-HON!

"Goddess," she murmured, "maybe it would have been better had You ... ah ... well ... that is ... I mean ..."

But the words would not come. She had been touched. There was no question about it, no doubt. Sari's own hands had felt the reality of her body just as they had felt the ponderous mass of the decidedly real rocks that had filled the Caves.

"Well ... all right."

Not feeling at all confident, she pushed off from the wall and started toward the market. She was an herbalist: with sufficient supplies she could set herself up in a small business and support herself—perhaps even move away from Beshur and his strange obsessions— while she looked for some way to fulfill the Goddess' commands. Given that herbalism now seemed to be a

forgotten art among Naians, she supposed that she
would be able to do reasonably well for herself.

She crunched along the sandy streets, passing among
jumbled houses and random shops. Above her head,
the roofs stuck up as though they were a blanket that
was covering something fairly bizarre, something with
many points and projections . . . and little purpose. Incense and wind chimes followed her.

Hunna-hunna-hunna-HON!

"It would work so much better if they only did it
right," she muttered as she stepped into the small
square that served as the market in the Naian Quarter,
and, truly, she was not sure whether she should laugh
or weep. Clear the Caves, indeed! At least her immediate goal was vaguely attainable!

Or . . . perhaps not. Though the market square offered a variety of wares, both Panasian and Naian, no
one seemed to be in the business of selling herbs. Sari
found resins (at an inflated price), jars of colored sawdust that she thought she recognized (and from which
she turned away with a shudder), and large, uncarved
blocks of fragrant wood (from which, as the merchant
enthusiastically told her, important things could be
carved), but no herbs. Neither fresh nor dried. None.

"None?" she wondered.

"Well," said the vendor of the uncarved blocks,
"people will not buy what they do not want or need,
and I am sure that even an attractive young girl like
you will understand that. While it is true that some of
our older residents still believe in the efficacy of vegetable matter of varying sorts, they are, you understand, quite old and therefore their judgment is not of
the best quality, unlike these magnificent blocks of
wood. Much better for illnesses of any sort are gem
elixirs, for stone is imperishable and cannot but influence the body to its betterment, for to put something
that is corruptible into something that is sick would be

as unintelligent as, for example, to use a magical tool that is consumable by the power supposedly controlled by it, and yet some people will do just that, though, as I said, they are usually old, and therefore their judgment is not of the best quality, unlike these magnificent blocks of wood. Why, I have heard of cures being performed by the gem elixirs that one can only call miraculous, yes, miraculous; and there was one time I was told by a friend whose cousin had an acquaintance whose father had been *raised from the dead* by an elixir of such potency that, well, it absolutely defies comprehension. I heard from this same friend that the mixture actually *smoked* when the physician pulled the stopper from the bottle, and that a drop, only a drop, under the tongue of the corpse, a single drop, mind you, brought the old man right to his feet, endowed him with the sexual potency of a camel in rut, and enabled him to work for five days without sleep, after which he sat down and ate an entire sheep for dinner. It was most remarkable, and I would have you know that this wood that I sell is of the very same quality, for it comes from trees that grow not on any ordinary ground, but upon soil from which those very gems were taken, and I am sure that even such an attractive young girl as you will be able to see the virtue in that, and therefore in the articles that you can make of this wonderful wood."

He looked at her expectantly.

Sari reached back, cleared her hair from the neckline of her shoulder cloth. "Does *anyone* sell herbs anymore?"

"Well," said the vendor of the uncarved blocks, "you might try the Panasian market in the city, for I have it on very good authority that even though the Panasians practice a religion that can only be dying, there are many interesting things there that you cannot buy elsewhere, but of course there is no wood of this sort, and I am sure ..."

A flutter of skirts, a swish of hair, and Sari bolted from the market.

Chapter Five

Clean-shaven, but a little disreputable-looking none-theless, the thief (for that is what he is) skulks (for that is what thieves do) through the shadows (though, since it is noon, there are not very many shadows near the base of the wall that separates the (unclean and super-stitious) Naian Quarter from the rest of the (virtuous and enlightened) city of Panas, Katha.

Or maybe that should be the other way around. Suit yourself.)

As is the case with most thieves, he is waiting for an opportunity. In this case, the opportunity involves climbing up and over the wall and thus effecting an un-observed entrance into the Naian Quarter. The fact that, were he to go straight up to the gate and present himself to the guards, he would be allowed to enter publicly and freely is of no consequence to him. He is a thief, and thieves have a certain pride, and they will not willingly do *anything* with official approval if they can help it.

Heat and fatigue and boredom being what they are, though, the desired opportunity eventually comes, and the thief, with a trot, a hop, and a quick scramble, gains the top of the wall; and with a swing, a hang, and another quick scramble (this last, unfortunately, ending with an abrupt *thump*), reaches the ground inside the Quarter.

Incense. Wind chimes.

Hunna-hunna-hunna-hon!

Smelling, listening, the thief gets to his feet. What?

Hunna-hunna-hunna-hon!

No matter: he is in the Naian Quarter now, and he has managed to get into it without so much as a smidgen of official approval (though here it must be remarked that, as the greater Panasian community is of the general opinion that nothing of any value—save, perhaps, an increased tax base—can come from the Naian community, the guards at the gate, if they are concerned about thieves at all, are more concerned about thieves who are coming *out* of the Quarter and *into* the greater Panasian community (though there is, admittedly, no record that any such thing has ever happened) than they are about thieves who, for some strange reason, insist upon breaking *into* the Naian Quarter from *out* of the greater Panasian community).

Hunna-hunna-hunna-hon!

But as he dusts himself off (the rubbish heap upon which he has fallen (Are those *crystals*?) being a rather dirty affair), he sees, coming down the crooked Naian street toward him, or, rather, toward the gate that leads out into the greater Panasian community, the woman for whom he has just skulked, climbed, and plummeted into the Naian Quarter!

Though she does not appear to be pursued, she is all but running, and her dark hair (the color of dreams about which, the thief is sure, Panasian law is very clear in one way or another) is streaming out behind her as she heads for the gate. This will not do. Not at all. The woman is obviously upset (bad), she is leaving the Naian Quarter (worse), and as she is looking only at the gate, she is paying no attention to the thief whatsoever (intolerable!).

Well, there is nothing for him to do but follow her.

Opting this time for speed rather than for pride, he follows the woman through the gate, only to discover that, though the guards are apparently bored enough (and mindful enough of a certain incident that took place at the gates of the city a week or two ago) to let the woman pass without comment, they are not quite bored enough to be free of curiosity about the thief.

"Are you not the idiot who climbed over the wall?" one of them asks.

"No," replies the thief with perfect equanimity, reflecting that it is not only in the nature of a thief to lie, but impossible for this particular thief to be an idiot. At least he does not *think* so.

"Oh ... all right then ..."

And now he is back in the greater Panasian community, which, a few minutes ago, by means of great patience and extraordinary effort, he left. Under other circumstances, this thief might be chagrined at the waste of time and energy, but, like the woman, he has other things on his mind. In his case: the woman.

But where has she gone?

Wagons rumble up and down the narrow streets. Weary oxen (Are oxen ever anything *but* weary?) plod along with baskets and panniers on their backs. Camels bob their heads and occasionally spit at the unwary. People—all men—go from place to place, not willy-nilly like Europeans, but with definite purpose. Somewhere among all of them is that woman ...

The thief plucks at the sleeve of a passerby. "Panas (blessed be He!) is good," he says.

"His chisel is hard and sharp," comes the proper reply.

"Have you seen a young Naian woman pass by?"

The passerby examines the thief for a moment. "Are you not the idiot who climbed over the wall?"

"No," replies the thief with perfect forthrightness (see above: *perfect equanimity*).

"Oh . . . all right then. She went up that street. I suppose she is going to the market."

"A thousand thanks. May Panas (blessed be He!) reward you, friend."

"And you also. Are you *sure* that you are not—"

But the thief is already jogging up the indicated street, reflecting as he goes that it is the nature of thieves to lie, that he himself cannot possibly be an idiot, and that the passerby is eventually going to miss his purse.

Dodging the aforementioned wagons, (weary) oxen, camels, and a host of people (all men) who are determined to get to where they are going to and thereafter to stay there until they have something better to do (at least in the case of the people (all men)), the thief makes his way along the narrow, crowded street, always straining his eyes ahead for a glimpse of the woman he has been following, though at this point, he cannot be said to be so much following her as searching for her.

But as he is a clever thief and a wily one, he catches a glimpse of her as soon as he reaches the market. There she is, hair and all, asking directions. Oh, gone again! No! Ah, there she is again, asking more directions and looking frustrated and agitated! Once more, she vanishes!

Where is she now? Over here? No. Over there? Yes? Maybe? No! Yes!

She has finally reappeared at a stall that seems to the thief to be a strange affair, for what else but strange is a stall that is, seemingly, stocked with bushes? Dried bushes, fresh bushes, cut up bushes, whole bushes . . . all bushes, everywhere.

And she is still not paying any attention to him!

But as he is a thief, and as he is a bit philosophical

(for a thief), he considers that perhaps it is better, over-all, if she does pay attention to him. Paying attention can come later. For now, it is probably to his advantage to remain, as the Europeans say, *incognito*. (Strange how such a disreputable-looking thief knows anything at all about what Europeans say!) And so, rather than making himself conspicuous to her (which is what he intended to do when he waited, climbed, and plummeted a short while ago), he instead loses himself in the crowd that has come to the market this morning, takes a moment to poke at a melon or two in a fruit stall (and is sternly reprimanded for his poking by the owner of the melons), and eventually drifts toward the stall of the bush-seller, nibbling a slice of purloined melon as he listens to the conversation between the woman, the bush-seller, and another woman (Another Naian? How strange!) who has also apparently decided that she is in need of bushes today.

Throughout her life as a Panasian, and despite her husband's disapproval, Sari had practiced her clandestine herbalism with a careful attention to detail and a breadth of knowledge that had carried over even into what had, a few weeks ago, turned abruptly into a rather bizarre version of old age. Hence, when she came to the stall of the herb merchant, she knew exactly what she wanted, and, without faltering, rattled off a list of her needs that included everything from common earfeather and sweetstraw (which, though legitimate additions to the cooking pots of the Three Kingdoms, seemed to be known to Naians only as *weeds*) to the more exotic sweetcandle and straxonephridia (which Sari was actually a little surprised that he had at all).

The merchant obviously thought very little of this Naian slut who had come to him for her purchases without even having the decency to cover her head

(Surely she could do *that* much!), but he cut and filled and tied up as quickly as she spoke. He was a big man, grizzled and massive, with a great, wide beard that appeared to have taken its inspiration from the plants he sold, for it exploded and twined in every direction like an exuberant mat of mixed moss and ivy, and when he bent to cut off a portion of one of the more robust examples of his wares (several of which had apparently been torn out of the ground in one piece, and it would not have been at all remarkable had he had an entire *tree* somewhere in that stall, so dense it was with vegetation), Sari was in some doubt as to whether a certain amount of outré cross-pollination was going on between the beard and the bush, and once or twice she found that she was actually holding her breath for fear that some sort of vegetable awfulness was going to take place ... until he at last straightened up without seeming much the worse for wear.

But Sari did her best to ignore not only his beard, but also his disapproving glances (She had not spent fifty years with a Panasian husband for nothing, after all.); and once he had packed her purchases into a large, cloth sack, and once she had paid him the agreed-upon price, she was just on the verge of congratulating herself on a successful expedition when, as she turned to go, she collided with a woman.

"Well," said the woman. "That is what one might expect today. Saturn *is* retrograde after all."

Charna.

Sari blanched.

"But," said the not-badly-aspected Naian leader with more than the usual undercurrent of sarcasm in her voice and a decided wiggle of her shoulders that was obviously for the benefit of the Panasian herb merchant (who continued to glare at both of the women without a shred of approval for these Naian sluts who would not even kneel to him (Surely they could do *that* much!)), "I see that you are new in Katha. I am Charna."

"Ah . . ." Not being able to think of a lie, Sari defaulted to the truth. "I am Sari."

Charna eyed her. "Really?"

"Well . . ." Well, it *was* her name after all. Sari squared her shoulders. "Is something wrong with my name?"

Charna smiled in a manner that Sari knew was supposed to be charming. "Of course not," she said. "It was just that I was thinking of another Sari that I knew once. Long ago. Very badly-aspected. Quite grotesque. You so obviously share none of those qualities with her. It was . . ."

Sarcasm. Sarcasm. Sarcasm. Sari carefully kept herself from wincing.

". . . such a curious coincidence . . ."

Recalling Charna's attempt to drug her, Sari carefully redoubled her efforts to keep herself from wincing.

". . . but then, you *are* an Aquarius, after all, and so well-aspected!"

Still (carefully) attempting to keep her winces under control, Sari now found herself simultaneously fighting with urges that pushed her toward doing something unfortunate with the large sack of herbs at her feet. But no: if she expected to be able to gather enough Naians together to unearth the Caves, she would have to be at least polite to this woman.

"How . . . ah . . . perceptive of you," she managed, though, in truth, she still had no idea what sign she was.

"Oh, it is all a matter of training," Charna replied smoothly. "My mother was an astrologer, and her mother before her. It is a family tradition, you know. Why, we can trace our lineage all the way back to the astrologers who crossed over the Mountains of Ern when Naia first brought Her people to this land."

Astrologers? The Hymns of Loomar said nothing about astrologers. In fact, now that she thought about it, Sari vaguely recalled that astrology—

"Oh! Hel-*lo*! You are new in Katha, are you not?"

As they had been speaking, and as the herb merchant had continued to glower at these Naian sluts who did not even have the decency to drop what they were doing and massage his feet (Surely they could do *that* much!), another woman had appeared at the stall.

"Oh!" said Charna. "What a pleasant surprise. How . . . nice to see you, Jeddiah. Sari, this is Jeddiah. Another . . ."

Sari had already recognized Jeddiah. She had met her at the gathering at Charna's house that had almost ended with a cup of drugged wine.

". . . leader in the Naian community."

Where Charna was sarcastic (and that quality was, to be sure, not missing from her introduction), Jeddiah was bubbly and vague. "Oh," she said, "thank you, Charna. Such a wonderful compliment! There are . . . so *few* leaders in the Naian community!"

Leaders. Yes. Sari remembered.

"Yes, of course," said Charna.

"But Naia is good!" Jeddiah burbled. "She has given me talents . . ."

"Yes, of course," said Charna.

". . . which I, to be sure, offer freely." Jeddiah nodded vehemently. "As a service to the community, you understand."

"Yes . . . of . . . course."

"I only ask that I be . . . reimbursed for my time. You understand."

"Yes, of course."

It seemed to Sari that Charna was now eyeing the

large sack of herbs as though herself considering whether to do something unfortunate with it.

"But you *must* tell me about your friend here!"

"My friend," said Charna. (Was there just a bit too much stress on the word *my*?) "Yes, my friend." (Yes, there was.) "Well, Sari is a distinguished visitor to Katha. An important person."

Distinguished visitor. Important person. Just as before. Sari desperately wanted to be away. Even *Beshur* was preferable to this.

"Another one?" said Jeddiah, with perfect disingenuousness.

"Another what?"

"Another important person? Why I recall that just a few weeks ago, you—"

"Yes." Charna uttered the word and all but closed her mouth with a snap.

The two women would have glared at one another but for the fact that Charna could only be offhand and sarcastic while Jeddiah could only beam. As it was, the Panasian herb merchant was doing more than enough glaring for everyone, having obviously become quite enraged by these Naian sluts who did not even have the decency to take off their shoulder wraps and rub their naked bodies against his face. (Surely they could do *that* much!)

"Ah . . . you must both pardon me," said Sari as she began edging away, "I must attend to my . . . ah . . . business . . ."

"Business!" cried Jeddiah, catching hold of her sleeve. "Why, you must tell me all about it! What do you do? Divination? Amulets? Card readings? Let me tell you about the powder that I make! I strew it about every morning, and it . . ."

Charna caught hold of Sari's other sleeve. "Sari and I have some . . . things to talk about, dear Jeddiah."

"Ah!" Jeddiah was fairly bubbling with vague delight. "But I'm sure that your sawdust and perfumes will keep for a bit, my dear Charna. Just until Sari and I have had a chance for a little talk." She shifted her beam to Sari. "You must tell me all about your business, Sari, and how you have gotten permission for such a thing from your husband." She paused. "You *are* married, are you not?"

The Retort Courteous

"Ah . . . no."

Jeddiah did not seem to hear her. "But what a wonderful name! Sari. Sari! Bright blessings to you, Sari! We have so much to talk about. Why, I'm sure that you will be a valuable person for my school. To teach, you know. The old ways."

Now Sari did indeed wince. "The . . . old ways?"

"Oh, yes," Jeddiah went on. "The old ways. Unlike some . . ." She looked at Charna, smiled at her. ". . . of the *newer* traditions, we will be teaching the *real* ways of Naia."

The Quip Modest

Caught, literally, between the two women, Sari could do nothing but refuse to yield to either while the herb merchant continued to glare at all three of the Naian sluts who did not even have the decency to lie down and allow him to violate them bloody. (Surely they could do *that* much!)

Charna would not relinquish her grip. "I'm sure that Sari will be more than happy to talk to you about your school, Jeddiah. When you actually have one."

The Reply Churlish

"Oh, but I am here as a representative of the Goddess," said Jeddiah, who would not relinquish *her* grip, either. "As a service to the community. The Goddess wants a school."

"And a temple, do not forget the temple, Jeddiah." Charna would have looked kittenish, but for the fact that there appeared to be a badger somewhere beneath all the mewing and fuzziness.

The Reproof Valiant

"Yes, the temple. You know, Sari, there are those of us in the community who continue to hold to spiritual goals, instead of to the mere acquisition of money. That is what I call serving the community." Jeddiah nodded and beamed vaguely.

The Countercheck Quarrelsome

Charna was ironic. Jeddiah was beaming. Sari was beginning to feel desperate.

The merchant continued to glare at the Naian sluts who ... etc.

"As it is," said Charna, "we were ... ah ... going to be discussing the meeting."

The Lie Circumstantial Declined

"Oh," said Jeddiah, "then you will want me to be present, since I am an important part of that committee."

"Oh, it is nothing that you need to bother with."

"Oh, I do not mind in the slightest!"

For an instant, the two women who held Sari looked very much as though they were considering King Solomon's solution to a difficult problem, but before they could put it into effect, a tall man appeared at the stall and went directly up to Sari (who was by now all but sus-

The Lie Direct Declined: and so they measure swords and part

pended between the equal and opposing
forces being exerted by Charna and
Jeddiah).

"Ah! There you are!" he said with a bright smile. "I
have been looking all over for you, my dear wife!"

"Wife?" said Sari, dazed.

He was dashing and he was handsome (despite the
fact that he looked as though he had been badly shaved
recently . . . which gave him a certain disreputable air),
and so great was the feeling of almost kingly presence
about him that Charna and Jeddiah did not protest
when he removed Sari from their grasp.

"It is terrible how the crowds in the marketplace can
separate a man from his wife," he said, smiling his
bright smile even into the face of the glaring merchant
. . . who found his glare somewhat blunted as a result.
"I have been searching for my dear wife for some
time, now. I'm sure you both know very well . . ."

He eyed them.

". . . that it is very dangerous for a Naian woman to
be wandering about in the marketplace by herself."

"Oh," said Charna and Jeddiah almost simultaneously, "no one ever bothers *me*!"

"And I can see why," said the man so smoothly and
with such a very bright smile that neither Charna
nor Jeddiah said anything about the less-than-
complimentary meanings inherent in his statement.
"Come, Sari!"

"But . . . but . . ."

He leaned down to her ear. "I am trying to get you
away from these *harpies*," he whispered. "If you will
just go along with me, I will help you."

Sari had no idea what *harpies* were, but she was
dazed and desperate enough to allow herself to be led
away from the stall. And surely she could not possibly
mind the strong hand of a handsome man on her arm
all that much, despite the fact that she could not but be

a little curious as to why such a handsome man would
be interested in an old ...

Oh. Oh, yes. That.

"But I am not your wife," she managed.

"Oh," he said, "I certainly will not hold you to *that*.
It was simply the best that I could come up with under
the circumstances."

"But ... who are you?"

He stood as though stunned, and Sari could not
fathom it. A simple request for a name, and here he
was, looking as though he had just discovered that his
(already eaten) dinner had been poisoned.

"Is there a problem, my brother?"

"I am ... ah ... that is ... I mean ... I ..."

"I am sorry. I should not have asked."

"I am the ... the ... the ... ah ... the ..."

"Really: it is perfectly all right."

Despite her reassurances, he was plainly desperate;
and, momentarily unaware of where he was going, he
ran directly into a cart full of roots and vegetables.

The cart tipped, and produce was suddenly
everywhere—rolling on the ground, falling on his feet,
skittering across the dusty pavement of the market—
and was being pursued by its irate owner.

Sari's rescuer looked down, and, suddenly: "I am ...
Potatoes!"

And as the owner of the cart, his wares snatched by
the hands and trampled by the feet of the crowd, ad-
vanced on him with what Sari could only suppose to be
some kind of vengeful purpose, there was a sudden
blaring of horns and a beating of gongs. Soldiers and
barefoot boys with powdered faces appeared, leading
into the market square a long line of camels, horses,
people, carts, wagons, canopies of brightly colored
cloth, gilt banners, and a hundred other magnificent
things. Oh, it was a grand and glorious procession that

had come to Katha this afternoon, a progress fit for a king, an emperor ...

... or even the Gharat Abnel himself, High Priest of Panas, Hicrophant of the Three Kingdoms.

The owner of the cart was distracted from his vengeance. The crowd forgot its snatched and trampled roots. The progress continued to enter the marketplace, to interfere with commerce, to arrest citizens who were unfortunate enough to be in its way (Panasian law was very clear about things like that.), and to make for the complex of priestly buildings that surrounded the Temple of Panas.

Shaking herself out of her astonishment, Sari looked at her companion. "Ah ... Potatoes?"

He cleared his throat. "Potatoes. Yes."

And so it was.

Chapter Six

It was a palpable hole.

At the site on the Promenade of the Justified Wealth of Merchants where once had stood a small embroidery shop (which had also sold doors (used and new), strange devices of a sexual (and crippling) nature, and explosive substances), there was now a deep pit. Actually, the entire Promenade of the Justified Wealth of Merchants had been replaced by the pit, for, as the late Citizen Valdemar had insisted, the goods he had sold had been of nothing less than the finest quality.

All around the pit, buildings had been thrown about like so many wooden blocks. Masses of stone that had, according to Panasian tradition, remained divinely situated and unmoved for thousands of years had been very much unsituated and very much moved. Entire streets of shops and houses had been flattened . . . including the one that had contained the dwelling of one Umi Botzu, would-be scientist. (But Umi Botzu is beyond caring about such things, and does not at present notice the disarray in which the explosion has left his rooms, his tables, and his precious curiosities.)

Haddar, shaven and shorn and looking very much forlorn which was sad for one so noble-born (Burton would have done it that way had he thought of it, all right? He did enough of that sort of thing as it was.

You should be grateful I am leaving it at that. Or did
you *want* the dot-of-ambergris-and-dimples-adorn routine?), and trying to ignore the stares (Is it still there,
Haddar? Better check. Yes? Good! Hang on to it this
time, dood. Pricks are funny things, you know. Ask Sir
Richard. He *knows*.), was inspecting the hole while his
masculine (Oh, yes! Very!) mind sorted methodically
through the possible causes and meanings of this disas-
ter.

About him, the survivors of the catastrophic detonation discussed how extremely fortunate they were to be
alive:

"Well, you see, it is only right that I petition the
king for what is left of your house, as mine is entirely
destroyed, and your ancestors were only allowed to
move within the city walls by royal decree ... and
only three hundred years ago. Now, *mine,* you see ..."

"Well, that is all very well and good, but three hundred years ago, your hovel was already in a sorry state
of decay, and you will have to talk to Panas (blessed be
He!) Himself about that, because I am sure that He
would not at all appreciate the fact that your family
took a house that was *divinely inspired,* not to mention
divinely *built* and turned it, in only a matter of centuries, into ..."

"A thousand pardons, but I feel compelled to add
my opinion. Is it not written in the Sacred Texts themselves that—?"

And here, this last speaker, on the verge of quoting
from the Sacred Texts, was grabbed and dragged off by
the religious police (Panasian law was very clear about
things like that). His wife, having suddenly acquired
the status of being married to a criminal, was also
dragged away, though in her case the dragging was
performed by a group of passersby who were more
than willing to administer to her the customary penalty.

"Now, I am not one to name names, but if certain

people had not *bought* their royal decrees with money made in a very dubious fashion while they were living in mud dwellings, then they would not be living in stone at all."

"But, as you mention mud dwellings, I should point out that ..."

Despite the maze of tortured logic exhibited by the bystanders, the situation was very clear to Haddar (and his masculine (Very!) mind): The Freedom Fighters of Khyr, having gained nothing through their periodic destruction of the mud dwellings that swarmed like an epidemic of poverty and ignorance about the outer walls of Nuhr, had turned to a more grievous crime: outright sacrilege. They had attacked the city within the walls, the fabric of stone laid down by the God Himself.

"Blessed be He," he murmured, causing the religious police to start toward him. Upon reflection, though, the police left Haddar unmolested and undragged, and instead returned their attentions to the common criminal who had quoted from the Sacred Texts (Well, *almost* quoted. It was close enough.) while the group of civic-minded passersby continued to attend to his despicable wife, whose shrieking crescendoed and then abruptly faded; and (Haddar reflected) was that not just like a woman? No stamina whatsoever.

Haddar was very glad that *he* was not a woman.

Really. He was.

(Still there, Haddar? Well?)

But, suddenly, he was gripped once again by uncertainty. Should he be competent? Should he be efficient? *Should* he be in charge, dictating to others (who were *certainly* more competent and efficient than he was, of that he was absolutely sure) what they should do and how they should do it? After all, the ache that had taken up what seemed at times to be permanent residence in his groin, and which was, even now, making him clench his teeth in an effort to keep from squirming . . .

Did anyone notice? Were they looking?

. . . was ample evidence of his weakness.

Not masculine. Not at all. And the very place in which he was standing—the remains of the Promenade of the Justified Wealth of Merchants—was a reminder of how he had come by that ache and what he had been doing when he had acquired it.

The woman's screams (the wife of a common criminal: just desserts to her) had stopped. Weak things, women. It was a very good thing that . . .

Haddar straightened up. He must be sure. He must be positive. He must be efficient, for to be otherwise . . .

"They must be punished," he said aloud. "And they will. If every Khyrling must be hunted down and impaled in the market place, we will find them."

Yes. Positive. Definite.

Haddar straightened his shoulders. The hot wind blew on his shaven face, and he felt a looseness about his belly that he immediately suppressed. Still, the thoughts came, unbidden. Why, he could wear the device *under his clothing,* and no one would know except him. How wonderful . . .

And the bystanders were still congratulating one another on their narrow escape:

"But if you ask me—"

"But I was *not* asking you."

"Well, if you *did* ask me, I would tell you that your house should now be mine, because—"

"I *have* my house, Panas (blessed be He!) be praised, and I intend to keep it."

"But . . ."

"It is the will of Panas (blessed be He!) that there be only so many houses of stone within the precincts of the city . . ." (And here the religious police were eyeing the speaker, waiting.) ". . . and that only those individuals of proven merit be allowed to have them. Is it not also the will of Panas that *my* house be still standing . . . ?"

"If you can call *that* standing."

"Well, it seems to be good enough for *you*!"

"It is within my power to restore it!"

"Oh, so you would interfere with the handiwork of the God Himself!"

"Handiwork! Handiwork! It was the handiwork of men that destroyed it! And as for interfering, why, is it not written that *Color and gold—*?"

And the religious police move in once more.

. . . must have it thought about. Yes. I will have it thought about. But it is Haddar who must think about it, and he has been . . . well, *squirming,* and that makes me nervous. I must have that thought about, too. But Haddar . . .

Pumice, I will have to have it thought about by someone else. But who? Haddar would know. But . . .

Pumice!

And why did he shave off his beard? I must admit that he does not look at all uncomely with a shaven face, but it is not at all customary, and it is so unusual for him to do something uncustomary like that . . . but . . . but that squirming. I must have that thought—

Pumice!

"We can only conclude," said Haddar as a kind of a soft shudder went through him, "that the explosion was the work of the Freedom Fighters of Khyr—so they call themselves—who say that by these criminal acts they are avenging the wrongs perpetrated upon their nonexistent country."

Squirming again. How can I have it thought about by Haddar if he continues to squirm? But Haddar is trustworthy, I think, but ... there, I must have *that* thought about also, and there is no one to think about it and ...

(Squirm!)

There it is again. And with Aeid gone, there is ...

But what about Aeid? And those books. Bakbuk told me about them. But now Bakbuk—

"I have not yet been able to determine just how the explosives were smuggled into the city ..."

—is gone, too. I sent him to protect the Gharat. Taxes. Blue Avenger. Avenger gone. Aeid gone. Taxes continue. I did not remember the Texts saying so. Wrong? But Bakbuk found those books in Aeid's chambers. What? Could it be? Should I mention it to Haddar?

(Squirm!)

But is Haddar someone to whom I should mention it? He is acting oddly, though I must have it thought—

Pumice!

"... though such a thing could only have been brought to pass with the cooperation of individuals in high authority."

If only Aeid were here. But Aeid ... republicanism. Those books. Would he?

And where is he?

What if ... ?

I must have—

Pumice!

Khyrlings!

High authority!

Aeid!

Ineluctable modality of womanhood. Held in my arms. Novices' house. Smucking. Giggling. No. Not her. Serious. Always serious. By the Goddess. Of course. What then of Panas? Consort. Cannot believe. But she is sure, standing there in her torn wraps, holding them to her breasts (!) like a woman caught. But she was not caught. I was. She caught me. Looking at her.

Beshur paced furiously back and forth in the room. He had gone out to carry shortly after Sari had left, and now, with sore shoulders, tired arms, and a pouch full of coins, he had returned. But no Sari. Only the cat was there to arch its back and lift its lascivious rump to his hand when he reached down to stroke its fur.

"Mrkgnao!"

—Did she come back, cat? Beshur said.

"'Gnao?"

Gone out. Was in trouble when I found her. Is probably in trouble now. What will she do? And that man. Blue. All blue. Sky God. All in blue did he cart the rocks down and build the cities. Will graven in stone. Forever. Chiseled out of universe. Blue. Wait . . . wait . . .

You do not suppose that *he* was . . . ?

No. Never. I do not believe. Oh, is he real then? Kisses are flowers. Mark of flowers. No flowers. Drought. Disappeared. None. Here, walk like this. What . . . ?

But where is she?

Do not care. By the Goddess. Let her rave.

His hand was closing on the latch of the door.

What is she to me? Nothing. A woman.

His feet were taking him down the stairs.

I should not worry. A Naian woman. Hah!

He was in the downstairs shop.

And I with more important things to do. Library. Must go to Nuhr. Find way in. Death. Do I care? Here, walk like—

Find out all. Secrets. Would not tell me, but I will find out. Best scholar of the school. All will be revealed to me. All! Woman? Pah!

—Where did Sari go? he said to the vendor of insignificant brassware.

"Well," said the vendor, "I do not know for sure, for

I am a professional, am I not? And therefore I must attend to my business, must I not? But I believe that she said she was going to buy supplies."

—Supplies?

Ignorant fool. Brassware like everything Naian. The girl. Sari. By the Goddess, she said. I do not care. Why should I care? More important things. Library.

"I do not know for sure, for I am—"

—What supplies?" Beshur said.

"Herbs, I believe," said the dealer, "or so she called them, though why she would want to buy weeds—"

Beshur was already out the door.

Herbs. Weeds. Next thing I know she will be eating grass in the square, save that there is no grass. No water. Clouds and rain in the mountains, but no water in the land. No flowers. Naia dead. No water, no woman. They told us that. Novices will believe anything. Texts say this. Texts say that. Texts never change. But they changed! Yes. And she was sent by the Goddess. Who would have sent her?

Those eyes!

Pah!

Out in the street, now, his steps crunching on litter and sand. Castoff crystals sparkled in the afternoon sun. Crooked streets opened up and took him in, digested him, moved him along as though with peristaltic contractions, excreted him in the—

Look, honey, I'm trying to get some work done. I can't help it if your boss is a dickhead. *My* boss was a dickhead, too, otherwise he wouldn't have fired me, but if *your* boss is a dickhead, it's no skin off my nose, on account of he's your boss and it's your job, and I'm trying to get this next scene down, and all your bitching and moaning isn't doing anything for me. OK?

So there was an earthquake. I know. I was here, remember? And everything's fucked up and no one can get anywhere, so everybody's in a pissy mood, but *I'm* gonna start being in a real good pissy mood if you don't leave me alone and lemme get some work done, on account of this thing's heating up, and if I just pull off this scene, I just know someone's gonna snap this up like a buncha Mexicans grabbing tacos. And then you won't have to worry about the rent, 'cause then I'll be making some money, and you can just concentrate on being my woman and taking care of me like you're supposed to.

See, things like this are kinda delicate. You don't just go pulling them out of your hat and throwing them on the paper. You got to handle them . . . like . . . correctly. OK? Got it? And I'm doing all this stuff *right*, so I *know* that this thing is really gonna take off. I got a college degree, you know, in Professional Writing. That's right: an M.F.A. And I'll tell you, that kind of thing opens up all kindsa doors, because I know what I'm doing, and they know I know, and I can just lead them around by the nose.

Take this thing here, for instance. See what I'm doing? This is all real good stuff. Like, I'm using James Joyce here, see? See, I've got this guy named Beshur. He's a real feep, I'll tell you. Fucked up from the word go. Well, he was gonna be a priest, only he got cold feet and dropped out. Now he's got this wild hair up his ass about finding out all the secrets of the priesthood and all that. 'Course, if you ask me, he could have just stayed in and found them all out, 'cause what does he care if he's a priest or not, huh? I mean, it doesn't make any difference, does it? If he wants to leave, he can just leave, right? Oh, they'd kick about it, but they're really too busy to worry about feeps like him, and, anyway, he thinks they're kicking about it now—runs around with one hand on his crotch, if you know what I mean—so what's the diff?

Anyway, he's like a real James Joyce character. Stephen Dedalus. Now, you don't know about Stevie-boy, but I do. Ties himself in knots, got guilt trips up to the eyeballs about God and all his brothers, but he thinks he's real hot shit on a golden platter intellectual-wise. OK? So what I'm doing is making this Beshur guy all like James Joyce would have done it. Interior monologue with lotsa big words (and I'm not gonna look 'em up, either, cause James Joyce sure as hell didn't!) and all kindsa guilt trips and stuff like that. And the best part of all is that I'm doing all his dialog in old J. J.'s style, without quotes. I just start it off with an em-dash ... 'course, you don't know what an em-dash is either, on account of you're a girl and that's writer stuff. Just take my word for it.

I'll tell you, this is going to be dynamite. And the best part of all is that when Beshur's with other people, they're all talking normal, but *he's* talking with those dashes! Yeah! It's really hot. It, like, clues everybody in on the James Joyce thing. Isn't it hot?

Oh, *yeah*! I'm doing this sort of thing *everywhere*! Lookee here in the first book: there's this question and answer stuff, like in that next to the last section of *Ulysses.* I never really read all the way through *Ulysses,* but I could tell that it was really hot stuff, and that's why I'm copping it. Got that? And I'm using this stuff like from that Molly Bloom monolog. You know, where she really tells what women are all about? Yeah. Now, I read *that*. And, boy-oh-boy, she was right on the money. James Joyce really *knew* all about that sort of thing. Sure he did! Hey, don't start squawking at me about it, honey. You haven't read it, so you don't know. And I can't help it if Jimmy pegged you gals the way he did.

And that's not all. There's this Umberto Eco dude

who's been getting all kinds of press with a couple books. Well, like you know, they're OK, and everything, but they're not real hot shit, either. It's really funny: he blows himself up with another book that's supposed to *explain* everything. Like, what kind of writer needs to *explain* anything? Huh? You tell me!

Anyway, I'm taking a couple licks at him, too. I've got mirrors in this thing already, and I'm putting in a library with all kinds of stuff in it, and . . .

What do you mean, screenplay? Oh, yeah. It'll be a screenplay. I'm a writer, and I'll figure it all out. It'll work, believe me. Just you wait and see!

—Naian market, where the stalls were just then beginning to close up. Wooden shutters clattered down. Donkeys stood silently while their backs were loaded. People (all men) stood about, discussing the day's events, arguing, occasionally falling upon one another with knives over some affair of honor (in the case of the Panasians), or talking their disagreements over like reasonable people (in the case of the Naians . . . and besides, they could always get back at one another in more subtle ways).

Ineluctable modality—no . . . used that before. All running about, going home to their wives, thrashed to pieces. Told us about that. Ah . . . that is camel dung and dried grass! Yes, clear my head. Sari. Why am I looking for Sari?

—Have you seen a woman pass through the market? Beshur said to a Naian merchant who was just putting away his unsold merchandise . . . which looked very much like uncarved blocks of fragrant wood.

"I have seen a few women in the market today," said the merchant, "and I must tell you that not one of them even stayed for more than a few minutes to examine these magnificent examples of wood, which, I assure you, will prove of no less than immense value in the fabrication of many useful things. Why . . ."

—This one did not have a man with her, Beshur said. Did she come this way?

". . . it is inconceivable that they would not buy. However, I have it on good authority that a woman who does not have a man with her is liable to be subject to all sorts of whims (on account of the heat of their vulvas, you understand, and excision is the only thing that can cure that, and why they will not submit to it, I do not know, being able only to account for it on the basis of their whims, which is the problem in the first place), and perhaps it is only the innate stubbornness of that sex that causes them to overlook such splendid blocks of wood as you see now before you. A fine young man like you could not ignore a chance like this, even . . ."

Blocks of wood! Pumice and tailings! What does he think I am?

—Have you seen her? Beshur said.

". . . if he demonstrates a most marked lack of discernment by ignoring these blocks of wood, which, as I am sure that I do not have to tell you, cannot but come from very extraordinary trees . . ."

Discernment? There is nothing wrong with my discernment!

". . . which is obvious to all but the most . . ."

The best scholar in my class! And they are not looking for me. No: cannot be true. They *must* be looking. Hidden. When I least expect it. But I can see . . . and my discernment cannot but be flawless, and . . . and . . .

—I am perfectly able to assay the quality of these blocks of wood, Beshur said. I do not need someone like *you* to tell me that they are very fine blocks!

". . . untrained and ignorant individuals who cannot know anything whatsoever of trees or of wood. Why, I was told once . . ."

—What is your price?

". . . that—" The merchant broke off, looked him up and down. "You want to . . . to . . . *buy*?"

—To buy! Beshur said. Name your price. I will show you who is ignorant of good quality wood!

"You want . . ." The merchant seemed dazed. "To . . . to *buy*," he said. "To actually . . . *buy*!"

—Pumice to you! You do not know your own wood!

And he turned away from the vendor of extremely fine uncarved blocks of wood and ran for the gateway that led to the greater Panasian community.

"To . . . *buy*!" said the merchant behind him, wondering.

No herbs here. Naia dead. Dead long ago. But Naians do not even know themselves what they practice. Copies of everything in Library. Must go to Library. Text changed: who changed it? Changes. Here, walk like this. Smucking. But bushes . . . I saw bushes in Panasian market. Sari there? Kisses. Flowers. Why flowers? Why. Ineluctable modality of the Panasian marketpl—No, not again! Only men. Women go only with men. What might she do? Must go to Library. Cannot leave her . . .

But bushes. Saw them. Did I? Discernment! Yes! Sari would go there. I do not care . . .

He ran to the gate, passed through. The guards seemed uninterested.

. . . about her. But she is alone and—!

Title: *That afternoon.*

Medium shot. Running from right to left is a street in Katha. Behind is the wall that divides the Naian Quarter from the greater Panasian community. In the middle of the wall is a gate. The wall is of white stone, polished to a matte finish. The gate is dark, but is flanked on either side by priestly guards dressed in identical outfits: green turbans, polished cotton shoulder cloths of a muted gold tone, skirts of the same fabric and color, and pointy-toed shoes of the best *Arabian Nights* vintage. The guards look very much alike. In fact, they might as well be played by the same actor.

The street is also of *Arabian Nights* vintage—the standard, narrow affair—and it is crowded with all sorts of people, from beggars to rich merchants, who, though they all appear to be going somewhere, never quite seem to be getting there. The overwhelming majority of them are Panasians, and are dressed in variations upon the theme of what the priestly guards are wearing (though with less of an "official" look). The Naians present are easily distinguished, for neither the men nor the (very few) women cover their heads, and the men are, as often as not, barechested.

There is, actually, only one woman: Sari. She is being escorted toward the gate by Potatoes. Though passing as a Naian, Potatoes at least keeps his chest decently covered. His face, though, has several cuts on it, giving him a rather disreputable appearance.

As they progress toward the gate, Potatoes is detained by a passerby.

Title. (Passerby) *Are you not the idiot who climbed over the wall?*

Potatoes explains that he is not, though the passerby indicates that, while this is all right, he is not at all convinced of it. Meanwhile, another passerby appears to be discovering that he has lost his purse. He wears the clothing of a fairly well-to-do Panasian. A large purse hangs from his belt.

Within a few beats, the crowd begins to scatter to

the sides of the street, and as the camera pans in the direction of the disturbance, we see that a grand procession, led by barefoot boys with powdered faces and servants blowing brass horns, is advancing along the street, and that the crowd is hastening to get out of its way.

Just then, Beshur comes sprinting out of the gateway. He seems quite distracted, and he becomes even more so when he sees Sari in the company of Potatoes. Before the guards can stop him, he is in the street, and, not being at all aware of where he is going, he crashes directly into the barefoot boys and the servants with the brass horns. Several immediately fall down, and the procession grinds to a halt.

A priestly guard in the procession (who is dressed exactly like the priestly guards at the gate, and who can also be played by the same actor) shouts in anger.

Title. (Guard) *Sacrilege!*

The procession is now in confusion. Brass horns have become locked together inextricably, and servants, still clutching them, fall to the ground like elk trapped in dominance combat. Wagons, carts, camels, asses, passengers . . . all are backing up and beginning to mill about as they find their way blocked.

Sitting amid the pomp of the increasingly disorganized procession, Mather squirms. Jenkins, beside him, looks at him in distaste. Abnel blandly peels a banana and eats it with an enigmatic expression on his face.

Title. (Guard) *Seize him!*

At once, a contingent of priestly guards (who are all dressed identically to the guards at the gate, and who can also be played by the same actor) advance on Beshur, who is trying to untangle himself from a heap of barefoot boys.

Sari has recognized Beshur. She turns to Potatoes in alarm.

Title. (Sari) That is Beshur!
Potatoes looks puzzled, then peers at Beshur.
Title. (Sari) *He is a friend. We must help him!*
Potatoes smiles and touches his forehead to Sari.
Fade out.

Chapter Seven

Pudda-pudda-pudda.

All in all, it was not a bad life for a ferret. Free run of the palace, all the raisins he could eat, a clean litterbox (which he used all the time ... unless he happened to come across a particularly attractive corner), a bed of soft rags to sleep in: Kuz Aswani could not have asked for more.

And yet ...

You don't love me anymore!

And yet there was a nagging sense of dissatisfaction about his routine (if a word like *routine* could ever be used with reference to a ferret) that manifested increasingly as the days went on (though, as he was a ferret, he had no real idea just how many days had gone on). For, though raisins were fine, and litterboxes (and, occasionally, corners) were fine, and soft beds of rags that he could crawl under and tuck in until he resembled nothing so much as one of the brown breakfast cakes (albeit a very large one) that he had once, as a Panasian husband, eaten with relish were fine ... there was nonetheless ... well ... something *lacking* in the life of a ferret, and Kuz Aswani found himself longing for the existence that he had left behind, the

human existence that had been so irrevocably ensorcelled away from him.

True, there was little that he could do about the en-
sorcellment, for Umi Botzu continued to keep careful
watch over his victim; and Kuz Aswani continued to
see the sorcerer everywhere: in distant doorways, peering out of windows, even dogging the footsteps of the
unfortunate Haddar, who was also—slowly but surely,
day by day—becoming increasingly ferretish, his recent attempt at removing the fur from his face an unmistakable sign of his frantic efforts to fend off the
inescapable change.

Poor Haddar! To feel the encroachments of the
metamorphosis so clearly and yet to be so powerless to
escape them! And Kuz Aswani could well sympathize
with the chief minister, for, like Haddar, Kuz Aswani
had once been in the grip of acute, incipient weaseliza-
tion, and he knew even better than Haddar that only
magic of an even more puissant nature than that
wielded by Umi Botzu could avert the fate that awaited
both of them. And where was such magic in a land
where magic was outlawed?

Nowhere. There was no such thing. Best to enjoy
what the life of a ferret had to offer, then, and be done
with it.

But of course I love you!

But still, *pudda-pudda-pudda*ing down the corridors
of the palace, leaping about with weaselish abandon at
the sight of a full bowl of raisins, even defiling a particularly choice corner that he had not visited before
(and in which the servants had neglected to spread paper and straw), Kuz Aswani would find himself
considering—in a ferrety sort of way—all the things
that he had lost. His books, his friends, his wife . . . all
these he considered; and he would, on occasion, find

himself gripped with a longing so powerful that, for an instant, he would see himself not as a carefree and happy ferret, but rather as a pitiful human figure who crawled, pale and naked, about the interior of the palace and attempted physically impossible feats of grooming and defecation as the result of an evil man's lust for power. And though, a moment later, he would jump up and wiggle with all the vigor of the best ferret in the world, still the longing would return, and in his own, ferretish way, he began to cast about in his mind for some agency by which he might be delivered from his present condition.

A few days after the explosion that had removed from physical reality the bodily presence of Citizen Valdemar, a number of his unsatisfied customers, and the entire Promenade of the Justified Wealth of Merchants, it was noticed that the resultant crater appeared to have quite a large amount of water in it.

It's very hard for me to tell sometimes.

The water went away after another few days.

Obadiah Jenkins could not for the life of him decide whether his current state of affairs represented the very best situation in which he could be—the culmination of all his dreams, wishes, and hopes—or the very worst of all un-Puritan and ungodly nightmares made real, concrete, and (worst of all) his personal responsibility.

That he should have found out about Mather's execrable vices was bad enough. That Mather was practicing those vices with the supreme religious leader of a heathen land was worse. That Jenkins himself was, at present, separated from his country and even from the small comfort of the military presence

embodied by the American ships was absolutely intolerable . . . not to mention terribly frightening, for what
with his acquaintance with Bakbuk and the subtle but
ever-present eroticism of the barefoot boys with the
powdered faces, Jenkins could easily fancy himself
adrift on a sea of rank perversion, kept from the unthinkable only by a tiny raft of determined virtue that
would doubtless not last more than a few days.

And yet, Jenkins had to admit that, looked at another
way, his position was quite enviable. Suddenly, much
that had been obscure had been made clear (though he
would never have put it that way to Mr. Wool, lest he
be answered by a multitude of Pauline quotations), not
the least of which was the strange and sudden willingness of the Gharat to cooperate with the American
embassy.

Why had Abnel agreed to take the heathen wool-
wearers to the holy city of Katha? Why, for the same
reason that Mather had suddenly become both ambi-
tious and rebellious! It all had to do with . . .

But here Jenkins could only clear his throat, unwilling to let the consideration of such un-Puritan
mechanics enter his mind.

What do you mean by that?

But though the mechanics involved in the sudden
alterations were, in and of themselves, abominable,
still there was a sense of godly purpose to it all, for
Jenkins was already seeing before him avenues and
paths of action by which he could accomplish what he
needed to accomplish. And as he watched Mather
make the final adjustments to the gravimeter in the pri-
vacy of their rooms in the priestly complex of Katha,
he could not but see the engineer—the toolmaker, the
tool adjuster—as something of a tool himself, nor

could he but marvel inwardly at the subtlety of the ways of the Almighty.

Tick-tick-tick!

Wegga-wegga-wegga!

The apparatus made its noises and swung its pendulums, and Mather, sitting behind it as though united with it in something akin to a bodily marriage (which made Jenkins consider, once more, certain un-Puritan mechanics that he did not want to consider), adjusted and moved and . . .

(Squirm!)

. . . occasionally squirmed.

You're just taking me for granted.

"Much better," the engineer muttered.

"Better for him that a millstone were hanged about his neck, and *that* he were drowned in the depth of the sea," responded Mr. Wool, whose position (behind low table, staring into space, eyes behind spectacles, knees above ear level, paper and pen before him) was little different from what it had been in Nuhr.

"Thank you, Mr. Wool," said Jenkins, who, despite the circumstances (Or perhaps *because* of them? It was becoming increasingly hard for him to tell.) was rather cheerful. He had Mather, and Mather did not know it. And if he had Mather, then he had the Gharat himself. And if he had the Gharat . . .

Why, the possibilities were *immense.*

Mather had looked up uneasily at Wool's words, but, with an expression of almost defiant resignation and one of his now-habitual . . .

(Squirm!)

. . . squirms, he settled back into his affair with the apparatus.

And once more Jenkins pushed the thought of un-Puritan mechanics out of his head.

"Can you gather enough information now?" he said.

Mather looked up indifferently (though Jenkins knew now that Mather was, in actuality, indifferent toward absolutely *nothing*) and shrugged. "It'll do," he said. "For now."

"For now."

(Squirm!)

I certainly am not! How can you say that?

Jenkins, though annoyed, restrained himself with a reminder that, given the physical effects that were in abundant evidence, Mather obviously *liked* to have various parts of his body twisted and battered; and though the ambassador tried very hard to keep the un-Puritan mechanics out of his mind, they insisted upon surfacing with alarming frequency and detail.

"For now we see through a glass darkly," said Wool, "but then—"

"Isthereanything—" Jenkins caught himself. Despite his unwillingness to allow Wool to continue, there was no sense in advertising that fact. "Ah . . . is there anything that would . . . ah . . . improve upon it?"

Mather almost sounded peevish. "Why . . ." (Squirm!) ". . . getting it up into the mountains would definitely improve upon it."

"Oh." Jenkins allowed the silence to grow, prayed that Wool would not break it with another one of his damnable utterances.

"But I'm working on that," said Mather.

Jenkins, elated, winced nonetheless. Mechanics. Well, no one had told him that diplomacy was going to be completely ethical and free from stain. He had known that from the start. Nonetheless . . .

(Squirm!)

. . . there *were* limits.

"Working on it?" he said, regretting instantly that he had said *anything.*

You never let me go anywhere!

"Working on it," said Mather.

14)   Besides ROMAN CAPITALS, it is necessary that the letter-cutter should know how to carve Roman small-letters (or "Lower case") and italics, either of which may be more suitable than Capitals for some Inscriptions.

Hearken all ye to the words of Panas, the Builder of the World, the Raiser of Cities, the Ordainer of Municipalities, the Shaper of Society. May His blessings be bestowed upon His people for all time, and in all nations may there be great and endless praise raised to Him.

Herein is revealed unto all, from the most devout of believers to the most abject of sinners to the most reprehensible of apostates and doubters, the mysteries of the holy. For has not Panas (blessed be He!) in His wisdom seen fit to separate that which is holy from that which is profane?

And where would you go?

First, though, before the separation of such things can be understood, it is necessary that their unity be clearly perceived, for as Panas (blessed be He!) carved all things in the beginning, so are all things sanctified, having been touched from the very first by the hand of God (blessed be He!) Himself (blessed be He!). And as is obvious, the innate holiness of such things is ~~in no wise~~ *not, for the most part,* an indication that all things are interchangeable in their place and position, but rather than all things have their purpose, and some are

more suited for certain actions and duties and purposes
than others. Therefore it is seen that the king rules over
his subjects, *the priests rule over the king,* and the laity
obey without question *the precepts of those who know
what is best for them.* And as the carver knows the use
of different kinds of letters, so does God (blessed be
He!) know the use of different kinds of men, and He
appoints them to such stations as they are suited, and
as pleases Him, and this appointment is eternal . . .

Jenkins looked at Mather for some time, wondering
whether he should be glad that Mather was "working
on it," or worried that Mather's "working on it" would
prove either dangerous (if Mather's method of "working on it" proved less than correct) or embarrassing (if
Mather's method of "working on it" proved overly correct) . . . and, in any case, he really did not want to
think about what "working on it" meant in Mather's
case.

"Working on it," he said again.

Hmmmph!

"Let him labor," intoned Wool, "working with *his*
hands the thing which is good."

Mather started visibly. "Really, Mr. Wool," he said,
"I wish that you wouldn't say things like that."

"One shall say, I *am* the LORD'S; and another shall
call *himself* by the name of Jacob; and another subscribe
with his hand unto the LORD, and surname *himself* by
the name of Israel."

There was venom in the look that Mather directed at
Mr. Wool.

*15)   Where great magnificence combined with great
legibility is desired, use LARGE ROMAN CAPITALS,*

Incised or in Relief, with plenty of space between the letters and the lines.

Hearken all ye to the words of Panas, the Builder of the World, the Raiser of Cities, the Ordainer of Municipalities, the Shaper of Society. May His blessings be bestowed upon His people for all time, and in all nations may there be great and endless praise raised to Him.

Oh, tell me!

And thus is the truth demonstrated so clearly that even those who would mock the sacred truths of God (blessed be He!) must be confounded. For here Panas (blessed be He!) reveals the essential truth that all things, great though they might be, must keep their distance from that which is greater, and that distance and spaciousness combine to offer the utmost respect to the kingly *and priestly* representatives of the power of God (blessed be He!). And therefore is the sacred, *for the most part,* hedged about and protected by space, that the will of God (blessed be He!) might be better and more clearly shown forth. The temple of Panas (blessed be He!) is kept separate from the laity, the quarries of Panas (blessed be He!) are isolated and visited only by the most pure among the priesthood, *the mountains themselves are, for the most part, kept in sacred isolation,* the king is attended only by the greatest of the nobility and the wisest of counselors, for only thusly is their magnificence shown forth adequately.

You get mad whenever I talk about it.

And this separation of the greater from the lesser is seen, too, in the separation of the rich from the poor . . .

* * *

"Not quote Scripture?" said Jenkins, distressed to find that, as a minister, he actually had to *defend* Wool's predilection for uninvited interjections when what he really wanted to do had something in common with the un-Puritan mechanics that he was trying (somewhat in vain) to avoid thinking about. "Why ... ah ... quoting Scripture ..."

Almost with a jerk, Mather went back to his pendulums and verniers. "I said that I'm working on it, Mr. Ambassador," he said petulantly.

16) Where great legibility but less magnificence is desired, use Roman small-letters or italics.

Hearken all ye to the words of Panas, the Builder of the World, the Raiser of Cities, the Ordainer of Municipalities, the Shaper of Society. May His blessings be bestowed upon His people for all time, and in all nations may there be great and endless praise raised to Him.

Tell me! Anything!

Here, yet again, the highest mysteries are hinted at, for clarity of purpose and position are herein put forth. As the king is distinguished from the common, as the priests are distinguished from the laity *and from the king,* so are the common and the laity distinguished from one another *on an individual basis,* for all have their purpose and their suitability, and all contribute to the everlasting glory of Panas (blessed be He!) ...

Tick-tick-tick!

What's the use? You'll just get mad.

Wegga-wegga-wegga!

* * *

17) All three Alphabets may be used together, as, for instance, on a Tombstone, where one might carve the Name in CAPITALS and the rest of the Inscription in small-letters, using italics for difference.

Hearken all ye to the words of Panas, the Builder of the World, the Raiser of Cities, the Ordainer of Municipalities, the Shaper of Society. May His blessings be bestowed upon His people for all time, and in all nations may there be great and endless praise raised to Him.

No. No. I promise. Tell me.

And here is the holiest of mysteries, for behold! All letters come together in the workings of God, and all contribute and share equally in the glory of Panas (blessed be He!). Therefore, let not the slave be downcast, nor the mud dweller abashed, for their station, miserable though it might be, even seemingly iniquitous, is nonetheless part of the plan of the Divine, an expression of the most holy will of Panas (blessed be He!), and though they are forever despised and rejected, cast out and reviled, it is fitting that slaves and commoners should rejoice in their misery, for nowhere is it better or more fully set out than here that theirs too is a situation not without its own kind of honor, *and therefore the priests may, from time to time, grant dispensations and permissions even to the most reviled of individuals, yes, even to foreigners who have no knowledge of the truth, for thus is the will of Panas (blessed be He!) revealed ...*

"Working on it ..." mused Jenkins. Silently. Mr. Wool stared at the wall.

You keep me cooped up here, and we never do anything.

Mather fiddled with his pendulums.
Wegga-wegga-wegga!

Dearly beloved, how wonderful are the ways of the
Lord. Wonderful I say, for what is not wonderful about
the fact that even in the midst of the unenlightened
darkness of heathens, the glory of God's mercy and
concord manifests itself? As it should. I mean the
glory ... no ... I mean the mercy and concord. Man-
ifest themselves. No ... wait ...

But what could we do?

Even, I say, among heathens, for what are heathens
but those who do not—nay, cannot!—acknowledge the
true goodness of the one true God. And surely there
are no greater heathens in the world than those who
dwell in the Three Kingdoms, to whose ears the godly
and righteous Americans have come to speak the
words of true enlightenment and truth. And yet ...

They are so grotesque. Fat and stupid, just like we were. Once. No more. Priests! But we will get what we want from them. Badly-aspected, every one of them. And gullible. The Gharat is a Taurus, unless I am mistaken.	And the Gharat came to me and said "Dress in my robes!" And so I did. And he said to me "Listen to the Naians," and so I am. But these women ... they are so tedious. And I know what to do with women. Oh, yes. I know.

... and yet God's goodness shines out among
them—I mean, the savages, not their ears—and so it is
with reverential awe that we witness the meeting of the
priests of Panas and the representatives of the Naians,
this convocation brought about as the result of many

days of labor on the part of the latter, and of great broad-mindedness and tolerance on the part of the former.

Well, you could let me go . . . somewhere.

And, indeed, it is labor and tolerance that have brought these two groups—so disparate in belief, and yet so united in their ignorance. . . . I mean, in their efforts!—together, for the work they both contemplate, warped and twisted through it may appear in the light of the truth of God, finds its counterpart in the godly and upright virtues of the Americans, for it is coexistence and recognition and mutual esteem that have so broken down the barriers of suspicion and distrust, and what could be more godly than that! I mean the coexistence and . . . no, wait . . . breaking . . . ah . . .

Where would you go?

But here are the Naians, who have been allowed on this day of all days to enter into the precincts of the temple complex . . .

Disgusting. That is all they are. And to think that we must come before *them* and ask *them* for favors! Well, people are bored with them. It is only a matter of time. And it is only a matter of time, too, before I finally can do something about Jeddiah, for she is, of *course,* right here, smiling

He-he! They think I am the Gharat. And they will let me do *anything*! He-he! Of *course* you can have anything you want. I can promise anything! And I will. Oh, and what if I want to *fart* right now! They will not say anything. No priests here at all, only slaves today, and the Naians do not like a piece of mutton fat on a plate. But Jeddiah does not know what I know, and she can go on about her school and her temple, if she wants. Disgraceful behavior in the market the other day. But I will deal with her. Later.

know the difference. Such simpletons! Yes! And we are better than they, for we belong to the priests, and are used by the priests, and the Naians belong to no one and are useless for anything. And I can *fart*!

. . . of Katha. Dignified and solemn, but dressed in the carefree and gay finery so characteristic of their rustic (though heathen) beliefs, they enter into the great council chambers of the temple, escorted, as though they are great nobles or foreign dignitaries, by priestly guards. And before them, wrapped in their tawdry religious habiliments, but regal for all that . . .

The question, though, is *What do they want?* And I have little enough time to decide. That Gharat. Taurus. Badly aspected. Fleshy. Food? Bribes? Disgusting that we have to bow before them like this, but we must be practical. This is the way the world works. A girl, maybe? Perhaps. What about that little thing in the marketplace the other day? Delusions of responsibility. Married . . . by no means. Was not her husband. I could ap-

He-he! But they are *disgusting* with their heads uncovered, and if I were the Gharat, I could do anything. Maybe the Gharat will let me do some things. Yes. I will ask. He liked what I did the last time he was here (though he is enamored of that *slug* of a foreigner). Might allow me a favor. This one here. I want her. I want her . . . and a knife. Yes. I could slide it just under the skin, and cut round and round. Oh! Excision! She would have to

peal to her sense of duty. do it, too, because
It could work. Find her. (he-he!) she wants some-
Bring her. Hmmm . . . thing. She will do it.

. . . are the priests, including—wonder of
wonders!—the Gharat of the Three Kingdoms himself!

You could let me go . . . oh, what's the use?

And truly it is a magnificent thing, for even here, in
this stronghold of darkness, light enters, and there is,
as has devoutly been wished by Naians and Panasians
alike, a coming to terms, a growing sense of felicity.
Yes, here in darkness, there is light, and where once
there was animosity, now there is . . .

Hmmm . . . Yes.   *He-he! Yes!*

. . . fellowship. And if God is so good as to grant
such grace even unto these, how much greater must be
His mercy and beneficence toward those who believe
truly and steadfastly, and whose lives are lived not in
darkness, but in the eternal illumination of Divine
Truth!

No, please. Tell me.

And so, let us go forth from this place rejoicing in
the goodness of the Lord, for where He might well
have brought destruction, He has elected to show forth
His kindness, and such grace cannot but be a lesson to
all of us!

Well, you could let me go . . .

I mean, a lesson to all of us *except* the heathens.
Who are savages.

Where? Tell me! Anything!

And are therefore incapable of learning anything.

You could let me go up into . . .

SO BE IT
ARDANE!

Chapter Eight

And what of Bakbuk?

Well, here he is (And, for anyone who ever had any doubt, it is most assuredly *he* these days, no limp-wristed coyness for this *man,* and do not forget that for a moment!), swaggering down the corridors of the priestly complex of Katha. Were there girls here, he would surely wink at them, perhaps do a little grabbing, even, under the right circumstances, go a little further than that (Who would be foolish enough to deny the wishes of the king's personal sworder?), and maybe a good deal further than that, for this is a man's man here, and he is (And that is *he*!), every crotch-hitch-and-swaggering inch of him, undeniably male. One hundred percent. Without a doubt. None at all.

But there are no girls in the priestly complex, only shaven-headed priests, and so Bakbuk (who has, for some reason, not seen fit to cut his long hair, even though it is most inconvenient to pile it up beneath the confines of his head cloth, even though it threatens to slither out and cascade invitingly down his shoulders and back, even though it is a constant reminder to him of *something else,* something he does not want to think about right now, because he is, after all, a *man* and *men* do not think about such things. Ever. (Do they?))

must leave his masculinity self-evident rather than actively proven.

And so, here is Bakbuk, and he is swaggering, and he is boyishly handsome, and he is most certainly *not* thinking about the Blue Avenger, other than (strictly) in terms of his suspicions regarding the true identity of the marvelous monad, suspicions that, to be sure, relate *only* to his present duty of protecting the Gharat from the attentions of that same Blue Avenger, and not at all to the fact that he still—

Swaggering, yes. *Yes!* A *man!*

Bakbuk, though, is having difficulty protecting the Gharat, owing to the fact that, day by day, it is becoming increasingly difficult for him to *find* the Gharat: and were it not for the fact that Abnel makes periodic appearances in the chambers of the Priestly Council of Katha (where he is both presenting his proposal for a universal temple tax and having difficulty keeping his temper in the face of the reactions of the council to that proposal . . . which appear to swing randomly between obviously patronizing and explicitly amused), Bakbuk, manly and swaggering (Yes!), would think that perhaps the Blue Avenger had been successful in prosecuting the designs upon Abnel's personal safety so fearfully hypothesized by Inwa Kabir. His (Yes! His!) inquiries are met with dumb uncooperativeness by the mute slaves who tend to the material needs of the priestly household, and even the palace guards assigned to the Gharat seem to be unable to help.

This satisfies Bakbuk not at all. Approaching the Gharat directly is no good: he has tried that already, and has met with an obfuscation that, as a subject under orders, he cannot question. It is, therefore, up to him to discover a method of interrogating the Gharat indirectly, and since climbing and being invisible are among Bakbuk's best talents, he intends to avail himself of them again.

Now, spying on the Americans or on a possibly errant son at the request of that son's father is one thing, but spying on the Gharat of the entire Three Kingdoms is quite another, and Bakbuk might be forgiven if he is a little giddy at the prospect. And yet that giddiness is, for him, a kind of a failing that goes beyond the mundane question of the bravery that a man, by custom and nature, is expected to exhibit. No, there is an essentially womanish cast to Bakbuk's giddiness, one that involves not only the anticipation of dangerous actions, but also the conviction (unfounded and disbelieved though it might be) that he, by custom and nature, is not at all capable of those actions, and even a tantalizing and groin-tightening apprehension of being *caught*, of having things *done to him*. . . .

And here he checks his thoughts and attempts to recover the manly swagger that has, of a sudden, been replaced by a girlish sway; and he clenches teeth behind lips that had, a moment before, gone slack and inviting.

He had been . . . so close. Right next to him. In the Gharat's tent. His side had brushed against . . . *him*!

Oh! Oh! Oh!

—Oh! Oh! Oh! Beshur cried from his bed.

"Oh! Oh! Oh!" Potatoes cried from his pallet.

Sari, holding a cup of water, stood in the middle of the room, wondering whom she should attend to first.

—Oh! Oh! Oh!

"Oh! Oh! Oh!"

To be sure, it was not an easy decision. Both men were severely battered as a result of their encounter with the Gharat's progress, though Sari judged that had Beshur not run in a direction that had taken him directly into the massed strength of the priestly guards, his injuries might not have been so severe. Potatoes, too, might have been spared, for the latter, gallantly attempting to rescue the former, had been forced to throw himself directly into that same massed strength.

Beshur eyed Sari, noticed that she was turning slightly toward Potatoes' side of the room.

—Oh! Oh! Oh! he wailed.

Potatoes, noticing that Sari was being drawn toward, Beshur's side of the room, made haste to answer.

"Oh! Oh! Oh!"

Sari, still holding the cup of water, drifted back to the center of the room and reached equilibrium once again.

—Oh! Oh! Oh!

"Oh! Oh! Oh!"

Sari put a hand to her head. "Oh, Naia!"

Both men fell silent, eyeing one another.

Sari looked at them. Bruised and battered. Very. But she noticed that both of them were watching her very carefully, almost eagerly, a fact that she found very curious, considering that she was such an old—

Oh. Oh, yes. That.

She dragged a sleeve of her shoulder cloth across her forehead. "I think that you should both rest," she said. "You have had a hard time of it. Beshur, Potatoes and I both thank you for providing a place for him to recover from his wounds."

—Oh! O—

Beshur looked carefully at Sari.

—It is the least I can do, he said. And my pleasure.

"Certainly," said Sari. Moving carefully, so as to make sure that she remained essentially equidistant from the two men, (which was no mean feat, considering that most of the floor space of the tiny room was now occupied by bedding of one sort or another), she went to her sack of herbs and carried it over to the upended box that Beshur used for a table. Silently, she began pulling out herbs, crumbling them, grinding them, and dropping them into a pot of water that she set over the brazier.

She felt the men watching her, felt herself growing a little warm. Oh, yes. That.

The water began to simmer. An odor that would one day be compared to moldy sweat socks began to diffuse throughout the room, and the cat, until now content to be an onlooker to the proceedings, immediately fled through the open window.

—Ah . . . what is that? Beshur said.

"Medicine," said Sari. "Very potent medicine. You have forgotten, perhaps, that I am an herbalist?"

—Why, no, Beshur said. I had not forgotten that. But . . . ah . . .

"You are both ill," said Sari. "This will help you." Both men were silent.

"How very fortunate," she continued, "that you have an herbalist as a . . ." She glanced at them. Oh, yes. That. ". . . a *friend*. I can provide for you very well."

The odor increased. The sweat socks were multiplying, compressing, fermenting: obviously, an entire football team was in spring training.

"*Very* well," said Sari.

"Ah . . ."

The odor of sweat socks increased. Doubtless, near the bottom of the heap, the formation of coal was in its initial stages.

"Ah . . . let us not be hasty," said Potatoes.

—I feel much better already, Beshur declared, heaving himself up on one elbow while wincing a great deal.

Sari gave the bubbling pot a stir.

—Much better! Beshur said.

"Indeed," said Potatoes. "I feel like a new man." And he too heaved himself up on one elbow while wincing a great deal.

"I am very glad to see that you are both recovering

so quickly," said Sari. "But I am sure that you will want to avail yourselves of the benefits of my herbs." A quick glance told her that both men were attempting, without much success, to rise. "Why, the infusion that I am preparing at present—"

"Wonderful," cried Potatoes. "Absolutely wonderful! Why, the mere odor of it has given me great strength!"

"I am sure that you could work for five days without sleep," said Sari. "It is truly a marvelous infusion."

—And I, Beshur said, have regained my strength also! Yes! Truly marvelous!

A knock came to the door.

"Let me get that," said Potatoes, still struggling to rise.

Beshur was also struggling.

—No, no, he said. It is my room, after all. Allow me. I feel quite well.

"Ah," said Potatoes, "but not as well as I!"

—Better!

"How would you know?"

—Believe me, I know! Beshur said with some heat. I know many things. More things, I am sure, than you!

"Ha! Pumice! Surely you will next be claiming to be a scholar!"

—Well, I *am* a scholar!

"And studied in the Great Library of Nuhr, no doubt!"

Now Beshur was quite angry.

—As though anyone like *you* would ever be allowed into the Great Library! he said.

"And *you* would be? Sandstone—"

The knock came to the door again.

"There is no need for such language in this room, brother," said Sari.

But Potatoes' wrath was not to be checked by a woman's voice. "—and pumice! Now it is obvious that you are quite deranged. No one is allowed into the Great Library! Only the priests may go there."

—Well, I . . .

But Beshur's words suddenly died on his lips, and he paled remarkably.

"Is something wrong?" said Potatoes. "Perhaps you need some of the wonderful infusion that Sari is brewing?"

—Ah . . . no . . . Beshur said quickly. By no means . . . I am quite well.

And he paled a little more.

"But tell me of the Great Library," said Potatoes. "You seem to know a great deal about it."

—Well, Beshur said. In fact, I do. Every true scholar knows about the Great Library.

"Even though you are not ever going to be allowed into it!"

—I could get into it if I wanted to!

"Oh?" And there was a flicker of real interest in Potatoes' tone. "May I ask how?"

The knock came yet again, and Sari finally went to the door and opened it.

"Now, Beshur," said the vendor of insignificant brassware, "I am a professional, am I not? And therefore I must make a living, must I not? And since I see that you now have yet another person living with you besides your wife—"

Potatoes yelped. "Wife!"

—Wife! Beshur said smugly.

Sari put a hand to her face, shook her head. "Wife," she said. And then, most uncharacteristically: "Pumice!"

"—why then it is imperative that I—"

—He is my brother, Beshur said.

"Wife!"

The vendor of insignificant brassware, caught between two inexplicable conversations . . .

—No, Beshur said. Brother.

"Oh, Naia . . ." murmured Sari.

. . . three inexplicable conversations . . .

"And what *is* that odor?" said the vendor of insignificant brassware.

"What odor?" said Sari.

. . . four inexplicable conversations, one of which was, in fact, his own, lost the thread of his queries and stood, finger upraised as though to make a point, completely uncertain as to how to proceed, particularly in view of the fact that he was about to be faced with . . .

"Ah . . . *brother*?" he ventured.

—Yes, Beshur said. He is going to be . . . ah . . . staying with us for . . . a few days. I am sure that you will not deny my brother a place to sleep, will you?

Needless to say, the odor of sweat socks had continued to build, and by now the room was thick with it. Obviously, the athletes had been training assiduously, and if coal was not starting to form in the lower strata of the pile, then fusion was surely imminent.

"But . . . that odor . . ." said the vendor of insignificant brassware.

"Odor?" Potatoes ventured, but then, returning to a former train of thought with a distinct start: "Wife!"

The vendor of insignificant brassware looked at him carefully. "Are you not the idiot who climbed over the wall?"

Potatoes looked up. "I beg your pardon. I was someone else at the time."

. . . five inexplicable conversations.

But the vendor forged on through confusion and odor alike. "Well, now, as I said . . . I am a professional . . . and . . . urk!"

"Ah!" said Sari, who, as an herbalist and a mother, was immune to most any kind of olfactory assault, "you are not well! I have just the thing!" And she went directly to the pot (which was, by now, spewing forth its anachronistic scent at a really alarming rate) and gave it a vigorous stir.

"No, really," said the vendor. "I really was just stopping by ... was I (Urk!) not? And so I will (Urk!) leave you with your (Urk!) family, will I ... I ... I ..."

—Just for a few days, Beshur said.

"Well, if that is the case, then may Naia bless you, and I will be going."

"Oh," said Potatoes cheerfully, even though he looked to be struggling to repress the same physical reactions as were gripping the vendor, "I beg you to stay. We were just going to ... going to ..."

He looked at Sari, then at Beshur.

"... ah ... have lunch!"

The vendor fled.

Potatoes looked at Beshur again. "Anytime you want?"

—What? Beshur said.

"You said that you could enter the Great Library of Nuhr anytime you wanted to. I would like to know details."

—Well, Beshur said, I am, after all, a scholar ...

"Are you not?" said Sari, who had found herself seized by a number of uncharitable thoughts that very much resembled those that had possessed her in the marketplace when she was in the company of Charna and Jeddiah.

Which brought her back to the first problem. The important problem. What *about* Charna and Jeddiah? As nominal leaders of the Naian community—insofar as the Naian community could be said to have leaders at all—they were people whom Sari would have to see again if she intended to carry out the Goddess' implicit command. And she did indeed intend to carry it out.

"Somehow," she murmured.

Beshur, as usual, misconstrued what she had said.

—It is not a matter of *somehow* at all, he said. I am a scholar. I *know* certain things.

"Certain things," said Potatoes. "As in: how to get into the Library. Of course."

—Well, yes, Beshur said. Do *you* want to get into the Library?

"Me?" said Potatoes. "Me? Oh, by no means. What would *I* want to get into the Library for?"

—Well . . .

"But I could if I wanted to."

—Oh, indeed!

"Scholars sit at home and read books," declared Potatoes. "People like me . . ."

"Yes?" said Sari, realizing that, aside from the fact that he was gallant and handsome (though a little disreputable-looking) and had gotten her away from Charna and Jeddiah, she really knew very little about him. "What about people like you?"

Potatoes, obviously caught (though Sari had no idea what he had been caught about . . . or in), fell back suddenly on his pallet. "Oh!" he said. "Oh! Oh!"

Sari watched him for a moment, saw that Beshur, not about to be outdone, was about to follow his example, and interdicted the display with another stir of the spewing pot. "Try some of this infusion," she said helpfully. "It will make you both feel better."

The curative properties of the infusion were indeed most remarkable. The mere mention of it, in fact, was enough to effect a complete recovery.

—Well, Beshur declared. I fully intend to enter the Library.

"You do?" said Potatoes.

—Yes. I am a scholar. It is my right. No . . . my *duty.*

Potatoes looked eager. "When?"

—Anytime you wish!

"We leave tomorrow!" said Potatoes. "*All* of us."

Sari, watching, listening, had set down the spoon and folded her arms. "*Both* of you," she said.

"What?"

—What?

"I was sent by the Goddess to do something," she said, "and I intend to do it. You can both do as you see fit. I have other matters to attend to."

Beshur and Potatoes eyed one another.

Oh. Oh, yes. That.

"But," said Potatoes with a dazzling smile, "as far as the Library is concerned, there is really no hurry. For me, that is." He turned to Beshur. "I assume that you find your explorations pressing, though?"

—Not at all, Beshur said. There is no need for me to be rushing off. Why . . . why . . . why, I am not yet healed.

He glanced at the still-bubbling pot, appeared to become aware once again of a certain odor.

—. . . ah . . . I mean . . . that is . . .

"Just so," said Potatoes. "And you need to rest. After all, your work—You are a porter, are you not?—requires that you be strong, and so you must rest and recover. Sari and I . . ."

Sari sighed.

". . . will be delighted to take care of you."

—Oh, but I feel fine! Beshur said.

"I thought you said a moment ago that you had not yet healed."

—A . . . a figure of speech, Beshur said. I am, in fact, much better!

"A false recovery, I am sure of it." Potatoes rose from his pallet smoothly (albeit with a certain amount of wincing). "Indeed, a classic case. Now is the most dangerous time for you, for if you strain yourself prematurely, it could be fatal. You must rest, and you must be sure to drink a great deal of this wonderful . . . ah . . . infusion that Sari has prepared."

—I feel fine! insisted Beshur. I am a—

"Scholar," said Potatoes, "and therefore you should know better than to tax yourself when you have not yet healed. Yes. And Sari and I . . ."

Sari had put a hand to her head again.

". . . will take care of you!"

Oh. Oh, yes. That.

Chapter Nine

Not quite every inch the Puritan for the present, Obadiah Jenkins stood on a rough plateau high above and half a day's journey to the east of the city of Katha, his thin, noncommittal body wrapped in the splendid garments of a dignitary of the Three Kingdoms. Nearby, a number of riding asses browsed on the leafless ground, and three priestly guards scratched at their shaven heads; both groups—browsing and scratching—occasionally looking up to watch as Mr. Mather, also clad in exotic habiliments, adjusted the gravimetric apparatus with efficiency, attentiveness . . . and an occasional squirm.

It was indeed an amazing turn of events, Jenkins considered as, for the third time that minute, he grabbed his head cloth to keep it from sliding off. (And how did they manage to keep those things on, anyway? Staples? Why, he had seen acrobats in the square doing *handsprings* without losing them! Bother!) A few days before, Mather had announced that he was "working on" the problem of getting the apparatus up into the holy mountains—mountains into which no foreigners (and, indeed, hardly any layfolk) were ever allowed—and then, quite suddenly, permission for the Americans to journey into the foothills had been granted.

Cause. Effect. Now, though Jenkins knew well what

the effect was (he was, after all, among the foothills, looking toward the immense, near-vertical slopes of the high, interior ranges, with even higher ranges, he knew, farther in), he was strenuously attempting to avoid thinking much about the cause . . . his efforts being largely thwarted by Mather's constant squirms. Still, even this was something relatively positive, for had Jenkins asked for a more conclusive proof that Mather was leading Abnel about by the . . . ah . . . nose (so to speak), he could not have gotten it.

"Ask, and it shall be given you; seek, and ye shall find," he murmured . . . and was immediately chagrined by the fact that not only was he uttering such things while wearing pagan garb, but that he was also, for all intents and purposes, taking after Mr. Wool (who, though also clad fantastically, was otherwise much the same as he was always: a few feet away, behind a low table, pens, paper, spectacles, and knees arranged appropriately).

"Ye have sinned against the Lord," intoned Wool, "and be sure your sin will find you out."

Mather started visibly, glared at Wool.

"Pay no attention to Wool, Mr. Mather," said Jenkins. "He is simply being a godly man." He caught his head cloth as it dived for the ground once again. "As we all should be."

"Yes," said Mather a little too hastily. (Squirm!) "Yes, of course. Yes."

The priestly guards scratched at their stubbly heads and stared with unabashed curiosity as Mather made his last adjustments. Then, with a turning of gears, a swinging of pendulums, a *tick-tick-tick* and a *wegga-wegga-wegga* the gravimeter was in operation, and the engineer was once again involved in what Jenkins could think of only as a kind of unholy union with a mass of metal, glass, and wire.

Now. Now. Now it was only a matter of whether

Mather's initial readings in Nuhr, confirmed once in Katha, were again confirmed by a field measurement. Here, actually *in* the mountains, the readings could not but be exact and unambiguous.

And Jenkins' thoughts—where they were not tripped up by his uncontrollable speculations about Mather and Abnel—were leaping ahead, for Mather, an experienced engineer, had been confident about his first two sets of readings, had, in fact, been able to modify the apparatus so that its precision had increased tenfold. Unless something had gone terribly wrong or the geology of the Mountains of Ern was so freakish as to disallow any kind of precision, the ambassador had no doubt that what Mather was now doing was but a necessary formality, that the plans of the Righteous States *could* move forward ... toward Bonaparte, toward Egypt ...

... toward the world.

Trade with the Three Kingdoms? Trade? He was no longer even remotely concerned with trade. He had Mather, and, through Mather, he had Abnel. What did he need trade for?

And just then his head cloth at last succeeded in leaping (Jenkins would have sworn—had he been a swearing man rather than a godly man—that it had leaped.) from his head and plummeting to the ground with an audible thump.

"How are the mighty fallen!" intoned Mr. Wool without a trace of an exclamation point.

Mather looked up in some annoyance. "Mr. Ambassador, please! You've ruined an entire set of readings!"

"Well," said Jenkins, "then do them over again."

"Do them over again! Do them over again!" The engineer's voice rose toward something approximating a soprano. "Do them over again! It's not just as easy as that! I can't just *do them over again*. I have to establish initial conditions all over again, and then I have to resolve the base magnitude of the reading all over again . . ." Mather's voice rose even higher, something Jenkins had not thought possible. ". . . and then I have to extrapolate those conditions and readings *all over again*—"

"Well, just *do* it then," Jenkins snapped, but he was suddenly alarmed by the fact that Mather's . . . ah . . . novel recreations (And there he was thinking about them again!) had apparently unbalanced him. This would not do. No, not at all.

Again, his fears rose about what "working on it" might mean when "working on it" involved Mather. And if he, Jenkins, depended upon the engineer (with all of his attached . . . ah . . . novel . . . ah . . . oh . . .) for his own kind of "working on it", what then?

"Feet of clay," he muttered, realizing as he did so that, yes, he was imitating Wool again. Drat that man!

Drat? Now he was even swearing! And he a minister! Oh, God!

But it was becoming obvious to Jenkins: Mather was only a beginning. Mather *had* to be only a beginning, because dealing with Abnel through Mather was tantamount to running the Righteous States of America by means of tiny notes passed through a hole in a wall. It would not do. It would not do at all. Jenkins was going to have to put his own hands on the reins . . . or, more likely, plunge them into the stink.

Shuddering at the thought, he bent to retrieve his head cloth, but as his hand closed around it, he became aware of a strange, almost subliminal rumbling that emanated from somewhere below his feet.

A short distance away, the riding asses suddenly milled, brayed harshly, and began to run away. And as the rumbling became louder and turned into a shaking, the priestly guards ran after the asses.

Dutifully, Wool was intoning: "For the windows

from on high are open, and the foundations of the earth do shake."

"An earthquake!" exclaimed Jenkins. "Mather!"

But Mather had risen from his seat behind the apparatus and was now jumping up and down in excited glee. "An earthquake! Just as I expected! And the gravimeter registered it a full minute before we felt it! It worked! It worked!"

The earth continued to shake, the asses continued to run away, and the priestly guards continued to run after the asses.

"Yes!" Mather was screeching. "Yes! A full minute! I *wondered* what that perturbation was! What luck! What excellent luck!"

And then the rumbling was augmented by a sudden roar. The asses ran, the guards ran, and, above their heads, a large piece of mountain let go . . .

"Look out!" cried Jenkins.

. . . and slid directly down onto the asses and the guards, burying them in an instant and raising a cloud of dust that cloaked everything in a haze of white and gray.

"Look out?" said Mather, now invisible in the thick clouds. "It's not coming this way: the gravimeter didn't say it was coming this way."

"Those poor devils!"

"Blessed are the p—"

"Shut up, Wool!"

"The apparatus said nothing about it! And the apparatus is accurate. *I* made it accurate, and therefore you have *me* to thank for that."

Jenkins, his eyes blind and stinging from the dust, was torn between horror at the sudden annihilation of the men, concern about how he was supposed to return to Katha without guides, fright that yet another part of the mountain (inconveniently located above his own head this time) might be coming down, and bewilderment at the hysteria of his engineer. "Those . . . those men are dead, Mather!"

"Dead? Of *course* they're dead. Dead as doornails, all of 'em. And the apparatus said it would be so! Yes!"

Jenkins decided that his estimation had been entirely correct. Mather was a blunt chisel that he would have to cast away. He would have to deal with the Gharat himself. But there was suddenly another roar, and Jenkins felt a spray of unaccustomed dampness on his face.

"Mather! Good God! What is this now?"

"Hmmm . . . entirely unexpected," came the reply.

"I shall come on thee like a thief, and thou shalt not know what hour I will come upon thee."

"Shut up, Wool!"

The dampness—*Water?* wondered Jenkins. *Here?*—increased, and the clouds of dust abruptly turned into a clinging mud that coated everything. Wool, sitting at his table, looked very much like a clay statue of a man sitting at a clay statue of a table (along with clay pen, paper, spectacles, and knees . . . arranged appropriately), so thoroughly besmeared was he. Mather looked much the same, and the apparatus was transformed into a strange network of earthen webs.

The spray, though, had cleared the air of dust, and Jenkins, wiping his grimy face, could now look up toward the higher slopes—What had Mather said? 40,000 feet at the interior peaks?—and see a jet of water leaping away from a cliff that must have been over a half a mile away. Caught by the breeze, it was showering down on everything to leeward of it, including the Americans.

"For we must needs die, and *are* as water spilt on the—uck!"

Jenkins, who was about to tell Wool to shut up for the third time, turned just in time to see that Wool had been struck to the ground. The old secretary lay sprawling in the mud to one side of his table, and the thing that had put him there lay beside him, squirming.

The water continued to roar and then, suddenly, as suddenly as it had started, it stopped. The jet was gone.

Wool floundered. The thing beside him squirmed for a moment more, then trembled and lay still.

Jenkins, his feet squishing in the tenacious mud that had formed from earth too unaccustomed to water to know exactly what to do with it when it actually got it, walked over to the secretary and looked at the thing on the ground.

"For he was cut off out of the land of the living: for the transgression of my people was he stricken," Wool was mumbling.

Mather, edging toward hysteria once more, was clenching his fists and shouting: "Stop that, Wool! Damn you! Stop it!"

But Jenkins said nothing, for the thing that lay on the ground beside Wool, the thing that had struck the elderly secretary to the ground, was a human hand and arm, and the lifeless fingers were still clutching a mallet.

Fakik kneaded the dough, trying yet another sweet-meat experiment. Surely this one would prove success-ful. To be sure, experimenting was a terrible trial, for when one was working with the established and true, one at least had some idea of what the end result would be; but when one was trying to create something really different, something wonderful, something un-like anything else, something that would catch the fancy and the favor of King Inwa Kabir, why then one was groping in the dark.

Eventually, though, something had to work. Regard-less of the burned exercises, the rocklike failures, and the completely inert essays, somewhere ahead (Fakik was sure of it.) was success, and a pleased king, and restored favors, and, perhaps, as his manhood was gone forever, one or two of those barefoot boys with the powdered faces . . .

The cat watched from its perch on one of the ceiling beams.

"That is good, cat," said Fakik. "I need you to stay up in the ceiling beams right now. Right now I do not need you to bother me, because I am still working on these sweetmeats, for I need a most excellent sweet-meat recipe. That is what I need now. And that is what I will get, if you only leave me alone and stay up in the ceiling beams."

Softly, almost subliminally, a distant rumbling began.

"And then, one day, I will bring the sweetmeats before the king, and he will find them good, and he will say to me 'Fakik,' (he will say), 'these are the most wonderful sweetmeats I have ever tasted, and for providing me with these sweetmeats, you are hereby restored to favor, and I will give you barefoot boys with powdered faces as well, to do with as you please.' Yes, he will say that, and then I will have favor, and barefoot boys, too."

The rumbling grew louder. In a pile of pots and kettles and utensils left over from the last royal lunch, a spoon began to rattle loudly.

"And then I will take marzipan, yes, and shape it into—"

And the pile of pots and kettles and utensils (including the spoon) abruptly began to rattle all together.

"—oh!"

The pile came down with a crash, and the cat leaped, and Fakik, losing his balance, fell face first into the pile of dough that lay spread out on the table before him, ready to be shaped into the most remarkable sweetmeats.

* * *

Upon being told that Sari had recently returned from the Caves of Naia, did Charna suspect that the young woman who sat before her over a luncheon of dried figs and rehydrated fish was none other than the old woman who had, on a previous occasion, sat before her over a luncheon of dried figs and rehydrated fish?

No.

Explain.

The magnitude of the violation of physical law necessary for such an identity being greater than Charna's credence could accept, the thought never entered her mind.

Did Charna, in fact, believe in the possibility of any violation of physical law?

No.

Did Charna have any difficulty reconciling her lack of belief in the possibility of such a violation with her avowed practice of a spirituality that, at the time of our narrative, placed a large emphasis upon potential violations of this sort?

No.

Explain.

There being no reason, in Charna's opinion, that the acceptance of any possibility of any violation of physical law, great or small, was necessary for what was, for her, merely a vehicle for societal interaction and a method of acquiring personal prestige, a reconciliation between her outward spiritual practice and her beliefs was therefore entirely unnecessary.

* * *

Did Sari know that this lack of reconciliation on Charna's part existed?
She suspected it.

Did Charna know that Sari suspected it?
No.

Did Sari know that Charna considered this reconciliation to be unnecessary?
She suspected it.

Did Charna know that Sari suspected it?
No.

Did Sari's suspicions influence, in any way, shape, or form, her presentation to Charna of her thoughts on the necessity for the unburying of the cultic center of Naianism known as the Caves of Naia?
They did.

Explain.
Given the quantum mechanical, chaotic, and interrelated nature of the physical universe (even leaving aside for the moment any considerations of superluminal communication or manifold realities), the suspicions, by their simple existence, could not but influence her presentation. But at another level, Sari's thoughts (and, therefore, her expression of those thoughts) had become, in many ways, imbued with a kind of spiritual despondency by her discovery that the dedicated elders of Naianism whom she had known as a girl had been, in the contemporary scene, replaced by individuals who would not believe, could not believe, and, in fact, did not want to believe in a spirituality that was, for Sari, an integral and growing part of her being.

* * *

How integral?

Integral by the fact that by spirituality had she been transformed in body from an old woman to a young one.

How growing?

Growing by the increasing conviction and urgency with which she approached the task that she had intuitively grasped as necessary and fitting.

Was Charna aware of this?

No.

What, in fact, was Charna aware of?

The presence, in close physical proximity, of a young female of the human persuasion, one who appeared to be naïvely concerned with the improvement of the spiritual life of her co-religionists, and who (again, naïvely) believed in her ability to effect this improvement. The utility of the fact that said female was attractive, and therefore likely to be seen as a potential sexual partner by members of the Panasian priesthood (who, though technically celibate, would, Charna assumed, be nonetheless interested in attaining sexual congress with young, attractive females of the human persuasion). The profit to be gained by such utility, in that, by means of the gratification of the urges toward sexual congress with young, attractive females of the human persuasion possessed by members of the Panasian priesthood, she would gain for members of her own religion certain concessions that, by their value and convenience, could not but increase her standing in the Naian community. The likelihood that this increased standing, if realized, would work to the detriment, not to mention the possible ruination, of a certain Jeddiah.

* * *

Did Charna consider the opinions of Sari in this equation of presence, pandering, societal profit, and belligerence?
Yes.

How so?
The proportion of willingness to unwillingness of the young, attractive female of the human persuasion in question bearing heavily upon the question of how easy it would be to bring said female to sexual congress with said members of the Panasian priesthood (the desirability of this congress being assumed by Charna both in terms of personal profit and priestly interest), Charna had considered Sari's opinions in great depth, and, in fact, was continuing to consider them.

To what end?
To the convincement of Sari to become a party to the attainment of such congress.

What probability did Charna ascribe to this convincement?
High.

Enumerate the factors that prompted Charna to hold the opinion that such convincement had a high probability.
Sari's naïveté (mentioned above). Her determination (mentioned above). Her beliefs (mentioned above).

Was Sari initially aware of Charna's plan for her convincement and her (Charna's) assumption that such convincement was of high probability?
No.

Subsequently?
Yes.

* * *

What brought about this sudden enlightenment?
Increasing interaction, veiled suggestion, continued verbal intercourse, and, finally, blunt exposition.

Describe Sari's reaction to this plan.
Indignation. Anger. Violence.

Violence?

As the door slammed, Charna looked down at the plate of water-soaked fish. It had been a particularly good batch, that. Unfortunately it—along with the dried figs that had accompanied it—was now sitting in her lap, upside down.

"Badly aspected," she muttered at the chair that Sari had, up until a minute ago, occupied. "Typical Gemini." The fishy water dripped through the cloth, ran down her legs, puddled on the floor. "I suppose that I will have to do it myself, then."

And I farted. He-he! And they said nothing! Yes. They could do nothing. And Abnel gave me permission. A knife! He-he! And she will let me! She will have to! He-he!

Chapter Ten

... and he will do anything for me since I but strap him in and he is quite happy and that satisfies me for now but what about Jenkins and I have no idea why he had to go up into the mountains but Rosebud wanted it and he was so wonderful the night before that I could not deny him but those bastards in the council will not listen to me even though those Naian WHORES go about without their headwraps *in the HOUSE* and I cannot understand their opposition they seemed so amused by my plan as though they had some kind of secret wonder what it could be a good thing they do not know about my secret but I know they do it themselves they have to but Rosebud wanted it in any case and so he can be trusted to keep his mouth shut and what am I worried about they cannot touch me for I am the Gharat and if they have any questions why they can consult the Sacred Texts themselves and they will find what I want them to find if I do not kill them first for their sacrilege and surely it was a small thing to change them so that Jenkins and Rosebud could go up there and that Wool I must not forget about Wool he is a strange one to be sure but I wonder but no matter what that earthquake might have done you do not suppose that but no I would have heard by now and they had guards with them but why have they not returned I am very surprised . . .

Good morning! A fine day in Katha! There has not been any rain for a long time, and the river is all but dry, and there was an earthquake this morning that toppled a few buildings in the Naian Quarter and sent down another one of those famous stenches (though no one really knows what they are or where they come from, and no one had better ask, because Panasian Law is very clear about things like that), and the women who are moaning in the square in front of the temple of Panas about having been impaled an hour earlier for various infractions of Panasian law are not at all happy (and no one had better ask about what becomes of all the men who are guilty of various infractions of Panasian law either, because Panasian law is also very clear about things like that), but they will not moan for much longer, and it is a fine day nonetheless, and surely there is no more splendid sight in the world than that of the morning sunlight on the spires and pinnacles of Katha, the gleam of semiprecious walls and windows, the flash of a blue-clad figure making his way across the rooftops—

Oh . . . wait a minute . . .

. . . but I have not heard anything and so it is only a matter of time before they return but what they want up there I have no idea and it is surely a good thing that the Quarries are well beyond their range of travel they would not recognize the Quarries for what they are in any case but they might see all that water and Jenkins is hinting at remarks about backwards nations and what right does *he* have to say anything about it he wears *wool* of all things and in public and then he goes on about backwards nations it makes me sick and if Rosebud were not so compliant I would have had them all killed for I am the High Priest and my word is law and I can even tell the king the will of Panas (blessed be He!) and since I am the high priest I cannot utter anything *but* the will of Panas and those WHORES who go about without their headwraps *in the HOUSE* will get what they deserve I will see to it even if the bastards in the council laugh at me and I do not know what they are laughing about but I know they are laughing about something but Jenkins is hinting at all those things and I am becoming very tired of his airs and what if he sees the Quarries and all that water and he would then have to admit that we are most certainly not backwards for I could ask him whether his Righteous States (bunch of heathen WHORES) is capable of anything like that but then he would say something and three hundred years of work would go to sandstone and I can certainly not have that but if he keeps on with his airs I will have to find something to do because I simply will not tolerate . . .

And, indeed, it is the Blue Avenger who is skulking (though the Blue Avenger would hotly deny that he ever skulks) across the rooftops of the priestly complex, peering across open expanses of marble and jasper, sidling along ledges, flitting along beneath the multiple, overhanging eaves. He is obviously new to Katha—or at least to the rooftops of the priestly complex—for he appears to be examining everything, orienting himself . . .

. . . looking for something . . . or someone.

And, strangely enough, for all his athletic prowess and his fine physical condition, this morning (And a fine morning it is, indeed!) the Blue Avenger is pausing now and again and putting his hand to various parts of his body as though he is in some pain. Now, if fortune had seen fit to grace us with a pair of binoculars—

Oh, wait. Here they are.

And, since fortune has seen fit to grace us with a pair of binoculars, we can see that these uncharacteristic pauses on the part of the Blue Avenger are accompanied not only by the putting of a hand to various parts of his body, but also by a decided *wincing* . . . at least as far as we can tell from the portion of his face not covered by his blue mask.

How very odd. One might well think he had been beaten.

. . . that sort of thing from a *foreigner* who wears *wool* and who comes from a country in which women go about without headwraps *in the HOUSE* bunch of WHORES and surely Jenkins cannot possibly harbor the delusion that the Righteous States of America is in any way superior to a land in which for three hundred years there has been but he does not know about that and I cannot tell him and surely there is some way I can demonstrate to him how vastly superior to his miserable and heathenish land we are but that would mean showing him something, and I surely cannot show him the Quarries or the workings, for that would mean the end of it all but perhaps there is something else I must think about this but perhaps there is something else yes there would be much arranging to do but I think I could manage it the pavilion would almost be enough but that would raise questions and maybe I will have to examine the Texts to see if there is anything I can do yes the pavilion but they would want to know where it went and I would have to answer lest Jenkins consider me backwards and would wonder why I did not know but I am certain . . .

IN THE NAME OF PANAS, THE BENEFICENT, THE WONDROUS, THE SHAPER OF CITIES, THE CARVER OF WORLDS, THE ARBITER OF THE

LIVES OF MEN AND THE SUBJUGATOR OF ALL
THINGS WEAK AND EFFEMINATE, FOR WHOSE
GLORY THE GREAT WORK OF THE PUMPS AND
RESERVOIRS GOES ON CEASELESSLY NIGHT
AND DAY, TO WHOSE CREDIT WAS THE FIRST
REVELATION OF THE GREAT WORK OF THE
PUMPS AND RESERVOIRS, IN WHOSE NAME
THE WRITER GREETS AND COMPLIMENTS THE
READER AS MANY TIMES AS THERE ARE
GRAINS OF SAND IN THE DESERT, PEBBLES IN
THE DRY VALLEYS, PARCHED FIELDS IN THE
WASTELAND AND HUMBLY OFFERS THE FOL-
LOWING INFORMATION.

Mishap: Earthquake

Pumps damaged: #2, #7, #18, #4652

Reason for damage: collapse of pump tunnels #7,
#18, #911

Slaves dead/injured: 290/657

Reason for death/injury: collapse of pump tunnels
#7, #18, #911; external breach in working #697

Percentage drop in overall capacity: 25

Estimated time until return to full capacity: 120
days

Damage to dikes, dams, and retaining walls: moderate

Collateral release of water before containment:
120,000 kils

Projected strength of repairs: good

IN THE NAME OF PANAS, THE BUILDER UP AND
THE WEARER DOWN, THE MUNIFICENT AND
THE PROFITABLE, THE POWER OF THE PRIESTS
AND THE FEAR OF THE LAITY, THE HOLY AND
THE RIGHTEOUS, THE SMITER OF ENEMIES AND
THE HELPER OF FRIENDS, SO CLOSES THIS RE-
PORT IN THE HOPES THAT THE READER MAY BE

SO MAGNIFIED AS TO BE GREAT AS THE
CLOUDLESS SKY, AS WIDE AS THE DESERTS, AS
HOT AS THE BURNING SUN ...

FORWARDED TO KATHA

Beaten or not, wincing or not (May I see those binoculars, please?), the Blue Avenger makes his way
across the many-terraced and multi-pinnacled roofs of
the priestly complex ...

"Here," said Sari, bending over Beshur. "Drink up!"
—Oh! Oh! Oh!
"Did Potatoes say where he was going when he left?"
—Oh! Oh! Oh!

... that I must say something because I cannot have
them thinking that we are backwards but we are obviously good enough for *them* to come to *us* with trade
and agreements, and we are good enough for *them* to
come to *us* and did he not look well with that snake
coming out the way it did and the *thread* was magnificent I hope he does not limp for very long but he went
along with it and I could tell that he wanted it and why
should he not after all it was all his idea or he would
not have come into the garden the way that he did I
could see it in his eyes when Bakbuk was bending over
him but I am not at all attracted to Bakbuk might as
well try to bed a barber's razor as Bakbuk cut to pieces
in no time much better my little Rosebud and that
snake was so nice I am getting no that will not do now
but what shall I show them ...

... drawing ever closer to what his instincts indicate
is the location of the Gharat—oh, excuse me: I mean

the lair of the parasitical excrescence upon the potentially-republican body politic of the Three Kingdoms. (Better?) But though every muscle, fiber, and sinew (The usual catalog. Take the binoculars and confirm it, if you wish.) of his body is obviously taut with attentiveness and caution, they are obviously not quite taut enough, for he does not notice the boyish (girlish?) figure that is now making its way from pinnacle to pillar to wall on another part of the multi-planar roof . . . nor, for that matter, does the girlish (boyish?) figure appear to notice the Blue Avenger.

. . . it must truly be something remarkable and it can surely only be the pavilion but that means that I must show them the Library too and why not the Library Jenkins has said that they have libraries in America but surely those libraries cannot compare with our Library for we have copies of everything including even the Hymns of Loomar which do *not* say anything about running about without a headwrap *in the HOUSE* just think of it the WHORES going about and not even excised we must do something about that there is no telling what they will get into next and their days are numbered but it seems so long and I will not see the day so who can blame me for attempting to shorten the time surely I am more intelligent than the old priests who devised the plan taking three hundred years mine but a generation but I must have the approval of the council and those bastards will not listen to me and they go on with their knowing smiles and what *do* they know anyway cannot be much of anything good for nothing but drinking coffee and smucking serves them right and if I can get Jenkins' help everything would change because I would have their guns and their ship and they would do what I want because Jenkins would want what I have and that surely is something to think about but how would I bring that to pass a minister in their heads surely Aeid is something of a usurper for he is but a prince and I am the Gharat and I know what the will of Panas (blessed be He!) is and it is what my will is because how can it be other than what Panas wants because I am the Gharat . . .

But the boyish . . . ah . . . that is, *girlish* . . . uh . . .

But Bakbuk, too, is engaged in figuring out the lay-out of the roofs and buildings that make up the priestly complex. Despite the teachings of the priests regarding its divine origins, the complex, seen from this perspective, is a rather haphazard affair, with buildings and roofs stuck alongside one another without much regard for such niceties as proportion or convenience (though it must be admitted that the convenience of individuals traveling by rooftop was, more than likely, not on the mind of the designer, whether human or divine). Bakbuk, though, having dispensed long ago with any sort of belief in anything save his duty and his loyalty (the latter still unblemished despite a few pressing conflicts involving his suspicions, Prince Aeid, and the Blue Avenger), does not find it overly surprising that things up here are haphazard. Everything is haphazard. Why should the priestly complex (or, for that matter, the mind of Panas Himself) be any different?

In any case, Bakbuk, who prides himself on being able to rise above such confusion, is examining the roofs and the buildings, and in a trice he has oriented himself. Since he knows where the Gharat should be (which is, admittedly, no real guarantee that the Gharat will actually *be* there) it is a simple matter to go to that location and look.

Bakbuk, however, is slipping a little here. But perhaps he can be forgiven the error: since the rooftops are thickly furnished with pillars and pinnacles and balustrades and various other appurtenances appropriate to a proper priestly-complex roof, it is virtually impossible for him to see (on a course that is, given the haphazard and random nature of Bakbuk's personal conception of a universe, surprisingly similar to his own), a figure—quite manly, really—clad in a strange costume of azures and blues.

Oh. And the mask. Do not forget the mask.

. . . and I want what Panas wants and that is so true and yet no one ever seems to remember it most of all the king who should remember it and if he does not remember it then he is breaking the laws of Panas (blessed be He!) and if he does *that* then what kind of a king is he and it is a very good thing that I am here because *someone* needs to know the laws of Panas if that were not the case then punishment would be swift and sure and if Rosebud does that again I will have to *punish* him swift and sure oh yesyesyes and that was so delightful when the snake crawled out and the thread I never thought it could feel that way but that is what the Americans have to offer to us and I wonder whether Jenkins has any idea or might be interested in joining us one cannot be too careful among people who do not recognize the supremacy of the will of Panas but such things could be found out and that thread was wonderful and I *know* that those WHORES who go about with their heads uncovered *in the HOUSE* could never appreciate anything like that . . .

And so, inch by inch, foot by foot, the Blue Avenger, having discovered as though by instinct the location of	And so, inch by inch, foot by foot, Bakbuk, having determined as though by intuition the whereabouts of

the Gharat,	the Gharat,
lowers	descends the
himself down	outer wall of
the face of	the main
the building,	building,
unaware that,	unaware that,
just around	just around
the corner,	the corner,
someone else	someone else
is doing	is doing
exactly the	exactly the
same thing.	same thing.

. . . but perhaps Jenkins would be unable to appreciate it and that would mean the end of everything but though Jenkins is a heathen he considers himself a good man and that is what I must find out a minister in their heads and they all obey because they cannot do otherwise because they cannot even conceive of doing otherwise I *must* find out about that and Jenkins would tell me all about it if he thought that I shared his sympathies and so I must win him over a minister in their heads yes I will work for that and even the king would do what was right then and there would be no more waiting and no more running about with their heads uncovered *in the HOUSE* for they would not even think of it and I can show him the pavilion and the library and then he will be impressed with us and he will help me and . . .

And, at precisely the same time, two heads (furnished, by necessity, with the eyes required for the subsequent operation) look directly into the room where the Gharat is standing, seeing (first) the Gharat, and (second) one another.

. . . GAAAH . . .

GAAAH!   Ooooooh! *Him!*

And, as one, the heads vanish, one to consider how
effectively it (along with its attached body) has again
been thwarted in its efforts at terrorizing the Gharat,
the other overcome by a wave of sensual emotion that
leaves it . . . no, him . . .

. . . no, *her,* dangling at the end of her rope, her body
afire with impossible yearnings, her mouth slack and
willing and ready for a kiss that will never come.

. . . and I must leave Katha for he has found me
and I am not safe here what can I do it is dangerous
and Bakbuk has not helped in the slightest the little effeminate traitor where is he when I need him and I
shall have him *punished* when I am in charge and
I must leave but if he finds that I have left then he will
follow me and so I must do it in secrecy I must make
arrangements Bakbuk can help me what a splendid fellow yes he is truly a good servant of the king and I
would trust him with my life and he will get me out of
Katha and back to Nuhr the fools here can only smirk
and can get nothing done and they will not approve the
tax and so I must try something else and if I can get
Jenkins on my side he will help me yes I can do that
yes . . .

"Wife?" said Ehar.

Yalliah was standing by the cooking pot, looking off
across the barren wastes toward the mountains. The
sun was setting, the shadows rising quickly. About her,
the caravan was slowly preparing for the night's
march. "Husband?"

"You are thoughtful."

"I was thinking of Sari. I often wonder whether she
reached the Caves. I wonder whether she found what
she wanted to find."

"I do not know, wife," said Ehar. "But we will be in Katha in another week, and I will make inquiries."

A camel spat at someone. A sharp *thwap* said that the beast did not go undisciplined.

"I miss her," said Yalliah. "I worry about her."

"And I also," said Ehar.

Chapter Eleven

Where was Aeid?

This question had come to trouble Haddar more and more, and perhaps his continuing beardlessness—a condition he diligently maintained by means of daily exercises with a razor (exercises that were, fortunately (or unfortunately, depending upon one's point of view) without any further concomitant penile pursuits)— amplified that sense of trouble, for it was an ever-present reminder of how woefully ill-equipped he was for his position at court, a position that demanded, as its primary prerequisite, the undisputed possession of a penis.

Who had caused the explosions in Nuhr?

This, too, was a burden for him, for though he had a good idea as to the general identity of the culprits, nonetheless, a good idea of general identity did not go very far toward presenting the actual, individual perpetrators (suitably shackled, tongueless, and eyeless) to King Inwa Kabir. The beard—or, rather, the lack of it—was intimately connected with this problem also, for it reminded him from day to day, indeed, from moment to moment, of his inadequacies, of his true, inward, and hidden (as carefully hidden as the device that he now wore constantly under his clothing) status.

What was the true identity of the Blue Avenger?

Now here, Haddar could claim at least a little success, for Kuz Aswani's conspiratorial wiggles had gone some distance toward convincing him that the counselor's derangement was no more than a sham designed to divert suspicion. And when he considered the fact that, ever since Kuz Aswani had been put under close observation by the palace staff, the Blue Avenger had made no further appearances (the tax collectors, admittedly, having been none too conscientious in the execution of their appointed tasks while the Gharat was away from Nuhr), Haddar's surety became ever more complete.

He is watching me. I know he is watching me. And gloating. There is no doubt about it. A terrible man, to so gloat over the misfortune of such as me, and even more terrible for his having been the original cause of that misfortune! And yet there is no escape for me. I have been ensorcelled, and I cannot escape.

But Haddar's case against Kuz Aswani lacked something by way of absolute proof, and because Kuz Aswani's afflictions (shammed though they surely were) had managed to find some sympathy among members of the court (not, to be sure, including the unfortunate—and unmanned—Fakik), Haddar, whose denuded face was an ever-present reminder of the precariousness of his hold upon his office and his power, was unwilling to act. (And was that not just like a silly woman? Yes! Yes! Yes!)

But I cannot live this way. I do not want to live this way. I miss my manhood! I miss my wife! I hate this smelly litter box; and corners, even without papers spread in them, attract me no longer. All is as dust. Haddar shuns me, my wife has left me, and Umi Botzu does nothing but gloat. And there is no escape!

Hence, since establishing Kuz Aswani as the Blue Avenger was the only goal toward which Haddar could move with any confidence, the minister had, with mixed feelings, begun to watch the counselor with increasing care and constancy, waiting for something to happen that might demonstrate unequivocally the validity of his thesis. Once again, though, Haddar found himself in conflict with himself, for if he proved that Kuz Aswani was the Blue Avenger, that meant that he was adequately performing his duties as chief minister. But if he were adequately performing his duties, then that meant that the denuded face that he bore was no more than a sham itself, and _that_ meant . . .

But . . . but I cannot allow him to do this. I want my life back. I will have my life back. And I am a man, and therefore I will fight. I will defy Umi Botzu. I will not let him have his way with me. Panas (blessed be He!) will surely aid His humble servant and protect him from the snares of sorcerers and magicians, and therefore I will put my trust in my God and I will fight!

And so it was that, one day, as Haddar was prowling the corridors of the palace, looking for Kuz Aswani, looking for proof that the counselor who was deemed unfortunate by so many was actually not unfortunate, but, rather, extremely clever (but, at the same time, not looking for proof at all, looking, rather for a consummate demonstration of his inadequacies as a man and a minister, and yet not looking for that, either, because the life of a woman was unthinkable . . . though (as he could not but admit) perfectly suited to him), he came upon a strangely stumbling, oddly ill-at-ease figure who was, despite his stumbling, most certainly bipedal and, despite his obvious discomfort with the external apparatus, most definitely clothed in a counselor's linen garments.

A silly woman! Yes! Yes! _Yes!_

Horrors!

Say this place isn't half bad, considering the price. No offense intended, you know, but it's not exactly, like, the Beverly Hilton, is it? Hey, you're a great guy! You know, some people would get pretty P.O.'d about a crack like that, but you've got a great sense of humor, and I can tell we're gonna get along real good. That is, if I take the place.

Well, hel-*lo*! You are Sari, are you not? I was sure that I recognized you, for we have met one another before. Oh, yes, I am sure of it. Charna was mentioning you to me the other day, and I was absolutely certain at the time that I knew you from a previous lifetime. Oh, yes! But, you know, you and I had a pact that we made at that time, and it did not involve Charna, and so I am rather surprised that Charna even mentioned you to me, because she has always been jealous of our intimate relationship—we are soul mates, you know—and has always resented the fact that our pact did not include her. And . . .

The Caves? What Caves? *Those* Caves? But . . . ah . . . *why*?

But, you know, it looks pretty good, and I'm kinda in a bind, considering that my old lady—you know, the *bitch*—just threw my ass out of my apartment. Can you imagine that? A guy gets home from a hard day of looking for work, and she's got all his stuff piled outside his door! She even changed the locks! Now, I don't have to tell a guy like you that I'm good for the rent, on account of you're a good judge of character, and, besides, I was paying *every last cent* of the rent on my old place. Yeah. You bet. The one she threw me out of. The *bitch*. Would you believe it? But, you see, I'd had a couple rough months, and I actually had to ask her to chip in on the rent for a while, 'cause I was out of work. And you'd think it was the end of the whole goddam world that she had to put herself out that way when number one I'd been supporting her for months on account of a receptionist doesn't pull in diddly, and number two all she'd have done otherwise was spend all her dough on herself. I mean, what do women buy, anyway? Perfume and stuff like that. Makeup. Pantyhose. You know: junk. So I had to ask her if she'd just, like, not waste her money on shit for a couple of months until I got back on my feet. Just for a couple of months. *Pow!* She goes and tosses me out. Can you believe that?

Well, hel-*lo!* You are Sari, are you not? I was sure that I recognized you, for I saw you talking with Jeddiah in the marketplace the other day, and Jeddiah told me all about you. You know, I think that it is wonderful that an individual like yourself has friends such as Jeddiah, and I would never think of intruding into any friendships because, after all, freedom and free will are so important, and it is the assiduous pursuit of freedom and free will that makes Naians so special, would you not agree? But I must warn you about Jeddiah, because she is very vested in undermining my dear friend, Charna. You know Charna, of course: everyone knows Charna. She is a leader—perhaps *the* leader—of the Naian community, and . . .

The Caves? What Caves? *Those* Caves? But . . . ah . . . *why?*

Now, I'm a quiet sort of guy. I'm a screenwriter, you know. Yeah. Oh, I've got scripts out everywhere. It's just a matter of time before something hits big, because I know the market. I mean, that's one of my *jobs:* to know the market. One of those babies is going to wind up on the right person's desk at the right time, and I'll tell you it's gonna be hats and horns then. You bet. So I won't be giving you any trouble, you know, with wild parties or anything. Nope. I don't have time for shit like parties, because I've got to keep turning things over in my head, just turning things over. It was like I was telling my old

lady—you know, the *bitch*—the night before she threw
me out all about this new idea I had for this project I'm
working on. It's just a scream. Everyone'll be eating out
of my hand once I get it down on paper. It's the funniest
thing that I've ever written. Hell, it's the funniest thing
that *anyone's* ever written . . .

"Here," said Potatoes, bending over Beshur. "Drink
up!"
—Oh! Oh! Oh!
"Did Sari say where she was going when she left?"
—Oh! Oh! Oh!

. . . and I'm not one to start bragging when what I'm
bragging about isn't true. But I'll tell you, it's so great,
I started laughing in the middle of the night, and I had
to wake up my old lady to tell her about it. Wouldn't
you know it, though, she didn't *understand* it. But
then, she just draws pictures, and she's just a dumb
girl—you know, she's a receptionist—and I guess
maybe she just can't understand things like that. Some
people can't. But I can, and you can, and that's what's
important, isn't it? (Yeah, you and me, guy!) But I told
her about it anyway, 'cause it was just too good not to
share . . . and you know I really loved her, which was
why I wanted to share it with her, just like I wanted to
share my bed with her 'cause I really loved her. But
she got real P.O.'d at me, and she threw my ass out,
and now I gotta look for a place of my own. Do you
believe that? What a fucking ungrateful *bitch*.

Well, hel-*lo*! You are Sari, are you not? I was sure
that I recognized you, for you were pointed out to me
one day as the woman who is living with the two men,
and I did so want to take the opportunity to tell you
that I perfectly understand your situation, for I myself
am part of an open relationship, and both of my men

love me, and I love them both. Is that not a wonderful thing? Love is such a precious thing, and it is obvious that we should not limit it in any way, and I am so glad that you agree with me. You know, there are many who will criticize individuals like ourselves for having the courage to express our love, but that is because they are cowards, and do not have the strength of character of individualists like ourselves. In fact, they—and I do not think that I need mention names here, do you?— are constantly plotting and undermining us, and I know this for a fact, because just the other day, one of my men started to argue with the other over me (and, to be sure, I can well understand why they might), but such a thing could not have happened except for the fact that our society is unwilling to accept . . .

The Caves? What Caves? *Those* Caves? But . . . ah . . . *why*?

Now, you're a shrewd guy, and I sure wouldn't have to explain anything funny to *you*, on account of you got smarts. I mean, you're going somewhere. So if I came to you with a story about this girl who's like, on a mission from God, only nobody understands her, you'd catch on right away, wouldn't you? You see, her name is Sari, and she's, like, been sent to clean up the shrine of the local deity. Oh, yeah, forgot to tell you: it's fantasy. *Arabian Nights* meets *The Scarlet Letter.* I used to do those dream tours down there on Santa Monica Boulevard—you know the place—and I got the idea from that. It's a gas! Anyway, she's trying to explain herself to the bimbos who dig this local deity, only she doesn't know it but they really don't believe the way that she believes. (You know, this is subtle stuff, and I guess I'm not surprised that someone who thinks that being a fucking *receptionist* is a good job isn't gonna understand a word of it.) I mean, they don't believe *anything* like what she believes. They might as

well be speaking, like, different, *languages* or something like that. But I've kinda established that already,
and the Big Scene comes when she's talking to this
guy. You see, I've already established that Sari, that's
the girl, is all into this feminazi stuff, and—Hey, you
dig Rush, too? Isn't he *great*? Yeah, I'm a dittohead
and *proud of it,* man!—but I play that part of her
strictly for laughs, and all those skankies with the hairy
legs can all go shove it, right, fellah? But, anyway, Sari
is big on this shit, and she thinks that women should be
respected and kowtowed to and all this other PC and
minority quota crap that's been coming down recently,
and leading up to the Big Scene with this guy who's
some kind of leader in the community are a bunch of
waddyacallem ... vignettes (Yeah, that's it. Man, this
is so *hot!*) of Sari just falling on her face trying to get
help with this mission from God that she's involved in,
but no one understands what the fuck she's saying,
and, like, they really don't give a shit anyway, and
that's what leads up to the Big Scene where this guy is
agreeing with everything that she says, and going on
about how women are just wonderful, and how he'll be
glad to help her and all that, and you can tell from
Sari's face that she's really digging his response and
getting all worked up over it—I mean, it's Nirvana for
her, dig?—and this goes back and forth for a while
with him cranking it out and her taking it in except that
now he's going on about how women are so wonderful
and it's so great that he's part of a religion that respects
women and stuff like that until it's kinda starting to
make you *itch,* you know, and then he's off on how he
wants to respect Sari and the audience starts to notice
that he's putting the moves on her, but Sari doesn't notice anything because she's so grateful that she's finally found someone who's willing to help her out and
he damn near *rapes* her before she realizes that what

he means by respect isn't exactly what she means by respect. *¿Comprende?*

Well, hel-*lo*! You are Sari, are you not? I was sure that I recognized you, for you have been much on my mind ever since Jeddiah told me that you wanted to be a part of her school. I cannot express to you how wonderful that is, because there are so few among the Naians who fully embrace the old ways, and the thought that you are among them is just so wonderful, particularly since, as Jeddiah told me, you recognize her as the true leader of the Naian people, and is it not wonderful that she does it all as a service to the community? Unlike Charna, who only acts for profit? I must warn you about Charna, to be sure, because it is well known that, unlike Jeddiah—

The Caves? What Caves? *Those* Caves? But ... ah ... *why?*

Yeah, isn't it great? Now, I didn't mean to give you the idea that I don't like Sari. Actually, for a girl, she's pretty neat. Lotta spunk, if you know what I mean, and I think you and I can both agree that we like our women spunky. You know, you want them to give you a little bit of a fight in bed, just so long as they know who's boss, right? Well, eventually you can see the light bulb go off, and Sari tries to talk him out of it, but it's no go because he keeps going on about honoring women and respecting them all the time he's pulling her clothes off, and man, you can really imagine how he wants to honor her, and with how much of it, right? Isn't that a *riot?*

Well, hel-*lo*! You are Sari, are you not? I was sure that I recognized you, for I have often noticed you going about on your business. Now, I think it is a fine thing for a woman to have some business to take care of, but I feel that I should tell you that Naia is, first and foremost, a mother, and that she thinks most highly of women who fulfill their natural role as mothers. That stands to reason, does it not? Men can come and go as they please—they are, of course, not important—but a woman's entire being is made for the bearing and rearing of children, and it is toward this end that she should put her strengths, which are, of course, not inconsiderable, though wholly oriented in the direction of home and family. It is all a very holy mystery, since the divine feminine supersedes and is preexistent to the masculine, and I always feel very strong in my womanhood ... and my husband, I should add, supports me in this—of course he does—and makes very sure that he takes care of me adequately, since he is aware that I am fulfilling my divine role. And that is also why I had myself excised, you see, because ...

The Caves? What Caves? *Those* Caves? I will have to ask my husband, of course, but ... ah ... *why*?

Really funny stuff. Like I said, I don't think that *anyone's* written anything this funny, even back when they were really writing comedy. This is *classic* stuff, and you better believe that I'm gonna be able to afford your rent, 'cause you can't possibly be asking very much for this dump, and I'm gonna have the cash just rolling in the day after this lands on someone's desk.

Well, hel-*lo*! You are Sari, are you not? I was sure that I recognized you, for who could forget such an attractive and beautiful woman, and I am, to be sure, very proud to be a part of a religion that honors and respects attractive and beautiful women, for truly, attractive and beautiful women are a perfect incarnation of Naia, who Herself cannot but be attractive and beautiful, and is it not wonderful that my religious duties

require me to *embrace* attractive and beautiful women
and . . .

Anyway, Sari just craters when she *parley-vous* what
this doob means when he says he wants to respect her
(and man, by this time, he's looking like he's gonna respect her real good, too), but she's got spunk, so she
doesn't just lie there and whimper about being a victim
like some of these libbers. I mean, you ever really listen to them go on? Bad shit, I'll tell you. But, anyway,
Sari doesn't do that. Nah, she eventually just loses
it, kicks him in the balls, and gets the hell outta Dodge.

. . . surely you are not protesting my need to fulfill
my religious obligations? After all, Naia is a woman,
and She knows about things like this, just as I know
about things like this, because I am a man who is in
harmony with the feminine side of my nature. You really ought to listen to me and take my guidance,
because—

Yowza! Man, they'll be rolling in the aisles when
I'm done with them. Just you wait and see!

—*Urk!*

Ineluctable modality of . . . No, used that *before*.
Agenbite of inwit . . . What? (Where did *that* come
from?) Feeding me on that wretched stuff, enjoying
himself watching me. He won the first battle, maybe,
but I shall triumph in the end. Unlettered. Sandwasher
like those Khyrlings. Not even smooth stones to clean
himself up. And yet . . . scholar! Scholar! He knows
about the Library! Thinks he knows more about it than
I!

Looking at Sari all the time. Know that look. Boys

in the Novices' House. Smucking. Shaving. Slip.
(Here, walk like . . . *NO!*)

—I feel much better, he said to Potatoes, who was,
though the room was much too small for pacing, pacing nonetheless.

Worried about Sari. Well . . . so am I. She has been
gone all morning, and I am confined to nursing this invalid who would not be an invalid . . . *Pumice!* . . . but
for my own princely cleverness. Naian women go
where they want. But that looks to be changing. Seeing
much in the marketplace. Think I am a Naian. Stupid.
Know little enough about the religion, but a few *Naia
bless you's* convinces them all. But . . . Beshur. Not a
Naian. Scholar he calls himself. Hmmm . . . but what
kind of scholar? Head cloth. I wonder.

"That remains to be seen," said Potatoes. He went to
the latticed window and looked out. "Sari will have to
be the judge of that."

Has me where he wants me. Invalid. In this bed.
What is he doing with Sari? Does she care? Womanflesh. Sinful. Water. Mutable. Not like stone. Sculptor
God rives the bones of the earth and builds cities. Naia
pours down rain and washes them away. Rain gone.
Water gone. Naia dead. Inconstancy. Runs after the
next hard prick. But she was alone with me, and I . . .
did not. Could not. Sari . . . useless womanflesh. Not
worth having. But Potatoes wants her. I . . . I . . . must
get out of this bed.

—I am sure that she will say that I am well, Beshur
said.

Wants up. Well, I want up, too. Out, actually. I
should be back in Nuhr. Cannot be any good here for
the Blue Avenger. Unfamiliar city means no escape,
and they would bring me before father and then he
would give me *that look*. I cannot risk it. Foolish to
come here. But found Sari. But left her with . . . *him*.
Must leave. Excuse . . . somewhere. Library in Nuhr

. . . and Beshur knows about it. Maybe something there. Hmmm . . . but Sari is here, and she will not leave. I will not leave . . . her with *him*.

"Of course," said Potatoes.

The door opened, and Sari entered pensively. Her clothes were in disarray, and her hair was mussed and disheveled.

—Sari! said Beshur.

"Sari!" said Potatoes.

Sari looked at them, and neither man had ever before seen such sadness in her eyes. "I think that I must leave this place," she said. "I cannot fulfill the tasks of the Goddess here in Katha."

Wants to go! Nuhr! Yes! Library! Keep her away from Potatoes!

Wants to go! Nuhr! Yes! Library! Keep her away from Beshur!

—But . . . Beshur began.

". . . where?" Potatoes finished.

Sari sat down, shrugged. She looked thoroughly dejected. "Oh, it . . . it does not matter. Anywhere. Someplace where there is a Naian community who cares about Naia."

Nuhr! Yesyesyes!

Nuhr! Yesyesyes!

"If there is such a place anymore."

Chapter Twelve

A hand and an arm ... and a mallet.

Jenkins had been determined to take the bizarre relic back to Katha, but after a day and a half of walking under a hot sun, Mather (with much pleading and sulking) and Wool (with several pertinent and nonpertinent Biblical quotes) had persuaded him to abandon, if only out of consideration for their own precarious hold on survival, what had become by that time a half-rotting thing resembled nothing so much as a large, decayed fish.

The guards and the animals had been killed, buried under several tons of fallen mountain. The supplies, including the water, had been on the animals, and were therefore inaccessible. There was, therefore, nothing for the Americans to do but walk slowly in the direction of Katha, hoping all the time that the miles would run out before their endurance did.

Mather, once his desires regarding the dead limb had been fulfilled, had lapsed into a sullen, worried silence that gave Wool scant opportunity for a pertinent (or even a non-pertinent) Bible quote. Jenkins, on his part, had decided that speaking would only waste air and, possibly, water—the latter being, considering their circumstances, a particularly precious commodity—and so they trudged along in silence. But the ambassador's thoughts were in more rapid motion than his plodding feet might have indicated, were, in fact, simultaneously moving ahead of him (toward Katha, toward Nuhr) and running well behind him (into the fastness of the seemingly impenetrable mountains), piecing together a tapestry of fact and conjecture that appeared to indicate not only that the aspirations of the Righteous States might well be fulfilled, but that there were at least a few things about the Three Kingdoms that the local representative of those same Righteous States might find it worthwhile to look into.

With regards to the former, though the apparatus had been lost first to muck, and then (since transporting it back to Katha was out of the question) to the inescapable corrosion that would result from its exposure to the sun and air, Jenkins now had no doubt as to the feasibility of the American plan. Once he could reach some kind of an understanding with the king—or, more importantly, with Abnel—other gravimeters could be brought, and surveyors and good, competent, Yankee engineers could fashion hard reality out of ephemeral readings taken from brass verniers and swinging pendulums. True, reaching that understanding would be difficult, and might involve (was already involving!) some ... ah ... un-Puritan matters that continued to make him shudder, but he had not been sent to the Three Kingdoms for a holiday. Not at all. This was business. Godly business. Cut-throat, God-fearing, grab-'em-by-the-ears-and-shake-'em-until-they're-dead business. And Jenkins was not about to throw it all over on account of a few shudders.

But it was the latter—that which bore looking into—that intrigued him most, for as the former was made up of near-certainties, the latter was full of conundrums and enigmas that the ambassador's mental bent toward calculation and prudence found at once repellent and fascinating. Though the hand and arm could have been present through some relatively innocuous confluence of events, Jenkins, even straining his imagination to its greatest degree, was unable to construct such a confluence, and therefore he had to begin considering confluences that were not quite so innocuous.

A hand and an arm. And, what was more, a hand and an arm that had obviously been torn from their owner's shoulder by some great force. The identity of the great force was clear: the jet of water released by the earthquake had been under tremendous pressure. But the circumstances that would have brought that hand and arm into juxtaposition with such a jet of water eluded Jenkins ... eluded him as much as any sane explanation for why, in a desert land, such an aqueous jet was present at all.

And it had dried up so suddenly ...

Striding ... or, rather, slouching toward Katha, Jenkins found his thirsty and sunstricken brain churning through possibility after possibility, unable to make sense out of any of it. Deserts and water. Earthquakes and arms. No sense. None. And yet sense and the rational had to come into play somewhere in the twisted equation. Something was happening here, and Obadiah Jenkins was going to find out what it was.

He would have to control Abnel. But in order to control Abnel, he would have to know ... *everything.*

Diplomatic, calculating, wily, Jenkins began to consider how best he might effect the seduction (and the word came to him accompanied by a distinct shudder) of the Gharat, unaware neither that the Gharat had, to a large extent, already accomplished that seduction without any outside assistance whatsoever, nor that he himself had, in fact, drawn very close to the walls of Katha. Mr. Jenkins discovered the walls of Katha (hidden in a haze of thirst and sun-blindness) by running into them. He discovered the seduction of the Gharat only much later.

* * *

"What are you doing with that knife?"
"He-he!"

Ehar entered Katha late in the afternoon. The last leg
of the journey had been a long one, and perhaps
Yalliah's concern about Sari—a concern he shared—
had caused him to push both the caravan and himself
just a little more than was perhaps wise. But though he
was no longer young, Ehar was nonetheless both a
Khyrling and a man of the caravans, and so, after a
few hours of sound sleep, he was up once again. He
left his tents and his camels behind and, after climbing
the long road up the slope of the mountain, passed into
Katha, which (though being to some a holy city and to
others the stagnant dwelling place of nit-picking scholars) was now not only a place to buy and sell merchandise, but also an opportunity to search out news of a
woman whom he had come to consider his friend.

"Hel-*lo*! You are new in Katha, are you not? How
wonderful to meet you. My name is Watersong. Of
course, that is not my real name. That is my spiritual
name, which I took in order to express my spiritual duty
to the world. It goes with my spiritual personality, you
see. And then, of course, I have a secret name, which I
do not reveal to anyone. Excuse me? Sari? An *old*
woman? You *are* a Naian, are you not?"

But Ehar was not a man who was used to searching.
He was a man of commerce, a trader. If one wanted to
trade, one went to the marketplace, and if one had to
search, it was only to find nothing smaller or more obscure than the proper section of the marketplace: the
rug merchants, for example, as opposed to the leather-
workers. This business of looking for news of a single
person among the crowded streets and shops and
houses of a city the size of Katha was not a task for

which he felt properly equipped, and yet both his promise to his wife and his own concerns prompted him to continue. And so, as the sunlight fell ever more obliquely upon Katha, he wandered, looking for Sari, asking questions.

"Hel-*lo*! You are new in Katha, are you not? Well, you will find an extremely active Naian community here. We are all very devoted to the Goddess, since we are the community that is closest to the Caves of Naia. What? An old woman? Who went to the Caves? Why-ever would she want to go and do something like *that*?"

He tried his trading partners and his acquaintances first, but it was not long before he became convinced that Panasians, no matter how well-informed they might be, could know nothing about the whereabouts of a Naian—particularly if that Naian happened to be a woman—and therefore he eventually passed through the guarded gate and entered the Naian Quarter, continuing his search for Sari.

"Hel-*lo*! You are new in Katha, are you not? Well, may Naia bless you! How wonderful! You know, we get many pilgrims to Katha, since the community in Katha is possibly the most important of all the Naian communities in all the Three Kingdoms. What? An old woman? A pilgrim? To the Caves? What Caves?"

"Psst!"

Ehar stopped in the middle of yet *another* maze-like street in the Naian Quarter (and, indeed, there seemed to be nothing *but* maze-like streets in the Naian Quarter, a fact which had speedily rubbed raw the nerves of the Khyrling caravan leader, who was used to open spaces and the ability to see clear to the distant hori-

zon) and turned to the mouth of the alleyway out of
which was coming not only a faint glistening (Were
those *crystals*?) but also the whispered call for attention. The sun, though, had dropped still further, the
brief twilight of the equatorial zone had been replaced
by night, and the speaker was cloaked in darkness.

"Pssst!"

"What do you want?" said Ehar, who, though he was
not a timid man, could not but wish that the genie who
lived in his gold earring would demonstrate some expertise with something besides approaching sand-
storms. Something like . . . say . . . identifying and
evaluating any potential threats inherent in *Psst!*s
and/or *Pssst!*s.

"Psssst!"

Annoyed by yet a third variant of the call, Ehar was
about to shrug and (with fists prudently balled) march
past the alleyway when a hand detained him. Well, not
so much *detained* as *seized him from behind*. And an
arm went around his throat. And, though the hand released him a moment later, it immediately returned in
a different incarnation, for a knife was suddenly prodding his back.

"You are the leader of the caravan that recently arrived outside the gates of Katha, are you not?" said the
voice that had previously spoken only in *Pssst!*s.

Ehar, wisely determining that, given both the absence of any technical expertise on the part of the genie and the presence of the knife, truth was probably
his best policy, nodded as best he could with an arm
half choking him.

The owner of the arm (and, doubtless, of the voice,
the hand, and the knife as well), appeared to be satisfied with Ehar's nod. "That is good. I wonder if you
would be interested in a little additional business for
your caravan?"

With the knife and the arm both continuing to attend to their respective duties, Ehar was very interested indeed, and the owner of the knife and the arm received yet another nod in response.

"That is also good," said the owner. "Come with me. We will discuss terms."

Considering the knife and the arm, there seemed little enough to argue about, and therefore Ehar found himself very amenable to the offer.

The arm was removed from his throat, but the hand refastened itself on him, and the knife remained where it was; and with the shadows of night deep about him, the caravan leader was taken down the alley, over a pile of what felt like gravel but which glittered a little too much in the faint light (Were those *crystals*?), and through a dark doorway. Once the door was closed, however, lamplight suddenly flared, and Ehar found himself facing, across a small table, an attractive . . . ah . . . a handsome . . . ah . . . well . . . that is to say . . .

Ehar was not sure what to make of it. The clothing said *male,* the demeanor said *female,* and the face said *decline to state;* nor was the good caravan leader helped in the slightest either by the creature's speech (which seemed made of equal parts alluring innuendo and masculine directness) or voice (which hovered somewhere in an androgynous alto range). Given the hand and the arm and the knife—and the certainty that all three were hovering somewhere nearby—Ehar devoutly hoped that he would not be called upon to offer any kind of an opinion.

"We understand that you will be traveling to Nuhr," said the creature with a move of its shoulders that indicated a willingness to be seduced, but a flash to its eyes that evinced a determination to instantly kill anyone rash enough to try anything so insulting.

Again, Ehar felt compelled to tell the truth. "That is true," he said, but the ingrained caution of a trader caused him to add an instinctive "maybe" at the end of the otherwise flawless statement.

The creature eyed him. "Would you care to be a little more clear?" it inquired, putting a hand to its sword.

Sword! Ah! A sword! It must be a male!

"Ah ..." began Ehar, reassured that he was dealing with a man. After all, they could at least understand one another, "... well ..."

But a moment later, a heave of what could only have been budding breasts beneath the creature's gilt shoulder cloth plunged Ehar back into confusion.

"... uh ..."

"No matter," said the creature. "We *know* that you are going to Nuhr. With rugs."

"Yes," said Ehar, stifling yet another unfortunate *maybe*. "To Nuhr. Baroz ... uh ..."

And was he now going to involve the unfortunate Baroz in this potentially lethal foolishness? Ehar cursed inwardly at his stupidity. Poor Baroz! And it was said that he was a nobleman who had fallen on hard times! He had enough troubles!

"The rug merchant, yes," said the creature with yet another heave of those obviously (from what Ehar could see of them) perfect breasts. "Yes, we know. We want you to take a guest with you."

"A ... a guest?"

"A passenger. Do not worry: you will be paid well. You will, in fact, be paid well enough ..." But though the words conveyed the essence of command and surety, a sudden catch sent them sprawling into a very womanly, tempting, spread-my-legs-I'm-hot-and-runny-come-and-get-me-heap. Ehar felt a certain ... stirring, which he immediately suppressed in favor of a certain crazed scramble for self-preservation. "... for you to feel no excuse to ask any questions about the identity or the business of the passenger in question. That is clear, is it not?"

"Ah ... very clear." But though Ehar gritted his teeth, still a wayward *maybe* forced itself from between his lips.

The creature eyed him with a flashing, imperious gaze that nonetheless gave a distinct impression of willingness ... for almost anything. "It had better be clear, caravan leader, for should it not be clear, your life is forfeit. You are a Khyrling, are you not?"

"Yes!" Ehar shouted and clamped his mouth shut before the *maybe* came out. (He was just in time.)

"Need I remind you of the recent activities of the Freedom Fighters of Khyr?"

Ehar could have sworn that a look of unalloyed lust passed across the face of the creature.

"No!" Again Ehar was successful.

"Your status within the Three Kingdoms is very uncertain, trader. A single accusation against you could result in ... unfortunate consequences."

"Yes! *Mmph!*"

"What was that?"

"Yes! *Mm—!*"

"What?"

"Yes!"

"That is better. Do we have an agreement, then?"

Ehar, judging that he was but agreeing to prolong his life—which, considering the circumstances, was not such a bad deal after all ... a bargain, in fact, in which any trader worth his camels might take pride—agreed wholeheartedly.

"Fine," said the creature, folding its hands. "Then I believe that we are done here. Expect your passenger ..." The dark eyes examined Ehar as though disrobing him. "... upon the evening of your departure. As far as your caravan is concerned, you have taken on a passenger, and he is traveling to Nuhr, and you know nothing about him beyond that. Do you understand?"

Ehar, not trusting his tongue, merely nodded.

"He is merely a passenger. No further comment is to be made about him or about any companions he might choose to bring with him."

Ehar nodded again, clamping his teeth together against the *maybe* that persisted in welling up.

"Good."

And, with that, the creature rose and left, but not without a final glance over its shoulder that Ehar could not but perceive as being imbued with a deep longing, an insatiable desire for something unspecified, yet very clear, something within arm's reach, yet absolutely unattainable.

A minute later, he was back at the mouth of the alley. Deep within the dark passage, the footfalls of the owner of the hand, the arm, and the knife were fading amid the glitter of a heap of something (Crystals? *Really?*) when, once again, Ehar felt himself grabbed, felt an arm go about his throat, felt a knife prick his side.

He sighed. Affliction had made him philosophical.

"Who was that?" hissed a voice in his ear.

"Who was what . . . ?" Ehar almost said, but though affliction had made him philosophical, it had not made him idiotic, and so, instead, he answered truthfully, "I do not know."

"You do not know?"

"Yes. May—"

He caught himself just in time.

"What?"

Ehar thought quickly. "May . . . may . . . may Panas bless you!"

Not quickly enough, it appeared. Here, in the Naian Quarter, he was invoking the blessing of Panas? But the new arrival did not seem to notice. "What did he say?"

"I ..."

"He wanted you to take a passenger away from Katha, yes?"

"I ..."

"He wanted you to take him to Nuhr, yes?"

"I ..."

"He wanted you to ask no questions, yes?"

"I ..."

"He promised you a good price, yes?"

"I ..."

"He has a companion, and you could not tell whether that companion was a girl or a boy, yes?"

"I ..."

"Would you be interested in taking another passenger to Nuhr?"

"I ..."

"The price will be good, but you must ask no questions, either about him or about his companions."

"I ..."

"That is all. Your additional passengers will arrive on the evening of your departure."

"I ..."

But the arm and the knife, not to mention the hand, were gone, along with their owner. Once more, Ehar was left alone outside the mouth of the alley. His isolated condition, however, lasted only for a minute, for the sound of rapid—very rapid—footsteps approached, and a moment later, both Ehar and the runner were sprawling on the ground.

—Did you see him? the runner cried.

Ehar, both philosophical and (now) unprompted by a knife, could at last afford to be cautious. "Maybe."

—Did he ask you to take a passenger?

"Maybe."

—Several passengers?

"Maybe."

—I will be one of those passengers!

"Maybe."

—And you *will* be paid well.

Ehar was suddenly despondent. "Maybe."

—We will be there on the evening of your departure. Do not forget!

"Maybe."

—I must go now. I must see where he is going.

And the runner got to his feet and sprinted off.

Incense. Wind chimes. The distant sound of *Hunna-hunna-hunna-hon!* Ehar, bowing to the inevitable, rose ... and waited. Sure enough, in the silence of the evening (broken only by the sound of wind chimes and the above-referenced *Hunna-hunna-hunna-hon!*) he heard another set of footsteps approaching ... one with a distinctly womanly sound to them. A figure materialized out of the gloom.

"Beshur?" came a young voice.

"No," said Ehar.

The figure stopped in mid-stride. *"Ehar?"*

Ehar blinked. It seemed that everyone knew more about him than he had ever dreamed, even his name. "Yes," he said, dropping his cautious *maybe,* "I am Ehar."

"But what ... what brings you to the Naian Quarter?"

"I am looking for an old woman named Sari," he said, deciding that, if the young woman with whom he was speaking knew his name, and the men (or otherwise) he had met knew his business and everything else, he might as well be open about his mission. In any case, they all probably knew about it already.

"Sari?"

"Sari."

A long silence. The woman seemed to waver. Above them, a rickety shutter was thrown open and then slammed closed: someone was curious about the meeting at the mouth of the alley.

Ehar shrugged inwardly. Though he was curious himself, he had no doubt that this fourth darkling visitant would also want passage to Nuhr.

But the brief light had revealed the woman before him, and she was lithe and lovely, her hair unbound in the fashion of the Naians. The bronze medallion above her heart glinted. Her eyes were searching, restless, and they had widened at the sight of Ehar.

"My ... my name is Sari," she said when the darkness had closed in once more.

"Ah," said Ehar, "but the Sari I am looking for is old, and you are young. You cannot possibly be that Sari."

Another long pause. Then: "Yes," came a soft voice, "that is true. I cannot possibly be that Sari."

Chapter Thirteen

This just in from our bureau in Nuhr:

In the wake of a crippling explosion in the heart of the Holy City, a spokesman for King Inwa Kabir this afternoon announced that a thorough investigation has attributed the widespread destruction to the work of the Freedom Fighters of Khyr, a self-styled revolutionary branch of the Greater Khyrling Independence Movement, which is itself a renegade offshoot of the Revolutionary Council for the Greater Work of Panas, which was implicated last year in the massacre of several hundred Kalashite pilgrims to the Peaks of Adamant. A minister of Khyr, speaking anonymously, suggested that strenuous efforts are now being considered to root out the influence of the Freedom Fighters, which draws most of its strength from disenfranchised young men of Khyrling descent. No details were given as to what methods might be used to accomplish this.

Coming up next: Last Quakers exterminated in Vermont.

Despite the efficiency inherent in preparations that have become, over the years, so habitual as to be well-nigh instinctive, there is a certain feeling of uneasiness about the caravan as it prepares to leave Katha. The leader, Ehar, a man of no small experience, seems hesitant and distracted, and if this is so obvious as to be immediately noticeable by such as ourselves—and from this altitude—then certainly his wife and his sons and his caravan partners cannot but perceive it even more clearly.

Indeed, Ehar actually appears almost *reluctant* to depart. It is as though there is something absolutely essential missing from what, to other eyes, is complete readiness. The tents are down. The camels are loaded. The provisions are carefully packed. The merchandise is stowed. What, then, could be lacking?

Ah! Here is something! As the evening shadows begin to fall across the breadth of Kaprisha, there suddenly appear from out of the just-closing gates of the city two groups of figures, one splendid, one not.

The splendid group consists of five men. Well . . . four men and one . . . ah . . . well . . . let us reserve judgment on that, all right? They come in elaborate clothing and bring with them much baggage . . . and obviously expect Ehar and his people to attend to it. The not-splendid group consists of two men and a woman . . . and Naians at that. They come in plain dress—shoulder cloth and waist cloth and sandals— and they do not seem to want to trouble anyone about the few small bundles they carry.

Questions on Chapter 13.

1) Note the study in contrasts between the splendid group and the not-splendid group. What is the author attempting to do here? How successful is she? What are your feelings about the members of the two groups? Expound upon the Christ-symbolism underlying this.

2) Does the use of the term "plain dress" in the above paragraph indicate any pro-Quaker bias on the part of the author? Ex-

plain the reasons for your answer, paying
particular attention to the underlying Christ-
symbolism.

3) Describe the author's use of narrative
tone in order to achieve a sense of frivol-
ity or lightheartedness to this section.
What techniques does she use to accomplish this? Compare with other authors and
other books. Include instances of Christ-
symbolism.

4) What does the author mean when she
uses the term "altitude"? Does this have
anything to do with social or class struggle? Why or why not? Describe the Christ-
symbolism of hot-air balloons.

Immediate resolution on the part of Ehar. Hesitancy
is banished. An abrupt transition from stasis to flow.
A cork might well have come out of a bottle of
champagne: the caravan is suddenly in motion! Individuals—including the members of the splendid
group—mount. Camels—one and all—rise. Others—
particularly those in the not-splendid group—shuffle
their feet and wait to be told which direction to go.

And, indeed, the direction of travel now appears to
be something of a matter of contention between the
leader of the splendid party (a round man named Baruch, whose head cloth does nothing to conceal the fact
that his scalp is, in fact, shaved in the manner of the
priesthood of Panas) and the leader of the caravan,
Ehar (who is tall and lean and wears a golden earring
that appears to have more significance to him than
mere ornament). Judging from the gesticulations that
we can see from here (and from what few words manage to carry through one thousand feet of clear air), the
leader of the splendid group earnestly desires the cara-

van to take the route that lies close to River Forshen,
while Ehar wants to strike directly off across the desert; and while the desires of the former appear to have
something to do with the availability of comparatively
large amounts of water from River Forshen (even
though Forshen is not an overly large river, owing to
the drought that has persisted for over three hundred
years), the opinion of the latter is based not only upon
the opportunities for trade afforded by the towns and
villages of the interior wastes, but also upon the danger
inherent in that same river, owing to its unpredictable
rises that follow hard upon the equally unpredictable
earthquakes that occur in this part of the land.

The difficulty created by this impasse appears to be
insoluble, but when the participants in the disagree-
ment have fallen into frustrated silence at the end of
yet another fruitless interchange, the individual about
whose gender we previously found it necessary to reserve judgment steps forward and speaks one or two
words to Ehar. Potent words these must be, for the
leader of the caravan, who, a moment ago, found nu-
merous compelling reasons for keeping the people,
animals, and merchandise in his care far away from the
dangerous uncertainties of the river, now finds the
river route very desirable indeed; though our guess
might be that this has less to do with the availability of
water than matters of personal survival and familial
safety.

Questions on Chapter 13 (continued):
**5) Discuss what threats or instructions
might have been uttered in "one or two
words." Draw parallels to the words that
Christ uttered in the Gospels, in particular,
the Seven Last Words. Is brevity a good
quality? Explain your answer, using examples of Christ-symbolism.**

6) What is the likelihood that the author, in choosing to describe a potentially unsympathetic character as "round" and a sympathetic character as "lean," is falling victim to an ethnocentric bias against the overweight? Discuss this possibility in light of Christ's injunction to "Go and teach all nations," and the lack of any specified height/weight ratio in this order. What Christ-symbolism can you draw from this?

7) Does the inclusion of an individual of ambiguous sexuality indicate any equivocation on the part of the author with regard to her own sexuality? Discuss the negative impact of homosexuality on society and suggest ways of combating it. Give three concrete examples of homosexual behavior and the Biblical condemnations of them. Be concise and clear, particularly with regard to Christ-symbolism.

And so begins the journey into the shadows of evening, and as a sun reddened with the dust of a drought-stricken land slips below the distant horizon (from beyond which such strange visitors have recently come to disturb the holy stasis of the Three Kingdoms ... and do not those three companions of the round leader and the androgynous assistant look a little *odd*?), the caravan sets off, with Ehar—looking inexplicably gloomy and preoccupied—mounted in the lead, guiding his charges across the dry wastes.

The route takes them southward, toward River Forshen, but the way to the river is not short, and long before the caravan reaches the bed of that river—a bed once full of rushing water but now no more than a dry valley occupied by a miserly trickle—the night ends, and a glow from behind the high peaks of the Mountains of Ern announces that morning has arrived in whatever foreign land lies to the east of those impassable ranges, and that caravan leaders who wish to avoid traveling in the heat of the day had best begin to consider stopping and making camp.

And so Ehar brings his caravan to a halt near a small, opportunistic spring whose existence out here among dry sand, gravel, tumbled rock, and blasted foothills no one (not even ourselves) would have guessed. Here the water bubbles up, sustaining a few stunted trees and a handful of herbs who know nothing more than a marginal existence bounded by arid death in all directions. And four out of the five members of the splendid group sit down and wait for their dinner to be brought.

The not-splendid group assists as it can in the making of the camp: the two men carry bundles to and fro and pull ropes to raise the tents, and the woman, though she is a Naian, nevertheless assists Ehar's wife, Yalliah, in the preparation of dinner.

And just as there was a vociferous and wordy interchange between Ehar and the leader of the splendid group at the beginning of this day's trek, so there is a curious but wordless interchange between Yalliah and the Naian woman here at the end, for after watching the Naian as she contributes her labor to the meal, Yalliah's face holds a curious expression that appears (as far as we can tell, it being difficult to ascertain for certain in the half light) to disconcert the Naian woman. The latter wanders off to collect her thoughts, leaving the former to stare after her for some time, as though considering some great enigma with which fate has presented her.

Questions on Chapter 13 (continued):
8) Note the change in the tone of this last section. What is the author's intent here?

Consider her previous use of the literary equivalent of the cinematic "smash cut," and discuss the likelihood of an extreme alteration in the narrative tone in the next section. Demonstrate the Christ-symbolism in this.

9) Is the fact that the caravan travels at night significant? Why? Give examples of other nocturnal/diurnal reversals in the course of this narrative and explain how the temptations of sin can cause otherwise evil recreations to appear desirable. Use Christ-symbolism to support your arguments.

10) What might Yalliah be seeing in the Naian woman? Comment on the author's use of the term "enigma," and discuss why she did not instead use the term "mystery." Can you find three parallels in Christ-symbolism?

11) What relevance does this section have to the overall narrative flow of the story? What relevance do these questions have to this section? Expound on the relevance of Biblical study for any true understanding of the author's work, with particular emphasis on Christ-symbolism.

DUE TO UNFORESEEN TECHNICAL DIFFICULTIES, WE HAVE TEMPORARILY LOST THE VIDEO PORTION OF OUR PROGRAM

"Mmmmph!"

"Ughughuhgughughugh!"

"Rosebud!"

"Ah! My own!"

Sccccccchlrrrrrpchchchchch.

"*Ow!* Yes!"

"Flowers, my rosebud. Flowers. It is said that His kisses are flowers!"

"Aaaaaaaaa.... rggggh!"

"Hah-hah-hah-hah ..."

"OW!"

"Flowers!"

"Yes! *OW!*"

"Flowers! Arrrgmph!"

"OW!"

"Arrrgmph!"

"OW!"

"Oh! What a pretty flower!"

"OW!"

"Here is another!"

"Yes! *OW!*"

"Flowers! It says so in the Sacred Texts!"

"OW!"

"Flowers!"

"UghughughughughughughughUGHUGHUGH-UGHUGH!"

"!"

"OW!"

Sari stood outside the tent used by the strangers from Katha, transfixed by the sounds. For a moment, she was still, and then, hand pressed to her mouth, she turned away, looking for something to do to take her mind off what she had heard. There was always something to do in the caravan. Always.

If only Yalliah ... but ... no ...

She did not see the thin, foreign-looking man slipping around the corner of the tent, his expression hovering between interest, disgust, and calculation.

Ooooooh! *Him!*

Bakbuk had fallen. Greatly. Indeed, she (and, despite her best efforts, despite her attention to and choice of

gesture, clothing, language, demeanor, carriage, gait
. . . in short, despite everything, the female pronoun
had become intrinsic to her view of herself, and she
could not now banish it) had never dreamed that there
were such depths into which to fall. But she had
suspended herself above all the petty concerns of sexuality, mocking them from a distance, aping and ridiculing the posturings of man and woman alike without
ever noticing just how frayed and worn had become
the rope that had supported her. Indeed, judging from
the immediacy and precipitousness of her plunge, it
must have been worn indeed, with scarcely a hair's
thickness left to take the unremitting tension.

No matter now: it had broken, and she had fallen.
She was Inwa Kabir's sworder, and she was as ruthless
as she was lethal and efficient, but she was, at heart, a
woman, and there was no escaping it.

Ooooooh! *Him!*

The thought had risen up unbidden, instinctively.
The Blue Avenger had appeared, and her body itself
had reacted, and so, though she might go about in
men's garments, and though she might clap her hand
on her sword and gaze directly into the faces of those
to whom she spoke, and though she might bear herself
as straight as any guard of the palace of Nuhr, she
knew that it was all a lie, knew that she should be
wearing other rags, be stripped of her sword, keep her
eyes humbly on the ground, and shuffle along bound
by ankle fetters.

Ooooooh! *Him!*

And the thought of what she was, of what she should
have been—and been doing—was a heat in her belly
and a tightening in her too-smooth groin. She wanted
it. She wanted to be bound, to submit, to be ordered
property and no more. The others, she was sure, saw it.
She *knew* that they saw it. The curious looks from the
caravan men. The amused looks from the caravan

women. Oh, certainly: here was someone's daughter done up like a boy, being transported in supposed secrecy like a piece of gold hidden within a sack of rottenstone, served up in male garnish (but deceiving no one) until it was time to strip her and put her in her prospective husband's bed for a proper blooding.

And yet the thoughts of what she wanted were at the same time a horror, not only because they were in and of themselves repellent to her sensibilities, but because they were also an inescapable finger of accusation pointing at her, confirming the falsehood of her existence. Everything about her was a lie. She had tried, and she had failed, and as there was no place in Bakbuk's self-esteem for even the slightest hint of failure, so she despised herself.

Going about among the men of the caravan, dreading (hoping) that an intrusive (welcome) hand might dart out (be invited) and explore her secrets (please!), she knew the depth of her shame, and could not but wonder whether her vengeful hand and dagger would be quite so quick, quite so vengeful anymore. She was, after all . . .

Ooooooh! *Him!*

"Another game of chess, Turtletrout?"

"I think I'd like that, sir."

"Fine day, ain't it?"

"Not much wind, sir."

"I warn't talking about the wind. Fine day."

"Yes, sir. A fine day, indeed."

Elijah Scruffy examined the harbor and the city that surrounded it on three sides. The sky was blue, but so hot was the sun that it had acquired a metallic glint, almost as though there were, beneath the blue, a burnished surface of bronze that had been bullied into azure only through the skills of a master enameler. The water reflected the sky, and it, too, shone like hot

metal, managing, despite the unearthly calm, to convey
a sense of liquidity through its precise replication of
the heat shimmers that rose from the otherwise rigid
walls of marble, granite, and jasper that surrounded it,
rose above it.

"Wouldn't like to have to get out of harbor in this."

"No, sir."

Scruffy examined the harbor again, but it offered
nothing more than it had offered before. Heat. Shimmers. Bronze. He longed for the cool hills around Bos-
ton and Bookshave, wanted to see trees—real
trees—with proper trunks and branches and green
leaves.

It would be a while. The ambassador was still away
with that crew of heathens, and what he was doing, or
even where he had gone, was beyond Scruffy's knowledge.

Again he thought of the secret orders. Again he
thought of Mather, the diplomatic assistant with the . . .
curious hobby.

"Don't like it, Turtletrout," he said. "Don't like it at
all."

Turtletrout looked at the city in his slope-headed
away and nodded. "Right, sir."

"I don't mean the city."

"Right, sir."

Scruffy, direct, to the point, and open in all facets of
his life (save one . . . or perhaps two), did not like it.
But he was an officer of the Righteous States of America, and therefore he could do nothing but follow orders. And his orders were, for the present, to stay in
the harbor of Nuhr—heat notwithstanding, explosions
notwithstanding, curious students of natural philosophy
who appeared obsessively interested and then disappeared notwithstanding—keep his increasingly restless
men on board, and wait for the ambassador's return.

"You don't suppose, sir . . ."

"Suppose what, Turtletrout?"

"That . . . well, sir . . . the ambassador . . ."

Scruffy immediately jumped to the wrong conclusion. "Ambassador Jenkins is as honest as the day is long," he said flatly, thus indicating without any doubt at all, even to Turtletrout, that he would not have trusted the ambassador with a burnt-out match.

"I meant, sir, that . . ." Turtletrout was looking at him. "You don't suppose that they *did* something to him." He blinked at Scruffy. "I mean . . . with him . . . I mean . . ."

Feeling that he had revealed just a little too much of something that he was himself not at all sure of, Scruffy turned pointedly back to the sea and the harbor. "Don't know, Turtletrout. *Can't* know."

"Yes, sir."

"Now about that game of chess . . ."

Turtletrout nodded. "My pleasure, sir."

Chapter Fourteen

You gotta listen to this. This is absolutely DY-NO-MITE stuff.

Truly, Panas cannot but be on our side.

See, there's a lot going on in this chapter, and I gotta show you things that you're not gonna follow real easy, so I gotta be cagey about it and kinda hold your hand. But don't worry about that, on account of I'm a real good writer, and I'm used to that sort of thing. Believe me, this is *nothing:* you want to see some real hand holding, you just try to pitch a script at some idiot film director who's all hung up on this *auteur* theory crap. Yeah, you know the kind. Head up his butt and all that. Thinks that he runs the film just 'cause he's got a chair with his name on the back, but he's full of shit and you and I both know it, 'cause the guy who runs the show is the *writer,* and that's a real important responsibility. And that's why I put all the camera angles and everything in my scripts, 'cause the feeps can't figure out what the hell's going on unless I help them out. Got that?

Panas is the liberator of stone from the embrace of the earth, and therefore He must encourage the liberation of all men . . .

OK, what's happening here is that Aeid (And for all you rubes who aren't too quick on the uptake, that's *Potatoes.*) knows real damn well that this guy in the caravan isn't any "Baruch" (And what the hell kind of name is that, anyway?) at all, but is really Abnel, the ... waddaycallim ... the Gharat. (And if you didn't figure *that* out, then I got no hope for you at all.) And Aeid is really getting antsy, 'cause what he wants to do is scare the bejeezus out of Abnel and teach him a lesson he'll never forget about trying to impose stupid taxes and stuff like that (and he thinks the tax is immoral, too, but what the hey, Aeid's pretty much a dweeb); but all this is just rubbing his nose into what he thinks is the real problem, which is his father. The old fart can't see beyond the end of his nose. I mean, reactionary city. The whole country is going to hell in a handbasket, and this dude is, like, doing *nothing* about it. Well, that's not quite right. He *is* doing something. But what he's doing is putting everything on terminal hold, and that sucks big time as far as Aeid is concerned. So the problem is his father, really.

... and so He must at the same time encourage our liberation from the evil conquests of the Kaprishan dynasty.

Now Abnel is thinking that Inwa Kabir is the problem, too, only he's coming at it from a different angle. You see (and go ahead and take notes if you have to: I know this is complicated.), Abnel is all eaten up with the headful of crap that Jenkins has been feeding him over the last couple of months. About how the Righteous States is so wonderful and everybody obeys the law because of this "minister in their heads" shit. And, yeah, it *is* shit, but Abnel is a real anal character—in a number of ways (He-he, that's a good one!)—and he's been stewing about what he thinks people have been getting away with for a long time, and, in any case, he's sure that Jenkins has been doing nothing but ragging on him about how backwards his country is (which he (I mean Jenkins) hasn't, but, like I said, he (I mean Abnel) is a real anal character (I can't believe how I can do this stuff sometimes!), and has gotten himself all fratchy about nothing), and now he's blaming it on the *king* for not going along with his little piddly ass temple tax! What a doob!

And the Kaprishan dynasty must be evil ...

So I figured that I'd do that parallel column thing again. You know, like I've been doing all along to show things happening at the same time? You could film it in, like, split screen or something like that, and you could take all the credit for it. Yeah, like it was your idea or something! Cool, huh?

... because what else but absolute evil would go against the decrees of Panas?

Anyway, here's what it looks like:

... but for all my focus on Abnel, is it not really my father who is at the root of it? The land dies, and nothing is done ... boys with powdered faces all out of tradition. Cannot but think—but no, that is unthinkable, and even Jean Jacques would not think of it ... would condemn it in fact. Yes, it *should* be con-

... a minister in their heads he said and he does not miss even a single opportunity to ridicule me for what he obviously thinks is my backward country but if he only knew that we are doing things of which he has not the slightest idea and would it not gall him if he found out what a great

demned, for that kind of relationship is the root of all sacred relationships, surpassing even the love of a man for a woman. (And Beshur . . . how to get her away from him: he is such a fool, and—by Panas! (blessed be He!) I handed her over to him! I!) And now I contemplate—but no, I will not contemplate it. And yet should I suffer all this to continue, I knowingly participate in the destruction of my lands and my people. And now I find that the Americans are right *here,* and it is absurd to consider throwing away this opportunity, but I do not trust them, for they appear to be friends with Abnel, though I do not understand how. Reaction . . . action . . . and they keep to themselves, and the one called *Mather* is . . . wounded. Must do something, but cannot. Opportunity. But the alternative . . . undertaking it is and perhaps I will reveal all to him so that this country can do more than suffer the Naians and a minister in every one of their heads and they would not ridicule me anymore for *I* would be in their heads and the Texts are just the first step and yet there is still the matter of the king and he will not allow the tax and the Council of Katha will not allow the tax (ow!) and since I cannot do anything about the council I must do something about the king it should have been me after all and if Aeid had even the slightest weight to his stones he would have attended to this earlier has happened before but it would be harder to dislodge Aeid so maybe that is for the best after all it has happened before seventeen kings ago was a priest . . .

And therefore, since the Kaprishan dynasty is evil, all those who acknowledge it by not warring against it agree with and encourage its evil . . .

And that's how it goes. You see how clever that is? They're thinking kind of the same thing, and I'm showing it together . . . and like at the same time. What a gas!

. . . and should be warred against by the true and righteous believers of Panas.

Anyway, that's not the whole thing by any means. There's more. (I *told* you this was complex stuff. See what I mean? Hey, I'm a *writer*!) You see how Abnel is getting all hot and bothered about what Jenkins is saying to him about how backwards the Three Kingdoms are? Well, like I said, the fact is Jenkins isn't saying any such thing to him. Jenkins is just trying to pin down what might be going on up in the mountains. You see, he's still thinking about that baking soda ad he saw up there (Clever, huh?) and is thinking that if he doesn't know everything, then his job is going to go to shit real fast. So he's not trying to rub it in at all, but Abnel is thinking that he is, and boy is he (I mean Abnel) getting steamed!

And, should they resist us, it is but a further expression of their support for absolute evil . . .

But I've already used those parallel columns, and I don't want to use them again, 'cause that'll confuse you, so I figured that maybe I'd do some Faulkner-type stuff here. I mean, I know Faulkner real well—I mean, I read *The Bear* in high school, and that about covers everything, doesn't it? Just a boy and his God . . . or something like that. (Aren't I hot?) So I won't get into the God stuff, but I thought some of the gimmicks he used were pretty cool.

**. . . and therefore should our efforts become
ever more strenuous in our quest to destroy
them.**

So try this on for size:

And Jenkins looking across the torchlit tent without
any pain or agony but only the dim remembrance of
his wild trek across the slopes of mountains yet
unclimbed by any save priestly feet; their secrets as yet
unpossessed by any save, as he thought, considering
out of a shrewd mind fueled by years of diplomatic
cunning and the exacting and involuted training of Puritan minds, other minds, yet minds linked to his by
the sinews of a shared faith held with all the zeal of the
doubting, a few priests and heathen bunglers of the
True Word: wondering what those secrets were, a hand
and arm pointing into the darkness, demanding with
unspoken imperiousness the answer to his questions,
and he knowing that the brown flowers of scabby
wounds on Mather's neck could mean but the signing
of a covenant between himself and the High Priest, itself signifying, as with all manflesh from the first
knowing of man and woman and the difference of
blood and flesh between the two, the contention between man and man, the struggle and the fury that
could produce only victor and vanquished coming
from his lips in the challenge of two simple words:
"Nice mountains:" and Abnel

"Very, my honored guest:" and he could only think
of how Jenkins unceasingly mocked him with his
knowledge, his canniness of the interior workings of
sacrilegious minds, and what profound fault he must
find, what mannish and genius lacking he could discover in the arid heterodoxy of the Three Kingdoms
and how he, Abnel, product of the perfumed and sanctified loins of royal concubines and brought to the position of his rank and his holiness by the full and

undoubted knowledge that he, and only he, possessed the spiritual potency necessary to bring to fruitful union the spreading openness of men's spirits to the descending chisel of Panas' love, must discover to him the true secrets of the mountains and bring him to wondering at the strength

his legacy; and his duty to all, and himself bound by that legacy to bring his own people to the openness of their spirits to that descending chisel by discovering the openness of a foreign land: and in a moment, he saw his path clear, sharp, the mountains of the breaking day outside withdrawing their shadows from the land as the shadows of his mind fled from the dawning light of his manly and coruscating knowledge, and Jenkins

"It was a hard journey out:" and Abnel

"Terrible, I am sure. I cannot but thank the divine beneficence of Panas (blessed be He!) for your escape, honored Ambassador:" knowing all the while that Jenkins was tormenting him with the failure of Kaprishan guards, the heterodoxy of Kaprishan people, the foolishness of the pomp of the court and the recalcitrance of King Inwa Kabir, offspring of his country and father to a wastrel of a prince whose new ideas, flourishing in the soils of foreign lands, could bear no fruit under the torrid sun of an equatorial realm, and Jenkins

"The lack of water was the worst:" knowing all the while that there was water, hidden and untapped, in the fastness of the mountains and desiring to find out about it, and Abnel

"I am sure that it was:" knowing all the while that Jenkins was ridiculing him, and he with the proud blood of kings flowing in his veins, yearning with all the royal imperative of a king for the protection of his land and the titles which by twist of fate or Divine decree he did not have, only this golden fillet around his infantile, shaven head prompting him to strive for

greater things still (else why would he have sealed the
changed manuscripts with his signet, calling forth the
duty to Panas and putting it upon the shoulders of all,
Naians grunting and heaving in the grip of their apostasy begetting more Naians and covering the land with
impiety now finding their own shoulders bent beneath
the wheel of godly work, their sullen natures brought
by force to glory) a protection of his land even from
the slightest taint of doubt, and of himself from doubt
and doubting, seeking to head off the clipper-and-profit
drive of the Yankee Puritan toward the secret, and yet
calling him in spite of it all toward that very goal, and
Jenkins

"I have heard about these ... floods that occur, and
how they suddenly inundate the land, and I do wonder
about this drought:" prying even further toward what
he wanted: the secret, vaginal and private, of the land
itself, thrusting his obedient mind toward its goal
through the mystery of water

there had been a parcel of land that he had come to
in the fullness of his comfortable manhood, be-
queathed to him by his father, Isaac, a great, roaring,
childlike man in whom the fervor of the Pilgrims and
the salt determination of the doughty *Mayflower* had
flowed inseparable with his blood, the determined sap
of zeal and devotion, the land lying hard upon the Mis-
sissippi, itself bounded by water, a tongue of land
thrust into a quivering loop of water that all but closed
on itself and the great house facing the water like a
husband who lacked nothing save the arrogance of
false humility, the way to the greater country stretching
behind the house perhaps a hundred yards at its widest,
flanked by water that curved away abruptly to either
side as though swerving from the hard hand of her
master, the tongue served only by a single road and all
going to failure because the man of the next plantation,
a traitor and deceiver, had come in the night and dug

a trench along the hundred yards between one curve and another, the water first trickling and then rushing and then roaring through, cutting a new bed, flooding what it could not cut, and the road and the plantation both broken by morning, and Isaac a ruined man with only his zeal for God to bear him up against the wiles of feminine water, and Abnel

"That happens often:" and Jenkins

"Why would you suppose that?" and Abnel

"It pleases Panas that it be so:" and Jenkins, thinking of Puritan troops and a trek across a thousand miles and a surprise attack

"We could help:" and Abnel gritting his teeth against the anger, remembered a time long ago when the priests had first devised ...

And now, three more of our own have fallen in the war against absolute evil ...

And so on and so forth. You get the picture? Abnel is convincing himself to do all sorts of things, and Jenkins thinks that he's finding things out, and neither has anything to do with the other. What a gas! Not to say that this kind of stuff isn't subtle, which is why I've gotta point it all out to you. But do you see it now? Sure you do. Hey, am I hot or what?

... and their deaths, because they served in the cause of absolute good, must be good in themselves ...

So you see the way it's shaping up. This is a big book—I mean, really big—with lots of stuff going on in just this one chapter, and I haven't even said a word about Sari and Bakbuk and about the fags on board ship, and all that other stuff.

. . . but better it is to destroy that which is evil, and which refuses to cling to that which is good.

The quotes? What quotes? Oh, you mean the ones in the funny print? You wanna know about the *quotes*?

Truly, the will of Panas is clear!

The moon was just a day or so past full, and the caravan was continuing on what, in Ehar's opinion, was a dangerous and—considering that the absolute lack of towns in the flood valley of the miserable remnant of River Forshen had afforded him not a single opportunity for trading—completely unprofitable journey. But though the lack of profit galled him, it was the danger that was most on his mind as he led his people along under a night sky, for the silver light turned the empty valley bed into a shimmering apparition so liquid in its appearance that it seemed to be made of water . . . a most unfortunate reminder of what could happen here. Did, in fact, happen here. Often.

Behind him, moving through the moonlit darkness, were his wife, his sons, his possessions . . . and, unfortunately, the strange individual from Katha named Baruch and the companions, one ambisexual and three obviously foreign, who accompanied him. The Naian and her friends were there, too, of course, but Ehar had no extraordinary worries about them other than that this girl named Sari seemed to be having a profound effect on his wife that he could neither pin down nor quite understand. But no matter: Yalliah was getting on, and she was no longer the silken thing she had been when she had first been stripped and brought to his bed: she was probably worried that a comparatively (No: completely!) undried piece of merchandise like Sari (And try as he might, he could not but think—and worry—about another Sari, one who had gone off to the Caves and who had been heard from no more.) might turn her husband's head in an undesirable manner (even though Sari, that is, this Sari, seemed completely uninterested in turning *anyone's* head, least of all the heads of the young men she was traveling with, both of whom seemed, on their part, very much interested in turning *her* head).

The old story. Very old. As old as ... well, as danger, and that brought Ehar right back to the silver moonlight that made everything look uncomfortably as though it were submerged in water.

And it was for this reason, perhaps, that, vigilant as he was, he nonetheless missed the glint, as of moonlight on metal, that flashed for an instant at the top of one of the valley walls. Unfortunate though this was, it was true, and Ehar continued leading the caravan along the river, wondering and worrying about the unpredictable surges that could sweep away a caravan in a heartbeat, about Baruch and his strange companions and the threats that accompanied him, and about an old woman whom he had befriended and taken under his protection (and Ehar, a Khyrling, took such things as protection very seriously: if someone grabbed his waist cloth and called for help, why, it was a done thing as far as Ehar was concerned).

But the one called Potatoes had quickened his steps and was now half jogging up to Ehar's position at the head of the caravan.

"I saw something," he said.

Ehar was immediately worried about water, but Potatoes quickly dispelled that fear, substituting for it another.

"A flash. A sword."

"A sword?"

Unfortunately, Potatoes' warning came too late, and there were suddenly shouts and the clash of weapons.

From the valley walls to the right and to the left (lowering themselves by ropes, slipping down slopes, tumbling over and over when a likely-looking foothold proved something less than reliable), and from behind and from before (running along and occasionally spraining an ankle in a hole left by some enterprising, drought-tolerant, and flood-ignorant rodent), came a host of men ...

Q. How many men in a host?
A. A great number.
Q. How many?
A. Say ... fifty, all right?

... all waving the short, curved swords favored by the men of the Three Kingdoms. They were shouting something about God and Freedom and Liberty, and not only was it very easy to tell that all three words were capitalized, but it was also very obvious that their arrival was not something the members of the caravan should look forward to.

"Swords!" shouted Ehar. (And he noticed with a sense of unease that Potatoes was suddenly nowhere to be seen.) "Swords out! Women to the center! *Ho! Brigands!*"

Yes, Potatoes was gone. Was he perhaps ... ?

No time for that. The brigands who were shouting about God and Freedom and Liberty (and, yes, all three were most certainly capitalized) were sweeping toward the circling-up caravan like a wave (And there was that disturbing image again!), breaking onto it from all sides, falling back as the swords of Ehar and his sons and his men demonstrated that caravan folk had a few things to show brigands about blades and metal, despite any shouting about God and Freedom and Liberty (even if they *were* capitalized).

But there were many brigands, and Ehar's was a

small caravan, and if something did not happen
quickly, then it appeared that God and Freedom and
Liberty (all capitalized) would triumph. But something
did happen, for the strange companion of Baruch—the
ambisexual one—was suddenly springing forward, a
sword (A sword! Surely that meant that—but no, Ehar
was not going to fall for that one again.) in ... well
(for want of anything better) *his* hand.

Ehar was not at all sure how the ambisexual one
managed it. For one thing, he himself was occupied
with spitting and slashing as many of the brigands as
he could, so he could not spare the time to watch carefully. For another, the ambisexual one seemed to be
everywhere at once, making observation difficult.
Nonetheless, everywhere that (for want of anything
better) he went, brigands were falling down and not
getting up again, and this was such a Very Good Thing
that Ehar was unwilling to question it at all, even
though he wanted very much to see what kind of miraculous technique the ambisexual one was using.

But even the ambisexual one had (for want of anything better) his hands full, for there were just too
many ...

Q. *How* many?
A. OK, a hundred, then.

... brigands for the small number of sword-wielding
men of the caravan to effectively handle, and the latter
were suffering as a result, the women, supplies, and
pack animals being compressed more and more in the
center of a tightening circle of defense.

And then, with a flash of silvery blue, a strange figure in tights and tatters, cape and mask (Do not forget
the mask!), swung ($T=2\pi\sqrt{\frac{l}{g}}$) down from some unspecified place, and, with an alliterative shout of one kind
or another, plunged into the thick of the crowd of brig-

ands who were still shouting about God and Freedom
and Liberty (all capitalized).

Immediate consternation on the part of the brigands.
Where they were certainly prepared to deal with the
swords of the men of the caravan, and willing at least
to strive against the sword of the ambisexual one, this
new arrival was tipping the odds in distressing ways,
particularly since he appeared to be just as good a
swordsman as the ambisexual one.

A thinning of the press allowed the blue figure to
wave his sword, point, and shout: "This way! Out of
the valley!"

Ehar did not need to be convinced. He had disliked
the river route from the start, and only the threats of
Baruch and his companions had convinced him to take
it. What with the brigands surrounding his people, and
the threat of the unpredictable floods still high (Earthquake or no earthquake: it did not take an earthquake
to make a flood, any more than it took a ruptured
maidenhead to make a baby.), Ehar wanted *out*.

So with much shouting and driving of animals by
both male and female hands, the caravan, still fighting,
forced a way through the thinnest part of the surrounding line of brigands (who were *still* shouting . . . capitalized . . . etc.) and began to make its way toward
higher ground. The blue figure and the ambisexual one
were everywhere, Ehar's sword was doing its share of
cleaving skulls, and (thanks be to Panas!) there had
been no casualties—

Spoke too soon. The one called Baruch, not being at
all willing to pick up a bundle and help with the fighting retreat of the caravan, found himself without
anything to put between himself and the sword of a
brigand who suddenly broke through the thin line of
caravan men. In an instant, Baruch was run through. In
another instant, the blue figure and the ambisexual one
converged on the brigand and silenced his shouts of

God and Freedom and Liberty (with or without capitals) forever.

Baruch, still alive, was seized and dragged up the
slope as the caravan continued to fight its way through.
There was the sound of a loud *crack:* one of the foreign men had pulled a thing of wood and iron from a
fold of his garments and had pointed it at an advancing
brigand ... with spectacular results.

And then, the sound that Ehar had been dreading. A
hiss and a rumble, a sudden roar ...

... and there was suddenly a wall of water advancing down the length of the valley, frothing in the
moonlight, smashing through dunes and rubble.

"Forward!" Ehar shouted as the caravan struggled
along a tortuously narrow and steep path up the side of
the valley. The brigands were pressing close behind,
and the water was coming on like charging cavalry.

The blue figure and the ambisexual one were fighting side by side at the rear of the caravan, but abruptly,
the latter lifted a foot, planted it in the middle of the
closest brigand's chest, and, with a cry of *"Bath
time!"*, sent him tumbling backwards down the path,
straight into the mass of his fellows (Yes, they were
still shouting about God and Freedom and Liberty (all
capitalized).), who, losing their balance as a result,
tumbled even farther down the path, to be instantly
buried beneath the wall of water, mud, gravel, and rubble that charged up, filled the valley for the better part
of a minute, and then, just as suddenly, dwindled into
nothing.

Ehar, counting noses, found that, with the exception
of the wounded Baruch, everyone was safe. Even his
possessions and merchandise and animals were safe.
And then he noticed that the blue figure was gone, and
that the ambisexual one was staring longingly off into
the distance, lips quivering as though a chalice of nec-
tar had been suddenly snatched away.

Chapter Fifteen

Throughout the ages, Divine Providence has been perceived as a deific force operating external to and outside of the laws of the mundane physical universe (a position it holds unique among all things, and is, by virtue of this, not only rendered unprovable and unmeasurable by any purely phenomenological analysis, but also removed from any possibility of external examination—experimental, heuristic, or otherwise—that might be brought to bear upon it, thus allowing any and all occurrences, regardless of how bizarre, unlikely, or inappropriate, to be ascribed to its machinations in one way or another) which constantly and in various ways interferes with accepted physical law—whether newtonian, quantum mechanical, or customized by end-user options—so as to bring about circumstances advantageous to human beings, these circumstances being subject to objective observations uninfluenced by any conscious or unconscious actions or thoughts on the part of the benefited human beings as well as perceived by the human beings who have supposedly benefited by them as being beneficial in one form or another (no matter how unlikely) only after they have manifested, and therefore ascribable only to the workings of that same Divine Providence (previously established as unprovable and beyond any exam-

ination, human or otherwise), and which extends its
benefits to human beings (who perceive those benefits
only after the fact) in a manner so unpredictable as to
be describable only in terms of the haphazard, capri-
ciously meting out blessings to the apparently unde-
serving and withholding them from those who are
obviously in need.

A perhaps classic example of this can be seen in the
events, processes, and discoveries that occurred subsequent to the unsuccessful attack by the self-styled
Freedom fighters of Khyr upon a certain caravan led
by a certain Ehar (himself a Khyrling and therefore,
under most systems of logic, exempt from attack, but,
unfortunately, not exempted under the political ratio-
nales openly professed by the aforesaid freedom fighters; said attack resulting in the loss of the lives of the
latter as a result of (1) the providentially skilled
swords of the individuals connected with the caravan,
(2) the providential arrival of reinforcement for the
caravan in the person of the Blue Avenger, and (3) a
providential flood (one which, in this case, providentially went unannounced by any earthquake or other
warning); and the providential wounding of only one
member of the caravan, an individual named Baruch,
who, though magnifying the general level of his un-
popularity among the members of the caravan by dis-
daining even the most elementary tasks that were, by
custom, expected of any and all members of the caravan (a self-sustaining community by necessity and isolation), tasks that, in the case of a bundle carried as
part of the general effort, might have resulted in the
availability of some article of some indeterminate use/
appearance/sort that could have been interposed between himself and the oncoming blade of a sword (but,
not being carried, was, therefore, not available, and
consequently could not be interposed), was nonetheless
spared instant death by the weapon's providential miss-

ing of any vital organs, which providentially left him
only wounded and therefore subject to the administra-
tion of aid by Sari, a Naian herbalist, whose providential presence was the result of her own providential
transformation from old to young, there being no rational reason for the simultaneous existence of the above
serendipitous happenings and circumstances save the
perception of them by the human mind (whose abhor-
rence of such things as vacuums has been well docu-
mented: witness the writings of Avicenna and the
equations of Einstein) as the workings of Divine Providence.

And the providence of this confluence and fortuitous
interpenetration of events is further amplified (thus
lending passing credence to the theories put forth by
those who have belief in such matters, theories that, at
times, become very understandable in light of the staggering coincidences that occur whenever any human
endeavors, large or small, are examined with sufficient
attention to detail) by the subsequent interaction of this
Baruch (who might have been expected, by those with
less than charitable attitudes, to have providentially
died, the fact that he did not exhibiting *par excellence*
the generally reported, contra-expectational outcome of
classic instances of Divine Providence) with this Sari
during the period of, first, a fever brought on by his
wounds *(see example #1)* and, second, his recovery
from the weakness brought on by wounds and fever
both *(see example #2),* both periods providing him
with greater or lesser opportunities to exhibit his reluctance to believe that any medicinal skills of any sort
exhibited by other than approved Panasian doctors
could not help but prove, in the end, deficient, and that
therefore his recovery could not be other than illusory
(see example #3). This prolonged interaction, unlikely
in the highest degree, particularly in view of the fact
that Baruch was actually the Gharat Abnel, High Priest

of Panas, in disguise, resulted in the utterance of several comments on the part of Baruch (Abnel) *(see example #4)*, several observations on the part of Sari *(see example #5)*, and several suspicions on the part of Obadiah Jenkins, a companion of Abnel *(see example #6)* and on the parts of Beshur and Potatoes (the latter being, in actuality, Prince Aeid in disguise) *(see examples #7a and #7b)* resulting from, in the first case, an overhearing of Baruch's (Abnel's) words by a third party, and, in the second case, a combination of the former with Sari's innocent repetition of her patient's words to her friends.

And mystery upon mystery arises when the random nature of words in general, and these words in particular, is examined, for, of all the words that could have been uttered by Baruch *(see example #8)*, in delirium or out of it, there were, among the usual dross of small talk and complaint likely to come from an invalid who had, for most of his life, been accustomed to a luxurious and relatively pain-free existence *(see example #9)* (though in the case of the latter, the pain-free aspect of the existence had to take into account Baruch's occasional choosing of pain as part of his personal, interpersonal, and recreational activities), several vocalizations of a most intriguing nature *(see example #10)*, words that, in a drought-stricken land beset by a combination of rising superstition and increasing priestly control, could not but cause individuals concerned about both the land and the drought to wonder whether said drought, underlying as it did all of the ongoing social, economic, and religious changes in the land, might not have, at its root, some element of human calculation and machination hitherto unthought of by any save (obviously) those intelligences responsible for that calculation and machination, yet wonder at the same time about their own sanity for suspecting any such thing, for the magnitude of the inferred calculation and machination would have to be, by nature, such that both would eclipse those involved in any other project ever undertaken by human ingenuity, no matter how large or pervasive, and thus any credence given to that calculation and machination would, by nature, have to be based on the suspicions of a mind that was something less than sound, a turn of events providential in both its aspects, for it allows the narrative of these events to exist in a pseudo-historical yet fantastical framework of natural and divine causality, simultaneously providing immediate entertainment in the form of anticipation and suspense and extending the action and the resultant intrigues in such a way as to mimic the apparent random and cross-purposed flow of human endeavor so as to present to the reader a simulacrum of reality, howsoever it is reduced to comprehensible terms by the artifice of literary conceit.

THE EXAMPLES:
Example #1:
Sari bent over the man. Baruch's eyes were half closed, fluttering, and his breath was shallow and rapid.

—I cannot understand this, Beshur said. He was fine yesterday.

"This happens frequently," said Sari, examining Baruch (who seemed aware of absolutely nothing), feeling his flushed, sweaty skin, laying a cool hand on his forehead. "A deep wound, and then a fever."

The strange, girlish companion spoke up. "Fever?"

"Yes," said Sari.

Example #2:
Tottering and lurching, Baruch moved from one side of the tent to the other. "I can hardly walk!"

Bakbuk gave a short, unconvincing, manly nod that reeked of feminine insecurity. "That is to be expected, Gharat—"

"Do not call me that!" Baruch sat down heavily, his chest heaving, his hand fanning his face.

"My apologies."

"I am not getting any better!"

"Oh, but you are," said the sworder. "Two days ago you could not stand up. Two days before that you could not even sit. You are indeed getting better . . ." There was a flash of irony in Bakbuk's eyes. ". . . Baruch."

Example #3:

"You unlettered fools are all alike!" Baruch was all but screaming at her. "You have your philters and your decoctions, and you administer them to anybody who is stupid enough to open his mouth! If I have managed to survive this long, it is surely not through any of your simpleminded efforts!"

"And I assume that you would prefer some gemstones soaked in water?" said Sari, who had all but lost patience with the demands and complaints of Baruch.

"That would be infinitely better! Anyone knows that gemstones soaked in water have worked miracles!"

"As opposed to herbs, which have saved your life."

"I doubt that greatly." Baruch coughed with emphasis. "As you can see, I am still sick."

"Well, you are alive," said Sari, and try as she might, she could not keep down an unspoken thought of *Would it were otherwise!*

"No thanks to you!"

"Then go soak your necklace in a waterskin and leave me alone!"

"And even if your concoctions *have* helped me," Baruch went on as though he had not heard her (which, Sari supposed, was more than likely the case), "the effects cannot last. Nothing that is vegetable can last. Only stone is imperishable, so say the Sacred Te—"

He caught himself.

Somehow, Bakbuk managed to look both girlish and ironic.

Sari shrugged. Since her transformation had ripped her away from her former life, the Sacred Texts had turned into nothing but words, and Baruch could quote them or not as he wished: it made no difference to her.

Example #4:

a:

"Water! Pumps! Oh, pump me! Pump the water! Up, up, up!"

"He is delilrious," said Sari. This happens often in a fever of this sort.

"Can you cure him?" said Bakbuk.

Sari shifted uneasily as she knelt beside Baruch's sleeping mat. Baruch annoyed her, but Bakbuk made her nervous. There was something . . . wrong . . . with Bakbuk. But: "I will try," she said. "I am an herbalist, and I will try."

b:

"Woman is water! Water! Destroy the water, and you destroy the woman! Yes! And then . . . then . . . then . . . *we* can be the woman!"

"He is still raving," said Jenkins. He had given up attempting to convince anybody that he was anything save a foreigner, and though his accent was terrible, Sari could understand his Kaprishan very well, and even found that she admired him for having taken the trouble to learn it.

"It appears so," she admitted.

"Will he die?"

Sari heard the eagerness in Jenkins' voice. "I . . . I do not think so," she faltered.

"Good. Good."

c:

"Oh," said Sari, who had become more than a little irritated by Baruch's constant mockery, "I suppose you will now be telling me about the demons of the desert."

"Demons?" said Baruch. He stopped eating his gruel and looked at her. "Demons of the mind, little Naian girl. Demons of the mind!" And he nodded smugly.
d:

"How much water?"

"What do you mean? It was a great deal of water. Enough to sweep away over a hundred men."

Q. *How* many?
A. All right, all right. A hundred and fifty. Satisfied?

"That is not what I want to hear," said Baruch. He thumped his fist on the cushion. "You ignorant camel drivers are all alike. And a Khyrling at that! I would be willing to believe that you are in league with—'

Ehar was indeed a Khyrling, and Baruch was his guest, but there were limits. "In league with . . . who?" There was an implicit threat in his tone, one that, coming as it was from a Khyrling, was dangerous to test.

"Never mind. How much water?"

"A lot."

"That is not good enough!"

"I happened to be fighting with ten men at the time," said Ehar. "You will have to be forgiving if I did not notice how many kils of water there were. I did not have a measuring bucket at the time. We are all lucky to be alive!"

Baruch's recent fever had left him weak, unsteady, and as he turned away, his entire body was shaking. "The fools," he said. "I hope they have the sense to document it. And not even an earthquake! What is the matter with them? What is going on up there?"

Ehar looked at Jenkins. Jenkins looked at Ehar.

Example #5:

"He is very tedious sometimes," Sari agreed.

In order to preserve Panasian sensibilities, she spent her nights with the women of the caravan. Her days, however, when they were not taken up with chores (which she did not mind) and nursing Baruch (whom she was beginning to despise) were her own, and she would frequently spend at least part of them looking for refuge from the invalid and his more mobile companions.

Today, she had found some of what she sought in the tent shared by Potatoes and Beshur. Beshur was off walking alone with his arms folded across his chest and his eyes staring intently at the sand as though to discern there some great secret . . .

—I am a scholar, he had said. I must think about certain things.

. . . but Potatoes was in the tent . . . and was very sympathetic.

"Terrible person," he said. And he sounded as though he meant it. He truly did. In fact, he sounded very much as though he would have liked to have slapped Baruch across the face, invalid though he was. "The world would be better off without the likes of him."

Sari was disturbed. "I would not go so far as to say that."

Potatoes shrugged, smiled at Sari.

Oh. Oh, yes. That.

Sari was even more disturbed, but she continued. It was a relief to speak to someone who seemed (She was not exactly sure how to put it.) so *above* everything. Unconcerned. Detached from everything.

Potatoes smiled again.

Well . . . *almost* detached.

"It is just that he seems to hate a great many things.

If I did not know better, why, I would think that he
hated the land itself!"

"The land itself . . ." Potatoes was suddenly thoughtful.

"And he is so . . . so . . ." She shrugged. She was
tired, and Potatoes was sympathetic, and so she was willing to talk. "I do not know how to say it. I cannot tell
whether he is still delirious or is just making fun of me."

"Indeed!"

"Yes."

"What sort of things does he say?"

"Oh, I asked him if he were going to try to frighten
me with stories about demons in the desert, and he just
smirked and said something about *demons of the
mind.*"

"What else has he said?" Potatoes was still smiling,
but he seemed even more thoughtful than before.

"He went . . ." Sari thought for a time. "He seemed
very concerned about pumps."

"Pumps?"

"Yes. I could not understand what pumps had to do
with anything, but he was very concerned about them.
And he goes on about women so!"

"Yes," said Potatoes, very sympathetic. "I know."
And he smiled.

Oh, yes. That.

"As though we are the land!"

"Well . . ."

"Which he hates!"

Potatoes smiled.

Oh, yes. That.

Example #6:

The hand and arm, and the hammer. And now Jenkins, standing outside the Naians' tent, was hearing of
ravings. Or were they ravings? He had heard Quakers
confess quite freely and willingly to their abominations

under torture, and so he was quite convinced that physical pain was wonderfully conducive to the revelation of truth. And here was physical pain, and here was the revelation of truth.

The little Naian girl was idiotic enough to want to nurse back to health someone who would be perfectly willing to impale her in the market square some fine morning (And Jenkins regretted yet again that the Fathers had abandoned that wonderfully effective practice and had settled instead for the ducking stool, the brank, the stocks, and an occasional noose.), but that was her affair and her idiocy. She was, though, proving useful, for if what she was saying to Potatoes was correct (And Jenkins assumed that it was, for women were born gossips, and could be relied upon to recount evidence verbatim, so long as it was damaging.), then there was a remarkable consistency in Abnel's spoutings, for Jenkins had heard some of them himself.

Consistency. Pumps. Land. Women. Water.

Example #7:

a:

Inelectable modality . . . curses! Shaved head. Given me away? Spies? Guards? Here, walk like this . . . not me. No. Unthinkable. How would they know? Take no interest in me. Possible, though. Pumps. Why pumps? Could hear him all over the camp. *PUMPS!* Why? Water. No water. Wants to pump water? No water to pump. What . . .?

b:

It is impossible to tell exactly what is going on, but I am becoming increasingly convinced that *something* is going on. Father does not know about it. Or does he? Would he tell me? Probably not. How could I find out, then? The Library? Hmmm . . . and Beshur wants to go to the Library. And now I have more reasons to go there myself. Death to enter . . . but there must be a way in, and I am beginning to wonder about Beshur.

Example #8 (a selection):

    Rhubarb.

    Calliope. *[Unlikely.]*

    Sandstone.

    Snake.

    Obstreperous.

    Dingbat.

    Panas.

    AMRAAM. *[Highly unlikely.]*

    Brf.

    Often.

    Tie.

    Coffee.

    Star.

    Indubitably.

    OW!

    Top.

    Bottom.

    In.

    Out.

    Intercourse.

    Me.

    Mine.

    My.

Example #9 (a selection):

    "Stop that!"

    "That hurts!"

    "I will not drink that!"

    "Sandstone to you!"

    "Leave me alone!"

    "To the demons with you!"

    "Nobody likes me."

    "I despise you."

    "Stupid Naian girl!"

    "You expect me to sleep on *that*?"

    "Don't go!"

    "Go!"

"Give it to *me*!"

"You cannot have *mine*!"

"That is *my* cushion!"

Example #10 (a selection):

"Pumps."

"Water."

"How much?"

"Reservoirs."

"Woman."

"In the HOUSE!"

"Naia."

"Minister."

"Soon."

"Sooner."

"As soon as possible."

"Must."

"End."

Chapter Sixteen

Pudda-pudda-pudda.

Kuz Aswani caught himself and looked around. Had anyone seen his lapse? At this point, lapses were a constant, nagging worry, and all the more so because, try as he might, despite his best efforts, he *did* relapse periodically. Why just last night, Sabihah—newly returned to him by order of the king and still a little nervous—had narrowly escaped being dragged into bed by the scruff of her neck. In truth, it was the only thing that still aroused Kuz Aswani (Oh, that feeling of soft, pliant skin between his teeth!), but it was most certainly not anything that a man (as opposed to a ferret) would do, and therefore, he would most certainly not do it.

But no: no one had seen. No one was about. He was alone in the gallery of the palace. But *alone* was always only a relative term as far as Kuz Aswani was concerned, because although he might be technically alone, he had always to contend with the constant presence and observation of his nemesis, his tormentor . . .

. . . Umi Botzu.

Feeling carefully for footholds, Haddar crept along the ledge that ran along just below the upper windows of the gallery. His stomach churned, for (just like a silly woman) he was dreadfully afraid of heights, but (like the able counselor that he was) he was determined to settle, once and for all, the question of Kuz Aswani's nefarious activities. He *knew* they were nefarious, for why else would a man first wiggle and writhe nakedly about the palace, defecate in corners, sleep in a foul pile of rags, and then, suddenly, turn completely around and behave as though nothing at all had happened? And had Kuz Aswani not come close to admitting openly that he had been the strange, blue apparition that had stormed through Citizen Valdemar's fitting room?

"Ow!"

Haddar stifled his involuntary cry as the muscles in his groin once again protested the presence of Valdemar's infernal device ... which Haddar himself, in contrast to his muscles, had found that he simply could not live without.

And then, below him, he saw Kuz Aswani suddenly bounce, wiggle, and, as though against his will, scratch himself behind his ear with one of his gilt-sandaled feet.

He knows. He must know. He cannot but know.

But: *Did anyone see me?* was the thought in Kuz Aswani's head as he lowered his foot, grimacing with the bitter pangs of failure. Yes, he had scratched behind his ear. He had failed. His devotions to Panas had proved deficient, the God doubtless finding in this poor excuse for a counselor some ingrained failing, some abominable flaw that, like a crack in a piece of stone, rendered the entire block worthless.

But stone, though sacred, was inert, while this poor counselor, Kuz Aswani, so ensorcelled that he could not walk five paces without the overwhelming urge to chitter and bounce, was, in contrast, alive, and therefore possessed of a capacity to grow and change. And while change was a bad thing when it came to such femininities as water and earth and mud and flesh, it was, perhaps, not such a bad thing at all when it came to souls, for if souls could change, then Kuz Aswani was determined that, with devotion and fortitude, he would so change his soul that Panas could not but be willing to take a hand in the welfare of His beloved son and save him from the wickedness of the sorcerer who, even now—

Yes! Yes! There he was!

He has seen me! And Haddar scrambled for one of the windows. But as he hauled himself over the sill, he found that he was suddenly staring straight into the face (or rather, the lack of one) of his penis.

Loose . . . *again*? No. It could not be. The device . . .

Now doubly frightened (And was that not just like a silly woman?), Haddar scrambled out the window as the penis reared up and spat at him derisively; and Kuz Aswani, with an involuntarily chitter, raced off down the hall, calling out to God.

But now there was another problem for Haddar: he was out on the roofs, and he had no real excuse for being out on the roofs. True, as chief minister to King Inwa Kabir, there was no real reason for him to need an excuse for being *anywhere,* but as a craven woman, he had to have an excuse for just about *everything* . . . not that excuses would do him much good. Panasian law was very clear about things like that.

Kuz Aswani was running. No trace of the old *pudda-pudda-pudda* here: this was a good, old fashioned, time-honored, human sprint, a dead-straight-ahead pelting designed to leave the wily Umi Botzu far behind him.

But running was but a temporary release. Running would only prolong the agony that was afflicting the soul of Kuz Aswani. And the counselor had no doubt that no human action would prove sufficient when faced with the diabolical machinations of Umi Botzu. No, only Panas could save him.

But would Panas look with favor upon a son who was so cowardly as to run away?

The thought brought him to an instant standstill, banished all thoughts of wiggles or chitters from his mind. By Panas (blessed be He!)! *No!* It could not be!

And with a sudden surge of very non-ferrety resolve (as opposed to obsession, which is very ferrety indeed), he turned around, turned *back* toward his tormentor. No, Panas would not, *could* not love a coward, for though a woman could not but be weak, and a ferret . . . well . . . ah . . . ferrety (whatever that was in this case), a *man* could not but be brave. And so, Kuz Aswani, with his pointed nose (and the rest of him following along behind), was returning to face the sorcerer, to—in fact—face him *down.*

Haddar was wandering across the rooftops, completely lost. He had discovered that while the layout of the corridors, halls, and rooms of the palace was very obvious when he was inside, directions outside became obscure and confused, particularly to someone who should by no means have been wandering about without the strong arm (and, occasionally, fist) of a husband for guidance. Worse, not only did his penis keep popping up from behind pillars, pinnacles, balustrades, and carvings to leer at him (as much as a penis could be said to leer) provocatively (He was, after all, a woman, and was therefore attracted to such things.), but, search though he might, he could find no way of getting back inside the palace, which was, he reflected, exactly what might be expected from a beardless counselor who wanted nothing so much as to be completely dominated by everything and everyone, as a proper woman should be dominated (And was he getting an *erection* now? All those thoughts of being *dominated* rising up, slithering down his belly, and loosening—)—

The penis poked up above a stone grillwork and

waggled at him. Caught in a moment of weakness, Haddar dived for it. "Come back here!"

It was off in an instant, Haddar chasing it across the rooftops, retracing, unconsciously, the path that had taken him away from the gallery window. Indeed, having led him back to the point where the chase had begun, the renegade organ dived (perhaps instinctively) for the aperture, and Haddar was right behind it, his hands inches from the fleeing, scrambling flesh.

"Come back here!" he cried, forgetting that, inside, there was only a narrow ledge below the window.

Too late! He toppled off the ledge and would have fallen the thirty feet to the ground (doubtless dashing his brains out . . . if women had any brains to dash out in the first place) but he managed to grab hold of the ledge and wound up with his feet dangling some twenty-two feet from the marble floor. (Haddar being in the vicinity of six feet tall).

And then Kuz Aswani showed up.

"I have become quite curious about your country's attitude toward sheep, my dear . . . ah . . . Baruch."

"In what way, my dear . . . ah . . . friend?"

"Well, I notice that it is rather . . . ah . . . ambivalent."

"Indeed?"

"Because you are neither hot nor cold—"

"Be quiet, Wool. I mean . . . well, you eat mutton . . . yes?"

"Well, of course."

"He-he! Eat! He-he!"

"Muth'n ith ue m'th cum'ndbl f'd."

"Eaten by both royalty and commoner alike, no?"

"Oh, yes."

"But wool . . ."

"Ith 'n . . . unclean fiber. Why, my dear ambassador, have you noticed how the animals *smell*?"

"But, the animals smell the same, regardless of whether we are speaking of meat or of wool!"

"I will go after my lovers, that give *me* my bread and my water, my wool and my flax, mine oil and my drink."

"Be quiet, Wool."

"I confess I do not see your point."

"The point is ... ah ..."

"Point! He-he!"

"... that ... ah ... wool is considered unclean and unfit for wearing as clothing. And yet, something that comes from the same animal ... in fact, that *is* the animal, is considered fit for eating."

"Just so."

"I do not understand."

"It is a matter of use. One would most certainly say that wool and mutton ... h'f v'bby d'ffunt ubtheth, 'od 'n ... not?"

"Well, that is true."

"And one would certainly not eat wool."

"No. One would not."

"No more than one would ... w'r muth'n. Correct?"

"Well, quite true."

"Well, then it is obvious."

"Ah ..."

"So you see."

"But the nomads ..."

"N'muds?"

"Well, they are on the rise. Very dispersed, unless I miss my guess."

"We 'r b'ndeth bthy theepeh c' ... c' ... commonalities than mere proximity."

"He-he!"

Combine:
1 part henbane
2 parts opium

3 parts cannabis
2 parts saltpeter
1 part water of emerald
Mix well and let dry. Burn as needed.

The first thing that Kuz Aswani noticed upon reentering the gallery was a pair of feet. It was, in fact, impossible *not* to notice them, because not only were they a palpably exotic thing to find hanging in the air in the gallery, but they were also flapping about frantically, as though they were sparrows caught by a young boy and destined for some truly objectionable fate.

But then Kuz Aswani noticed that the feet belonged to Haddar, and that put an entirely different—though not particularly correct—perspective on the entire affair, for Kuz Aswani immediately came to the conclusion that Umi Botzu had once again been up to no good, and that in this case he had done something to Haddar that conceivably had much in common with the abovementioned objectionable fate of sparrows being held in captivity by a young boy.

"That fiend!" he shouted. "Haddar! Haddar! Was he here?"

"Here? He?" The chief minister looked around frantically, finally craning his neck enough to see past his feet to Kuz Aswani. "Yes! Yes he was! He spat at me!"

"Terrible! Terrible!" said Kuz Aswani, finding in himself a previously unknown capacity for emphatic repetition. "He will stop at nothing!"

"I profoundly wish that he would just stop!"

"Are you growing fur yet?"

And at this, Haddar looked down at Kuz Aswani, realizing that *he* in one instance might not mean what *he* meant in another instance, and in any case, what was this *growing fur* business?

But Kuz Aswani, all afire with righteous and religious wrath, did not notice Haddar's confusion. "He has done it! He has done it!" he cried, continuing with his rhetorical discovery. "And only the might of Panas can save us."

Haddar was attempting to remain calm and logical, but, femininity getting the better of him, he could manage only a squawk of: "Get me down from here!"

"Truly, Panas (blessed be He!) is great!"

"His chisel ..." Haddar glanced up at the window again. "... is strong and sharp! Get me down from here!"

"You must remember, Haddar," said Kuz Aswani, "that we cannot climb. It is unwise to climb, save only upon very low things. Running about on window ledges is not something that we can do." But righteousness suddenly rose in him once more. "But with the might of God, we will run on window ledges again!"

Haddar looked down past his feet. "Window ledges?"

"That is, if we want to."

"Again?"

"Though I cannot think of a reason that I would really want to ..." Kuz Aswani admitted. "I mean, I never really wanted to run about on window ledges. That is, *before*. And I cannot think of any good reason that I would want to ... well ..."

Before? After? Haddar, realizing that he had started Kuz Aswani on a dangerous train of thought— particularly since Kuz Aswani might ... know ... certain things or might ... be ... a certain person—made haste to turn the counselor's locomotive onto an opportune spur. "Get me down!"

"Never fear!" cried Kuz Aswani.

"Immediately!"

"Is he coming back, then?"

Frightened, Haddar looked up at the ledge. How would he explain? And a lack of explanations would result in ... well, unpleasant things, any of which might lead to . . . even more unpleasant things. Panasian law, after all, was very clear about things like that, even if the things themselves were not very clear at all.

But, hanging as he was, Valdemar's device was settling into new and unpleasant positions, and pain was building in much more than his hands and arms. "Ow!"

"See how he afflicts you even from afar!" said Kuz Aswani. "Truly he is potent!"

Between the pain in his arms and the pain in his groin, Haddar knew that he would not be able to endure his present position for long. "Will you . . ."

"But with Panas (blessed be He!) on our side, we will triumph!" Considering for a moment, Kuz Aswani decided to avail himself once again of his new mastery of rhetoric. "We will triumph!"

". . . get me down from here!"

"It would give me the greatest of pleasures," said Kuz Aswani, "to thwart, in any way, his terrible and evil designs." And he glanced up, down, right, and left as though really *seeing* someone there.

Frightened, Haddar glanced up at the window ledge. But no. Nothing.

So far.

"And demonstrate the righteousness of Panas (blessed be He!) to all!" (Kuz Aswani being just a little bit disingenuous here, since he was not so much interested in demonstrating the righteousness of Panas to all (that righteousness being, in his opinion, completely self-evident) as in demonstrating his own righteousness to Panas in the hopes that He might be thereby induced to intervene on the behalf of his (demonstrably righteous) son.)

"Yes, yes, of course," said Haddar, whose hands and arms (and groin) were by now on fire. "Now get me down."

And Kuz Aswani, ever aware of the conventions of palace conduct, and more than usually determined to follow them to the letter (for men followed conventions while ferrets did whatever they wanted), bowed. "I await your orders."

At first, Haddar was speechless, and then—

📺 NEWS FLASH 📺

We interrupt this program to bring you a special bulletin.

In response to the recent wave of violence in Nuhr, all Khyrlings living within the bounds of the city of Nuhr are, by royal order, hereby confined to their enclaves. Commerce between the enclaves and the greater urban area is prohibited, and any Khyrling attempting egress from the enclaves is subject to summary trial and impalement, with the exception of any female Khyrlings, who are subject only to impalement.

We now return you to our program, still in progress.

—finally found Fakik, who was up to his elbows in yet another batch of experimental sweetmeat dough. "Fakik!—"

📺 NEWS FLASH 📺

We interrupt this program to bring you a special bulletin.

Due to widespread Khyrling outcry over the recent proclamation regarding the restriction of all Khyrlings to their enclaves, the royal decree has been amended to provide six hours of safe conduct for all Khyrlings who might have been outside of their enclaves when the proclamation was made, six hours being deemed sufficient for all Khyrlings to return to their enclaves.

We now return you to our program, still in progress.

—the camel, though, had other ideas, and insisted upon getting its feet into positions that were incomprehensible both to—

▓ NEWS FLASH ▓

We interrupt this program to bring you a special bulletin.

An anonymous, high-ranking priestly consultant said today that the amendment to the royal decree restricting all Khyrlings to their enclaves, which provided for six hours of safe conduct so that all Khyrlings who might have been outside of their enclaves when the proclamation was made could return to their enclaves, did not apply to Khyrling females, who are subject to impalement, but not, as per the original decree, to summary trial.

We now return you to our program, still in progress.

—sticky mass of—

▓ NEWS FLASH ▓

We interrupt this program to bring you a special bulletin.

In response to the anonymous, high-ranking priestly consultant who stated earlier that the amendment to the decree restricting all Khyrlings to their enclaves, which provided for six hours of safe conduct so that any Khyrlings outside of their enclaves could return to their enclaves, with the exception of Khyrling females, who were still to be subject to impalement, but not to summary trial, a member of the priestly council of Nuhr stated that such distinctions, based entirely upon sexual characteristics, were contrary to the will of Panas, and that, therefore, neither male nor female Khyrlings could be subject to summary trial, but only to impalement.

The official went on to hold responsible for the recent upsurge in violence the general degeneration of the morals of society, particularly in view of the fact that it is well known that Khyrling females go about without their head cloths "in the house," and that the stigma associated with this omission is no longer applied as vigorously as it was in the past.

We now return you to our program, still in progress.

—positioning, but the camel, realizing that Fakik had no intention of parting with it, reared abruptly, and planted one of its large—

🔲 NEWS FLASH 🔲

We interrupt this program to bring you a special bulletin.

Magistrates in Nuhr were grim today as the tide of protest against the widespread Khyrling impalements rose. Police barricades have gone up in several sections of the city, and public unrest has reached the point at which officials are calling for a dusk to dawn curfew in the Khyrling enclaves. From the royal palace came word that law-abiding citizens should stay out of the Khyrling enclaves in order to avoid violent confrontations with civil and religious authorities as well as unwarranted impalements.

We now return you to our program, still in progress.

—lost his balance, and, after flapping his arms frantically for a moment, toppled face first into the—

🎴 NEWS FLASH 🎴

We interrupt this program to bring you a special bulletin.

The order confining all Khyrlings to their enclaves has been rescinded by royal decree. All entrances to the enclaves have been unsealed, and magistrates and police have been ordered to allow all Khyrlings free access to the greater urban area, with the exception, of course, of Khyrling females, who are still subject to impalement, though not to summary trial. Khyrling community leaders, presented with the news, were guardedly optimistic, and expressed hope that any remaining impalements found to be necessary might be performed over the next few weeks, and only upon Naians, who, as is well known, go about without head cloths at all times.

When asked what steps might be taken to prevent further explosions in Nuhr, a palace spokesman stated, unofficially, that it was being thought about.

We now return you to our program, still in progress.

—of the camel, which immediately bolted, just as Haddar landed heavily but, as had been the design all along, without injury.

"Ow!"

Chapter Seventeen

27) *Take paper and pencil, or what you will, and write out the words of the Inscription in Capitals, or small-letters (or both), without any regard to scale or the shape of the space the Inscription is to go in. The carver will then see easily of what letters and words his Inscription is composed. Next draw the shape of the Inscription space, and in that space set out the Inscription, either "Massed" or "Symmetrical," as has been decided. The drawing should be neither scribbled nor elaborated. The carver will thus be able, after a little experience, to calculate quite easily what size he will be able to carve his letters, what space he will be able to leave between the lines, and what margins he can afford.*

Hearken all ye to the words of Panas, the Builder of the World, the Raiser of Cities, the Ordainer of Municipalities, the Shaper of Society. May His blessings be bestowed upon His people for all time, and in all nations may there be great and endless praise raised to Him.

And thus in his infinite wisdom does Panas (blessed be He!) hereby command us to gather together such knowledge as is ours to gather, without stinting in any way upon the gathering, whether that gathering might be perceived by some as *massed* or *symmetrical* or *what you will,* and store it away in such edifices of learning as can be kept free from interpretation of that knowledge in any way, for only Panas (blessed be He!) is worthy to interpret knowledge, all human endeavor, by necessity, falling into that which is *scribbled* or *elaborated, with the exception of the endeavors of the priesthood, and, in particular, of the High Priest himself.*

And when this edifice of accumulated knowledge is finally realized by means of the paltry efforts of human beings, *under the supervision of the priesthood, and, in particular, of the High Priest himself,* so may it be kept, *for the most part,* sacred and apart from the mundane concerns of the laity, for as Panas (blessed be He!) has commanded that it be made, and as the words of Panas (blessed be He!) are to be kept apart from and unsullied by the tongues of the laity, so are those devices which are commanded by His holy words to be kept apart also, for *space* and *margins* are of the greatest concern here, and no transgression of either can be tolerated, ~~which is the cause and origin of the universal application of the temple tax.~~ Therefore, though this edifice be as grand and magnificent as anything so ordained by the will of Panas (blessed be He!) ~~and it is the will of Panas (blessed be He!) that the responsibility …~~ must be, let it also be guarded day and night, that its holiness may be magnified by its isolation, and that its sacredness never be profaned by a touch of a mundane foot or its contents sullied by the glance of an eye that can see but not comprehend *unless the priesthood, and, in particular, the High Priest himself, sees fit that the decree be set aside for a time, so that the temple tax …*

~~And it is seen here also how Panas (blessed be He!), in His infinite wisdom, has ordained that the wearing of women's clothing by certain members of the priesthood is indeed a worthy and just thing, highly commendable …~~

*   *   *

Of all the outcomes of Abnel's journey to Katha that
King Inwa Kabir had dreamed about—or, perhaps, had
ordered dreamed about for him—this was the most unexpected: the Gharat returned from Katha alone but for
Bakbuk and the Americans, a virtually anonymous
member of a minor caravan. And, wonder of wonders
(and despite his insistence that he had been wounded
in a terrific battle with brigands in the middle of the
desert, a battle marked by his own uncommon hero-
ism), he actually looked reasonably fit.

*. . . and not a bit of good she did it is a good thing
that I have a strong constitution or she would have
been the death of me but I have failed now and now the
king will not grant the tax and those fools in Katha
with their knowing looks effeminate every one of them
and she without even a head cloth* in the HOUSE
and . . .

"It was the will of Panas (blessed be He!) that the
council of Nuhr hardened their hearts against the will
of Panas (blessed be He!)," said Abnel. "The reasons
for this are obscure. Perhaps it is a . . . a . . . a lesson
of some sort."

"I assume," said Inwa Kabir, "that the tax collectors
of Nuhr have been notified that the temple tax no
longer applies to the Naians?"

"May it be . . . as though it has already been done,"
said Abnel promptly, though there was a trace of reluctance in his voice.

*. . . they giggling behind my back and Jenkins laugh-
ing at me when what I could show him and I will show
him but what of it if the king is not on my side I
know my plan is much better and the king would have
been me but for twist of fate but he is king and I am
Gharat but there have been precedents even up to old
Abramelin's time and what if . . . what if . . . what if*

*something yet that is possible I could arrange it but
then . . . what if . . .*

At the same time, though, quite unexpectedly (and in
marked contrast to the Gharat), Bakbuk, ever the epit-
ome of either sensuous femininity or dapper masculinity (depending on the whim of the day or, perhaps, the
positions of the moons of Jupiter), actually looked hag-
gard, distracted, even drawn, despite his obvious efforts to the contrary. Indeed, he was swaggering and
blustering as well as ever.

But no, that was not quite right. Inwa Kabir had seen
Bakbuk swagger and bluster much better (though, in
order to be completely sure, he would have to have it
thought about): there was a sense of insincerity about
him now, one that said that he was being not at all
forthright about . . . well . . . about being a he, that, in
fact, the sworder did not believe a word (or, rather, a
gesture) of any of it.

*Him! Him! Him! He was right beside me, and I
could feel his hip pressing against mine! I cannot stand
this. I am nothing. What can I do? Stupid, stupid girl!
That is all. A girl! Nothing! And he did this to me! I
cannot be anything! Clean! When I was a boy! Off!
Nothing left but swords and knives, and now not even
those. It is a good thing that they cannot see. And even
if he knew! I will never know when he might reappear,
but I know that he will indeed reappear and that will
be the end of me.*

Really, though, this was a little too much thinking
for the early morning, perhaps for any time at all. Inwa
Kabir would have it thought about.

"Bakbuk," said Inwa Kabir.

The sworder shrugged his shoulders in what was obviously an attempt to look determined, but succeeded
only in appearing delightfully helpless, the sort of
young woman that any man . . .

Inwa Kabir resolved very quickly to have that thought about by someone else.

"May the king live forever," said Bakbuk, looking— No, by someone *else*.

"Were you troubled by the Blue Avenger?"

"Ah . . ." And now Bakbuk was appearing even *more* helpless than before. Indeed, Inwa Kabir half fancied that the sworder was going to swoon right there. ". . . ah . . . well, he appeared . . . ah . . . once or twice, All Highest."

Very curious. Very, very curious. Even at his most poisonously feminine, Bakbuk never *ah*'d. "And you defended the . . ."

Given the temple tax, its inception, its history, and the reluctance with which Abnel had agreed to its cancellation, defending the Gharat was not what Inwa Kabir felt comfortable in talking about, but, like musicians with brass horns and barefoot boys with powdered faces, defending the Gharat was a tradition sanctified by the words of Panas Himself. Indeed, Inwa Kabir had sent Bakbuk to Katha for the express purpose of defending the Gharat, though he supposed that he could have *that* thought about by someone else, too.

". . . the Gharat?"

"Ah . . . he did appear to be interested in the whereabouts of the Gharat, All Highest, but he did not attack him. Actually, in the affair . . ." Bakbuk colored, looked away. ". . . with the . . . ah . . . brigands . . ." And he had unconsciously allowed his hip to sway out to one side. Simply delight—

No. Someone *else*.

". . . he was something of a . . ." A swallow. ". . . a help."

I cannot live like this. I will not be ridiculed. I must destroy him. Death to him! Death!

Curious. Very curious. Quite unlike Bakbuk. It

would have to be thought about. By someone. Else. Perhaps Haddar could think about it.

But Haddar, who was standing near the window, suddenly shuddered and glanced outside quickly as though he expected to find a very large spider (or something similar) crawling into the room; and this made Inwa Kabir reconsider. No, Haddar probably ought not to be the one to think about it. Haddar had become ... well ... rather *strange*. It was more than his squirms, more than his beardlessness (though this was, in itself, strange enough). No, the man had become ... well ... nervous. Very nervous. Hardly a minute went by during which the chief minister did not jump or twitch or look apprehensively over his shoulder as though afraid that something or someone was approaching him.

Is it ... there? Surely that was it. It is out there, looking for me. And how would I explain it? Crawling around. Topaz! It might well get among the women! And then what would I do? Would they ... would they know that it was ... mine? And then what would happen? But Kuz Aswani ... does he know? Is he simply biding his time? True, he was very helpful when I was hanging from the ledge, and he managed to deal both with the camel and the sweetmeat dough, but perhaps that was only a ploy, a sham to make me lower my guard. And then he would have me. And yes! There it is!

No, Haddar would not do at all. But what of Kuz Aswani, who, having apparently fully recovered from his madness, was now standing very attentively to one side, examining Bakbuk and Abnel with an air of astuteness that made him very much the picture of the perfect counselor?

"A help?" said Kuz Aswani. "That is strange news."

Where is he now? At the window? Did Haddar see him? Is that why he looked so startled? Poor Haddar!

To be so ensnared, and to not even have the hope that Panas (blessed be He!) can save him! But then again, Haddar was hanging from that ledge, and it was only at the mention of the Blue Avenger that he started. Now, I am a counselor, and I am wise as only a man (and most certainly not a ferret) can be. And from Haddar's actions, I, a counselor and a man (with the help of Panas (blessed be He!)), can draw certain inferences.

"Strange indeed," said Haddar.

And look at him, pretending to be innocent. "That is strange news," he says, and tries to look as though he knows nothing.

"Yes," said Kuz Aswani.

"Strange indeed," he says. But a wise counselor (and a man at that) would be able to do more than simply stand about and utter responses to his king. He would be able to do something. Something great. And Haddar jumped at the mention of the Blue Avenger. Hmmm.

And Inwa Kabir turned to Haddar, who was still looking very nervous, though he seemed divided in his mind as to whether he should look nervous because of the window, because of Kuz Aswani, or because of his king. "And what of Aeid?" said Inwa Kabir.

"Aeid, All Highest?"

"My son."

"Ah . . . just so."

"He has disappeared."

. . . good riddance to him a puerile excuse for a prince should have been me a mistake of fate which could be rectified in a moment there are precedents after all old Abramelin knew about that it is in all the texts and no one would smirk anymore and the tax would be a matter of fact for both Panas (blessed be He!) and the king would support it, and then . . .

"That is so," said Haddar.

"Have you found anything out?"

"Ah ..."

Must be him. Can only be him. And I touched him. And he touched me. I cannot live this way. I must do away with him. From now on, the Blue Avenger ... but if the Blue Avenger is ... then ... oh ... oh ... oh ... !

"... not yet, All Highest."

"Why not?"

And he stands there, looking very innocent. It can only be him. Wiggles, and twitches ... a ploy. He knows. He saw me. And now he is biding his time, assuming the role of counselor again now that he thinks he has deceived everyone.

It seemed obvious to Inwa Kabir that he was going to have to have matters thought about by someone else. Haddar ... well perhaps Haddar was tired. After all, matters had become very complex since the Americans (And where *were* the Americans, anyway?) had arrived, and the Khyrling freedom fighters (And what about the Khyrlings? Should they be confined to their enclaves? That would be one solution. But it seemed to Inwa Kabir that he had tried that already, and that it had not worked. He could not be sure. He would have it thought about.) had not helped things at all with their explosions. And then the Blue Avenger showing up ... well, it was obvious that Haddar had extended himself a little too far, and perhaps it was time for a new chief minister. Which was in itself, something to be thought about. By ... ah ... someone ...

Aeid? Looking very innocent now. No, Aeid is but a deception. Something unfortunate has happened to the prince. Could it be the work of Umi Botzu? Is our beloved Crown Prince rolling about and eating raisins somewhere? Horrors! What an awful fate, and how ter-

rible that Haddar is making use of his misfortune to cast suspicion on him in this way!

"Never mind," said Inwa Kabir. "I will have it thought about."

Precedent!
Death!
Saw me!
Blue Avenger!

IN THE NAME OF PANAS, THE BENEFICENT, THE WONDROUS, THE SHAPER OF CITIES, THE CARVER OF WORLDS, THE ARBITER OF THE LIVES OF MEN AND THE SUBJUGATOR OF ALL THINGS WEAK AND EFFEMINATE, FOR WHOSE GLORY THE GREAT WORK OF THE PUMPS AND RESERVOIRS GOES ON CEASELESSLY NIGHT AND DAY, TO WHOSE CREDIT WAS THE FIRST REVELATION OF THE GREAT WORK OF THE PUMPS AND RESERVOIRS, IN WHOSE NAME THE WRITER GREETS AND COMPLIMENTS THE READER AS MANY TIMES AS THERE ARE GRAINS OF SAND IN THE DESERT, PEBBLES IN THE DRY VALLEYS, PARCHED FIELDS IN THE WASTELAND AND HUMBLY OFFERS THE FOLLOWING INFORMATION.

Mishap: structural failure
Pumps damaged: #41, #86
Reason for damage: collapse of pump tunnels #3, #124, #89
Slaves dead/injured: 10/34
Reason for death/injury: collapse of pump tunnels #3, #124, #89
Percentage drop in overall capacity: 8
Estimated time until return to full capacity: 15 days

Damage to dikes, dams, and retaining walls: light
Collateral release of water before containment:
10,000 kils
Projected strength of repairs: excellent

IN THE NAME OF PANAS, THE BUILDER UP AND
THE WEARER DOWN, THE MUNIFICENT AND
THE PROFITABLE, THE POWER OF THE PRIESTS
AND THE FEAR OF THE LAITY, THE HOLY AND
THE RIGHTEOUS, THE SMITER OF ENEMIES AND
THE HELPER OF FRIENDS, SO CLOSES THIS RE-
PORT IN THE HOPES THAT THE READER MAY BE
SO MAGNIFIED AS TO BE GREAT AS THE
CLOUDLESS SKY, AS WIDE AS THE DESERTS, AS
HOT AS THE BURNING SUN . . .

~~FORWARDED TO KATHA~~
FORWARDED TO NUHR

Had they all become that lax?

It certainly looked to be so, for as Aeid—ah . . . I
mean Potatoes—no . . . I mean the Blue Avenger made
his way along the rooftops that overlooked the
crowded market square of Nuhr, he could see not a hint
of any guards, disguised or otherwise. Which meant, to
be sure, that they had either become lax, or . . .

. . . well, perhaps they had just gotten to be very
good at *hiding*.

This possibility brought A—, ah, P—

Let me try that again . . . ahem . . .

This possibility brought the Blue Avenger up short,
for since he had been absent from the city of Nuhr for
some time, almost anything might have happened. The
entire population of the market square (which could, I
suppose, be conveniently referred to as a "milling

throng") might well have been made up of a large, specially-deputized group of guards, all ready to pounce on the Blue Avenger the moment he appeared. Surely, though, he would have heard of such a plan . . . but, then again, perhaps he would not have heard of it, for just as surely as he had but recently returned to Nuhr, so his customary methods of gathering information had all fallen into weeks of disuse (And who had Shandar found to exchange insults with? The poor old man! Really, the Blue Av—, no A—, I mean P— . . . *(Rats!)* . . . Baroz would have to do something about that.)

But for now, he (Hah!) peered over the edge of the roof. Just a crowd. Or was it? Fumbling into his belt he extracted a large gold coin. A princely sum, but there were many others where it came from, and so he could easily spare it. With a flick of his thumb, then, down went the coin: spinning and tumbling and glinting straight into the crowd.

The effect was instantaneous. Grasping. Shouting. Scooping up the fallen coin. Punching one another in the face. Deprecations that involved one another's grandmothers and grandfathers and great-grandmothers and great-grandfathers, all of whom apparently had various kinds of illicit liaisons with various kinds of draft animals and fish.

The Blue Avenger smiled. No. There was no plan. They had really become that lax.

But upon gaining the roof of the temple, he discovered that the long tables with the stacks and heaps and baskets of (in his opinion) illicitly gathered coins were gone. There were no tables. There were no tax collectors, nervous or otherwise. There were no Naian men standing before those tables and tax collectors considering whether a life of abject poverty or of Panasism was preferable (and surely it was not something that was going to hurt *them,* was it?), though, to be sure, there were quite a few less Naians in evidence, the matter of poverty or Panasism having been coinciden- tally settled in favor of Panasism by just that number of formerly-Naian men (and surely it had not been something that had hurt *them,* had it?) who demon- strated equally good sense when it came to recognizing that apostasy was a grievous crime against Panas ... and Panasian law was very clear about *that,* too.

It was quite obvious what had happened. Abnel, having been unsuccessful in his efforts to gain the backing of the priestly council of Katha, had given up on the tax. But what, the Blue Avenger wondered, was next?

Lifting his eyes from the grasping, shouting, scoop- ing, punching crowd that was screaming deprecations ... etc., he found that he was looking at the gleaming alabaster structure that was the Great Library of Nuhr.

Pumps. Water. What *was* going on? And *why* (Curse him!) had he once again left Sari alone with that ... that ... ?

Fakik had ached before, but that was as nothing compared to his pain now. The hooves of a camel, though designed for treading the sands of the interior wastes without a misstep, were quite capable of bruis- ing a man to a degree to which men (at least, those in their right minds) did not wish to be bruised. And when the camel was maddened by an application of sweetmeat dough where sweetmeat dough had no busi- ness being applied ... well ...

"Mrkgnao!"

"Go away, cat. I do not need your help. I have never needed your help. If you could keep Kuz Aswani away, I would be glad of your help. If you could keep Haddar away, I would be glad of your help. If you could keep camels away, I would be glad of your help. But since you cannot, you have nothing to offer me, and I do not need your help."

"Mrrk?"

"Go away, cat. I need you to go away. You will help me by going away. I am almost ready with my sweet-meat dough, a dough that will surely please the king enough that he will restore my honor to me (though he cannot ever restore my manhood, save by perhaps procuring for me one or two of those barefoot boys with powdered faces, and surely he would not miss one or two, and I would promise him that I would take very good care of them) and make me once again someone to be reckoned with, and perhaps he will finally punish Kuz Aswani for spoiling that raisin compote that was the beginning of my ruin."

"Mrkgnao!"

"Go away, cat. This is almost ready, and when it is ready, it will surely please the king and restore to me my fortune."

"Mrkgnao!"

Chapter Eighteen

V̥: People of Naia, it grieves me to bear to you the news of a great catastrophe. All of you know of the holy Caves of Naia, where our ancestors once worshiped after they had crossed the Mountains of Ern and had reached this land, which was, at the time, fertile and green and a true paradise. The Caves are our treasure and our spiritual wellspring. It is, indeed, as though their water is the lifeblood of Naia, poured out upon the earth to nurture Her Children.

As I said, it grieves me to bear to you such evil news, but I must tell you that the holy Caves are no more. It was my fortune to journey to them, but my misfortune to discover that a landslide has buried them beneath many thousands of kils of rock. No more do the waters of life flow from the Caves of Naia, and no more is there a holy place to which the Children of the Goddess can come so as to tread in the footsteps of their ancestors and offer worship and homage to the Greenest Branch.

But as it was my misfortune to witness the ruin of the Caves, it is my fortune to come to you, people of Naia, and ask for aid. With much work and great perseverance, the Caves may be cleared. True, it will take many months, perhaps many years, but what are years to the Goddess who is forever, or to a loving people who wish to retain the spiritual treasures of their heritage?

And so I come to you now to ask you for aid, not for myself, but for Naia, who has nurtured Her Children throughout many ages of the world, and who now is Herself in need. By helping Her, we help ourselves, and, indeed, we help the land, for it is through Naia's water that we live, and so what greater goal could there be than to seek to return Naia's grace and gifts to a land that is sorely in need of both?

Therefore I appeal to you: come to the Caves with me, and help me to clear them.

R̞: Well, at least *I* know better. Though she might well find some willing listeners around here somewhere, it still surprises me that more people do not know that the Caves were an elaborate fiction concocted by a secret order about one hundred and fifty years ago and designed to keep the more dangerous secrets of power away from the masses. The references are available, but no one bothers to go and look at them. Well, sometimes they do not bother. Other times they have bothered and the records have been destroyed by some people who find it profitable to continue the deception. But the information is there, and I have researched it thoroughly, as can anyone who wishes to take the trouble to do it.

Actually, this "Caves" rumor is making its second appearance. The whole delusion had pretty much died out in my grandfather's time, but recently it has been gaining ground again. I think that it was restarted at a festival two or three years ago. They did not invite me, but I found out from respected third parties that a certain individual from one of the towns in the interior wastes had claimed it as a discovery he had made from some "ancient texts." Now, for all I care, anyone can believe anything that they want. I am very open-minded about that. But to try to pass off something that someone made up—probably some drummer who was attempting to prove that his guild was older and more "traditional" (whatever that means) than someone else's—as genuine history is, to my mind, reprehensible, though some people these days are making a tidy profit from it. Not that I think that this girl is that sort. No. She is probably someone's wife or bedmate who has been deluded into believing all these things about the Caves. Poor thing.

Anyway, I am glad that *I* know better.

R7: What a lovely girl! Oh, but she is beautiful! (Hand over her mouth, she struggles but I shove her down and will not hurt her unless she needs it.) I could easily see her in my worship group. Yes, she would fit right in. I can tell. (Pinning her, a knife to her thighs, she would open right up for me, and I will not hurt her unless she needs it.) She has that kind of appreciation of the divine that is essential to a worship group. (And then that soft moistness closing around me, slipping up and down, tickling until it rises like fire, and she with her back arched, wondering when the blade is going to start cutting, but I will not hurt her. Unless she needs it.) It is very easy to fall into rote custom, and new faces and new ideas are so often needed to spark that inner perception of the Goddess. (And I can do it as hard as I want because once you break them they are yours forever, and I like seeing that frightened look in their eyes when I am through. But I do not hurt them. No. Unless they need it.) And my wife would go along with it. Yes, she would. She knows what the group needs. And she is getting a little tired these days, what with all the children, and I am sure that she would not mind stepping aside now and then to allow someone with such an obvious devotion and such new ideas and such a wonderful inner perception to take over. Now and then. (And they like it, I know that they do. They need mastery. And there is no better mastery than that. Smother them. That melt just gushes about once I pin them properly and they see that look in my eyes that I am perfectly serious and will hurt them. But I will not hurt them. No. Not at all. Unless they need it.) And I am sure that she would come to like it, and would let someone new simply take over. I could explain. I am sure that she would understand.

R₇: Oh! The Caves! Oh! How terrible! Something must be done. We must do something! Oh! Such an awful stroke of fortune to befall us, but I am sure that something can be done. There are so many individuals and groups here in the community that do not do enough for anyone, and I am sure that they would be glad of an opportunity to help with the Caves. And they should! Oh, yes! I would help with the work myself, but my time is so limited. Why, tomorrow, I have some students coming. They are so eager to know about Naia, and yet they are so demanding. Next week, the group of interested individuals who are planning the recreations for the next seasonal festival are meeting, and there is so much work to be done there! Oh, yes! And then there is the matter of the proper traditional costumes for the members of the drummers' guild, which I and a number of others are working on. And the women's group that we are forming. And the group that is discussing the mass ritual for next year is getting started, and there are just so many things to do! Something definitely needs to be done about the Caves, though, and, as I said, there are so many other groups and individuals that are not doing *anything* at all, and they need to be spoken to, because what is by nature the primary shrine of our religion is certainly an important thing to be attended to. Oh, yes!

R₇: It is obvious that we must do something about the Caves. They should definitely be cleared, and as soon as possible. And in order to make sure that the work is done as quickly as possible, it is important that the

right group of people be put in charge of the effort.
This is true. They must be the proper people, because
it is important work, and it would be very important to
exclude certain individuals whose approach is just not
correct. Bepha, for example, I could never work with,
because I do not like his ideas about certain things
which I am not at liberty to discuss because of an oath
that I took. This is true. And Depha is not someone
that *anyone* would want working on this sort of thing,
because she once worked on a project of similar importance (which I am not at liberty to discuss because of
an oath that I took) with a friend of mine, and you simply would not *believe* what she did to him. If you knew
what had gone on, you would understand, but I make
it a point to never spread malicious rumors (as some
people do) in the community. This is true. In any case,
Depha is good friends with Jepha, and so I do not think
that Jepha would be interested, because we would have
to exclude Depha, you see. And if Jepha will not participate, then I think we can safely assume that Nepha,
Shepha, and Tepha will not either, which is probably
just as well, because they are not quite, well, ethical,
you know, but I am not at liberty to discuss that because of an oath that I took when I was working with
Zepha, who knows all about it. This is true. But we
definitely need to do something, because something
must be done. It is just so very important, you see, that
the right people do it.

R7: Well, you can get involved if you want, but I have
had a few bad experiences, and I really should tell you
that I have gotten involved in things like this in the
past, and every single time matters turned out against
me. You can do it if you want. I will not judge you
in any way. Everyone has to make his own decisions,
and I would be the last person to say anything different
than that, but one time that I became involved—and it
was with something *just* like this—I wound up losing

a great deal of money. Not that this was by the design of the individual involved. No. While some people might see deceptions such as this as a way to take money away from others, I do not think that this was the case with my experience. Some people are simply *careless,* and as a result they do things that work to the detriment of others. They do not live in the real world. I cannot judge them, for that is simply the way they live.

Another time, I became involved, and wound up with someone living at my house for many months. It was a very disagreeable situation, I can assure you, as they became increasingly demanding, and I wound up having to move in order to be rid of them. They still do not speak to me, but what of that? But I do not think that there was anything overtly malicious in their behavior: it was simply that some people are careless, and they wind up doing things that work to the detriment of others. They do not live in the real world. And then there was another time, and that was so awful that you simply do not want to hear about it. But yet I do not think it was out of malice that any of this happened. Some people are simply careless, and wind up doing things that work to the detriment of others. I will not say that *this* individual is careless, but one never can tell, and, as I said, I have had many experiences that make me cautious.

R7: Well, this is all very well and good, but I notice that she only speaks of the Goddess in Her female aspect, giving no thought to the Goddess in Her male aspect. This is a very serious omission, as it puts her completely out of balance with the natural aspects of the Goddess, and though I have heard that it is very popular with some of the eclectic traditions of Naianism to utterly ignore this, I, for one, hold to the old traditions and attempt to maintain balance. After all, there are two kinds of people in the world, male and female, and there are examples everywhere of opposing qualities that are embodied by them. Light, dark. Dry, wet. Active, receptive. Dominant, submissive.

As Naia is a Goddess, so She must have a male aspect, a God, to counterbalance her qualities, otherwise the world would remain sterile and there would be no fertility at all. And it just does not make sense to me that some people can so blithely ignore this, and go on as though there were only one sex in the world. Greenest Branch, indeed! Everyone knows that a branch cannot live by itself, but needs a tree to support it, just as a woman cannot live without a man.

This sort of muddy thinking is a *fine* thing for someone who presumes to speak of "our ancestors" and what they did in the past! Why, you might think she was an elder of some community instead of some young thing who shows up without any kind of proper introduction and insists that we obey her! "Come and clear the Caves," she says, and tells us all about hard work. What does she know of work? Young, that is all. Just a young woman who has not realized that she needs a man in order to complement her natural inclinations and moderate her excesses. And perseverance? Why, it has taken me twenty years to bring some people in the community around to my way of thinking, and if you do not call that perseverance, then you might as well start considering going off to those Caves—whatever they are—with this girl.

R7: Her intentions are very good, very good indeed. I am afraid, though, that she misses the point. Naianism is a very animistic religion, but not at all in the way that the ignorant Panasian priests think. We perceive all things as being embodiments of the Goddess, and as such, they take part in Her life. Therefore all things are alive. Now, one of the qualities of life is self-determination. As men, we make constant decisions about our wants, our needs, and our preferences. But even animals make these decisions. The ass decides to eat. The dog decides to gnaw his bone. This is quite obvious to anyone who pays any attention at all. Plants, too, exhibit self-determination. Some decide to grow; others decide to wither. This also is obvious. But just as men and animals and plants demonstrate their self-determination, so do apparently inanimate objects, and if our perceptions are so coarse that we cannot readily see those constant demonstrations (which must be there, because all things partake of Naia's life), then that is certainly not Naia's fault.

So the question again becomes one of choice, and it is very obvious to anyone who pays any attention at all that the Caves chose to be buried under the landslide, in accordance with their self-determination (which, we might repeat, proceeds directly from Naia herself). And as this is the case, we have very little right to interfere with that choice.

It is unfortunate that she has gotten this all wrong, but those of us who are deeply religious can perceive things with a clarity that those who are merely intellectually spiritual cannot.

R7: I notice that she uses the term "Children of the Goddess" very freely, without paying much attention to the contradictions that arise from this. For one thing, how can she specify any particular people as "Children of the Goddess" when, in fact, we are *all* children of the Goddess in one way or another. Hence, her separation of Naians from the rest of the population is inaccurate, and can only lead to divisiveness. On the other hand, used in its strictest sense, "Children of the Goddess" can only truly be applied to those Naians who have accepted themselves as "Children" of the "Goddess," which means much more than simply assuming a title. The worship of Naia as mother must be paramount, of course, but there are also several other requirements that must be fulfilled for the individual to be really qualified. Now, some would say that only the very first Naians to arrive at the Caves were really entitled to be called "Children of the Goddess", and some will say that only those among them who actually touched the waters of the spring are entitled to it, but I will not split hairs, for that would lead to divisiveness. Nevertheless, I must insist that some kind of discrimination must be applied when using terminology, as there are many Naians whose practice does not qualify them for the title of "Children of the Goddess", and incorrect usage can only lead to divisiveness.

Inel—*No!*
Come this far. To Nuhr. Miserable room in Naian Quarter. Smells of fish. Fish? Seacoast. Fishers. Diving down into water. Water. Salt. Mineral. Stone. Undrinkable. Knowledge. Unknowable. Hidden from me. Would not take me back now even if I ... if I ...

Here, walk like this.
Beshur cast about in the tiny room, reached out with a foot to edge Potatoes' pallet a little farther away from Sari's, and went to the window. Off in the distance was the wide, pinnacled form of the Library, the hot sun trickling gleams down its sides.

Death to enter. Hidden. Secret. Mysteries to all save priests. But they know. Or do they? Kept from all. No understanding. But I understand. More than they know. Guilty. Apostate. I understand.

He leaned his hands on the sill.
—Why did they change? he said.
Does not answer. Mute stone. Cannot read stone. What is inside, though. Inside. Death. Is it even possible? How? Potatoes says that he knows a way, but Potatoes ...

He turned away from the window and shoved Potatoes' pallet a little farther away from Sari's, shoved his own a little closer.

. . . is someone I do not know, and besides . . .

A light footstep on the stairs leading up from the fish shop below. Sari entered, eyes downcast.

Beshur gave his pallet another shove.

—How did your visits go?

Sari shrugged. "Well, they listened to me." She looked distractedly first at Beshur, and then at the window. "I think."

The Americans were back in Nuhr, in the same rooms, with the same guards and the same servants. The same food (too sweet, too frequent) was served, the same routines (meaningless and intricate) were followed, the same boys (barefoot, powdered) and musicians (braying, brass horns) escorted the ambassador wherever he went. Everything was the same. But not quite.

Mather came and Mather went. Jenkins had given up trying to keep track of him. The engineer-cum-diplomatic-assistant vanished at odd times, under really impossible circumstances, and Jenkins had finally come to the conclusion that customary forms of entry and egress were not involved. No: this was Nuhr, and this was Africa, and this was the devious African mind in action. Doubtless the walls were virtually honey-combed with passageways and cul-de-sacs and corridors and secret orifices, one of which led to the chambers given over to the Americans. Well, Jenkins reflected, at least Abnel was not demanding that Mather appear habitually as some plump, pocked, and not-very-androgynous houri with kohl-rimmed eyes and diaphanous veils . . .

Jenkins shuddered at the thought, and was immediately horrified to discover that he was . . . was . . .

He looked around quickly. Had Wool noticed?

Wool gave no sign. The secretary was sitting in his usual place behind the (same) low table, his knees up above his ears and his eyes swimming like two goldfish behind his thick spectacles. His pen was in his hand and his paper was before him, and Jenkins was quite convinced that, had he done no more than coughed or sneezed, Wool would have taken down the vocalization with excruciating exactness, translating it into his vermiform shorthand while simultaneously annotating it with some appropriate Biblical quote.

And then there was Haddar. Or, rather, there was *not* Haddar. Jenkins had, in fact, not seen the chief minister since that last, belligerent interview before Abnel and his progress had left for Katha. Instead, Haddar's place had been taken by a certain Kuz Aswani, who, in marked contrast to Haddar's decided opinions about Americans and all the unfortunate things that should be done to them, seemed to have no particular opinions about anything at all, save for a peculiar obsession with raisins and a bent toward scratching his head with his foot (and Jenkins never ceased to be astonished by the flexibility he thereby demonstrated) ... a bent in which he seemed to indulge both unconsciously and guiltily, for he would invariably catch himself midway through the procedure (usually with his big toe just beginning to probe behind his ear), and, with a sheepish "You must, of course, forgive your humble servant" expression, lower his foot to the ground and attempt to carry on as if nothing had happened.

Regarding such things as trade, maps, and fishing rights, Kuz Aswani seemed to be very easygoing: so long as trade, maps, and fishing rights demanded no commitment of any sort from him, his monarch, or his country, Kuz Aswani was very willing to go along with just about anything, giving Jenkins the impression that he was dealing not with a seasoned counselor of the

Kaprishan court, but rather with a large, anthropomorphic custard.

But no matter: Jenkins was no longer working toward trade, maps, or fishing rights (though, for Kuz Aswani's sake, he would continue to pretend that he was), but toward the very heart of the Three Kingdoms. He could see that Abnel was desperate for . . . something, that Abnel wanted . . . something; and though the inexactness of this perception was, for a man who was used to understanding the depths of even complex and deceptive matters of diplomacy, an irritating barb, its sting was somewhat blunted by the hard edge of suspicion and knowledge that had come from his overhearing of the Gharat's fevered ravings, and by his surety that Abnel was desperate enough to do . . . anything.

But the echo of Abnel's words nagged at him, blunting any sense of satisfaction that he might have felt. Pumps. Water.

Very strange, very unknown . . . and very possibly dangerous.

"Hello," said Mather from close behind him.

Jenkins all but jumped. Only years of finely-honed discipline saved him from revealing that he had been startled. He looked over his shoulder, noticed that Mather reeked of perfume, was bruised, and had traces of something (Oh, dear God, was that *kohl*?) around his eyes, but said only: "Ah, just as I expected."

"And they shall be afraid and ashamed of Ethiopia their expectation, and of Egypt their glory."

Jenkins decided upon the simple expedient of ignoring Wool.

Mather limped toward a cushion. Since the loss of the gravimeter, he had had nothing mechanical with which to bond (though Jenkins suspected that Abnel possessed more than enough mechanical things with which Mather could bond (had bonded, was bonding)

... and about which his own stoutly Puritan mind fervently desired to remain ignorant ... and *had* Wool noticed?), but he did not seem to mind. He was not in the Americans' chambers for more than an hour or two each day, in any case.

"Ah ... Mather ..." Jenkins chose his words carefully: he neither wanted to reveal himself nor miss the opportunity. "What was your final determination regarding the mountains?"

Mather flopped down, the cushions squishing beneath his ample (and, Jenkins assumed, well-perfumed) buttocks. "I told you that," he said sullenly.

"Behold, I have told you before," came the mournful intonation.

Jenkins frowned. "Tell me again. A great deal has happened since that last measurement, and I want to refresh my memory."

"Oh, the mountains are there, but it shouldn't be too hard to find a passage through them," said Mather.

"For the mountains shall depart, and the hills be removed ..."

Jenkins determinedly did not listen to the rest of the quote, but out of the corner of his eye, he noticed that Wool was writing again. Drat!

"It looks as though what we're dealing with is a few very high ridges that give way to a shelving plateau. The ridges will be the hardest to get through, of course, but the engineers ..."

Mather preened just a little.

"... will be able to manage it. Not at all the problem it would be if there were just one set of ridges after another."

(Squirm.)

"Thou waterest the ridges thereof abundantly ..."

Jenkins had learned to ignore Mather's squirms. "So I can safely communicate with President Winthrop that the plans can proceed?"

"Oh, yes."

For a moment, there was a rumbling. The floor swayed. Jenkins looked wildly for an escape, but the rumbling and the swaying were gone in a moment.

"Another earthquake," nodded Mather with satisfaction.

"Ah . . . yes," said Jenkins. "Just as I expected."

"I'd think you'd be used to them by now."

"What?"

"Well, we get them now and then in the States."

Jenkins frowned at the potential heterodoxy. "So I've been told, Mr. Mather. I confess I never felt one until I came here."

Mather preened just a little more. "Well, they're small, but they're there. It's the earth rebounding from the weight, you know."

"Then the earth shook and trembled; the foundations of heaven moved and shook, because he was wroth."

Jenkins continued to ignore Wool. "What weight?"

"Of the glaciers. During the last Ice Age, glaciers covered all of the Great Lakes area and even extended south from there. Immensely heavy. All that ice. Now that they've receded, the land is springing back. It goes in fits and starts. Earthquakes."

Jenkins looked at him. Mather was crucial to the success of the mission, but doctrine and truth were doctrine and truth. "I would think," he said, "that it was the weight of the Flood that had been removed from the land."

Mather shrugged. Or perhaps it was a squirm. It was difficult at times to tell. For a moment, Jenkins toyed idly with the thought that perhaps *all* of Mather's gestures and expressions had come to be only slightly transmogrified tremors of discomfort.

But a thought suddenly struck him: Pumps. Water. The Flood. Did it make some kind of insane sense?

"And, behold, I, even I, do bring a flood of waters

upon the earth, to destroy all flesh, wherein *is* the breath of life, from under heaven; *and* every thing that *is* in the earth shall die."

"Whatever," said Mather with a carelessness that was all but infuriating. "You can think what you like."

Chapter Nineteen

"Mrrrk?"

"Go away cat. I do not need your help. My sweet-meats are done, and I am going to take them to the king, and when he tastes them he will call his servants and he will say to them 'Who was it made these wonderful sweetmeats?,' and his servants will say 'Fakik, who was your head cook but who is now in disgrace over the matter of the raisin compote . . .' (Cursed be the name of that Kuz Aswani!) '. . . made these wonderful sweetmeats,' and the king will say, 'Bring Fakik to me,' and they will come to me and say, 'Fakik, the king desires your presence,' and I will say, 'Oh, I cannot think of why, as I am in disgrace over the matter of the raisin compote,' and they will say to me, 'He wishes to reward you for your wonderful sweetmeats,' and I will say, 'As the king commands, so may it be as if it is already done,' and I will go to the king, and he will praise me and reward me and restore to me my honor (though even he cannot restore my manhood), and perhaps I will then have the use of one or two of those boys with the bare feet and the powdered faces . . . or perhaps the use of three or four. Truly, these are uncommonly good sweetmeats, and so I can well imagine that the king might even give me the use of five or six. But you must go away now, cat, for I can-

not have you tripping me as I am carrying this tray of
wonderful sweetmeats to the king, and . . .

". . . is that the Gharat?"

"Mrrk?"

. . . much better than theirs, and could arrive at the
result in just a few years and those WHORES who go
about without their headwraps *in the HOUSE* would
keep their heads covered already but for the idiocy of
a recalcitrant king who will not listen to anyone not
even the word of Panas (blessed be He!) Himself can
sway him and would have been me but for a trick of
fate should have been me and Mather with that smirk
once I gave him that drink and the snake he did not
mind at all and old Abramelin knew best of course he
took matters into his own hands as I shall if I could
only find the proper way and there is that cook with a
tray of something like that little Naian WHORE telling
me that I should watch what I eat as though she would
recognize decent food if it were stuffed down her
throat and she went about without a headwrap *in the
HOUSE* I would do something about that and he tells
me that he is taking these to the king and they are for
the king only and he seeks the restoration of his honor
and I have an idea I will take them and present them
to the king myself and put in a good word for poor
Fakik who was unjustly accused because of the actions
of that wretched Kuz Aswani who lost his mind or perhaps he only pretended to lose it but no matter I would
wager that his WHORE of a wife goes about without
her headwrap *in the HOUSE* and she will be among
them when a minister in their heads yes I can do it I
shall do it put in a good word for Fakik and restore
him to favor though what he would do with one of
those boys I do not know not very good for anything
they scream a great deal and not much else but he
gives me the tray and I reassure him and he kneels to

me and I bless him just as I will ha-ha bless these sweetmeats and make sure that they are ha-ha even more suited for a kingly mouth than they are already and then since Aeid is gone they will come to me and I can easily have Aeid taken care of and if he had a wife I would wager that *she* would go about without her head cloth *in the HOUSE* and soon I will have everything as I want it and we can dispense with the pumps never believed they could do the work properly and if Kuz Aswani so much as looks at me I will have him blinded and his tongue cut out but what better than to have him take these to the king now that they have been properly ha-ha blessed and made ha-ha fit for a kingly mouth and I can see that he is eager to do such a thing especially when I tell him that they are for the good of the king and have been specially blessed with much holiness for the protection of the king and yes I will yes . . .

It is a terrible thing that has befallen me, but who should I tell about it? It is death to meddle in magic, and I have meddled in it indeed, or, rather, magic has meddled in me, which is not the same thing at all. It is a very good thing that I can tell the difference, though, for it shows how far I have come. A ferret would not know the difference, but a man would. And I am a *man*.

Is that him? Yes! There he is!

But it is so hard, sometimes. Why, just this morning I was talking with that American, and I found that I was scratching my head with my foot! Again! He pretended not to notice, of course, but I know that he noticed. I cannot imagine what he must think of a *man* scratching his head with his foot, but he is a foreigner, and perhaps he considers it but a local custom. Still, though the strength of Panas does not fail me, my own strength does, particularly when Umi Botzu is near

(Yes! There he is again! How he gloats! But I shall defeat him, I and the strength of Panas (blessed be He!)!), and then I lapse. Would that I would not lapse, and that I could enjoy my life as a *man,* along with the attentions of my lovely wife (who, I can tell, is still suspicious, but I really only meant that as a love bite this morning, and not as preparation for a good drag about the room)!

A good drag! Panas (Blessed be He!) have mercy!

And in answer to my prayers (Yes!) here is Abnel with a tray of sweetmeats, and he is telling me (Yes!) that these sweetmeats have been specially blessed (Yes!) in order to add to the spiritual fortitude of the king, and would I, as acting chief minister, be willing to present them (Yes!) to Inwa Kabir with the compliments of the chef?

Perhaps he simply does not know. Does Panas (blessed be He!) tell his priests *everything*? Surely not. (And I am glad that I am a *man* and not a ferret, for a ferret would not understand these subtleties at all, and would simply be obsessed by the fact that there are *raisins* in the sweetmeats.) For if He did, then Abnel would understand that these sweetmeats have obviously been brought to me for the express purpose of aiding this humble son of Panas (blessed be He!) in his struggle against the snares of the diabolical Umi Botzu (Yes! There he is *again*!), and that they are not destined for the king at all, but for *me*!

Take them to the king? Of course I will take them, my honored Gharat! I shall be happy to take them! I would take them a hundred times! And when I appear next before the king, the sweetmeats will be in me, and I will therefore take them to the king, who will, thereby, be graced with the presence of a fine and sturdy counselor who is a *man*!

* * *

Sabihah honestly tried not to think about very much, because it did not pay for a woman to think. And besides, when she did *not* think, she was treated well enough, and that, she supposed, was the best that one could ask for ... besides such necessities as rubies and feathers ...

But something of a dent had been put into Sabihah's world, not only when it came to rubies and feathers, but also to thinking (which, unfortunately, she was starting to do), for the former had been taken away from her by the unexpected absence of Prince Aeid, and the latter had in many ways been thrust upon her by the sudden alterations in fortune and lifestyle resulting from her husband's sudden madness and his equally sudden recovery.

Well, his *apparent* recovery. Though she thought (And there she was *thinking* again!) it something of a relief to have him back at her side at night, Sabihah was still unnerved and alarmed by his habit of scratching behind his ears with his feet, and when he was excited he would ... well ... *chitter* in a way that would make her clap her hands over the scruff of her neck and flee the room. For the most part, though, she thought (Eek!) that he seemed normal enough, and so she was willing to put up with the scratching and the chitters ... so long as she had some assurance that it would go no further than that.

Today, though, Kuz Aswani entered their chambers, and while his hands bore a silver tray piled high with sweetmeats, his face bore an expression that Sabihah found truly terrifying, for it seemed to embody in its every angle and feature all of the scruff-draggings and chitterings and wigglings that she had come to loathe and dread in the past.

But once she noticed that there were raisins in the sweetmeats, she had no doubt as to the cause of her husband's relapse. And so, after Kuz Aswani had set down the tray of sweetmeats (with raisins) and had gone into another room in order to wash his hands (declaring, as he went, that a *man* washed his hands before eating), Sabihah, making a quick decision that (for once) did not involve rubies or feathers or nocturnal trysts with the Crown Prince, seized the tray, carried it to the door, and handed it over to a servant with a request that it be deposited someplace exceedingly far away from her, the chambers, and, especially, Kuz Aswani.

Yum! Yum! Yum! I *love* sweetmeats, especially sweetmeats with raisins! What a good stroke of luck! Me! Sweetmeats! A whole tray of sweetmeats! Yum! And they are fairly *dripping* with honey! My favorite . . . though I would think that sweetmeats such as these should have just a bit more *sugar* sprinkled on them.

But I cannot eat them here. I must take them elsewhere. And elsewhere must be private. I will not share my fortune. Not where raisins are involved. (Oooooh! Yum!)

No, not the corridor. Take them outside. Out the back way. I can circle around behind. Yum! No one else but me. Why, there must be at least (Yum!) twenty sweetmeats here, and they look very fine indeed! (Raisins!) Yes, out the back way here, down the stairs, and across the courtyard, where no one will see me but the man who brings the water, and he will say nothing because I am a servant and he will assume that I am taking them somewhere, and, yes, I *am* taking them somewhere! Somewhere private! Yum!

But who is that? Oh! Must hide these. Under this cloth on the water wagon. Yes. He will be here for a while, and I can get them in a short time, when no one will see me. Oh . . . !

* * *

Hmmm ... hah ... PIGS! Will not buy water from
a holy man! *No, not today,* hah! PIGS! What do they
know of water! Hobble about now with only one leg,
all on account of that powder! Introduced, it said! Introduced! Hah ... ah ... PIGS! But they tell me they
do not need water, and so I will go. I will not stay to
have them tell me again that they do not need water.
PIGS! They know nothing of water, and they know
nothing of holy work. Hah! PIGS. And they discharged
me because of that powder. Would have sent me to the
pumps, but I escaped, and they will not look for me because they are too busy with their own water.
Hmmm ...

PIGS! Brimstone and pumice, I will leave, and the
devils who made that thing on the island will not find
me, not that they are looking for me at all, for there are
many water sellers, and many of them are selling water
because they are missing something inessential ... as
opposed to something *essential,* hah!, that some do not
have, and so they let them among the women, but I
have what is essential ... um ... eh ... urg ... PIGS!
... and I will sell water along with the best of them,
but I will not stay if they do not want my water, and so
here I go out through the gates and into the city where
they will want my water soon enough, and some will
want it for free, but I will not give it to them unless
they pay me, for it costs money to live and they are
certainly PIGS who would send a man out to an island
with powder and bruising and wads and cheeses and
then discharge him for losing his own leg (And what is
that PIG shouting about? Pumice and brimstone, he is
only a servant, so what do I care?) because he tried to
do his job smartly. Hah! I am intelligent, and so I did
it smartly, and that infernal thing took my leg. Run
out? I cannot "run out" for anything now, because I
only have one leg! But I escaped, and go away, boy, I
will not give you water because you have no money

and because you are a PIG and go away I say and get
your hands off of that (I cannot run because I have
only one leg!) and leave that alone and what is that—?

He cannot catch me because I am young and he has
only one leg! But it is very strange that he did not
know that this was under the covers of his cart, but
perhaps he is stupid. I am sure that being stupid would
be a terrible thing to be, but I am young, and I cannot
be stupid because I will grow up to be like the Crown
Prince who is not stupid at all. I wish I could meet
him! I am sure that he would like me! And perhaps we
could . . . do things together. He could take me up on
his fine horse, and we could hunt. Oh, my, yes! And I
could grow up to be like him, for he is handsome and
smart.

But for now, the very best thing for me to do is
to take care of my mother, for the Crown Prince would
take care of *his* mother if she were as sick as *my*
mother is, of that I am sure, because that is just something that the Crown Prince would do. And these
sweetmeats are just the thing for a sick mother to have,
for she needs something that will make her feel good,
and for that I cannot think of anything better than a
fine tray of sweetmeats, and so I will take them to her
immediately because I am going to grow up to be just
like the Crown Prince.

Oh, my! She is in the other room. She did not hear
me come in! Mother! Oh, she must be asleep. I will set
these sweetmeats down here on the table and go and
fetch her, and what a wonderful surprise she will have
when she discovers what her little Crown Prince has
brought for her! Oh, my!

No medallion. Well, she did not *have* a medallion when
I was done, but no one took that into account, did they?
And how was I supposed to know about the Blue

Avenger? Everybody talks about the Blue Avenger here in
Nuhr (which is very funny, because no one has seen him
recently), but no one had even *heard* of him in Katha.
And so how was I supposed to know that he was the Blue
Avenger, and how was I supposed to pay much attention
to him at all when I was staggering about after that Naian
slut rapped my stones? But they blamed me, of course,
and how was I supposed to say anything against it? I was
just a guard, and was just doing my work, and this Naian
slut raps my stones, and then this man who looks like a
dyer's nightmare shows up and spirits her off. And what
was I supposed to do about it? But they sent me off and
told me to go away and that I was lucky that I was not
deprived of my stones for having had them rapped by that
Naian slut. And what was I supposed to do other than
come to Nuhr?

But there is nothing for guards to do in Nuhr, and
how am I supposed to earn my bread save in any way
that I can? And how am I supposed to do anything at
all save by keeping my eyes open, and I am sure that
he took this turning. I know a beggar-boy when I see
one, and beggar-boys have no business with silver
trays, and so I will relieve him of that silver tray. And
how am I supposed to do any different? I am very hungry, and I must eat, and that tray will feed me for several weeks.

Ah! Here is the house! And *there* is the tray! And
how am I supposed to resist the chance of feeding myself for several weeks? So I climb in, and I take the
tray (Are those *raisins*?), and I climb back out, and
now I am away, and the beggar-boy will have to remain a beggar-boy, for how else am I supposed to take
care of myself after that Naian slut rapped my stones?

Surely there is providence in the world, for here is
the tray, and here are sweetmeats, and I am hungry,
and . . . my, but they are good sweetmeats! Oh! And
how am I supposed to keep from eating another, seeing

as how the first sweetmeat was so good? Clearly, I am *not* supposed to keep from eating another. And another. And, my, but these are good sweetmeats, and this tray (And another!) will feed me for several weeks. Indeed, it has already begun to feed me, and how am I supposed ... supposed ... supposed ... t—

Urk!

Money.

Everything is money. In all my forty-two years, that is the clear, essential thing I have learned. Everything is money. I know that. And if everyone was honest with himself, he would know that, too. Take those priests, for example. Spirituality? Spiritual welfare? Pah! It is all money, and it was obvious even before they extended the temple tax to the Naians, who are a bunch of idiots and who do not know the slightest thing about money and we would be much better off without them.

Everything is money, and praise be Panas (blessed be He!) for that, because that makes everything so simple. It is all buying and selling. I want, so I buy. You want, so I sell. This is clearly obvious to anyone who thinks about it, and only those stupid Naians do not understand, and we would certainly be much better off without them.

If I want, I buy, and this is a good thing. And I sell to whomever I want, and this is a good thing too. And if an opportunity arises that was previously unlooked-for, like this corpse in the alleyway with a silver tray of sweetmeats at its side, who am I to pick my nose at it? Well, I buy what I want, and I want this tray, and so I will buy it from this corpse. And since corpses have no need of money, I will buy it very cheaply. It is all a matter of good business, which the Naians do not understand, and we would indeed be much better off without them.

And as I want to sell this tray, and as I understand that the foreigners on their ship will pay money for things which they do not have, so I will take this to the foreigners on board their ship, and, since *I* am most certainly *not* a corpse, I am sure that I can get a good price for this tray and the sweetmeats both. And perhaps my wife will begin speaking to me again if I give her some of the money, though I really cannot understand what she is so upset about, it was just a small cut, and besides, it was not something that hurt *me* in the slightest . . .

Avast thar, and shiver me timbers, if it ain't a bumboat of the foreign extraction a-clawin' its way out across the catspaw and a-fixin' to make fast to us! Why, I'll bet my bullybeef she's come to trade, and caul or no caul I'll be jiggered if I don't get off this ship and put my yardarm into some fine little sling ashore, and no bucko of this man's navy is going to keep me from cutting my painter and unlatching my pawl and springing out of this joggle that's been keeping me bottled for a long trick indeed!

Aye, mate! I'll be blown a'fore His Nobs knows it! Why, here's a bugger with a plate in his hand and a fine piece of duff a-sittin' on it climbing over the gunnel with a face like a league of puddening and an eye that'd lose us the wind in a whistle, and if it warn't for His Nobs bein' ashore, we'd be keelhauled by now, but since His Nobs is, we won't, and sure but we can sail right afore the wind can't we? No closehaulin' for this man, ain't that right? And aye, that's a fine piece of duff he's runnin' up the yards, expectin' to see 'em all salute, and I'll tell you, I'd do some serious donkey riding with that wadding in my cake-hole, you bet your wheels, no matter how many!

Ah, but now we're athwart his hawse, and he's going to be raked. And sure enough, his duff is hauled down and he's ducked, ducked, ducked, and in a minute they'll mate him with a gunner's bride and turn his innards into a fine pendant! But I'll just grapple this plate and this duff alongside and bring 'em aboard, and then I'll take this bumboat myself, and she'll sail under no colors but my own, and I'll find a fine little deadeye to fit my sheet in tonight!

Excerpted from "The Memoirs of Shaka Shik: Constable of the King"

That afternoon, I was proceeding in a southwesterly direction along the Byway of Magisterial Indifference when I observed a suspicious-looking individual of about man-size loitering in the vicinity of a large excavation in the ground that had taken the place formerly occupied by the Promenade of the Justified Wealth of Merchants. The individual in question was garbed in a manner which, upon consideration, I found strange and foreign, and when I approached in order to ascertain whether he had legitimate reasons for being where he was, I observed that he was in the process of utilizing and employing a certain silver tray that was itself encumbered with a number of what I deduced were pastries in order to obtain certain favors from a female citizen of the city.

I attempted to obtain informationary knowledge from him, but as he expressed himself only in an unknown tongue, I was left with no alternative but to believe that his conduct and designs were unlawful. Attempting to place him under arrest, I was struck in a hostile manner several times by said individual, but in the end I managed to subdue him by means of my truncheon and the approved constabulatory measures.

The woman involved made use of the resultant confusion in order to depart from the scene, and the silver tray disappeared, possibly appropriated by an individual who thereafter concealed himself in the crowd of citizens attracted by the disturbance. When, in accordance with correct procedures, the suspicious looking individual was taken before the magistrate, Nash Shar, he could make no case for himself beyond some kind of shouting, and so the magistrate in question, unable to ascertain what his business was, sentenced him to the customary punishment, of which it would not do to speak.

(In the space below, the reader is invited to exercise his or her own fancy to link the previous whereabouts of the tray of sweetmeats with the subsequent episode. If more room is needed, separate sheets of paper may be attached to this page. Incidentally, the speed of light, c, is approximately 186,000 miles/second in a vacuum. This should not be forgotten, nor should the various relativistic effects that arise from extended periods of travel at velocities approaching c be ignored.)

. . . forcibly ejected from the airlock, and, catching the barest edge of the anti-gravity beam, descended rapidly, though without mishap, through the quantatran, arriving back on the streets of Nuhr at about the same time that Shandar, a merchant, was just passing by. Now, to be honest, Shandar had done something smack now and again in his life, but if he knew anything, he knew about loyalty to friends (though, to be honest, he had occasionally done something smack to one of his friends, too), and it occurred to him that perhaps he not only could share his find and his fortune with his old friend Baroz, who, as he had heard, had returned to the city after a long absence, but could also, perhaps, make a fair profit from selling the tray to him once its contents had been consumed.

It is time to contact my father. Jean Jacques, you were so right about fathers and sons, and about the natural bonds that link a man with a man, bonds which supersede even the affections of a man for a woman.

His false beard itched. He was not sure why he had thought that Baroz the Rug Merchant would be able to find out anything more about anything—Valdemar, pumps, water, the Americans, or the Library—than Potatoes the Thief, but he had decided to try; and, surveying the marketplace with an aged but virile eye (and noting as he did that many of those in the marketplace now and again looked up toward the surrounding rooftops as though in the hope that they might espy either a dashing figure garbed in azure or the glint of a descending gold coin (preferably the latter)), he pondered the links that he had established between the Gharat and the Americans (disturbing), between the Gharat and pumps and water (vague), and between the Americans and the Three Kingdoms (suspicious).

There must be something in the Library. They put everything else in there. Even father, I am sure, does not know. All priestly secrets. Abnel would not tell. No. I will have to enter the Library. Take Beshur with me and, if caught, say that I was apprehending him? (Unworthy plan. No. Will not do that.) Have to take him with me, though, to keep him away from Sari. There is no telling what might happen if I left him alone. No, I could tell. He would theorize about it constantly and do nothing. Fool.

I must speak with father as soon as possible, and therefore—

But here is Shandar . . . bearing a silver tray that can only have come from the palace!

"You old scrofulous monkey!" shouted Baroz, reaching out to embrace Shandar in an affectionate hug that, administered to another man, would have broken several ribs. "How are you?"

"You miserable excuse for a decayed mackerel," bellowed Shandar, returning the embrace. "I am as fine as Panas was the day he chiseled the cities of Kaprisha out of the stone of the Sacred Quarries themselves!"

This outburst on the part of Shandar was deemed by the religious police (who were admittedly having a slow day) to be sufficiently close to blasphemy. (Panasian law was very clear about things like that.) Baroz the Rug Merchant was therefore left not only with no need to think up any further insults, but also with a silver platter heaped with glistening sweetmeats that had obviously come from the palace of Inwa Kabir.

"Mrrk?"

Chapter Twenty

The woman sitting on the stool wheezed out her words like an old bellows. "There was a doctor I saw some years ago," she said, "he told me to use elixir of diamond. And I did. And it seemed to help for a time but then it did not help anymore. And so he prescribed carnelian, but I did not trust the carnelian at all and so I did not take it. Then my husband moved, and there was a doctor in that city, and he said that I had the 'airs,' and so he prescribed something (I cannot recall what it was now.) for the 'airs,' and that really did not help. I do not have much hope anymore but . . ."

She was not the only one without much hope. A sense of futility had been creeping up on Sari ever since she had arrived in Nuhr. No, that was not quite right. Since she had reached Katha. Well . . . no, that was not right, either. Since she had left her village? Perhaps that was it. First Ayesha and Rhydi . . . or was that Zarifah and Golfah? Maybe. It was hard to say exactly when it had started. In Halim, she had still believed in . . . something. But, somewhere after Halim, that belief had gone away, and here in Nuhr, it had pretty much unequivocally stated that it had no intention of returning. Naianism? What Naianism? For that matter . . . what Naia?

The woman—who had been continuing her tale of

other doctors, other remedies, other cities, broke off suddenly and began to pant, sucking in large gulps of air and expelling them in small, gale-force gasps. Her eyes grew large and began to protrude.

"Is something wrong?" said Sari, seriously alarmed. "Can I get you—?"

The woman stopped gasping. "No. These are my breath exercises. Another doctor prescribed them for me. I do them every day at this time, though I cannot say that they have ever really helped me. As I said, I have very little hope, but I heard that you had opened up an herb practice, and so I am willing to inquire about some of the more primitive methods."

And, once more, she broke off and began gasping and sucking again, blasting small storms across the room.

"I really think that I should get you something," said Sari. "Do you need water?"

"Oh, no. As I said, these are just my breath exercises." And thereupon the woman began snorting rapidly, closing off each of her nostrils in turn. "The doctor who told me to do this was very skilled," she managed between blasts, "though I had no faith in his chalcedony preparations. Still, I do his breath exercises faithfully . . ."

Seeing clients, counseling, prescribing herbal concoctions that everyone should have known and used as a matter of course (but did not): Sari earned a little money this way, contributed to the rent on the small room that she and Beshur and Potatoes (And where *was* Potatoes?) had taken above a fish shop in the Naian Quarter, attempted to make it evident to everyone, including herself, that she was an independent woman who was on a mission from Naia (instead of—as was obvious from the knowing winks of the owner of the fish shop and everyone else with whom she came into contact—the young love-toy of two men who doubtless had some arcane method of establishing whose turn it was going to be on any given night), and grew increasingly depressed. What did prescribing herbs for people who had turned sickness into something bordering on a vocation do for the Caves of Naia? For that matter, what did it do for anyone?

". . . though I cannot say that they have ever really helped me."

Perhaps, Sari thought, she gave her clients something to talk about when they visited their next practitioner: *Oh, yes, and then I saw this Naian girl—a love-toy of two men, you know—who fed me weeds three times a day. I still take them when I can find them, though I cannot say that they have ever really helped me.*

And yet there had to be some point to it all. Naia had transformed her, and since Naia was certainly not offering any further advice as to her actions, Sari could only suppose that Naia, in some way, approved of them.

To be sure, it was a little hard to tell. She had, after all, never actually *met* Naia. She had only seen the incontrovertible results of what had obviously been some kind of meeting. And since Naia was willing to change an old body for a new in order to prove Her point (whatever it was), then She was also perfectly capable of making known Her other wishes, too.

But despondency was growing on Sari, and, little by little, as she came to realize that her visits to Naian households and Naian shops and her discussions with weighty members of the Naian community were accomplishing nothing, she had begun to withdraw. Now her visits were less frequent, her plans less convincing . . . even to her own ears.

Naia wanted the Caves cleared. But . . . but . . . did Naia *really* want the Caves cleared? For whom would She want them cleared? Was, perhaps, the idea of

clearing the Caves not Naia's at all, but rather just one
more delusion in the mind of Sari—formerly old, now
young—who had run away from the house of her dead
husband without even mourning him and had transformed her desperate flight into (or perhaps justified it
by) a search for purpose, meaning, and the remnants of
a lost, childhood faith?

The woman closed both nostrils and held her breath
until Sari was sure that someone—perhaps the woman,
perhaps herself—was going to faint.

Another blast. "I do them, but I have no real faith in
them."

"Yes," said Sari weakly, "just so." And she wondered then whether Naia had made her young because
she, having blasphemed so virulently, was supposed to
devote the rest of her life to clearing the Caves ...
alone.

"Will you be coming to the festival?"

"Festival?"

"Why, what kind of a Naian are you that you do not
remember the festivals?"

Half-despondent, half-frightened that some particle
of the old ways had escaped her (Should she have been
keeping *festivals* all this time?), Sari searched frantically through her memories.

"It is the dry season festival that we always have,"
said the woman after a particularly tremendous snort
that left Sari breathless. "We sing and dance all day
long, and then, when it grows dark, we exchange
gifts."

"Gifts?" said Sari, feeling a sudden upwelling of
hope. "Oh, what a lovely custom!"

"And I never feel more like a woman than when I
am exchanging gifts."

"You ... ?"

"With a man."

Sari felt a chill. "Ah ..."

"It is the most meaningful duty of a woman: to exchange gifts." And another snort swept through the small room.

"Yes," said Sari, with a fresh gust of cold that had nothing to do with the snort. "I had entirely forgotten."

"Well, I am sure that you would find many young men with whom to exchange gifts at the festival," said the woman. "And you would feel very much like a woman by doing it, too, though I am sure that you already feel very much like a woman every night. Even several times a day."

"Oh. Oh, yes. That." But Sari's reply was absent, half hearted, for she was looking out the window. Just over the rooftops of the Quarter, she could see the high peaks of the Mountains of Ern. She had, in effect, been born there. She would return there. She knew now that she would return.

Potatoes. Where is Potatoes? I need him to get into the Library. Could get in myself, but easier this way. Will keep him away from Sari, too, and then ... maybe say that I apprehended him in the Library? Bad idea. Would probably not believe me. Impale us both, or worse. Why no men impaled? Do something else with them. (Here, walk like this.) NO! Inelucta—grr! NO! Potatoes ...

"What are you doing here?" said the priestly guard.

Beshur thought that his truncheon looked a little excessively large, even though truncheons were *supposed* to be large.

—I ... ah ... that is ...

He backed away from the gate of the Library.

—I was just ... ah ... passing by, he said.

"Well, continue to pass by, then, and the blessing of Panas (blessed be He!) upon you, though it does not look like you would know a blessing of Panas (blessed be He!) if it fell on your head."

—Thank you, thank you, Beshur said, moving away.
Bless you.

"Go on."

—Yes, yes, Beshur said. Bless you.

Here it is afternoon, and here is the palace, and here
is Aeid showing up in the king's chambers (after en-
during "the soldiers of the All Highest" who sincerely
"wish the Prince of the Three Kingdoms a long life
and a happy one" along with the rest of the subsequent
compliments, interchanges, and other interminable aspects of royal protocol). No: explanations are not going to be forthcoming, not to Fakik (who was, a few
minutes ago, very surprised to find the Crown Prince
himself entering the kitchen with a tray of sweetmeats
in his hand), not even to Inwa Kabir, even though it is
to his father that Aeid has come. And moreover, without any prelude, the prince, ignoring the counselors
and the servants and all the rest of those who are as-
sembled here in the king's chambers (including two or
three of the traditional barefoot boys with powdered
faces whom Inwa Kabir keeps about for the sake of
tradition), launches directly into an overview of his
concerns regarding the Gharat Abnel, the Americans,
and . . .

But here Aeid's plan breaks down. Or, rather, it
broke down some time earlier, but so occupied was
Aeid with the Library (and with a few other things . . .
such as an attractive young Naian woman by the name
of Sari) that he did not realize it. No matter: he is realizing it now. For one thing, he has nothing concrete
to present with regards to the Gharat save a few words
that were shouted in the throes of delirium and a curious taste in traveling companions. For another, coming
to his father with even a faint accusation regarding the
Gharat is a serious thing indeed, particularly when (1)
he has only the abovementioned shouted words and

taste in traveling companions as evidence, and (2) he himself is under something of a pall of suspicion, given not only his sudden, lengthy, and unexplained absence, but also any number of other princely irregularities . . . such as (he suddenly realizes) his complete lack of a beard.

And so, halfway through his presentation, Aeid notices that only Bakbuk is listening with anything resembling interest (and from the expression on Bakbuk's face, the sworder would be interested if Aeid did nothing more than read from the accounts for the royal stables, though it is a peculiar sort of interest indeed that can seemingly waver between the rapt fascination of a woman and the intent fascination of a would-be murderer).

Fortunately, at this point, Fakik brings in a tray of sweetmeats. Everyone, including Aeid, is relieved at the interruption, though when Inwa Kabir takes this as an opportunity to order that the room be cleared of all save himself and his son, Kuz Aswani appears to be noticeably upset, and Fakik looks close to tears. But the king's word is the king's word, and the counselors and servants and assistants and barefoot boys with powdered faces and even trusty Bakbuk (the latter with a longing look over his shoulder that Aeid prefers to leave unthought about) file out of the room, accompanied by compliments, interchanges and other assorted and interminable aspects of royal protocol.

"Kuz Aswani?"

The acting chief minister has been lingering beside the tray of sweetmeats, and he looks imploringly at the king, who, if he had it thought about, would be presented with the conclusion that the counselor longs for one of the pastries. But since Inwa Kabir is, at present, fresh out of individuals by whom to have matters thought about, and since Kuz Aswani, who is, for the present, supposed to be taking care of the thinking-about, is otherwise occupied ... apparently by the sweetmeats (Are those *raisins*?), the King only points at the door, and the chief minister follows his fellows out, accompanied by compliments, interchanges, and other assorted and interminable aspects of royal protocol.

Was that a hiss?

No matter. Inwa Kabir is alone with Aeid, and Aeid perceives very clearly that, despite what Jean Jacques might have said about the natural bonds of paternal and filial affections, there are potential outcomes to this interview that are not at all pleasant. His father is still, after all, the king, and he himself is still, after all, the prince.

He finds himself looking at the tray of sweetmeats, finds himself wondering whether Fakik had the foresight to prepare another batch, or if these are the same sweetmeats that Shandar (There is no telling what has happened to Shandar now, and it would not do to speak of it in any case, but how did *Shandar* of all people get his hands on them?) brought to the stall of Baroz the Rug Merchant.

No time for that. His father is already talking.

"My son ..."

Not bad for a start—

"... I am aware of certain books that you have in your possession ..."

—but going rapidly downhill—

"... and should like you to explain why you possess them."

—indeed, bottoming out.

Aeid finds (with annoyance) that he is looking at the (Are those *raisins*?) sweetmeats again.

"Ah, Father ..."

Not bad for a start—

"... it seemed to me that it was wise for one who would someday ascend the throne ..."

—but going rapidly downhill—

". . . but who does not necessarily *want* to ascend the throne . . . ah . . . of course . . . ah . . ."

—indeed, bottoming out.

Inwa Kabir does not look convinced. Well, that is to be expected, for Aeid admits that he has not said anything that would convince anyone . . . save perhaps Beshur, who seems to have a knack for convincing *himself* of just about anything. (And if that flea-infested, arrogant excuse for a pseudo-scholar so much as *looks* at Sari with anything but the purest, most brotherly thoughts in his head, Aeid fully intends to . . . to . . .)

". . . unless it is absolutely necessary, that is . . ." he continues, noticing that his father has picked up one of the sweetmeats and is examining it with some curiosity. Indeed, it looks like a very fine sweetmeat. One of Fakik's best, to be sure. Perhaps it might even win back some of the kingly favor the chef lost as a result of the unfortunate incident with the raisin compote.

Aeid plunges on. ". . . to . . . ah . . . to have some knowledge of the outside world, particularly since the outside world appears to be . . . ah . . . coming to us these days."

"The outside world?"

"Yes."

"What outside world?"

"Why . . . ah . . . the . . . outside world. The Americans."

"What Americans?"

Obviously, Inwa Kabir is having the matter of the Americans thought about by someone else. But by whom?

Abnel? By Panas!

"There are . . . ah . . . movements that are sweeping the world."

"Movements?" Inwa Kabir touches a forefinger to

the glistening surface of the sweetmeat, brings it to his lips.

"Movements," Aeid insists. "Movements that are written of in those books. The dignity of man. The ability of individuals to govern themselves . . ."

In the distance, he hears a commotion. Screaming. Draft animals. Fish. It is obviously coming from the marketplace. Has someone dropped a coin?

". . . ah . . . wisely."

Inwa Kabir nibbles experimentally at the edge of the sweetmeat. "And what does this have to do with the Americans?"

Aeid is distracted, worried. "What Americans?"

And then, not having anyone else available to think about the matter of the sweetmeat, Inwa Kabir tries a small bite.

Aeid collects his wits. "Oh, *those* Americans. Why, they represent the world. That has come to us, I mean."

"I should have had their ships burned and their men sold into slavery."

"Father, *no!*"

Inwa Kabir sets the rest of the sweetmeat aside. He is not used to hearing any kind of a negative from anyone, and, in addition, Aeid realizes that he has now put himself in the position of defending the Americans . . . in whom he has no confidence whatsoever.

"I mean . . . I mean . . . I mean . . ."

"What do you know of the Freedom Fighters of Khyr?" Inwa Kabir's voice is very grave. Aeid has heard his father speak this way before, and the tone has invariably preceded something unpleasant . . . usually of the sort that it would not do to speak of.

"I . . . ah . . . well, I know *of* them."

"Hmmm . . . I will have that thought about."

Inwa Kabir is agitated. He picks up another sweetmeat and seems on the verge of taking a bite, but he puts it aside and goes to the window.

"Why did you flee the city?"

This puts the situation in an entirely different light, and Aeid flounders. Flee? Flee from what? What and how much does his father really know?

"I was . . ." Jean Jacques was very clear about such things as truth, and how the truth would never hurt anyone save the oppressor, and yet Aeid is quickly coming to the conclusion that Jean Jacques would not last ten minutes in the court at Nuhr. "I was pursuing . . ."

Pursuing? A bad choice of words. Very bad.

"Ah . . . seeking to accompany . . ."

Quickly now . . . accompany who? The Gharat, or the Americans? (What Americans?)

But Aeid is saved from any further racking of his brains, for just then his father suddenly straightens as though he has been struck by a thought. "Urk!"

"Father?"

"Urk!"

And Inwa Kabir, King of Kaprisha and of the Three Kingdoms, suddenly stiffens and topples straight into the arms of his son. Aeid, about to call instinctively for help, hesitates, for he recognizes the effects of poison when he sees them, and two questions have immediately arisen in his mind as a result. Who? And how?

Who: Who did it? Who would profit by it? Who had access to the sweetmeats? (Oh, by Panas! He *himself* was seen bringing the sweetmeats into the palace!) Who would want the king dead? Who would actually *do* something in order to kill him?

How: How to help his father? How to escape the inevitable accusation (particularly since—Oh, by Panas!—he *himself* was seen bringing the sweetmeats into the palace!)? How to keep Abnel (Abnel!) from seizing control while Inwa Kabir is incapacitated and the Crown Prince is under suspicion of attempted parenticide?

Aeid acts quickly. After lowering his barely breathing father to the ground, he picks up a sweetmeat, tears it in half, and carefully rubs a few crumbs onto his lips. One half he drops on the floor, the other he flings out the window ... where it is immediately caught by a very unfortunate pigeon, which promptly (with an avian equivalent of *Urk!*) folds its wings and plummets to the ground, dead.

Aeid follows its example, but his *Urk!* is of a more human and intelligible variety, the ground is much closer, and he, like his father, is not dead.

He does manage to fit a *"Help! Guards! Treachery!"* in there, too.

Chapter Twenty-one

"Captain Scruffy," said Jenkins, "please be so kind as to call Mr. Turtletrout into the cabin."

Jenkins was as stiff and as straight—and as noncommittal—as ever. Several weeks among the savages of the Three Kingdoms had not changed that in the slightest. Gray wool, gray hat, gray shoes. And now he wanted Turtletrout. For a moment, Scruffy considered all the reasons that Jenkins would want a third individual in the tiny cabin—particularly when that individual was, specifically, Turtletrout—but if he blanched inwardly at two or three of the reasons (and the disastrous possibilities inherent in them) he gave no outward sign. No. Time enough for the future when it arrived.

Scruffy sidled around the table upon which rested the steam engine and a partially reconstructed Leyden jar, and despite his more pressing concerns, he could not help but wonder again what had happened to Umi Botzu. Such a promising student! But then, the heathens of these lands appeared to make a virtue out of obsessions, and, doubtless, Umi Botzu was pursuing some other mania at present.

Annoying. Very annoying. Very much against the grain of a scientist; but Scruffy, still outwardly calm, went to the door and opened it. "Pass the word for Mr. Turtletrout."

"Yes, sir," came the reply. "Passing the word for Mr. Turtletrout."

In a few minutes, feet clumped down the short companionway that led to the cabin door. Turtletrout knocked and entered without waiting for an acknowledgment, and, in his dull, slope-headed way, stared at Jenkins for almost a quarter of a minute before he realized that his presence in the cabin was official, rather than recreational. Slowly, almost absently, he refastened the loose buttons of his coat.

Scruffy swallowed. Matters had become a bit lax on board *Seaflower*. It was hard to avoid it. The heat, the isolation, the inevitable resentment that welled up in the men as the result of land that was within sight and yet forbidden them: all these could not but fray tempers and loosen the morale and readiness of a crew. So far, only one deserter, though. That was good. But if the situation continued ...

"Mr. Turtletrout," said Jenkins, "you are here as a witness."

Turtletrout had finished fastening his coat, and now (to Scruffy's mild mortification) he slid his hands into his pockets and leaned toward Jenkins with his usual dim expression of bewilderment. "Of course, sir," he said.

"Witness, Mr. Ambassador?" said Scruffy, trying to keep his mind off of what he wanted to keep his mind off of but was not keeping it off. Of.

Jenkins cleared his throat. "Mr. Turtletrout is here as a witness to the instructions which you are about to receive, Captain Scruffy. In accordance with your sealed orders, which you opened in my presence shortly after we arrived in the harbor of Nuhr, I am the authority on board this ship, and you answer to me."

Turtletrout was nodding slowly, albeit without much

of an air of comprehension. Well, thought Scruffy, that was understandable.

"Yes, sir," said Scruffy. Though relieved of his fears, he still understood what was going on no better than Turtletrout. Well, at least it appeared that it had nothing to do with ... ah ... chess.

Jenkins reached into an inner pocket of his coat and extracted a sheaf of folded papers. He handed them to Scruffy. "Read," he said. "If you have any questions, ask."

Scruffy opened the papers, examined the first paragraphs. "Home!" he exclaimed involuntarily.

"Home?" said Turtletrout.

"Home," said Jenkins. "And you are to deliver the attached report—the attached *sealed* report—to President Winthrop, as per your enclosed instructions."

There was more going on, Scruffy knew, than Jenkins was telling. This was, to be sure, not unusual in the military, but something about the situation bothered him. *How* many soldiers? *That* many?

"Questions, Captain?" said Jenkins, and there was suddenly a certain dangerous impatience peeking through his noncommittal mask.

"None, Mr. Ambassador," Scruffy said quickly.

He suddenly noticed that Turtletrout's shirt was partly untucked, and that the rebuttoned coat did nothing to disguise it.

Jenkins was nodding. He appeared to be satisfied. "I am appointing you, subject to President Winthrop's confirmation, to the overall command of the operation."

But, then again, perhaps Jenkins only *appeared* to appear to be satisfied. And perhaps . . .

Scruffy caught himself. "Yes, sir."

"When you return with the men and equipment, you will answer to the local authorities."

"To . . . to the local authorities?" said Scruffy, trying

to keep his eyes off Turtletrout's shirt. Yes, that part of the orders had indeed puzzled him. But then again, maybe it was only supposed to *appear* to puzzle him . . .

Jenkins gave no sign that Scruffy's question was anything more or less than what he had expected. "Yes," he said. "I assume that you have no quarrel with your orders, Captain Scruffy?"

The barb in Jenkins' words was unmistakable, and it brought Scruffy back to his senses. "No, sir," he said. "No question at all."

"Excellent." Jenkins looked him up and down. "As I expected."

There was a curious sort of backhanded praise in his words that was utterly lost on the bluff Scruffy.

"Mr. Turtletrout," said the ambassador, "you have seen me give Captain Scruffy his orders?"

"Yes, sir."

"And you have heard my verbal confirmation of his orders?"

"Yes, sir."

And *still* with his hands in his pockets. And that shirt . . . This enforced confinement in a foreign port had turned discipline into warm milk. Oh, well, Scruffy considered, at least Turtletrout had managed to get his coat buttoned.

"Very well," said Jenkins. "I will expect you back here with men and equipment as soon as the President and the Synod deem it possible."

It took a moment for Scruffy to comprehend the meaning of the ambassador's words. "You're not coming with us, sir?"

"That is correct. I am needed here."

Scruffy stared.

"You should probably know that the king has been taken ill. So has his son."

"The prince? Prince Aeid?" Scruffy had never met

the king, had not, in fact, even seen him. But the prince had been pointed out to him once or twice during his first weeks in Nuhr, and, even from a distance, Scruffy had taken an immediate liking to the man. Possibly it was because the Crown Prince was an exceedingly well-put-together young fellow, but more likely it was something more general, something indefinable, something Scruffy generally referred to as *dash*. "Saw him once. Fine-looking lad."

Jenkins looked at him carefully. "Well, he's not so fine-looking now," he said after a pause that gave the captain a chill. "In order to preserve the security of the Three Kingdoms, the Gharat has taken charge. Temporarily. He has asked me to stay on as an advisor. I was honored to avail myself of an opportunity to bring our countries closer together."

Scruffy looked again at the papers in his hands. "But . . . all these men . . . ?"

"Follow your orders, Captain," said Jenkins. "Just follow your orders."

"But the local authorities . . ."

Jenkins was still looking at him carefully, knowingly; and Scruffy suddenly wondered how much Jenkins knew . . . and about what.

"There is no telling who will be in charge when you return," said the ambassador. "The king and his son are not expected to live."

Turtletrout suddenly appeared to became acutely conscious of his untucked shirt, and Scruffy, for a brief, panicked instant, thought that he was going to undo both his coat and his trousers and attend to the matter right then and there. But Turtletrout only nodded in his slope-headed way and rechecked the buttons he had fastened a few minutes before.

"A terrible shame," said the ambassador, with just the right amount of noncommittal, diplomatic regret in his voice. "We will have to leave our options open."

* * *

Hunna-hunna-hunna-HIN!
DUM-dum-DUM-dum-DUM-DUM-dum!
Hunna-hunna-hunna-HIN!
DUM-dum-DUM-dum-DUM-DUM-dum!
Hunna-hunna-hunna-HIN!
DUM-dum-DUM-dum-DUM-DUM-dum!

It was the night of the festival, and, having settled the pressing questions of whether public nudity constituted a legitimate expression of religious devotion, whether the possession of illegal substances that varied from (proscribed) drugs to (proscribed) magical charms was required for the proper expression of religious devotion, and whether flagrant trespass and breaking of the general curfew in the Panasian parts of the city were inevitable byproducts of proper religious devotion (not to mention other concerns that had to do with everything from mistreatment of dogs to coerced infidelity and forcible rape), the Naian community of Nuhr had abandoned itself to its carefree celebration of sacred mystery.

Hunna-hunna-hunna-HIN!
DUM-dum-DUM-dum-DUM-DUM-dum!

And Sari was hiding in the room above the fish shop.

Overheard:

(1) "Well, I do not think that you have any right to attack me for this. You are obviously attempting to take away my personal power and substitute your clumsy authority for my freedom. You are obviously very lacking in any kind of faith or sacred experience, or you would understand that I mean only the best for you."

(2) "So it was *you* who put that jar of mummy ash outside my doorstep! Do not lie to me! I *know*. Someone came and took away the jar, and someone else must have spilled water on it so that it appeared to be

dog turds, but I *know*. It was you! You have been attempting to bring misfortune upon me! Admit it!"

(3) "You certainly do not know anything about relationships! My partners and I have had a relationship for the better part of a week now, and we have always trusted one another with the understanding that all of us were free to choose other mates during that period of time. We are mature, responsible adults. And yet you meddled with what we had, and intruded into our relationship, and all because you lusted after one of my partners! How dare you!"

(4) Assorted animal noises.

(5) *Hunna-hunna-hunna-HIN!*

(6) *DUM-dum-DUM-dum-DUM-DUM-dum!*

(7) *Click.*

Click?

In the darkness of the room, Sari, exhausted from a long day of attempting to heal where healing was not desired, and trying, despite the noise, the confusion, and the occasional scream, to sleep . . .

. . . sat up. She was alone, for Beshur, with declarations as to the necessity of "examination" and "research", and reiterations of his responsibilities as a scholar, had left several hours before to mingle with the celebrants outside and pursue "examination" and "research" and other work pertinent to and understandable only by one who willingly shouldered the weighty responsibilities of a "scholar".

And there it was again. The noise outside was terrific, but the sound, close as it was, was clear. The window? The door? Sari could not tell. Groggy with fatigue, she put her hands to her face and listened, but then someone screamed outside, and she was on her feet in an instant. Was that laughter? Whose?

"Potatoes?" she said, but her voice was soft—too soft to carry over the oppressive noise.

The click came again. It was definitely the door, and

for a moment, Sari thought that what she was hearing was indeed Potatoes returning after his mysterious and comparatively lengthy absence. But there was something furtive about the sound that was decidedly uncharacteristic of Potatoes, who was always (or at least, always *seemed* to be) direct, to the point, and reasonably open and honest—though Sari had come to realize that such things tended to be somewhat relative where most people were concerned.

Wrapping a sheet about herself, Sari stepped through the darkness and approached the door. What looked like torchlight was flickering through the crack along the threshold, and someone was fumbling clumsily at the fastening.

"Ah . . ." She hesitated.

(8) "I told you, she is someone that you will very much want to exchange gifts with, and I am sure she will want to exchange gifts with you, too, once you . . ."

The sound of explosive snorting came from the far side of the door.

(8 cont'd.) "I am sorry. It is time for my breath exercises. I must do them at this time every day, though I cannot say that they have ever really helped me. In any case, she will surely want to exchange gifts with you, because you are someone with whom women simply want to exchange gifts, and our relationship is a sacred one, and is able to encompass this sort of gift giving."

(9) [See 4.]

(10) [See 7.]

The door began to swing inward. It *was* torchlight outside. Torchlight and . . . several figures.

"No!" said Sari, and, throwing her shoulder against the door, she managed to push it closed again. Unfortunately, the latch was nothing to speak of, and there were several people outside, any one of whom was perfectly capable of forcing an entrance.

She leaned weakly against the door, her back to the wood. "Oh ... Naia ..."

(11) [See 6.]

(12) "How wonderful! She is reenacting the tale of Naia's flagellation! The part where the Goddess learns love by being beaten by a man ..."

More explosive snorting.

(12 cont'd.) "... after which She serves him, because She thereby discovers Her proper place in the universe."

Sari's eyes widened, and she whirled on the door and screamed at it: "I will not submit!"

(13) [See 4.]

(14) [See 5.]

Oppression, threat. For a moment, she thought that perhaps it would be easier for her to give in, to give them what they wanted. They would leave her alone, then, and after that, she could return to the Caves and ... well ...

(15) "You see? I told you that she was reenacting it! Ah, so knowledgeable for one so young. Who would have thought it? And the next thing she will say is—"

"Go away!" Sari shouted, her voice almost lost in the drumming, the chanting, the screams, the animal noises.

(15 cont'd.) "—*Go away!* See? I told you!"

And now the door began to press inward. Desperate now, she looked about for something heavy to drag in front of it, or, that failing, for an escape. But there was nothing large enough to provide any sort of impediment to the opening door; and as for escape, though there was a window, the cacophonous revelry outside deterred her from using it as much as did the twenty-foot drop down to the street.

"Oh, Naia! It is happening! It is all really lost!"

The door pressed inward a little more, and at last was heaved open. Arms flailing, sheet flying loose, Sari was propelled across the room. By the time she came up against the far wall, the door was fully open, and torchlight was spilling in.

(16) [See 6.]

Sari, naked now but unaware of it, was already looking for something large and heavy.

(17) "And as you can see, she is all ready for her part in the rite! And in another moment she will scream—"

Rite? Sari wondered. But she had found a stool, and it immediately hurtled in the direction of the dark figures entering the room. "Stay away from me!"

(17 cont'd.) "—*Stay away from me!* She is very intelligent for one so young! Very well trained!"

(18) [See 4.]

The stool shattered against the wall. Sari looked for another.

Snorting and gasping.

(19) [See 6.]

(20) "A gift! A gift!"

Sari, giving up on stools (there were, in any case, no more to be had), turned to the window with the decision to take her chances with the drop down to the street (not to mention the current goings-on *in* the street). Before the intruders could cross the room and lay hold of her, then, she had jerked the lattice open, and was just reaching for a handhold by which to pull herself out when she realized that she was staring into a girlish face, a face she dimly recognized.

She screamed. Under the circumstances, this was perhaps understandable.

(21) "You see? First she makes as if to escape, and now she screams! All a part of the rite. Such an intelligent girl!"

"Good evening," said Bakbuk. "Or should I say, *May Naia bless you, sister?*"

And now even screams were no longer appropriate. Sari could only watch, wide eyed, as the slender Bakbuk swung into the room and dropped down noiselessly between her and the intruders.

There was a flurry of motion.

(22) [See 4.]

(23) Assorted screams.

(24) Loud thumping.

(25) A crash.

(26) A slithering sound.

(27) [See 5.]

(28) [See 6.]

The door closed, and the girlish figure reappeared in the spill of light from the window. Sari felt the sheet drape about her shoulders. "I have heard that Naians are casual about nudity," said Bakbuk with an irony so cold that Sari shivered, "but I am sure that there is, perhaps, such a thing as being too casual."

"Yes . . ." said Sari. "Yes. Thank you."

Bakbuk's eyes were a little too bright, but Sari finally made the association. Of course. Bakbuk. Baruch's traveling companion. The one that no one could ever tell . . .

But . . .

But what . . . ?

"I am here to bring you a message," said Bakbuk as though reading her mind.

"A message?" Sari felt numb, weak. She clutched at the sheet.

"A command, rather. From the Crown Prince of the Three Kingdoms."

"The . . . the Crown Prince?"

(29) [See 4.]

"Yes. The . . . Crown Prince."

Why the hesitation in Bakbuk's voice? Why the

catch? And why was the androgynous servant of a mysterious (and exceedingly spoiled) merchant bringing a message from, of all people, the Crown Prince to, of all people, a Naian woman?

"You must come immediately to the palace," said Bakbuk. "Prince Aeid and the king have been taken ill, and the prince has requested your aid."

"*My* aid?"

"Yours. Are you going to question the will of the prince?"

"No. I mean ... yes. I mean ..."

What *did* Naia want?

Bakbuk's eyes were still too bright. "Doubtless you are confused from the attack. I am very glad that I was able to offer some ... support."

Sari nodded.

"But you must come to the palace. Tonight. You must wait upon the king and the prince. You are an herbalist of some skill, and the prince has no confidence in his physicians."

"I ... ah ... I mean ... but ... Beshur ..."

Bakbuk's eyes became even brighter. "You mean the apostate priest?"

Apostate priest?

"He will be attended to. But you must come. Now. Fear not: you are under King Inwa Kabir's protection."

(30) [See 5.]

"And mine, too."

Chapter Twenty-two

The figure is bright, blue, and, by now, well-known (to us, at least). What is less well-known (to us, at least) is the environment in which he has made his appearance, for instead of haunting the pinnacled and balustraded rooftops surrounding the market square or the pinnacled and balustraded rooftops of the great Temple of Panas, the Blue Avenger is, today, haunting the pinnacled and balustraded rooftops of the palace of King Inwa Kabir!

He is obviously quite familiar with the external layout of the building, for without any hesitation, he scampers, flits, and tiptoes with the assurance of a man who knows exactly where he is going. No hesitation, no bewildered glances from right to left, no hurried rushes to the edge of the roof so as to orient himself by means of some well-known landmark in the city (such as the Library . . . and do not worry: we will get to the Library soon enough). No. The Blue Avenger obviously knows very well where he is going. It is as if he has been on these roofs many times before. Which is very much the case, as is well-known (to us, at least).

Toward the western wing of the great, sprawling, ornamented building he goes, his blue garments bright against the agate and the jasper and the onyx and the marble that surround him. His step is quick, direct;

and only when he stumbles upon the realization that he is not alone up on these roofs does he acquire anything resembling the guilty stealth of a thief.

He crouches warily behind a secondary roof, for, ahead, a figure in white linen is making its uncertain way along a line of pinnacles. Peering more closely into the glare of the sunlight, and shading his eyes with a hand while attempting to keep from knocking his mask (Do not forget the mask!) askew, the Blue Avenger realizes that it is Haddar.

The former chief minister is all but slouching along. He moves slowly, casting a serious eye into all the crevices, cavities, and niches provided by the rooftop (and, to be sure, there are many). He looks between each upright of a balustrade, examines pinnacles from all sides, pokes his nose into gutters and drainpipes that have not carried anything more than dewdrops (and precious few even of *them*) for the last three centuries.

And then the Blue Avenger realizes with a start that Haddar is carrying a *net*.

"Come here. Here. Now. I command you. Come."

The Blue Avenger sticks his index fingers into his ears and wiggles them (his fingers, not his ears) in order to make sure that he is hearing properly.

"Now. I am the chief minister. You belong to me. Yes. Me. You will come. You are *mine*."

The wiggling (of his fingers, not his ears) having not changed in the slightest what he is hearing from Haddar, the Blue Avenger must, by necessity, accept that what he is hearing is accurate and true.

And then Haddar's manner turns furtive, sly, and his eyes are fixed most earnestly upon a patch of flat rooftop that is, as far as the Blue Avenger can tell, quite vacant. No matter: Haddar is creeping cautiously toward the empty space, net at the ready.

And then a sudden spring, and the net, with a loud *thwap*, claps down onto the vacant roof.

"Missed! No! Come back! You are mine!"

And Haddar is off among the pinnacles and balustrades at a run, net held high as though he is chasing butterflies.

A little shaken, the Blue Avenger stands up from behind the secondary roof. His way is clear now, and, though he wonders about Haddar and the net (and what the net is *for*), he returns to his journey across the rooftops, which, fortunately, takes him in a direction opposite to that of Haddar's pursuit.

Here is the edge of the roof, then, and here is a drop . . . and—Oh!—here is a rope. And, with a surety that would be truly amazing were it not for the fact that we have often seen him demonstrate it before, the Blue Avenger descends rapidly down the outside wall of the palace ($T=2\pi\sqrt{1/g}$) until he reaches a window that (from the inside, at least), looks out in the direction of the harbor of Nuhr. Were he to look in that same direction, he would notice that the American ships are gone. But he does not look in that direction. Instead, he concentrates on the window, or, rather, on what he hears coming out of it:

"Ugh, ugh, ugh, ugh . . . ! Aaaaaaaaack!"

"Some water for the king."

"Urrrrrrk!"

"No. Better: some wine for the king."

"Eeeeeeech!"

"Is that herbalist going to come?"

"Arrrrrrg!"

"She is being purified, chief minister."

"Eeky! Eeky! Eeky! Eeky!"

"Well, hurry up and purify her, and bring her here. The Crown Prince has ordered her to help."

"Oook!"

"And while you are bringing her, bring some . . . ah . . . raisins, too."

"Erk!"

"Raisins? For . . . for the king?"

"Aaaaaga!"

"Ah . . . no. For me. You see, I have had no breakfast."

"Wrg."

"By the way: how *is* the Crown Prince?"

"Ookook!"

"I would think that he is much the same as the king."

"Waaaark!"

"Same poison, same effects. Well, at least they are both alive. Go see to the prince. And hurry up with those raisins."

The Blue Avenger swarms back up the rope. Very quickly. His reasons for such haste, though, are well-known.

To us, at least.

There was a commotion in the market square of Nuhr. The tax gatherers were again setting up their tables.

"That is very true, but I have it on good authority that the prince was seen entering the palace with a tray of sweetmeats in his hand."

"I still like the idea of a conspiracy better."

"Simplicity! Simplicity! It is much easier to account for the prince's actions if we assume that he acted alone, for then all becomes clear. He caused the sweetmeats to be made, and then he poisoned them, and then he brought them into the palace."

"It would be sensible to ask the chef. *That* would make everything clear."

"But the chef is dead. Panasian law is very clear about

things like that. Which leaves only the prince, who poisoned the sweetmeats and then brought them into the palace."

"What if he poisoned them *after* he brought them into the palace?"

"That, too, is possible, but it is much more likely that he poisoned them *before* he brought them into the palace, as there would be a danger of his being observed, you see, if he poisoned them *after* he brought them into the palace."

"But if he poisoned them *before* he brought them into the palace, he still would have been seen *bringing* them into the palace. It is the same thing."

"It is not the same thing at all."

"Why, yes it is. And, in any case, the king is still alive. Now, the prince is intelligent ..."

"Oh, intelligent! To be sure! To allow himself to be seen bringing a tray of poisoned sweetmeats into the palace!"

"We have not determined whether the sweetmeats were poisoned or not at the time he brought them into the palace. They might have been perfectly innocuous sweetmeats, until they were poisoned ... by someone else, for example."

"Someone else! Who else would poison them?"

"Well, the chef."

"Your conspiracies again! In any case, the chef is dead, and it makes much more sense for the prince to have poisoned them."

"In any case, the prince would have made sure that the king died from the poison, would he not?"

"But if he allowed himself to be seen—!"

"But the king is alive. And, besides, the prince is ill from the poison himself!"

"Well, he might have consumed just enough of the poison to make himself ill, so as to divert suspicion from himself."

"A fairly intelligent action for someone who, as you have said, was foolish enough to be seen bringing a tray of poisoned sweetmeats into the palace in the first place!"

"So you admit that they were poisoned *before* he brought them in!"

"I admit nothing of the sort."

"It is self-evident."

"Self-evident! The prince's illness is self-evident!"

"I tell you, he is alive by his own design!"

"Well, the king is also alive. Are you saying that he is alive by *his* own design? Is that self-evident?"

"What is self-evident is that the prince brought the sweetmeats into the palace himself."

"That is hearsay."

"That is *not* hearsay. That is *fact*."

"Just as it is fact that he poisoned the sweetmeats *before* he brought them into the palace?"

"Now you *admit* that he poisoned them."

"I admit nothing."

"Yes, you do!"

"No, I do not."

"Yes, you do!"

"No, I do not. What if the *king* poisoned them? And only ate enough to make himself ill?"

"Are you saying that the king—?"

(Here the discussion ended. Panasian law was very clear about things like that.)

"Ugh, ugh, ugh, ugh . . . ! Aaaaaaaaack!"

Sari felt as though she had entered a dream. From a wretched, smelly room above a fish shop in the Naian Quarter, she had been suddenly transported to a world of jasper and agate, of ivory floors and emerald windows. Guards were (well, besides being condescending) resplendent in their livery, counselors were (well, besides being condescending) glorious in their habiliments, and even the servants were (well, besides being condescending) arrayed in finery such as she had never thought to see in her life.

"Urrrrrrk!"

And she herself now partook of that dream, for after Bakbuk had brought her to the palace (somehow managing to guide her safely through streets packed with very spiritual Naians), she had been attended to by the female servants of the palace who (well, besides having been condescending) had bathed her, perfumed her, arranged her hair, and garbed her in polished cotton . . . somehow having managed to accomplish it all despite the fact that Sari had been willing neither to give up her Naian medallion nor cover her head and face. She had made herself very clear: if the prince wanted her, then the prince would have to take her as she was: a Naian and a woman. True, she did not know the prince, but she did know Naia (Indeed, her knowledge was a bit overly intimate for comfort.), and whether the Naians were Naians or were not Naians, she was a Naian, and therefore she would be a Naian.

"Eeeeeeech!"

Or something like that.

"Arrrrrrg!"

And, so, bareheaded and barefaced, she was brought to the king's chambers, and there, in the king's bed (which, surprisingly, was no more than a thin sort of pad on the floor), she found a grievously ill man who hardly knew where . . . or who . . . he was. Perhaps he did not even know that he was a man. He certainly did not appear to know that she wore no head cloth or face cloth.

"Eeky! Eeky! Eeky! Eeky!"

"As you can see," said the chief minister, Kuz Aswani, who was eating raisins from a bowl, "he is ill."

"Oook!"

"Poison," said Sari, for she had instantly recognized it as a more-pernicious variant of the drug that Charna had attempted to administer to her.

"Erk!"

"Well . . ." Kuz Aswani looked very uncomfortable, and, for a moment, appeared to be on the verge of attempting to scratch his head . . . with his foot. "Well . . . that is so, I fear. I thought that was well established."

"Aaaaaga!"

Sari examined the king, and, with a glance for permission from Kuz Aswani, felt his pulse, his forehead.

"Wrg."

"Can you do anything for him?"

"Ookook!"

It was a terrible poison. As little as another mouthful of whatever had contained it would have proved instantly fatal, and Sari knew that she might well be able to do no more than hold off death for a week or so. This she carefully explained to Kuz Aswani. "I believe I might be able to help a little," she finished. "I *might*. If you will give me permission to do my best, I will do it. But I can promise nothing. Now take me to the prince."

"Waaaark!"

"Immediately!" said Kuz Aswani.

"You do not understand. It is very clear from all historical experience that the hair of a woman, uncovered, emits strange and magical rays that overpower the senses of a man. It is obvious, is it not?"

"That might be so, but if you ask me . . ."

"I am not asking you."

". . . the danger lies more in her mere *presence* in the palace. It is unseemly and dangerous for men and women—particularly Naian women—to coexist in the same physical space . . ."

"And the next thing you will tell me is that the devil smiles at such things."

". . . for the devil smiles at such things. Magical rays from women's hair, indeed!"

"Tests have proven it. Would you dispute *tests*?"

"Tests! Oh, of course. Tests. To be sure."

"Well?"

"Their presence is worse. And a Naian at that!"

"What difference does it make whether she is a Naian or not?"

"Well . . ."

"Or . . . is it, perhaps, that her hair is uncovered?"

"Certainly not!"

"Oh, really now! Then it is her bronze medallion that you find so attractive?"

"Naians are . . . well, Naians. She goes about without a face cloth. In the house!"

"And without a head cloth. Do not forget that."

"And so you are saying that it is her hair. Magical rays? Pah!"

"Well, *you* were the one who brought up the matter of how she was dressed. And if her back is turned, then you cannot see her face. But you can see her hair!"

"You . . . prefer women with their backs turned?"

"You know very well what I mean!"

"I know that you go on about magical rays from women's hair."

"It is true! All true! There are tests to prove it! Only a single strand can destroy a man!"

"A single strand?"

"Tests prove it!"

"What about half a strand?

"Well . . ."

"A quarter perhaps?"

"I will not go on splitting hairs with you. What I have told you is the truth. Proven! By tests!"

"But your tests say nothing about the devil. How curious."

"The Sacred *Texts* say nothing about the devil!"

"Well, they say nothing about women's *hair,* either!"

"What do *you* know about the Sacred Texts?"

"I know a great *deal* about the Sacred Texts. I *memorized* them when I was a boy!"

"Well, *I* memorized them, too, and it is quite clear from the third verse of the fifth chapter that women's hair—"

(Here the discussion ended. Panasian law was very clear about things like that.)

And, once again, Naian men stood before the tables of the tax collectors, weighing lifelong poverty against religious conversion. And besides, it was not something that was going to hurt *them,* was it?

"Ugh, ugh, ugh, ugh . . . ! Aaaaaaaaack!"

"Your Highness," said Sari, bending over the bed, "if I could but see your face . . ."

"Urrrrrk!"

The prince thrashed away from her, still holding the sheet tightly over his features.

"Eeeeeeech!" he screeched hoarsely. "No! Never!"

"I will say," said Sari, running a hand beneath her long hair and tossing it back (as, behind her, guards flinched, Bakbuk smiled ironically, and even Kuz Aswani—who was occupied with his bowl of raisins— looked very uncomfortable) so as to keep it from falling into the cloth-shrouded face of the prince, "that your symptoms look to be very similar to those of your father."

"Arrrrrrg! Fine! Fine! I trust you! Just give me what you—Eeky! Eeky! Eeky! Eeky!—give him!"

Very curious. She felt his pulse (as much of it as she

could through the cloth wraps that the prince had pulled tight against himself).

"Erk!"

"Well," she said, "you are very fortunate, Your Highness."

"Aaaaaga! That is good to hear!"

"You are much better off than your father."

"Wrg. Good! Good!"

"You can save the prince, then?" said Kuz Aswani, who had paused with a raisin halfway to his lips.

"Ookook! Yes! Can you . . . save me?"

Sari could not but wonder who (other then Charna, of course) could possibly have the cruelty to administer such a drug to anyone. "I can promise nothing," she said. "I will do my best. That is all I can say."

"Waaaark! That is why I sent for you!"

Sari looked down at the cloth-shrouded face. Very odd, indeed. But if wrapping up made the prince feel better, then she would let him wrap up. There would be time enough for unwrapping later. "Thank you, Your Highness," she said. She tossed her hair back once more and sent two guards fleeing down the hall. (They were caught and punished: Panasian law was very clear about things like that.) "I will do my best."

17) All three Alphabets may be used together, as, for instance, on a Tombstone, where one might carve the Name in CAPITALS and the rest of the Inscription in small-letters, using italics for difference.

Hearken all ye to the words of Panas, the Builder of the World, the Raiser of Cities, the Ordainer of Municipalities, the Shaper of Society. May His blessings be bestowed upon His people for all time, and in all nations may there be great and endless praise raised to Him.

And here is the holiest of mysteries, for behold! All letters come together in the workings of God, and all contribute and share equally in the glory of Panas (blessed be He!). Therefore, let not the slave be downcast, nor the mud dweller abashed, for their station, miserable though it might be, even seemingly iniquitous, is nonetheless part of the plan of the Divine, an expression of the most holy will of Panas (blessed be He!), and though they are forever despised and rejected, cast out and reviled, it is fitting that slaves and commoners should rejoice in their misery, for nowhere is it better or more fully set out than here that theirs too is a situation not without its own kind of honor, and therefore the priests ~~may~~ *must*, from time to time, grant dispensations and permissions even to the most reviled of individuals, yes, even to foreigners who have no knowledge of the truth, for ~~thus is~~ *it is necessary, indeed, it is of the utmost importance,* that the will of Panas (blessed be He!) *be* revealed . . .

"Hmmm . . ." said Captain Elijah Scruffy.

Turtletrout knew the ways of his captain, and it took but one *Hmmm* . . . to bring him to Scruffy's side at the weather rail of the quarterdeck. "Sir?"

"You see that cloud, Mr. Turtletrout?"

Turtletrout bobbed and nodded his head in the direction in which Scruffy was pointing. "Off the port beam, sir?"

"Yes. That one."

"I do, sir."

"So it's not my eyes, then . . ." Scruffy looked again. "Hmmm . . ."

Turtletrout knew the ways of his captain. "I'll fetch Mr. Crane directly, sir."

"No matter, Turtletrout. We can't go and look. But I'll bet a barrel of bounceberries that there's an island out there, an island that's not on any chart that the Righteous States of America has."

Turtletrout nodded.

"Have to look in on that one," said Scruffy. "Later."

"Yes, sir."

"Later ... hmmm ..." Scruffy examined the cloud again. "Later."

Chapter Twenty-three

"ROTTENSTONE RECTAL REAMINGS TO THE REPREHENSIBLE REPRESENTATIVES OF REPRESSION!"

Thump. Whoosh. Crash.

Grasping. Shouting. Scooping. Punching.

Deprecations: draft animals and fish.

"You want *what*?" said the new head chef (who had a habit of keeping his legs pressed tightly together).

"Herbs," said Sari. "I believe that most of what I want are used occasionally for cooking."

She reached back and cleared her hair from the collar of her shoulder cloth. The chef looked on the verge of fleeing, but the sight of two members of the religious police loitering just outside the door of the kitchen apparently made him reconsider.

"Yes," he said, looking at Sari's list. "Yes. I have these."

"Good," said Sari. "Bring a tenth of a kil of each to the chambers of the king and the prince."

"A tenth of a kil?"

"And a kettle full of water and something to build a fire in."

"You . . . you . . . you cannot do that in a palace!"

(And here the new head chef ventured a glance down into the depths of his waist cloth.)

"I have been given permission by the chief minister."

"What about the . . ." (The new head chef looked up from the depths of his waist cloth, apparently relieved about something.) ". . . king?"

"He is not in any condition to give anyone permission to do anything." Sari glanced at the religious police, who had stirred. "It is the *truth*," she said.

The police blinked. "Truth?" said one.

"Truth?" said the other.

The chef (still keeping his legs together), glanced at the list once again. "It shall be done," he said.

"Immediately," said Sari. "There is no time to lose."

Dearly beloved brothers and sisters in Christ, is not ministry a wonderful thing? Yes, it is! But be assured that, when I speak of "ministry", I am not limiting myself only to the ministry of the soul. By no means! Ministry, in fact, reaches into every facet of our existence, in accordance with the teachings and actions of the Most Holy Savior, who most certainly did not confine Himself only to parables and spiritual teachings, even though, to be sure, those parables and spiritual teachings are of the utmost importance to the benighted souls who creep across the surface of this world. By which I mean us. Ah . . . I mean *we*. No . . . *us*.

In any case, Holy Scripture tells us that the Savior ministered to the body as well as to the soul, freely distributing the miracle of healing throughout His life. I mean, His *human* life. I mean, to *others* throughout His *human* life. And therefore, with such an example as this to guide us, is it not incumbent upon us to take every opportunity to minister to one another in such a

way as to bring comfort to the body as well as to the
soul? Within reason, that is. I mean, you would not
want to ... That is ...

Well ... you understand, I am sure.

And so, as we witness today the devoted ministry of
a trusted, personal servant to his ... ah ... yes, *his*
master, a ministry that extends well beyond all questions of what is required or expected of servitude, extends, yes, even unto the solicitude one might well
expect to see exhibited by a mother toward her child,
can we not see, concealed within that service, the ministry so instituted and sanctified by Our Savior?

Ha! He is here now. But he was not here an hour ago. And where was he? I think I know. But ... oooooh! He is so close. So close! I could ... and if he were indeed poisoned, he would not know. Anything! And I could ...	*Bakbuk. Looks like a boy, today, but it is diffi- cult to tell with him. Pum- ice, but it was difficult to keep him from recogniz- ing me during the cara- van trip! Avoiding him all day long. And he acting so strange ...*

See with what solicitude the servant comes to the
master, kneeling by his bed and examining him with an
earnest eye filled with nothing but regret that events
have so transpired as to place such an affliction upon
the one who commands him. And thus do we see the
virtue of fidelity, for was not Jesus faithful to His dis-
ciples, in that all that He promised to them actually
came to pass? Ah ... that is, *most* of what He promised ... ah ... no ... *all* of what He promised came to
pass. With the exception of the end of the world, which
we are still waiting for. But it will come. After all, Jesus promised it, and so it must be. But to return to my
example ... ah ... I mean, my story ...

... kill him, and every-one would think it was merely the result of the poison, except that he is not poisoned, or he would not have been gone, but my disgrace would be over, and I would be free, and no one would know!

... recently and I do not like the way he is looking at me. Something is wrong. I can tell that something is wrong. But here I am, having to pre-tend that I am sick, and now I have to keep Sari from recognizing me!

... here is the virtue of Our Savior made real once again in the virtue of a servant, and true virtue it must be, for what heart, however inured to the ways of evil and deception, could falsely counterfeit that suppliant, earnest, passionate expression of spiritual and physical interest. Ah ... I mean *platonic* physical interest.

But I would know, would I not? Every day I know, and I yearn. And what could I do? Killing him would do nothing, for I am drawn ... even though I can do nothing. It is all I can do to keep myself from ... lying back ...

Pumice! What does he want? I can tell he wants something. That expres-sion. That look. Never seen that before. Does he want me to die? What was the plot? Who poisoned the sweetmeats? Surely not Bakbuk! But ... who ... ?

And as the welfare of the body of the afflicted is so assiduously sought after by those about him, so the welfare of his soul, even in these pagan, benighted, savage lands, is looked to with no less earnestness! And surely it is an irrefutable demonstration of the all-encompassing love of the Most High that He, in His infinite goodness, so allows His beneficence to mani-fest not only in the most Righteous States of America, but even in the comparative and general ignorance of the priestly hierarchy of the Three Kingdoms!

. . . idiot cannot even get an entire sweetmeat in his mouth without failing miserably how did the kingdom even survive until now with his constant have it thought about what I shall do next must have it thought about . . .

It all becomes quite clear. He does indeed want something, and he thinks that I can give it to him. Perhaps I can. That remains to be seen. (I wish Mather would stop squirming.) But I can use this, and I can use him.

And so it can readily be seen, dearest brothers and sisters in Christ, that the world is as an open book to he who would read therein, and in that book (The world, I mean.) is written . . . ah . . . writ . . . ah . . . put down the story and the elucidation of God's will and goodness for all people. Saving the heathens, of course, who will burn in hell . . . but even the heathens are of use because they elucidate . . . ah . . . they show God's goodness. Without actually taking part in it. God's goodness, I mean.

. . . will die soon enough just have to wait and then they are already collecting taxes will show those effeminate so-called scholars in Katha who they will reckon with might even help them along there is more where that came from . . .

There should be no trouble with that. The mission will be a success. Scruffy will return in a few weeks with the men and equipment, and Abnel will be firmly in hand by then, so there should be no trouble. Just as I expected.

JILL REDROSE AGENCY
18576 WESTERN AVENUE
NEW YORK, NEW YORK 10045

April 7, 1994

Mr. Bud Leopold
978 South Hobart Avenue
Los Angeles, California 91721

Dear Mr. Leopold:

Thank you for the opportunity to examine and critique your manuscript. While we regret to inform you that the subject matter of your novel does not fit our present needs, we do feel that there are some worthwhile parts to it that might eventually prove to be profitable to you. We encourage you to continue writing. We will, of course, be glad to examine any further work you might care to submit to us.

The most problematical part of your trilogy occurs near the end of the second book, when you attempt to convey the many deceptions that are going on at this point, as well as continue other plots and sub-plots. Prince Aeid is deceiving the palace by making everyone think that he is ill, and is also carrying on further escapades as the Blue Avenger and even, we suppose, as Potatoes. (You are forgetting here to account for Beshur. Bakbuk said two chapters before that Beshur would be attended to, and Bakbuk has been strongly established as a character who follows through. To have Bakbuk not follow through at this point is a serious departure from his character, and a flaw in the book.) Bakbuk is attempting to deceive everyone into thinking that "he" is a he, Abnel is pretending that he is innocent of the poisoning, Jenkins is covering up his ulterior motives, Scruffy has left for America. Not to mention Haddar, Kuz Aswani, and any number of other characters.

Your writing here becomes choppy and hard to follow, and you neglect to give sufficient reasons in the text to justify this. (Not to mention Bakbuk's curious failings. There does not appear to be any reason for "him" to be so distracted.) Furthermore, you seem committed to indulging in various literary "effects" which you obviously think will add some depth to your work, and your attempt to explain how Bakbuk (established as being a keen observer) failed to notice that one of the members of the caravan was actually Prince Aeid is very unconvincing, as it consists of a single throwaway line.

Your work, in general, shows promise. Please keep us in mind in the future.

Sincerely,

Audrey Puff for Jill Redrose

Jill Redrose

P.S.: Thanks for the $50, sucker.

"Ugh, ugh, ugh, ugh . . . ! Aaaaaaaaack!"

Her young face serious, her eyes intent, Sari bent over the steaming pot while, nearby, the king writhed in his poison-induced delirium.

"Urrrrrrk!"

"Is there anything else we can get for you?" said Kuz Aswani, who, immediately after uttering the words, stuffed a handful of raisins into his mouth.

"Eeeeeeech!"

"This should be sufficient," said Sari. She stopped, sniffed the vapors rising from the kettle, stirred and tasted the brew. "Almost."

"Arrrrrrg!"

"Alphrmstht?"

"Eeky! Eeky! Eeky! Eeky!"

Sari was used to working by instinct, and the chief minister's questions were distracting her. Nevertheless, she knew that she could not very well send him away, and, in any case, she needed to be polite to everyone, to smile at everyone, to try, as best she could, to keep everyone on her side. To have been brought in to tend a possibly dying monarch was a very dangerous situation: as many as there might be who wanted the king dead, there were certainly more who wanted him alive, and though success might make her enemies, failure, even despite her initial cautions and explanations, would surely prove to be a death sentence for the miserable Naian herbalist.

"Oook!"

"Almost ready." She stirred, tasted, added several pinches of herbs from the orderly piles arranged on the low table near the cauldron, tasted again.

"Erk!"

"Oh. Oh! Good. Good. Care for a raisin?"

"Aaaaaga!"

"No, thank you."

"Wrg."

"Really: they are the best raisins."

"Ookook!"

Sari ignored him. Ladling a small amount of the infusion into a wide dish, she swirled it until it cooled, and then, with a glance at Bakbuk for permission (it was useless to ask anything of Kuz Aswani), she poured a spoonful of the liquid into the open mouth of the king.

"Waaa—! Waa ... waa ..."

The king blinked several times, looked up at Sari. She saw his vision clear for a moment.

"What has happened?" he said.

"All Highest?" Sari bent over him. "You have been poisoned. Do you hear me?"

The king's vision clouded again. "Ugh, ugh, ugh, ugh . . . ! Aaaaaaaaack!"

Sari looked up at Kuz Aswani, but the counselor was involved with another handful of raisins, and so she turned instead to Bakbuk. "There is hope," she said.

"Urrrrrrk!"

Bakbuk nodded with a face that was as serious as Sari's. "We will continue the treatment."

"Eeeeeeech!"

"I will go to the prince now," said Sari. "Naia is good . . ." (And here, though the religious police started forward (Panasian law was very clear about things like that.), they stopped before they had taken two paces, for they saw the look on Bakbuk's face. Panasian law was not clear about things like *that,* but Bakbuk's dagger was very clear. And very sharp.) ". . . and with a cup of this infusion every hour, we may be able to save them both."

"Arrrrrrg!"

"It shall be done," said the sworder. "I shall see to it."

"Eeky! Eeky! Eeky! Eeky!"

"Now, let me be sure that I understand you perfectly, my dear Ambassador," said Abnel. "Your Sacred Texts are available to all? In printed form? And individuals in your country not only memorize large portions of them, but also quote them to one another?"

Jenkins suppressed a wince at hearing the Holy Scriptures referred to as though they were nothing more than a variation on the deluded, pagan writings of a heathen imagination. Why, there was no comparing the two at all! One was a compilation of the very words of God, the other was mere scribbling. But,

"Yes, Honored Gharat," he said smoothly. "That is true."

Abnel appeared to be considering this carefully. He put one elbow on the arm of his chair (which was a little smaller, a little forward of, and a little below the throne in the audience hall that was, under normal circumstances, occupied by King Inwa Kabir). "A minister in their heads," he said.

"So to speak."

Mather tottered in about then, and, after bumping vaguely into several pillars and fluttering blindly through the pools of bright sunlight cast across the floor by the semiprecious windows, he thumped down on the floor beside a pillar. He seemed oblivious to everything save whatever discomfort was presently afflicting him, for beyond an occasional squirm, he stared blearily off into space from out of a scratched, cut, and bruised face.

"He-he!" he mumbled. "He-he!"

Jenkins tried very hard to ignore him. Even though, given his rising suspicions about the hidden workings of the priesthood and the Three Kingdoms, an engineer, particularly one with some knowledge of geology, would have been desirable to have about, Decrease Mather was a very small price to pay for the success of the entire mission.

"Published," mused Abnel.

"You must understand, my dear Gharat," said Jenkins, who wanted very much to keep Abnel happy, "printing is a tradition in my country. A . . ." He gritted his teeth. Bloody heathens! ". . . local custom. No more."

Abnel continued to muse, but there was an agitation in his expression that made Jenkins wonder again exactly *what* the man wanted. Why did he not just come out and say it? Money? Power? Another one like

Mather? (Jenkins supposed that anything could be arranged.)

"You do not think us worthy, then," said the High Priest.

His statement caught Jenkins completely off guard. Worthy? Worthy of what? Saying—or not saying—grace? "By no means!" Jenkins hastened to say, even though he had no idea of what means he was talking—or not talking—about. "I think no such thing!"

"You do not respect us at all."

Jenkins was now thoroughly awash. "But of course I respect you!"

Abnel sniffed. "It is very hard for me to tell sometimes."

"I do not understand."

"You have accepted our hospitality, but you think little of us. You take us for granted."

"Honored Gharat! I must protest! How can you think such a thing?"

"You ask many questions, but you tell me nothing!"

Oh, Righteous God! Had Abnel somehow *found out*? But Jenkins kept his head. This was, after all, an ignorant heathen he was talking to: no match at all for a godly American. "And ... and what could I tell you, my dear Gharat?"

Abnel, however, clung to his moodiness. "Hmmph!"

"I beseech you, my friend. Name it ..." A few reservations here, but, then, as Jenkins knew well, diplomacy was built upon reservations. "... and it is yours."

"You mock me whenever I ask about it."

"Mock you? Tell me!"

Abnel waved a perfumed hand. "What is the use? You will simply mock me."

Jenkins, faced with the failure of his mission, with disgrace, ruin, and the possibility of physical threat in a foreign land, allowed himself to wager a bit more than he really wanted to. "No. No. I promise. Tell me."

Abnel seemed unconvinced. "You never tell me anything."

"But what could I tell you?"

"Well, you could tell me . . . the secret."

"Secret . . ." As far as Jenkins knew, it was *Abnel* who had the secret. He felt his expression turn suddenly very blank. A fatal flaw in a diplomat. "What . . . ah . . . secret?"

"You could tell me . . ." But then, on the verge, as it seemed, of uttering his desire, Abnel turned away from him. "Oh, what is the use?"

Jenkins swallowed hard, pressed on. There was no going back now. Not with Scruffy already en route. "No. Please. Ask."

"Well . . . you could tell me . . ." Abnel broke off again.

"My dear Gharat! Ask me! Anything!"

But Abnel swung back to Jenkins suddenly, his face determined. "I will demonstrate," he said, flaring, "just how worthy we are. Tomorrow night. I will send for you, and you will come. Bring Rose—" He caught himself, cleared his throat. "Bring Mather and Wool, if it pleases you."

"Of course," said Jenkins. And, all overconfident, he had sent *Seaflower* and *Speedwell* away! "Of course."

"Tomorrow night!"

"Of course."

"And then you will explain all to me!"

"Of . . . of course!"

"He-he!" mumbled Mather. He slumped against the pillar.

"Ugh, ugh, ugh, ugh . . . ! Aaaaaaaaack!"

The prince still insisted upon keeping the sheets of his bed pulled tight against his face, and, for a moment, Sari dithered over how to administer an infusion to a man whose mouth was covered. "Your Highness!"

"Urrrrrrk! What?"

"I have a remedy you must take if you wish to become better!"

"Eeeeeeech! Fine. Fine. Just leave it, and I will take it—Arrrrrrg!—later."

With an apologetic look at Bakbuk (who was staring at the cloth-shrouded figure on the bed in a manner so earnest that it made Sari uncomfortable), the Naian grabbed an edge of the sheet, jerked it up so as to reveal the prince's mouth, and, as his lips parted in astonishment, managed to get half a cup in.

"Gak! I mean . . . I mean eeky! Eeky! Eeky! Eeky!"

"Verthy gooth," said Kuz Aswani, his mouth full of raisins.

"Oook!"

Though she could not help but wonder why the Crown Prince of Kaprisha had affected the habit of shaving off his beard, Sari allowed him to pull the sheet back over his face. "My apologies, Your Highness."

"Erk!"

Her brow furrowed. "Odd . . . it worked on his father," she murmured.

"Aaaag—! What? Oh! Oh, I feel much better! I feel . . . ah . . . quite well!"

Sari nodded. "Good." She ran a hand back through her hair and sent another two guards fleeing down the hall. (Panasian law . . . etc.) "We will continue the treatment."

"Wrg. Much better!"

Bakbuk's eyes held a strange expression. Sari became even more uncomfortable.

"Ookook!"

"I will . . . see to it," said the sworder.

"Waaaark! Better!"

Chapter Twenty-four

Bakbuk has to sleep sometime, and apparently that time is now, for the sworder is dozing soundly (though not at all peacefully) beside Prince Aeid's bed when the latticework over the window to the prince's chambers, propelled from the *inside,* swings silently open, and the agency responsible for the propelling (as we must infer, else all sense of cause and effect is forever banished from the universe) steps onto the moonlit ledge on the *outside,* rope in hand, ready once again to demonstrate the laws of physics involving gravitational constants, pendulum lengths, and periods of oscillation.

But this is not the Blue Avenger: rather, it is the thief, Potatoes. Clean shaven, dressed in nondescript garments, he leans out, casts a loop of rope up toward the roof (where it falls over a strategically-placed bit of ornament), and, swinging gently (see *constants, lengths,* and *oscillation* above), pulls himself up toward the roof, unnoticed by all . . .

. . . except . . .

Sari was not sleeping well. The danger inherent in her proximity to the plots that, by nature, twined about even the faintest semblance of royalty (and there was certainly more than a semblance of royalty in the palace of Nuhr), the uneasy oppression that went hand in hand with a failed assassination attempt, the fact that she was a Naian—and a woman—in a stronghold of Panas . . . all these did not make for easy dreams, and, indeed, Sari was not even getting as far as dreams, for sleep was elusive, and the best she could manage was a light doze visited only by fatiguing worries about the day's events.

Dead if she saved them, dead if she did not: Bakbuk's assurances about her personal safety did nothing to blunt her knowledge of these potentials. But, as far as she could tell, death would be far more likely a result of failure than of success, and so concerns about the composition of her herbal remedies and the quantity being given to her royal patients (Could the servants be trusted? Poison in the sweetmeats . . . what about poison in the remedies?) were well represented among her restless visions.

Too much? Too little? What if . . . what if . . . what if . . .

Near midnight, fear drove her up from bed, into her clothes, and out of the chamber that had been given over to her use. The hallways of the palace were brilliant with torchlight by night as well as by day, and the guards outside her door not only allowed her to pass, but offered no objection to her unaccompanied departure (Bakbuk having made this necessity very clear to them . . . Panasian law notwithstanding). In any case, they knew where she was going.

And they knew correctly, too, for a few minutes later, Sari was treading the inlaid, ivory floor that led to the chambers of King Inwa Kabir. At her approach, the guards at the door straightened up (though they were supposed to be straight already: Panasian law was very clear about things like that).

"The guards of King Inwa Kabir greet—"

"Thank you," said Sari. "I will see my patient."

Protocol having devised no appropriate response to the unequivocal statement of a female Naian commoner, the guards, in confusion, allowed her to enter.

The king slept. No thrashing, no strange noises, no glazed looks. Just common sleep. This was a decided improvement. With gentle touches, Sari examined the monarch, looked to the kettle of infusion being kept warm on a tripod next to the royal pallet, exchanged a word or two with the slave who was tending the fire, the kettle, and the infusion, and left the room reassured . . . but not by much.

"The guards of King Inwa Kabir say farewell to—"

But Sari was already gone, passing down one corridor and then another, coming, finally, to the door to the chambers of Prince Aeid. Here, by long-standing princely orders, there were no guards to greet, question, or interfere. Here there was only a door . . . and Bakbuk's vigilance within.

But when she entered the rooms, she found Bakbuk asleep, found a figure leaving by the window, found the prince's bed . . .

. . . empty!

Aeid . . . ah . . . Potatoes makes his way across the roofs of the palace. As was the case with Aeid . . . ah . . . the Blue Avenger a day or two ago, he moves with an air of confidence, exhibiting the demeanor of a man who knows exactly where he is going. But there is obviously more to his errand than can be accomplished in . . . or, rather, *on* the palace, for, after traversing roofs—not to mention climbing walls and shinnying down buttresses and drainpipes—he is descending the outer wall, and without any explanations at all as to how he can manage to fasten a rope to a strategically-placed something-or-other securely enough that he can safely lower himself to the ground and then, with a mere *flick* of his hand, cause the whole length of the line to fall into neat coils at his feet (Sometimes it is best not to ask.), he reaches the city streets.

This time, the gates to the Naian Quarter are shut, and so, this time, he climbs the wall into the Quarter for more reasons than simple, thievish pride. If the guards at the gate notice that there is some idiot climbing over the wall, they say nothing, and, once again, Potatoes, a thief, finds himself plumping down in the middle of a heap of ...

Are those *crystals*?

And, once again, a flick of his wrist and the rope falls at his feet in neat coils. (Don't ask.)

Now he is among the incense and the sounds of wind chimes. A distant *Hunna-hunna-hunna-HIN!* drifts along on the darkling breeze as, with stealthy steps, he makes his way along the street, toward a certain fish shop.

Sari—as he was half afraid—is not there.

But neither is Beshur!

Ineluct—!

No!

Try again.

Hidden. All hidden. But I shall find out. I will enter. I am a scholar. I was the first in my class. I have the right to enter, to know all. The Library contains everything, and I shall know everything. Sari might be with *him,* but I will demonstrate to them my superiority, for while they rut and sweat in their fornicative (Is that a word? It must be: I am a scholar.) bed, I will learn ... many things!

Here, walk like—! That servant of the merchant ... was he ... ah ... she ... ah ... ?

Darkness, moonlight. The shadows of the buildings were like ink poured into a kingly trove of silver. Beshur kept to the ink, to the darkness. Slipping along, wary, he approached the outer wall surrounding the mammoth bulk of the Great Library.

No. Shall not be caught. I am clever. I know many things. Sari and Potatoes know nothing but each other. She would only know that, because she left me for ... for him! And what else can you expect of someone like Potatoes? But I will have more important things. I will have knowledge! I will learn about the Texts! They changed ... why—?

A movement ahead. A guard? Possibly ...

Here, walk like this.

No!

Keeping his thoughts very firmly under control, Beshur crouched low in the shadows. There was a way in, and he would find it. He was, after all, a scholar.

It was a very easy mistake to make. The darkness was profound, the moonlight almost dazzling, and once Sari was out on the streets of Nuhr, wandering alone, wondering what had become of the mysterious figure that had first left the prince's room (The prince? Surely not! But who, then? And where was the prince?) and then scampered across the rooftops as she, outside and at ground level, tried as best she could to follow (An assassin? But there had been no body! And Bakbuk there, asleep. Foul play? Whose? And they would surely blame her!), she had taken a wrong turning and had picked up the trail of what was, unknown to her, a *second* mysterious figure who was shuffling along through the shadows, heading rather clumsily in the direction of ...

The Great Library!

But as Potatoes climbs back up the rope by which he has reached, entered, and exited the window of the room above the fish shop, it strikes him that as the confusion now surrounding the palace and its occupants has resulted in the slackening of the vigilance of the palace guards (as has been amply demonstrated not only by his own stealthy escapades on the roofs of the palace, but also—though he does not know it at present—by Sari's unchallenged and unnoticed departure from the palace precincts), it might also have produced something of the same effect in the guards who watch over the entrances to the Great Library. This, then, is perhaps an opportunity for clandestine research not to be missed, and since his father is, under the influence of Sari's potions, regaining his strength and his health (and since he himself is *supposed* to be doing the same), there might not be another such opportunity for some time to come.

And therefore, Potatoes swarms back up the rope to the roof of the room over the fish shop (pausing there just long enough to give a flick of his wrist that results in the rope lying in neat coils at his feet (Don't ask.)) and crosses the rooftops back toward the wall of the Naian Quarter, his footsteps masked quite effectively by both the continued clank and tinkle of wind chimes and the ever-present sound of distant chanting:

Hunna-hunna-hunna-HIN!

"I wonder why they cannot ever seem to get that *right,*" he mutters to himself as he slips and slides up the pile of . . .

Are those *crystals*?

Darkness. Hides me. Hides the intellect from the light. No. Hides the light from the intellect? No . . . that is not right, either. Perception of the farraginous interpolative interplay of modality, but confined by the fleshly bounds to a plenum characterized by an absence of luminous fluid?

Not quite. But better.

Ah . . . guards fewer now. Not attentive. Could get in. Wandering. Gate . . . unguarded? Slip in? Then what? What if guards inside? Doubtful. Why should I care? Sari with *him* (not that *I* care). Nothing to look forward to. Carrying. Rest of my life. And I a scholar! The best! If I could stay hidden, could find out. Die knowing instead of unknowing. Yes.

Sari looked into the darkness, squinting into the shadows that all but totally concealed the figure of a man. But why would someone do something (She assumed that someone had done something.) to the prince, fairly dance across the rooftops, and then come to a shuffling, clumsy halt outside the walls of the Great Library?

If she had ever had any faith in Bakbuk's assurances of safety, they were gone now: Bakbuk had been asleep in the prince's chamber, and someone had come in and *done* something with or to the prince! Without any response from Bakbuk! This was simply too much. Well, she had fled before—from her husband's dead body, from what she had assumed was the pursuing arm of the law, from the insanity of Charna and her plots—and now she would flee again. But before she did, she was determined to find out who and what this figure was. Time enough for flight tomorrow, when the gates of the city would open. For now . . .

But the figure straightened and stood up (taking a misstep as he did so and nearly falling over), and the moonlight revealed his features.

Beshur!

Beshur! It *is* Beshur! Potatoes, staring down from the rooftops, recognizes him instantly and recalls the obsessive mania with which the would-be scholar regards the Great Library. Yes, and so it has come to this. But at least Beshur is not with Sari. Did they put her in a room in the palace, then? He supposes so, but cringes at the thought of how dangerous the situation is for her: to be at hand to care for the king (and the prince, too: he must not forget the prince, after all), but to be at hand also for any retribution that might result from either her success or her failure.

Still, Sari is safe . . . for now. And Beshur . . .

A plan, formerly held to be dishonorable, but now undergoing a revival, begins to take shape in Potatoes' head. It is still not the most honorable of plans, but, Beshur is not the most honorable of individuals, being but a common porter with delusions of scholarship. Still, Beshur seems bent upon putting himself in such a position of vulnerability that the thief cannot, for a moment, believe it; but whether he cannot believe it because it smacks of a degree of stupidity (on the part of Beshur) incomprehensible to the mind of an average human being or because it is the embodiment of a such a stroke of good luck (on the part of Potatoes) that it defies understanding, Potatoes is not entirely sure.

Beshur wants into the Library, then? Well, as a sometime prince, Potatoes . . . ah . . . that is, Aeid is in the business of giving his subjects what they want, and so Aeid . . . ah . . . that is, Potatoes will assist Beshur in the realization of his dreams. Up to a point. After which, Beshur will be on his own.

Until the guards find him, at least.

With a growing feeling of horror and distrust, Sari watched Beshur enter the outer gates of the Library. Towers, walls, pinnacles, and columns cast black shadows across the courtyard within, and it was almost impossible for her to follow his movements, but follow them she did, and not only with her eyes, for her concern and agitation were so great that, without realizing it until it was too late, she actually went in after him.

Shaking, she paused in the crisscross darkness. It was a bit confusing. Here was Beshur about to enter

the forbidden Library. And yet it had apparently been
Beshur who had left the prince's bedroom via the window after doing something with/to/upon/(other distressing preposition) the prince. And yet, that itself was
impossible, for Sari knew well that Beshur could no
more climb a rope than he could fly. (Actually, when
she thought about it, she had to rank the relative probability of Beshurian flight somewhat higher than that
of climbing.) And so someone else must have been
leaving the prince's bedroom. But who?

And then she remembered Bakbuk's cryptic remark
about Beshur. The apostate priest. Priest? Apostate?

And *then* she remembered. Katha. Water. The badly-
aspected Virgo postulant ...

This was more than she could bear, and she was
about to give up and turn back toward the city when
there was a blaze of torchlight from the gate behind
her. The portals were flung open, and there were suddenly far fewer shadows in which to hide.

Instinctively, she gathered up her waist cloth and
bolted for the darkness of the doorway, hoping that
whoever held the torches would be so dazzled by their
light that they would not see her sprinting across the
marble and onyx pavement.

Darkness ... and no guards? A trap? No. I am too
clever for a trap.

Beshur groped his way through the doorway. It was
dark inside, darker than shadows, darker than the night.
High above, a slit of a window was letting in a sliver
of moonlight, but far from illuminating anything, it
simply made the darkness darker, though Beshur was
not exactly sure how anything could manage to do that.

Light. Far away. Very high.

How big is this room?

* * *

Exactly the same question has occurred to Potatoes, who, after overpowering both guards, tying them up, and dragging them off into a corner, has preceded Beshur into the apparent vastness of the inner room. Yes, there is a slit window up above, but it is very far away both horizontally and vertically, and the moonlight coming through it is shining on nothing save the opposite wall of the room. As far as he can tell, there are no shelves, no cases, no books, no manuscripts . . . there is nothing, in fact, save that slit window in the distance and that rectangle of light on the opposite wall.

He hears Beshur entering. Footsteps echo against what can only be bare walls, bare floor, bare ceiling . . .

What? *Nothing?* But this is the Great Library! Surely there must be some . . . well . . . *records* of some sort here. Or something appropriately old. At least there must be a few other guards inside—somewhere—who will obligingly take Beshur into custody and deliver him to the representatives of Panasian law (which is very clear about things like this)!

But no. There is nothing. Certainly there are no guards. Only a vast, empty, echoing room.

Light from the doorway . . . from outside the doorway, actually. More footsteps . . . very close. Potatoes runs to the door, brushing by Beshur (who, unhelpfully, shrieks loudly).

"Shut-up, idiot!" Potatoes hisses.

But then he himself almost shrieks, for at the door, he runs into someone else. Someone soft, someone deliciously fragrant, someone, in fact . . .

"Sari! What are you doing here?"

"What? Potatoes? Where is Beshur?"

—Here I am, Beshur says. Sari! You came looking for me! Of course you did! Where have you been?

Potatoes groans inwardly, but there is hardly enough

time even for groans, for torchlight and moonlight clearly show what appears to be a formal procession of twenty or more figures crossing the courtyard toward the door.

—What are you doing here, Potatoes? Beshur demands.

"What are *you* doing here, Beshur?" Potatoes responds, realizing with excruciating clarity how absolutely useless any revelations of the kind are going to be in another few minutes.

Sari is much more to the point. "We must escape. And quickly. They are coming."

—Who?

This last question—another on the part of Beshur—is as unhelpful as his first. For that matter, it is as unhelpful as his initial shriek . . . which, fortunately, appears to have gone unheard.

But the light is approaching the door. So are the footsteps. There is no choice but to plunge deeper into the darkness.

"There is a door on the far side," says Potatoes. "Let us try to reach it."

—How do you know there is a door on the far side? Beshur asks suspiciously (but still unhelpfully).

"I am a thief. I know these things."

—A thief?

"Perhaps you have heard of me." Potatoes is anxious to be off. The light and the footsteps come still closer.

—No, Beshur says. Never.

"Well," says Potatoes, who has taken hold of Beshur's arm and is attempting to move him bodily away from the door (which is beginning to fill with the light from the approaching torches), "then it is quite obvious that I am an extremely good thief, since you would have heard of me otherwise."

He has succeeded in dragging Beshur (with some help from Sari) out into the room, which still obstinately refuses to demonstrate that it contains anything at all. There is, as far as the three intruders can tell, absolutely *nothing* in the room save the floor, which, as far as Potatoes is concerned, cannot really be said to be *in* the room, since it forms part of the boundaries *of* the room.

But while he is occupied with both his pulling (of Beshur) and his reflections (on the floor), he runs into a railing, topples, and falls part way down a flight of stairs.

Light . . . filling the doorway. There is no time to cross the room.

"Down here!"

—Where? Beshur says, holding to his tradition of unhelpful questions.

"Here!" comes Sari's voice.

Potatoes hears the two beginning to descend. "Just as I . . . ah . . . expected," he manages.

—You . . . *expected*?

"Pumice! Just come down the stairs, will you? It is our only hope."

Groping in a darkness even deeper than that which already seemed to be absolute (and which itself seemed deeper than that which previously appeared to be impenetrable), they descend. But the stairs go on and on, stretching downward monotonously until, when even Potatoes' alertness has at last been dulled, he finds that his nose is abruptly stopped by a wall. "Trapped!" he says, fingering his nose to see if it is broken. (The wall, being made of stone, needs no such examination.)

"No," says Sari with a tug at his shoulder cloth. "Another flight. Here: to the right."

But as they descend farther and continue down and down, they hear, from above . . .

. . . footsteps!

"They are coming!"

—Coming?

"Just continue, Beshur," says Sari. "Come now. More steps."

And more. And more. And after what seems like hours of descent, they at last reach what must be the bottom, and the walls fall away to either side.

Beshur stares, his unhelpful questions temporarily silenced. Sari murmurs a prayer to Naia. Potatoes searches desperately for something to say . . .

"Ah . . . as . . . as . . . ah . . . as I expected," he manages.

Beshur whirls on him.

—As you . . . *expected*?

It is, perhaps, still not a particularly helpful question, but it is indeed an understandable one, for here, before them, illuminated by three or four dim, red lamps, is another colossal room. Far from being empty, though, it is occupied by what, at first glance, appears to be some kind of large, ornate pavilion, but which, upon closer examination (And the three have moved away from the bottom of the stairs, since they can now plainly hear the sound of descending footsteps and the murmur of voices coming from above and behind them.), turns out to be some kind of boat, for there is a broad channel in the living rock that makes up the floor of the room, a channel filled with water, and it is upon the glassy surface of this water that the pavilion floats at its mooring.

Potatoes straightens up, gives a nod which he hopes looks very definite. "Yes. As I expected."

"Yes," says Sari, glancing back at the stairs. The footsteps have grown louder. "Yes, of course."

But there are only the pavilion, the channel, and the water. And the footsteps and the voices are still descending.

"Get on board," says Potatoes.

—On board? Beshur says, finding his voice and his unhelpfulness once again.

"On board," says Potatoes. "We must hide."

Large as the pavilion appeared from a distance, it proves to be even larger once they have climbed the cedarwood gangway and boarded it. The wide deck sparkles with gold where it is not covered with costly rugs, and to either side of the central tent, companionways lead down, their railings encrusted with gems. At the prompting of Potatoes, the three descend one of them and find themselves once again in darkness.

"Down farther," whispers Potatoes, for, outside, the footsteps and voices are growing louder, more distinct.

—Farther?

Down, and down again. Yes, it is a huge pavilion. Now they have passed the upper decks and the lower decks, and they have come at last to the storerooms and the bilge.

They crouch in the darkness. Voices from above:

"Now do you see that we are worthy, my dear ambassador?"

"I will call upon the Lord, *who is worthy* to be praised: so shall I be saved from mine enemies."

"Be quiet, Wool. Yes, my dear Gharat. Very impressive. Very, very impressive!"

"Worthy of . . . of *all*?"

"Worthy of . . . well, of a great deal."

"He-he! Man work!"

—What are they saying?

"Shut-up!" Potatoes attempts to shout and whisper at the same time, nearly sending himself into a fit of coughing.

"And you shall see even more, my dear ambassador!"

Footsteps on the decks above. Murmured orders. A swaying.

And suddenly the pavilion is in motion!